Run For Your Life

Lessons Learned From Going the Distance

Larissa Soehn, Christy Holt, Zoe Antaya, Stephanie Krebs, Tania Jacobs, Austin Sedgwick, Sarah Hughes, Olena Sadovnik, Morrie Ripley, Dave Madole, Herbert Camat, Priscilla Forgie, Ed Bickley, Dennis Kreba, Daryl Lang

Paperback ISBN: 978-1-7380421-6-6
eBook ISBN: 978-1-7380421-9-7

Published by Next Page Publishing Inc.
Red Deer, Alberta

NEXT PAGE
PUBLISHING INC.

Contents

Sponsors

A huge thank you to the sponsors of this project. On behalf of our authors and our entire Alberta running community, we are so grateful for you. Without organizations like yours, we would not have the events that we do, nor would we be able to do projects like *Run For Your Life*.

Run Calgary

Servus Edmonton Marathon

5 Peaks Trail Running Series

Read more about our Gold Sponsors

Run Calgary

RUNCALGARY

For those who aren't familiar with Run Calgary, we are a local non-profit organization with a mission to enrich lives and foster community through exceptional fitness experiences, including the Calgary Marathon. We believe that running can be a lifelong journey, and we aim to be a part of this journey for everyone from first-time runners to elite athletes.

With a long history that got its start back in 1963 at the very first Calgary Marathon (the longest-running marathon in Canada!), we've learned how to embrace original ideas, challenge ourselves, and use our passion and collective knowledge to enhance the participant experience. We hope this passion and history can be seen not only by participants at our events but also by volunteers, sponsors, charities, and stakeholders throughout the city.

The running community spans far and wide here in Calgary, but there is always room for more! We connect people, charities, and local partners through year-round collaboration and vitalize our community by promoting healthy, active living and fun social engagement. Whether it be in-person races, virtual races, ale trails, curated pop-up events or interactions with the community, we stay true to our core values. These values include community, integrity, innovation, social responsibility, and safety.

We continue to foster community on a daily basis through three community-based pillars: youth, corporate, and charity.

Youth are an important part of Run Calgary's ecosystem and integral in achieving our vision of growing lifelong runners. With a combination of reduced youth pricing, kids race distances, and contests for youth groups/teams/schools, we are making progress towards reducing barriers to entry for youth and families.

Corporate engagement is another way for us to connect with companies throughout Alberta while contributing to the improvement of employee health and wellness. The Corporate Team Challenge that occurs as part of the Calgary Marathon supports company wellness initiatives inspires employees to get active and encourages teamwork. Corporate teams are also encouraged to fundraise for a charity that is meaningful to them, which ties into our final pillar of the community, charity.

All Run Calgary races throughout the year are tied to a local charity. From local LGBTQ+ organizations, to youth programming, support for seniors, or animal welfare, we aim to support a variety of community groups throughout Calgary and beyond. The Calgary Marathon itself supports over 90 charities annually through the Charity Challenge.

While many of our programs and initiatives are large-scale projects with long-term goals, we know it is also incredibly important to work with small businesses in our community. We believe there is truly space for everyone in this industry. Whether it's local independent running stores, run crews, coaches, or even local publishers, there are always opportunities to collaborate.

By supporting projects like *Run For Your Life: Lessons Learned From Going the Distance*, we hope to elevate the stories and experiences of those within our running community and further strengthen the bond that running has created between us all.

Servus Edmonton Marathon

For over 30 years, the Servus Edmonton Marathon has celebrated the city's community and sporting spirit. It's an event that has become an Edmonton summer staple and one that local and international athletes, volunteers, and community leaders look forward to every year.

The event has grown to not only become an annual tradition for thousands of Edmontonians, but also a premier race, attracting participants from around the world.

Known as "the Friendly Marathon," the event is one of Edmonton's signature athletic and community events. Runners love the fast, flat course, historic neighbourhoods, and scenic views of the beautiful river valley. The inclusion of the Half-Marathon event (21.1K), Army 10K, and the Family Fun Run/Walk 5K reflects a commitment to inclusivity, catering to athletes and families of all ages and abilities.

Since 1991, the Edmonton Marathon has raised several tens of thousands of dollars for local charities. In 2023, the Edmonton Marathon also partnered with Ever Active Schools to help collect used running shoes to donate to communities in need displaced by summer forest fires. The Edmonton Marathon is made possible thanks to hundreds of volunteers every year, many of whom come back year after year. It's also an opportunity for local community leagues, sports teams, and non-profit groups to volunteer and, in turn, raise money for their respective organizations.

While the Edmonton Marathon attracts elite athletes from around the world, it also attracts runners with impactful stories. Every year, there are countless stories from people running for a cause. For example, in 2023, Eileen Chan, along with about 50 family members and friends, ran in honour of her sister, Kelli, who passed away shortly after her 48th birthday in September of 2021. The group wore matching yellow shirts and raised money for charity to honour and celebrate what would have been Kelli's 50th birthday. Previous years included runners in the Half-Marathon distance pursuing Guinness world records, like Natalie Shanahan pushing a double stroller with twin daughters and Noel D'Arcy in full firefighting gear. Chris Koch, an inspirational marathon competitor born with no arms or legs, completed the marathon, propelling himself on a longboard with one leg stump. A particularly heartwarming scene was when Milania Cadrain, a six-year-old from Saskatoon who had both legs amputated at birth, finished the 5 kilometer event also using a longboard and was met at the finish line by Chris Koch, who had earlier finished his marathon. The duo raised funds for The War Amps. Like the runners in the *Run For Your Life* stories, the Edmonton Marathon planning and organizing crew are a dedicated and committed team, with many having been involved for several years. They come from all walks of life, including teachers, health care, first responders, business people, moms and dads, aunts and uncles, brothers and sisters. The team shares the same excitement and enthusiasm, seeing new and familiar faces at the start line every year and being able to congratulate the runners with their finisher medals when they cross the finish line with a giant sense of accomplishment.

5 Peaks Trail Running

5 PEAKS
trail running series

5 Peaks is a trail running community that extends throughout North America. Our goal is to provide safe, sustainable opportunities for people of all ages, abilities, and ambitions to access the outdoors on foot. Our core trail running events are organized by region, with five series events in each region. These events offer a variety of distances for kids and adults alike, between 1 and 21 kilometers.

In addition to our signature 5 Peaks Trail Running Series events, we host a variety of other trail running adventures that provide additional opportunities to gather with like minded adventurers and test oneself. While most of our series events max out at a half marathon, some of our non-series events, like the Powderface Mountain Marathon, Stoked Ultra, Stoked Scramble and the TranSelkirks Run, offer distances up to and beyond a marathon.

Fast Trax Run & Ski Shop

AmSteam

Kevin Cheung Photography

Read more about our Silver Sponsors

Fast Trax Run & Ski Shop

Fast Trax Run & Ski is Edmonton's exclusive independent, locally owned and operated establishment dedicated to running and cross-country skiing and we're firmly entrenched in the fabric of the surrounding community. As fervent advocates for an active lifestyle, we take immense pride in having an integral role within a thriving network of local organizations committed to enhancing community well-being. We are actively involved in local running and skiing events, as well as our valued partnership with the Edmonton Nordic Ski Club.

Our differentiation is driven by our passionate staff, who have a love for and expertise in all things running & skiing.

Transcending the traditional retail experience, when you shop with us, not only will you receive great gear, but should you need it, advice towards your goals and adventures.

Embracing a holistic approach towards community engagement, we host bi-weekly run groups designed to accommodate all levels of runners, all free of charge. While fostering camaraderie, forging friendships, and gaining training & racing insights, most of all, these runs are welcoming and fun!

And in our commitment to giving back, Fast Trax actively contributes to the community by regularly donating new running shoes, as well as gently used footwear from our generous patrons to local organizations in need. Our philanthropic endeavors extend to supporting entities such as local shelters, hospitals, as well as athletics clubs catering to low income families.

It is our pleasure to be involved in *Run for Your Life*.

Thanks, Simon

Fast Trax Run & Ski

AmSteam

As I entered my 40s, I found myself in a comfortable yet mundane routine. Over the previous two decades, I had built my local carpet cleaning and restoration company, AmSteam, into a solid, flourishing brand in the Edmonton area. As my business expanded, I was spending 50+ hours per week at the office or in the field. While I found my work fulfilling, I knew something was missing.

One Saturday morning, while camping with my family, my sisters, Jocelyn and Jessica, invited me to join them on a run. My ignorance and ego got me to lace up my shoes (or rather, my sandals - the only footwear I brought), but the aches and hobbles I experienced afterward were enlightening. That felt horrible - shortness of breath, burning in my legs and tightness in my shoulders was all I could feel physically. Yet, I couldn't stop thinking about it. Did I just run...and actually like it?

That grueling five kilometer run on a sunny Saturday morning ignited my search for more. I soon signed up for a local half-marathon in Edmonton, called the Moose is Loose. Again, the burning and discomfort came. But it continued to fuel my passion to go further and delve into the warm and encouraging community I could see around me. I joined a running group at a local running store, Fast Trax. People seemed more cheerful, open, and supportive than anywhere else I had noticed. It became obvious to me how running touched everyone's lives in some way.

Not only has running improved my physical health, it has been invaluable for me mentally. Time spent in my running shoes allows me to unwind and reset after long days and provides me with the clarity needed to prioritize my life. I still love my work, but now I recognize when it's time to disconnect and focus on myself and those who are important to me. After cleaning carpets and performing flood restorations for 25 years, I've learned first-hand how hard work often pays dividends. My dedication to running has not only filled my cup but has also allowed me to be fully present in other areas of my life. I truly feel that my work, my family and friends, and my community all benefit from the better version of myself I've found through running. I'm so proud of where the sport has led me, and I am honoured to lend my support to this book, another opportunity for the running community to come even closer together.

7 Summits Snacks

North Sun Ultra

Read more about our Bronze Sponsors

7 Summits Snacks

You know the feelings - both of them. Several hours into a run (yes, I said hours), you're either feeling deliriously grumpy because that branch jumped out of the earth and tried to trip you OR your mouth is so sore and puckered from the too many gels you've been slurping back on that endless energy roller coaster. We've been there, and guess what? Distance running does not have to be that way.

Co-founder and triathlete Leanna posed the question to chocolate scientist, marathon runner, and sister Kristyn: "Can we eat chocolate when we run?" After a critical thought pause, Kristyn realised, "Yes! Chocolate has a superb balance of carbs and fat for a steady energy release." It is a perfect fuel for endurance sports, allowing you to have that steady stream of energy required to "fuel your next adventure." Oh yes, and it's also delicious. So the sisters tidied up the ingredients in a regular chocolate bar, packaged it in a familiar pouch, and launched 7 Summits Snacks.

7 Summits Snacks is a women-owned, Edmonton-founded company. Using ethically sourced chocolate and superfoods, 7 Summits Snacks provides you with food your body knows how to digest so you can focus on running kilometers and not running to the bathroom.

At 7 Summits Snacks, adventure, challenge, and community are at the heart of our values. The spirit of adventure guides us as we seek out challenges that will inspire us all to grow from the roots in which we are planted. Our ever-growing, endurance-loving community is the nourishment we use to reach higher and spread our branches. We value the support you show us as a seedling business, enabling us to root deep and grow on a global scale as a sports nutrition company.

North Sun Ultra

Four passionate trail runners in Edmonton founded the North Sun Ultra (NSU) in 2020 to showcase Edmonton's extensive trail network and inspire more people to pursue the adventure of trail running. Our 50 kilometer route weaves iconic single-track trails from east to west, creating an outstanding course finishing in the heart of downtown Edmonton. Established during a global pandemic, NSU began as a "choose your own adventure" event and has evolved into one of Edmonton's only trail ultramarathons, now including a shorter 30 kilometer distance as well. NSU is a fully not-for-profit event that aims to promote adventure, encouraging runners to discover new or revisit favourite trails within Edmonton's river valley. We believe in a commitment to community and donate our race profits to local charity organizations.

As participants navigate the course, they are greeted by enthusiastic volunteers who support aid stations and direct key junctions throughout the route. Racers are fundamental, but our volunteers are equally essential and serve as an integral pillar of our event. Recurring volunteers who choose to support NSU yearly deserve special recognition – we appreciate you! Our fantastic network of sponsors who have supported NSU has enabled us to deliver incredible prizes and an unforgettable finish-line experience, including physiotherapy, food/beverages, and music for participants and their friends and family. Thanks to sponsors, we can increase the amount of funds donated back into our community.

As directors of NSU, we believe wholeheartedly that trail running and ultra-marathon events are for anyone who chooses to participate. The sport is not reserved for elite athletes. Our goal is to attract those who are seeking a sense of personal achievement and an unforgettable experience. Our race is meant to be accessible to seasoned trail runners as well as runners seeking their first trail race experience.

Foreword

by Larissa Soehn

A season, a reason, or a lifetime. That is one of my therapist's favourite sayings. "Larissa, people, and opportunities come into our lives for a season, a reason, or a lifetime. You have to decide which one it is."

Running, for me, was a season and a reason. I was in my early twenties when I started running. I was insecure, overwhelmed, and on the verge of being very depressed when I happened across a book at my local library that would instigate a ten-year and counting love/hate relationship, *Chicken Soup for the Runners Soul (2010).*

As I poured through the pages, tears streaming down my face, I felt a deep urge to connect with every one of those brave souls who dared to share their stories. I wanted to be closer to something so transformational. Later that day I laced up my sad old runners and jogged around my block. After I was done lying on my floor and feeling like I was on the verge of death, I smiled. Not an, 'Oh thank goodness I'm alive,' kind of smile, but more of an 'I get it' smile. I felt the rush of endorphins the runners from the book had talked about. I wanted more.

Fast forward ten years and now I have an entire wall in my basement dedicated to finisher medals and a graveyard of dozens of shoes that have been worn through the toes.

I don't run anymore. Certainly not at the distances or intensity level that I did in the past. My knees say an emphatic no thank you to that. Shout out to those who said I should stretch more, you were right! Running will always be in my blood. The lessons it gave me have shaped who I am and who I want to become. That is why this book exists.

When Christy Holt and I discovered that we both had a love for running, we immediately knew two things: One, we love running for very complex reasons and two, we love to talk about it! We were pretty sure those two facts were relevant across the entire population of people who called themselves runners (or those who self-identify as plodders).

We were right! From a thirty-minute conversation, a community was born. We reached out to our fellow Albertans and gave them the opportunity to share their stories about their love/hate relationship with running. It was a full-circle moment for me as I watched these incredible people come together and tell their stories with the same laugh-inducing, tear-wrenching passion that I found over a decade ago. Just like those stories, these runners, and now authors, are proving that running has very little to do with the physical sport and so much more to do with the lessons we have learned. Yes, we sweat, bleed, and limp through our sport, but we also cry, hug, and rejoice.

Collectively, we know: *It's about more than the miles.*

As you pour through these pages, know that a community of kind-hearted, funny, and determined people wait for you on the other side. If you are already a member of the running community, we thank you. Community is what makes our sport possible. If you are not yet a runner but are looking for a deeper reason to jog that first kilometer, then I know you will find inspiration in these pages.

Lastly, this book is dedicated to all the support people who make it possible to run seemingly insane distances. So, to my husband, who despite having food poisoning after eating a sketchy Caesar salad, still got on the *extremely* hot bus to watch me take off from the start line at the Honolulu marathon, I adore you. Your sacrifices have not gone unnoticed. Trust me, everyone noticed you throwing up in the bushes thirty feet from the start line!

Cheers to all the runners, aspiring runners, and support people! This book is for you.

Regaining Hope: Running is my Coping Mechanism for the Trauma of War

by Olena Sadovnik

Dedication

Dedicated to all mothers who took their children to safety and people who helped them in new countries.

Присвячується всім мамам, які вивезли своїх дітей в безпеку, та людям, які їм допомагають облаштуватися в нових країнах.

As we locked our apartment in the besieged Kyiv, Ukraine's capital, I heard the fast-approaching and terrifying sound of a military jet. I grabbed my three-year-old daughter, Malenka, firmly by the hand and readied ourselves to run, knowing that we might not get another chance. Our friend had agreed to take us out of the bombarded city and every second counted - we had to make it to the nearest metro station. It was an 800-meter journey. That was it. Nevertheless, it was the longest, most dreadful and terrifying run of my life.

I have lost friends to the war. Their lives were taken in an instant. I left my husband and tore our daughter from his loving embrace, not knowing if or when we would see him again. I took my toddler to three countries before finding refuge in Calgary, Alberta. My push to survive was not for me. It was for my daughter. I could not, and would not fail my child. For her, I had to find strength and new bearings to keep her safe.

It feels like a lifetime and the blink of an eye since that day, that I ran a death defying 800-meters with blaring air-raid sirens and a crying toddler in tow. Now, I am 9,000 kilometers from my home, a home that is being torn apart. Here I am today, and now, I find myself running for an entirely different reason.

My name is Olena, and this is the story of how I, as a refugee, found peace through running.

-- Struggling with Settling In --

I was finishing my coffee when the chair I was sitting on collapsed. It folded beneath me, screws falling out and rolling away as I landed on the floor with a thump. It was one of the few pieces of furniture in our new apartment in Calgary. A mattress, another chair, and a yoga mat, which served primarily as our dining table, were all we had.

I was sitting on the floor motionless and did not feel like getting up. This was literally the lowest point in my life. As I sat covered in coffee, I thought back to my life in Ukraine. I used to have a loving family, a fulfilling job, a home, friends, a hobby and my routine. Now, I had nothing. My days were filled with sitting alone in my flat and sobbing for all that I had lost.

I had not seen my hubby, Volodia, for eight months and did not have a clue when we were going to meet again. The uncertainty of it all was the most depressing reality. It was March 3rd, 2022, at the Slovakian-Ukrainian border when we kissed a quick goodbye. I was rushing to cross the border with Melanka on foot. Volodia remained in Ukraine because men of military age could not leave due to martial law. Back then, I did not think a lot about us or about our relationship. Horrified by the war, my only priority was bringing our daughter to a safe place outside Ukraine, far from missiles, explosions, and violence.

Now, sitting on the floor in this empty apartment far away from home, I was thinking about my husband. We were both humanitarian workers and met through work, in a conflict-stricken Eastern Ukraine in 2015. Volodia was searching for an office with a bomb shelter in Severodonetsk town, where I surveyed a local community about the risk of mines and unexploded ordnance. We both loved helping people to normalize their lives after what they had been through. The front line was roughly 30 kilometers away.

Ironically, the war that brought us together has now torn us apart. It was merciless. We had never been this far apart for so long. Many women with children had already returned to Ukraine, regardless of it being constantly targeted by Russian missiles. The pain of separation from loved ones, multiplied by refugee life hardships, takes over the fear of attacks. I, too, found myself with the obsessive thought of going back.

A plan of returning home was like a sweet delusion. It was like a constant sparring match in my head: Do I stay or do I go? Yet every time I thought about going home, I remembered how many people helped us come to Canada. My friends from all over the world, from the United States, Georgia, Croatia, Poland, Germany, Sweden and the United Kingdom organized a fundraising campaign to help us buy tickets to Calgary. I could not give up.

I felt miserable. I needed help, which brought me to the doctor again. I explained that there is a genocidal war enacted by Russia against Ukraine with ongoing fighting in the territory which also is the location of one of the largest nuclear power plants in the world. I tried to explain that there may be a catastrophe worse than the Chornobyl[1] disaster. I tried to elaborate: "I can't sleep, can't focus, can't look for a job in this state of mind." The herbal anti-stress drops, melatonin and over-the-counter sedatives that were first recommended were not helping.

I left the doctor's office empty-handed. The doctor didn't prescribe medication. I repeatedly reproach myself for not having enough sadness in my eyes during those visits, for holding back my tears, and for not getting it all off my chest. The doctor told me to listen to music before going to bed, "At least for half an hour."

Devastated and lost, I returned to the condo while my daughter was still in daycare. I curled up on the floor and cried. This was my only option for venting emotions. I could not cry

---

1. No, this isn't a spelling mistake. Russians use ChErnobyl - they deny the existence of the Ukrainian language, replacing geographical names in Ukrainian with Russian versions of them. This happened to the town of Chornobyl during the Soviet Union. Another example is Kyiv, referred to by Russians as Kiev. Unfortunately, many outlets such as BBC, CNN, and Hollywood follow the Russian version.

in front of her. Only once did I cry in front of her. She became so worried that I had to soothe her for a long time afterward.

I understood that I could not continue like this, but I did not know what to do about the situation I was in. My perception of life, of humanity, was shattered into pieces. I could not find myself in this new reality. It was not supposed to be like this! There was a deep wound inside of me, unable to heal.

How would I lift myself up out of this depression?

While I was still in Germany, waiting for our visas to go to Canada, my friends tried to support me in every way possible. They knew about my jogging hobby and offered to stay with my daughter while I de-stressed a bit by running. They even bought me a pair of running shoes and a jacket. At first, I loved the idea and went to a second-hand store to get a T-shirt and leggings. However, when it came to babysitting, Melanka became hysterical. She was terrified that I would leave her for good, and who could blame her? She was missing her daddy, grannies and grandpa. No amount of explaining was going to reassure a three-year-old that I would be back soon when everyone else in her life was just suddenly gone. As a mother, I could not do that to her again. I could not put her through that, even if it was just for thirty minutes. Jogging would have to wait.

-- My Last Run at Home, in Ukraine --

The memory of my last run in the pre-war city of Kyiv is vivid. It was on a Sunday in February 2022, four days before the large-scale war started. The mood in the city was already so tense one could cut through it with a knife. At work, we were preparing an evacuation plan and packing first-aid kits and emergency bags in case of an escalation. Russia had attacked southern and eastern Ukraine back in 2014. Now, the Russian military had concentrated massive troops alongside the Russian and Belarusian borders with Ukraine. It was bizarre. How could one country attack another in the twenty-first century?

I got ready for my winter run, which meant layers of clothing. We had just moved into our dream apartment after two years of waiting. Among our unpacked boxes, I found my running hat, buff and gloves. I spent some time rummaging through piles of clothing in a walk-in closet, looking for my favourite orange jacket I had bought in Poland on one of my business trips.

I really needed to go for a run to relieve the tension. It was going to be a tough week ahead. There were a lot of deadlines at work, and my mom was scheduled for a double surgery on Friday. I remember her asking me if my sneakers would stop the snow from getting my feet wet. Running was not common in the village she raised me in and the whole idea of running for fun was a bit strange to her.

I ran one lap around the nearby Teremky lakes and a cathedral. I heard the word 'war' a lot from many people I ran past. They spoke to each other while walking, talking on their phones or sitting on benches. There was no other topic but war. I was running a second lap and heard that someone had already left the capital. Some were hesitant about what to do, and others were saying, "It's just media hype and everything will be fine soon."

Bells on the Cathedral's Bell Tower rang non-stop. It felt as if they wanted to warn us about something... The incessant loud ringing made me anxious. My stomach was in knots as my breath quickened, not from the running but from the feeling of impending doom. I stopped to take a video, a part of me hoping that this madness would pass and the video would serve as a reminder of how we were on the brink of something horrible, the other part of me knowing that would not be the case.

At some point, the running chemistry kicked in, and I returned home in a much lighter mood. This was the first winter when I decided not to give up running because of the weather and cold. I was planning to run a half-marathon in April. I spent the rest of the day putting family pictures up on our walls, trying to push away the negativity and create a home for me and my family.

-- The Escape --

There was no spring for us. It was stolen by the war that came to our doorstep. Day and night became one. On one of those day-nights, I realised that my training schedule was already down the drain. Suddenly, the possibility of running a half-marathon became something unthinkable. The life that we knew had come to a standstill. I had been in a war zone before, but this time, I was a mother, and this was a game-changer for me. I had to get my daughter out of this madness.

Had we taken the usual road to the west, there would have been a high chance of me not writing these lines. This was the road that many were daring to take while trying to flee the almost encircled Kyiv. We could have become additional statistics as that road was notorious for attacks. Just another civilian car gunned down by Russian soldiers on the Zhytomyrska Trasa highway.

Calgary became a safe haven for Melanka and I. After a period of many tears (hers flowing freely while mine hid behind closed doors), fear and anxiety, I decided to start running again. Before the war, running was associated with some sort of peak in my life. I became a runner after the COVID lockdown and after the birth of my daughter. I started as a very slow jogger, motivated to return to my pre-baby body.

While working on shedding those itching kilos off, I noticed that after a run, my brain felt like it was wired differently. Running provided a feeling of lightness in my head. It allowed me to become present in the moment. It was truly empowering. Perhaps it could be compared with the feeling you get after the first glass of wine, except that it lasts longer and doesn't harm your body! I fell in love with this after-run feeling and continued with jogging after I reached my goal weight .

Today, running is one of the few parts of my identity not taken by the war. It is something I carried over with me to Canada as if it were a treasure trove of resilience and stability.

-- My First Run in Canada --

It was supposed to be my first run in Calgary after a substantial break. I took my daughter to daycare and, from there, walked to the Bow River's embankment. When I reached that point, I did not have the energy to actually start running.

In the middle of the night, the fire alarm had gone off in our building. My first thought was that a nuclear war had begun. At the time, the Russian propaganda was at its peak, saying how they would launch nuclear warheads on NATO countries.

It was a false alarm, but I could not go back to sleep. The anxiety and fear kept me awake and I was doing myself no favours as I lay in the dark of my bedroom, scrolling through the news from Ukraine. Ukrainian Armed Forces had just liberated the town of Izium in eastern Ukraine. They found over four-hundred bodies in several mass graves. Most with signs of torture.

I had been to Izium a few years prior with a group of journalists to cover stories of people from the war-ravaged Donetsk and Luhansk regions who found refuge in this small town. I remember each family we interviewed. I could not sleep that night.

In the morning, I felt sluggish and could not switch from walking to running. When I reached the pedestrian Peace Bridge between the Eau-Claire and Sunnyside, I remember feeling like I could scream. The name of the bridge sounded so ridiculous. The feelings of injustice, pain, and horror over the war crimes Russia were committing every day in Ukraine with impunity were too much.

My daughter and I are two among over seven million Ukrainians who crossed the border into the unknown, searching for safety. I loved my life back in Ukraine and never planned on leaving until the Russians invaded. They made us homeless.

I suddenly began to run. I attempted to run a sprint, putting 100% force into my steps. I was quickly out of breath, my body reminding me that eight months is quite a long break. I slowed down with my heart pounding in my ears.

I started noticing bright yellow leaves under my feet. Looking up, I saw trees with golden foliage that beautifully contrasted with the turquoise waters. It was a gorgeous fall day. When I reached a pedestrian bridge between Crescent Heights and Downtown, I could feel a warm wind blowing pleasantly. What a view – vast river to the right and left with Prince's Island Park and shining high-rises in front of me.

For the first time after so long, a spark of joy fluttered through me. The bliss of being able to observe this splendid autumn had me breathing deeply. I only wished I could have been there with my hubby. I stopped to snap a picture and sent it to him. That was all we had for now. It was the best I could do to include him in this rare moment of peace. As I walked across the bridge, I finally felt a bit of tension leave my chest. I felt myself enjoying the view of the river and being fully present in the moment of this beautiful, peaceful day. I slept well that night.

A new routine was born that day. Take Melanka to daycare and go for a run. I am not a fast runner. Add sleep deprivation and weight gain to that and, I'll be completely frank with you, I hated running. Nevertheless, it had a therapeutic effect on me, on my mental strength and resilience. Jogging lifted my spirit and gave me hope that things would get better. After completing my five kilometer morning run, I started to have energy for my daily tasks.

As running became easier physically, I learned to dream again. I imagined my hubby joining us and showing him everything around here. Jogging helped me discover the city; a city with so much beauty that deserved to be shared. A beauty that I knew my hubby would love.

My favourite path is Lawrey Gardens along the Bow River. It reminds me of my favourite place for running in Kyiv – VDNKh Park. It used to be my place of strength. Similarly, the Lawrey Gardens have tall leafy trees that form perfect shade and keep you cool on a hot day.

Some people asked me if I run to forget...no, you cannot simply forget that you have been torn apart from your soulmate while your friends hide in trenches or have been declared missing, likely taken into Russian captivity. The war is breathing down my neck, even if it is more than 9,000 kilometers away. You do not forget that.

I run to find the strength to move forward.

-- Refugee Life --

I grew up in a poor family in the early nineties, right after the collapse of the Soviet Union and the economic turmoil that followed. Like many people back then, my parents would not get paid for six to eight months.

We lived on vegetables we grew in our garden. We lacked basic things. My first pair of sneakers were two or three sizes too big. They were ugly and I felt like a clown. I really wanted the white sneakers with the gummy bear on the Velcro that were a perfect fit, but my mom insisted on buying the bigger ones because my feet were growing fast, and we could not afford to buy new shoes every season. When I wore those ugly sneakers to the hilt, they were still too large for me.

Throughout my life, I took very calculated steps to lift myself out of poverty, first with my parents' help and then with international scholarships. I was able to succeed in education and land a good job in Kyiv.

I did everything possible so that my child would not feel the same level of poverty that I went through as a kid. And yet, here I was in Canada, applying for Food Bank support and buying my daughter shoes that were two sizes bigger than she needed.

Meanwhile, Melanka began to forget her Dad. She was becoming less and less interested in talking to him through the phone screen and she no longer asked me when Daddy would be coming home. It had been ten months since she had seen him in person. For a three-year-old, that is one-third of her life.

The separation turned unbearable. By early November, before the clocks changed to winter time, the mornings in Calgary were especially dark, with 7:30 A.M. feeling like the deep night.

"Mommy, I'm scared." Melanka's voice was small as I pushed her stroller through the dark streets.

"Sweetheart, I do not like darkness either, but the dawn will be here soon." Although, even my eyes nervously scanned the empty streets, looking for signs of life.

Each day, I took the C-train to work and back, picking my daughter up ten hours later only to go home in the same darkness we had arrived. With the nine hour time difference with Ukraine, and the full-time job, keeping in touch with my hubby was challenging and the loneliness was all consuming.

There was no more room for running either. I was left to live on the lingering fumes from my gorgeous autumn runs along the river and dream about my husband joining us so that I could go back to jogging again.

-- The Reunion --

On December 21, 2022, my hubby arrived. It was a true Christmas Miracle. Two hundred ninety-three days of separation disappeared in the airport as our family of three found ourselves together again. Melanka clung to her Dad for an entire week. Memories of her loving Daddy flooding her body with the instinct to never let go taking hold. The three of us are now together. Life goes on, but so does the war.

-- What Comes Next --

Saturday jogs are the hardest for me. In the mornings, we call our family and friends. The news they share with us is always death, funerals and injuries. After these calls, I usually go for a long run, desperate for anything to dispel the sadness and feelings of being homesick for a country that would likely mean death if we were to return.

Sometimes, I feel like I am not living my own life. Surreal feelings come forth as if there was a malfunction in the matrix and everything went wrong. Needless to say, I was not ready for the hardships of refugee life. Losing my identity and financial stability and embarking into complete uncertainty upended my sense of normalcy. Who could really be ready for something like that?

Running helps me to ease this anxiety and remain grounded without worrying too much.

Before the war, I was focused on losing weight, running techniques, and getting better results. Now, the physical side is way less important for me. I run for the sake of decompressing; it gives me a sense of ease and normality. I came into running in search of a stronger body but continued for the sake of not losing my mind. Every step is a reminder that if I can come this far, I can go further, regardless of how hard life becomes.

Running Through Grief

by Tania Jacobs

Dedication

For my village, who scooped me up in their loving arms when I needed it most, and for my Run Family, for inspiring me and giving me somewhere new to belong.
Thank you, and I love you all.

I wanted to scream. My body felt like a pop bottle that had been shaken up; fizzy bubbles coalescing into a mass of pressure, an explosion begging to be released. Bubbles of anguish, despair, anger, frustration, sadness and overwhelm were all swimming in a sea of numbness. Somehow, screaming felt like the answer. Maybe alone in the ravine, I could let the scream out.

I laced up my shoes and pulled on a toque and gloves. "I'll be back in 45 min," I said to my mom, who was hovering anxiously in the kitchen, wiping already clean surfaces with a damp cloth. "Ok," she trailed off reluctantly. Unable to resist, she added, "Are you sure you should be running? You're barely sleeping or eating." I resisted the urge to roll my eyes and closed the door, throat constricted with the contained growl of frustration, pretending I hadn't heard her. I ran down the deserted paved trail into the ravine; the puffs of my breath making small clouds in the cold January air. For a moment, I appreciated the sound of my breathing. I wasn't sure I would ever take healthy breathing for granted again. I looked around for dog-walkers and stroller-pushers. The trees were too naked. I wanted more cover. Seeing no one, I opened my mouth to release the scream but only a small sound came out. Frustrated, I tried again, but I couldn't overcome my self-consciousness. What if there was someone just out of view? What if I scared them? What if they called 9-1-1? Could you get a ticket for public screaming? Instead, I ran harder and sprinted up a set of stairs, leaking out small, anguished sounds as I went. I would later read about other cultures that encourage wailing and audible carrying-on as a way to honour the dead and I would think about how poorly we do grief as a society. We wouldn't want to make anyone else uncomfortable. I couldn't quite release the scream, but the run helped me to re-enter my body and enjoy the basic sensations of firing muscles and a pumping, healthy heart. Sweat met cold. Frost kissed my eyelashes. Breathing hard felt so satisfying when it seemed that nothing else did. The world I had known was completely destroyed.

My 39-year-old husband Trevor had died the Sunday before, leaving me a 37-year-old widow and single mother. A week before that, he'd been completely fine. We had mundanely been cleaning up Christmas decorations, parenting two snotty and coughing preschoolers, and trying to figure out why the check engine light kept coming on in my vehicle. Looking back, that seems oddly prophetic. Trevor had developed flu-like symptoms midweek. After less than 48 hours in the hospital on life support battling what turned out to be an invasive Group-A strep infection (the same bug can also cause strep throat, scarlet fever, or flesh-eating disease), he was gone. His organs succumbed to toxic shock as the antibiotics failed to kill the bacteria fast enough. I was in shock - feeling mostly numb, punctuated with surges of intense emotion that I couldn't seem to release. I was exhausted but could only sleep for a couple of hours at a time; I'd get hungry, but after only a couple of bites, nausea would win over. For the record, my doctor said running was the best thing I could do to battle the flood of stress hormones coursing through my body, which disproved my mom's concerns about my coping method. I didn't cry much, which mostly just made me feel like I was doing grief wrong. Running seemed to be the most effective remedy.

It might sound weird, but an incredible amount of beauty came out of Trevor's death. After watching him struggle to breathe on his own, then watching a machine breathe for him, and then witnessing his lungs stop functioning entirely, breathing now felt like a privilege. Being alive felt like a gift; an opportunity not to be wasted. I now understood that the end could come at any time and damn it, I was and am really grateful to still be here. Each moment feels precious. I am going to get to watch my babies grow up, barring any unexpected event like the one that ripped away my partner without warning. I am going to enjoy living in this body and experiencing as much of what the world has to offer as I can. In the immediate aftermath, his death also brought people together. The morning of Trevor's celebration of life, the river valley was painted white with hoar frost. I met with a group of running friends, many of whom I hadn't seen in ages. Everyone held me gently as we gathered at the trailhead, watching me carefully as if I were an egg in danger of cracking. The reunion created a vaguely inappropriately festive feel. As we started to run and the group stretched out along the single track, I felt the stirrings of loneliness. This empty void within was a feeling that would become a regular companion over the coming months. Even within this group of friendly faces, I now felt strange. Where did I belong? I was coming home to something I had not had the freedom to be a part of in a long time - a group run with other adults. I am so grateful to my family for watching my kids. It felt exciting but also as if I were missing a limb. I could already feel that I was irrevocably changed by widowhood. There was no way to avoid becoming a different version of myself. Nevertheless, as I focused on my footing and navigating the trails, all of that faded away. Someone ahead gave a whoop and a bunch of us whooped back. "Trevor would have loved this," I thought. He would want me to enjoy the moment of frolicking on the trails as a light snow fell. If all I had to do right now was run, I knew how to do that. One foot in front of the other, coordinated muscle movements to keep me upright, on the trail, and moving forward. This was simple. I was even able to allow myself to have fun.

Prior to this, I had been slowly easing back into running after five years that included two pregnancies and a lot of breastfeeding and sleepless nights with small kids. The summer before, in the middle of a very soggy camping trip with friends, Trevor and I plotted our return to the Canadian Death Race (CDR). This 118 kilometer ultramarathon in Grande Cache, Alberta, passes over three mountain summits and includes over 17,000 feet of elevation change. You can run it solo or as a relay team of up to five runners. We had both done the latter a few times prior to having kids. We entered a relay team including ourselves, our friends and Trevor's sister. I was now missing a team member not only for this race, but for an entire future that I had been looking forward to enjoying together. The thought never entered my mind that we wouldn't still go to the race. Instead, it quickly became a memorial team. We would run the race in his memory.

CDR 2017: The race weekend was everything we'd hoped for - a beautiful day, the usual vibrant race atmosphere and solid performances by everyone on the team. A lot of planning had gone into this - finding hotels, designing matching t-shirts with Trevor's silhouette on them and my eldest was going to run the kids race. In the months since Trevor had died, I had found it very difficult to plan anything. This was no small mental feat to organize with the rusty planning gears in my brain grinding their way back to life. Having this goal on the horizon also gave some shape and respite to those early days of grief, where I often felt like a bit of a zombie floating through the strange landscape of my new life. I increased my run mileage and frequency. I repeatedly discovered that whatever turmoil I was currently experiencing would fade away as I moved myself down the trail; navigating roots and other natural obstacles, one foot in front of the other, muscles working and lungs breathing smoothly.

The night before the race, I imagined Trevor was there watching over us as I spied a huge raven perched on an impossibly thin branch at the top of a pine tree near our hotel, pink clouds decorating the sky as the sun traded places with the moon. Trevor loved ravens and somehow that made it feel as though he was close. I knew he would be happy we were there. I don't know what I believe about what happens to someone after death, but perhaps he had a hand in making us all fleet of foot. We finished at the top of the team podium that year! I stood at the finish line, waiting for Trevor's sister to arrive, the evening light golden as the sun made its descent over the mountains. I was super proud of my performance on Leg Two earlier in the day - I had felt strong and precisely nailed my goal time of four hours for the 27 kilometer leg, which summits two peaks. Riding the endorphin high, and possibly under the influence of a celebratory beverage, I looked at our friend Andrew, who had run Trevor's assigned leg of the race, and asked, "Do you think I could do it? I mean, the whole thing?"

"Solo the race?" he replied, eyebrows shooting up. "Yeah, you could. You totally could. Do it!" He had soloed a few years earlier, so I knew his opinion was valid. He grinned and gave me a high-five. I grinned and sipped my prosecco, my heart swelling with equal parts hope and nostalgia. *Trevor should be here for this,* I thought to myself. But if he were, I probably wouldn't have had the conversation. At that moment, I was struck by how weird life can manifest. A glimmer of possibility sprang to life within me, transforming rapidly into something more solid. I knew at that moment that I was going to cross this finish line by myself. I would never have uttered those words out loud at the time, but inside, I knew.

The first time I attended the Canadian Death Race in 2010, I was blown away. Relatively new to trail running, I was running a 21 kilometer section, which would be my longest distance to date. Soloing seemed absolutely unfathomable. I may have even said, "these people are crazy!" And yet, Trevor and I were there on relay teams alongside a friend who was soloing. I'd been watching him train for months: getting up early to run repeats of the ski hill in our hometown of Edmonton, Alberta, and running for hours every weekend. Frankly, it sounded like way too much work. However, watching him cross the finish line in an impressive 16.5 hours, throwing down his trekking poles and exclaiming, "Fuck! That was hard!" struck some kind of chord inside. I had always been someone who loved conquering hard things. "Maybe when I turn 40," I'd flippantly said, easy words for someone on the eve of her 31st birthday to throw around.

Now, my 40th birthday was just two years away, and I was also a very long way from being ready to run over 100 kilometers. Suddenly, and for the first time in a long time, it felt like there was something in the future that I could see clearly.

The early stages of widowhood are like running along a familiar trail, knowing absolutely where you are going and what it will look like. You barely even notice the turns and you can run this way on auto-pilot. Most unexpectedly, a bomb goes off on the trail just ahead of you. You pick yourself up and dust yourself off, realizing with relief that you are physically unscathed. For a while, you stand there, ears ringing, unable to see anything at all. You know you are in a familiar place, but as the dust begins to settle and you look around, you feel completely disoriented. Nothing looks familiar. Which way do you go now? The trail that you were on is gone. I was parenting by myself. I'd stopped working, not knowing at that point if I would ever return to my career as a Registered Psychologist. I was 37 and single again. I was a social oddity; some of my friends were going through a divorce, but no one had a dead spouse. I could barely figure out what was for dinner, much less what the rest of my life was going to look like.

Setting that goal to solo the Canadian Death Race felt like finding a new trail leading out of the bomb site. This wasn't the way I'd been planning to go, but it held promise. I tentatively started to walk away from the explosion. The further away I got, the more interesting the path became. I met fantastic new people and discovered that there were constant opportunities for side journeys on this trail: other races and adventures that I needed to do in order to prepare my body for an ultramarathon, but that also deeply fed my soul and healed some of the grief. These included running the Skyline trail in Jasper, Canmore's "Triple Crown," and Rim2Rim2Rim in the Grand Canyon. Standing in some of the most incredibly beautiful places the world has to offer, having arrived by the combined power of my own body and my will, made me feel more alive and more like myself than anything else had in a long time. This was exactly what I wanted to be doing with my life, but it is strange to think that I likely would not have experienced any of this if Trevor was still alive.

Arriving in Grande Cache to solo the Canadian Death Race in 2019 was incredibly exciting. I remember milling around the race expo with a tummy full of butterflies. I was ecstatic to see many familiar faces of the run community I belonged to and jazzed to be tackling this HUGE goal just a couple of days shy of my 40th birthday. I felt as ready as I was going to be. Mixed in were some teary, reflective moments as I decorated a prayer flag to hang at the top of Mt. Hamel - the summit on the fourth leg of the race. It said, "Trevor Nickel - Forever in our Hearts." My heart overflowed with emotions: at this point, every run was a celebration of being alive, but this one was going to be next-level epic. Trevor was missing it, and we missed him; yet I had so many people here to support me. All of the feelings and the moment itself were almost too hard to take in. I was happy and sad, wistful and excited, nostalgic, confident and incredibly grateful all at once.

Time seemed to accelerate the closer we came to the race start, and while I wanted to savour it, I was also keen to get running. My crew had decorated my running pack with a ribbon and a sign that said, "I'm turning 40, wish me a Happy Birthday," so for the whole of the race, my fellow racers wished me happy birthday, creating connection and conversation with total strangers in a 118 kilometer-long party. My non-running friends thought this was a strange way to celebrate, but I knew better than anyone that turning 40 is a privilege not everyone gets to experience.

The course was very wet that year, adding massive puddles and rivers of flowing mud to the list of obstacles on the trail. For the first couple of legs of the race I cruised along, executing my race plan to perfection and feeling strong. I saw plenty of familiar faces, and it truly felt like a celebration both of having survived the past two-and-a-half years of widowhood and of my hard work in preparing my body for this. As soon as I began the third leg, the crowd thinned significantly, and I started to experience long stretches of time on my own. While I did not feel despair, the "high" of the party was definitely over. I turned into Goldilocks, fussing with my gear: I took my jacket on and off a half dozen times as rain showers cycled overhead, and I felt too cold, then too hot. I stowed my trekking poles and took them out again, not liking the way they jostled in my pack. I was hungry but not hungry, and none of the snacks I could find seemed just right. It got harder and harder to convince my body to run. I just wanted to walk. These doldrums are where an ultramarathon gets real. Thankfully, I knew what to do and I'd had plenty of experience with grief: hunker down, keep moving forward, one foot in front of the other. Find something small to appreciate in the present. Find something to look forward to.

My kids, my parents and my best friend were waiting for me at the next transition area. They were my motivation.

For me, one of the most significant moments of the race was reaching the top of Mt. Hamel on the fourth leg. It had been a long climb up; some of the trail was a rivulet of flowing mud, and as I neared the top, the rain clouds disappeared, pushed away by a strong wind. I cinched my hood as tight as I could against the chilly wind howling in my ears. Euphoric at having reached the top, I turned to the summit as a running acquaintance caught up and we paused together to admire the hundreds of prayer flags flapping in the wind. It was emotional to think that Trevor's flag was in there somewhere among other remembered loved ones'. My loss, while significant and meaningful, was also part of the collective human experience of connecting with others, of loving and grieving. "I think we're a bit closer to those lost loved ones up here, don't you?" he asked me. I smiled and took a big breath, nodding my agreement but unable to produce any relevant words. I hoped to keep up with him for company, but he jogged ahead, buoyed by the impending descent, so I shouted, "Go Death Racer!" in encouragement, settling back into my own rhythm and battle to keep moving forward.

Finally, after many more hours of slogging one foot in front of the other, I emerged from the dark forest into town. Slightly disoriented, it took me a moment to realize that I was only a block and a half from the finish line. I could hear the cheering, and suddenly, I got a burst of energy, picking up my pace from a tired shuffle to a surprisingly smooth run. Tears filled my eyes. I had successfully soloed the Canadian Death Race! Trevor would be so proud of me. I looked up, and spanning the area under the start/finish arch, a dozen giant sparklers lit up the dark, and I realized that there, at 4:15 am, were all of my people, singing Happy Birthday! I fell into their collective waiting arms for a massive group hug and thought to myself, "What a great day to be alive!"

A Summer of Miles

by Ed Bickley

Dedication - Credit Where It's Due

My organizing committee – Blaine, Megan, Jeremy, and Jody, were all there with help through the entire adventure – from the initial brainstorming through the arranging of events and group runs during the summer. It could never have developed into what it became without their help.

My wife, Michelle - who helped with many of the group nights in the sun and rain, put up with modifying many of our vacation and personal plans through the summer, and endured my focus on the enterprise. I owe her for this and a lot of other things.

My son, Brad - who supported me by running 60 sub-5 minute miles. He also helped bring about the two Kelowna group nights at the Apple Bowl and introduced me to that community.

My regular training buddies who got me through a lot of the miles on 'non-group' days, including Cesar Martin who joined for a lot of them and became an honorary mile streaker.

CanadaHelps made the process of customizing a '60 in 6' donation website easy.

And, obviously, all the people who joined, encouraged, or donated.

On a cool morning in September 2018, I'm running on an asphalt path in Central Park, New York City. There are many other runners in sight but I'm effectively alone in the big city. I breathe in the crisp autumn air, appreciating the unique scenery and urban sounds of the park. I'm warming up mentally and physically to run 1 mile at a sub-6-minute pace. I'm also rolling memories around in my mind, musing about the challenges and significance of the events of the past months that lead me here.

A year prior, I had started considering how I might mark my then-upcoming 60th birthday. I could ignore the milestone but then I'd likely end up with regrets if it just passed by. Should I throw a party? It would be fun to spend time with the right set of people. Should I do some sort of long running or race-related stunt? The longer I thought about it, the less those ideas felt right.

As background: I'm a competitive age-group runner, I married early and well, making my personal and family life pretty great. For forty years, I had a good I.T. career, so financially we were in fine shape. And yet, I could see retirement looming. My family was grown, and I was frequently being treated as 'an older person.' I started running about 35 years ago. Initially, running began as a one-time marathon challenge and later as a source of stress relief, personal accomplishment and social interaction. I'd run hundreds of road, cross-country and track races across North America and other parts of the world. I had logged the equivalent of more than three trips around the earth, collected four shoe boxes full of race medals and finished 110 marathons with 50 of them under three hours. My running library had grown into more than 100 books on training and performance theory and I'd done some informal coaching. I've done this running thing about as completely and whole-heartedly as anyone, while working full-time and helping to raise a family. I was enjoying it as much as ever, although my race times had been following a typical age-grading curve[1] downward and I had more difficulty recovering from hard runs or workouts.

I should have been happy approaching another birthday; most runners look forward to being instantly-competitive in a new age-group. This one seemed different as it came with the threat of looming decisions and changes which I'd been postponing for a long time. Yet, I still felt like I was just getting started with life, with running, and with accomplishing things in the world.

---

1. 'Age grading' is a mathematical technique that calculates, based on a race time and your current age, what a corresponding time would be for a younger person in their prime. Based on the average performance curves of a large population sample over time, it's a way of equalizing race results across age groups.

I've always been motivated by setting goals, so some sort of stretch goal that would be different from the cycles of training programs and races I've filled the previous decades with seemed in order. I had some criteria. One: it would need to re-connect me with some of the people I've run with in the past. As an introvert, you need to force yourself to 'get out there' once in a while. Two: I wanted a goal that was about something bigger than just me, as a lot of my running and training in the past had been just for myself.

One evening, an idea dropped in my lap in the form of an article on the internet: "A Crazy Speed Streak: Man Going for a Sub-5:00 Mile 105 Days in a Row".[2] It described how a post-collegiate runner in his twenties, Patrick McGregor, had broken his former coach's record for sub-5 minute miles on 105 consecutive days. I was drawn to this for several reasons: those miles are fast, the mile as a track distance is cool to me, and staying focused, healthy and non-injured for that length of time would be a great challenge.

This led me to set a personal target for a mile-a-day streak (age-graded to 6:00/mile for age 60) for 60 days ('60 in 6').

---

2. https://www.runnersworld.com/news/a20853025/a-crazy-speed-streak-man-going-for-a-sub-5-00-mile-105-days-in-a-row/

I would officially start on my 60th birthday in early July and proceed through the rest of the summer. In western Canada, this would be the only time of year when the weather would consistently allow running quickly outside. I asked people I had run with before to join me for at least one of the miles, by 'streaking' through the summer at their own pace, and/or by fundraising for charity. Since I'm compulsively competitive, I also set a private personal objective of running those miles for 120 days to adequately match McGregor's streak.

There didn't seem to be any way to successfully pull this off without a bunch of help. I had built a network of local runners over the years, so I was able to pull together a group to bounce ideas off. They quickly became an ad-hoc 'organizing committee.' They were so supportive and positive, that they were soon encouraging me to think bigger. With their enthusiasm and arm-twisting, I was soon locally 'outed' as something that was going to happen in the running community. This created some unease for me as I hadn't really done anything like this and wasn't sure I was the right personality to be in the spotlight organizing and marketing a charity effort.

We selected the charity we would fundraise for. I initially thought that we would have each person who joined me for a run pay $60 (like a race fee). If we could sell all 60 miles, that would raise $3,600 which I would match to raise $7,200. To achieve this level or higher, we expanded beyond my immediate network; arranging sponsorships to fund T-shirts and other prizes to attract more donors and participants.

On the morning of May 14, 2018, I was alone at the 'Apple Bowl' track in Kelowna, B.C. It was part of a visit with my son and his wife, who live there, and I was facing the first of my many 1 mile time trials. After a 20-minute warm up, I banged out a fairly easy 5:47 mile, and then cooled down a few minutes. This formed the template for the days to come. Running a mile on a track is a bit different than the experience of running one on a 'point-to-point' pathway or road. The track constantly gives you checkpoints about your pace and lap-times. The first lap is mainly about setting your pace, the second about holding it, the third about hitting the '600-meters-to-go' point at the right 'split' time and the fourth is about pressing back hard against the fatigue that's building in your legs.

I continued fitting daily 1 mile efforts in through May and June. By the start of the official charity effort, I had already notched 49 unofficial bonus runs with little or no physical wear and tear on my body. This even included a road mile race where I set what was to become my fastest mile of the year (5:24). I also picked up some daily pacing help from people in the group I regularly ran with.

Concurrent with May and June's unofficial runs, was the setup of a website for donations, design of a logo and order ing of T-shirts; all with the help of my organizing committee. I scheduled the upcoming summer runs as much as possible around the travel we had already planned. This allowed me to publish a July/August calendar so donors would know where and when to join me. I created a '60 in 6' Facebook group- the focus was to publicize and market, get people interested, and persuade them to start donating. I also wrote an article about my plans for a local fitness magazine which was published in their April issue.

When the start of my official '60 in 6' runs (my 60th birthday) arrived – it was time to take charge and 'lead' the donors and groups through the warm-ups, miles and cooldown debriefs, and to take photos documenting the event. I gradually grew into this role as the summer wore on. Things were going surprisingly well, and many donations were collected. Another bonus was the 'swag packages' for the donors. I had run in different towns with various groups over the years, so we had scheduled out-of-town Group Events which turned out to be highlights of the series, as well as a couple of special 'road mile' races in the United States.

-- Some memorable moments --

- Kick-off night in Invermere with the local running phenom, Kuba, flying around the track on his own
- My son and David Guss sprinting the mile on a rainy July group night in Kelowna
- An appearance by Ted Jaleta[3] at the track in Regina
- The Bow Valley Harrier nights at Calgary's Glenmore Track featuring both costuming, big 'Ed Head' cut-outs and stroller competitions
- 'Ladies night' in July, where I had the privilege of being passed on the track by most of the Phoenix Ladies Track team and a big gathering of other estrogen-powered athletes

The miles flew by and my confidence grew with each day.

Suddenly, things became more complicated. I had gone into the summer with a minor nagging sore ankle, which seemed manageable enough. However, during a mile in mid-August, with just two weeks remaining, it flared up. My ankle was aching

---

3. https://sachm.org/virtual-museum/category/ted-jaleta

for the rest of the weekend whether I was standing on it or lying down, and I looked like I was much more than 60-years-old limping around on it. The next morning was a dilemma as it didn't seem wise to try to run on it when I could barely get down the stairs. Still, with barely ten days left to go, it would have been very disappointing to just stop – I had come so far and so many people had joined along the way. I was publicly committed to this and virtually everyone I knew was following along.

My wife Michelle came to my rescue by saying she was afraid that I'd feel devastated if I didn't finish the streak. I knew she didn't really want me to try to run that day but her support was unwavering. This was a bit like the 'bell ring' moment in a Rocky movie. I knew I had to give it whatever I could muster. I waited until late in the afternoon, got my running gear on and loosened up the ankle by walking a mile, then jogging a mile slowly, then running one easy. At that point, although the ankle hurt, there wasn't any additional pain when I put weight on it. So, despite starting the mile at what felt and looked like a 'fast limp.' I was able to squeeze out a sub-6 mile without making the injury any worse.

After that, the next week brought a string of other pains. These were probably the result of an unnatural gait due to the ankle, but I was able to get under the time goal each day. I spent each day hoping to feel a bit better the following day; a wish that eventually started to come true the last week of August. On Day 60 of the official effort, at the local track, I and a big group of supporters ran a 'Friday Foothills Finale' – a beautiful morning at the track with a big group of people who had participated throughout the summer.

To conclude my private 120 mile streak, I continued on my own for ten more days, allowing my wife and me to travel to New York City to incorporate the Fifth Avenue Mile road race into the streak as my second-last mile. This was a fantastic book-end to the effort.

The next morning, on my solitary run in Central Park, as I prepare to finish mile #120, I'm still processing the events of the previous months. While I was explaining my streak with a fellow at work, he asked, "Is that hard to do?" I assumed the disclaimer "for a runner like you", or worse, "for a person your age" was implied. He isn't a runner so, without a point of reference, he may not have known whether a six-minute mile was difficult or not. Still, I was a little frustrated with the question. A six-minute mile pace is close enough to race pace for me that, while not a flat-out effort, it's difficult enough that a distraction, injury or illness could make it very difficult. I've since re-casted his question as one about the overall streak.

Looking back, there were a series of 'hard' and 'not so hard' aspects:

-- Hard Parts --

Acting as the 'Social Director'

Although these events mostly arranged themselves and while I got a lot of help from my 'organizing committee', these added a lot to the summer's duties. It took time and energy to get people out and to ensure they felt included; I was happy when the larger events came together successfully.

Being Driven by the Calendar

For example, driving all night from Salmon Arm, British Columbia, to Calgary, Alberta, to get to the Calgary Kick-off the next morning. Various other trips to runs across British Columbia and Alberta, coupled with the weight of having a timed mile as a daily commitment, turned life into a bit of a 'treadmill'. As the summer went on, it turned running into something resembling a second job.

Air You Can Taste

In early August, the now-annual Alberta forest fire season started. Most days, the runs were in air you'd find in a 1970's bingo parlour. I don't think this slowed any of my runs but I did notice some 'wheeziness' in my breathing during the last quarter of some of the smokier miles. Worse, it may have discouraged some people from coming out who otherwise might have joined.

-- Not So Hard Parts --

Re-connecting

One of my original goals was to use the streak to reconnect with the people I've run with over the years and it became a great way to do so. Many of the running communities and clubs in Calgary, Kelowna, and Invermere came out, had fun and ran the miles with me.

Travel

It was a great change of pace for me to run in unusual venues and at different times than I would have normally. Some memories included: early morning miles at Foothills Track (some solitary, some with others), a hot afternoon on the track in Regina, the Pearl Street Road Mile Race in Boulder, a two-loop mile around McGuire Lake Park in Salmon Arm, the Rails and Trails Bike Path in Kelowna, and, of course, the Fifth Avenue Mile in New York City.

Fundraising

Originally, I had assumed I would have to drag donations out of people, but the running community, my social circle and my co-workers all stepped up with very little persuasion. In early planning, my stretch target was pretty modest – the final fundraising count was over $26,000!

Was it hard to run any specific sub-6:00 mile? They all had me a bit nervous at the start line and usually left me doubled over my knees at their end. Some of them were relatively easy, some were difficult, some were in tough weather and some were 'down to the wire' (a couple of 5:59 times). Overall, what made them worthwhile were the people who joined and others who encouraged me with their words or donations. For them, I'm honestly grateful as they made the summer fly by. So, the answer to the question 'is that hard to do?' became, like everything else in life that's worth doing, 'yes and no.' There were lots of hard parts. However, with enough people helping, a bit of luck, and some effort, things turned out bigger, better, and more fun than I would have ever expected. This ended up dwarfing my birthday and became a much bigger life highlight for me.

Now, it's time to focus and finish that last mile...

Finding My Fire

by Priscilla Forgie

Trigger Warning
Reference to sexual abuse

Dedication

For all the children who kept quiet to survive.
I hope one day your voice can set you free.

Acknowledgements

Thank you to the running community - you got me out the door more days than you'll ever know.
Most of all, thank you to Dan - for sharing your light when mine was too dim to see.

My mind is on fire. Or, am I just feeling the sun in the Arizona desert? It's tough to tell, and frankly, I don't really care. I just want relief.

I breathe in deeply, hoping to settle the blaze between my ears. Instead, I choke on the hot, dusty air. No relief comes, just more burning and regret. The desert is so unforgiving. My brain is unrelenting.

The laboured breathing and heavy footsteps of other runners in the Javelina Jundred race have trickled away as the gap between us widens. I feel abandoned; their presence was a melody and a stark contrast from the insidious screeching inside of me. The front of the pack is long gone and I chastise myself for slowing down. A self-fulfilling prophecy festers and my tainted beliefs soon morph into my reality as I fall back. The desert landscape spans ahead, replicating my emotional state - barren and detached. For an area so physically foreign to me, I consider how ironic it is that I can relate to the desolation so well.

Alas, I carry a darkness into this race. The sun shines fiercely, yet a cloud looms over me, and each step forward feels like an effort to outrun its shadows. The rhythmic beat of my running shoes on the dry trail attempts to drown out the haunting whispers of my past. Still, the voices grow louder, echoing from a deep, dark place that I buried long ago.

My mental agony and physical exhaustion become intertwined. Before I can grasp a new distraction, my mind makes a U-turn that feels illegal to my body. I'm too fragile to withstand it. Every step I take loosens the latch on the door I was certain I had deadbolted. There is a frog in my throat so large I anticipate any words to be replaced by a ribbit. Instead, I gag. I try to suppress the vomit that rises but the memories boil into my mouth as if I'm a kettle about to burst. My eyes well with tears, forming puddles that are held back by the concrete walls I have built within. The tears threaten to overflow, taunting me to reveal my weakness. I long for them to drown me and put me out of my misery.

Departing from my dissociative state, I imagine the discomfort of coming across a photographer at this moment. My smile would twitch, it's fraudulent nature quivering at the thought of exposure. I envision the photographer attempting to uplift my spirits while adding another photo of a teary-eyed runner to their portfolio. If only I was out here crying over my relaxed training plan or the audacity of the race director to allow any wintered Canadian to step foot on this Mars-like trail. I'd do anything for my body to be aching instead.

Just then, I catch something out of the corner of my eye. Not a photographer, but all eight eyes are tracking me. My first ever tarantula sighting. Such a sweet and fuzzy creature, so underrated. The tarantula exudes an unexpected peacefulness. He is content with his existence despite the negative reputation so often associated with his kind. I aspire to be like him; my sense of self unaffected by the external influences surrounding me. Yet, I'm allured to the idea of seclusion beneath a rock, sheltered from the grave world. I snap back to reality, telling myself that the desert is this tarantula's bed, not mine. The beautiful warning lingers as I trudge ahead smiling. I am grateful for his existence, allowing me to escape my pain for just a moment.

That October morning, I had toed the start line to race a flat 100-miler, but in my mind I negotiated a full obstacle course. Stomach-churning memories plagued me for the whole race. ..or at least the part I was able to complete before I decided to drop out. I sat there in the dark, cold desert with my blistered feet diverting me from the lesions inside my mind. As I assured others I was fine, it was just one thought that incessantly repeated.

I was no longer fixated on the memories, but rather, the person who left those memories seared permanently into my brain. Did they take running away from me? And would I ever get it back?

My mind was on fire and I couldn't blame the sun any longer.

-- Finding my Fire --

I may have not finished the Javelina Jundred race, but I was only just embarking on the most difficult journey of my life. Months before the race I began a relentless battle with Post-Traumatic Stress Disorder, or PTSD, from long-suppressed memories of childhood sexual abuse. In 2022, at 31-years-old, the latch on the door I had carefully kept locked creaked open. Unraveled from within was a spin top of tightly wound up events and emotions that my brain had kept hidden in order to protect me. The tormenting memories clawed at the edges of my consciousness, revealing that my fears as a child weren't confined to the monsters creeping inside my closet, but the one that laid in my bed.

My childhood and adulthood minds collided, like two estranged souls reluctantly reuniting in a claustrophobic battle for space. This realization of my suppressed memories was too big and too frightening for me to hold onto. I was left plagued with fear, confusion and mourning of the life I once knew. So, I turned to something comforting; seeking solace in a familiar refuge.

I ran. And I ran a lot.

This story is about my path through trauma. A woven pathway that I will likely continue to traverse throughout the rest of my life. I've been running a lot of miles and through a lot of pain, ultimately, in hopes of finding peace.

PTSD manifested like shadows within me, unleashing unforeseen shrieks throughout the day and night, frightening me beyond repair. The unpredictability of when a flashback or nightmare would leave me frozen kept me in a constant state of unease. My soul felt trapped in a dark hole of my past while my body floated lifelessly in the present and my mind itched for the distant future.

Processing my trauma felt akin to an unscalable mountain. It was never the mountain peaks, harsh weather or the burn of lactate in my legs, but the stillness that scared me the most. By being present, I was forced to face the realities I had spent my whole life avoiding. Having mastered distracting myself to keep my feelings at bay and reality far away, the thought of doing the opposite felt disjointed. Talking about my memories triggered a visceral response - my skin crawled, waves of nausea felt like they were drowning me, and my chest tightened like an automatic corset pulling me tighter and tighter. Nevertheless, to get through this I needed to dig deep and allow those feelings to trickle to the surface. To manage the exposures, outside of therapy my focus shifted to things that brought me true joy. That sounded so simple, but for a long time I wasn't sure if there was anything that would bring me happiness again. Practicing mindfulness, journaling, baking and being with animals became my anchors; fueling me for my next therapy session. One of the tools I eventually connected with most was anything but static. I gravitated towards an unpredictable constant, a moving presence and an energetic calm.

What manifested, of course, was running.

When I first began running consistently in 2018, I was convinced it had to be some kind of sorcery. How could something be simultaneously loathed and loved? Why was the spectrum of opinion on this sport so wide? Were runners just cast into some kind of nasty spell to enjoy this torture? Perhaps it was as Dean Karnazes said, "There is magic in misery. Just ask any runner."

Whatever sadistic witchcraft is going on, I've seen runners do just about anything to lace up their shoes. They will run through injuries, countries, holiday gatherings, and, even funerals. A seemingly 'easy hike' morphs into an unrelenting 40 kilometer mountain pass with scrambles, bushwhacking and a query of survival. Limps and hobbles are dismissed as mere sore muscles, a blind eye taken to the neglected hamstring and dust-collected dumbbells. Icicle eyelashes and beards are donned in bone-chilling -30 Celsius temperatures, all in pursuit of the long run. For the true runner, running is rarely just about the running.

Running reshapes our souls with every pulsating step. It creates space for us to open ourselves to one another, building connections we never knew possible. Running happily unleashes strengths within us and is quick to reveal weaknesses that drive us to improve. "It's not about the run," my friend Steve would say. Running is healing, and that is exactly what I needed.

Despite my confidence in the gifts of running, what once felt like a graceful dance turned into an uncomfortable cadence in my new reality. Frantically, I reached for the tried and *untrue* formula familiar to many trauma survivors - to literally run away from my problems. Desperation stewed within me as my mind salivated for a quick fix to taste normalcy again, whatever that was. Nevertheless, the further distances my feet undertook and the harder I sought to escape my truth, the less in touch with myself I became. Focusing on morphing my trauma into an ultramarathon was distracting me from where the actual work was required.

Similar to my training, to brave the actual race, I needed to slow things down in order to speed things up. When processing my trauma, if I went too fast or tried too hard, I would lose control.

Training offered me a reason to wake up, attend to my well-being and fuel my body. The long miles mirrored the long healing journey ahead - slow, arduous and not always comfortable. The time on my soles offered me time to reconnect with my soul. I concentrated on my movements; how my feet felt on the soft dirt, my hair grazing the nape of my neck and the unrelenting strength of my legs pulling me up the hills. Modifying my schedule to what I could manage, I did things each day that brought me happiness and growth. When I had the capacity, I toyed with my limits. When I needed the space, I held myself back - using that time to regain energy, find comfort in rest, and remind myself of how important it was to be gentle with myself. I opted out of group runs when I felt too overwhelmed and sought out connections when I needed the energy of others to lift me up.

I became aware that competitions generated my highest inner doubt, where I questioned my strength and abilities the most. So, I developed a mantra for the darkest of times:

"You can do hard things."

This mantra was countlessly repeated in my head and out loud throughout the year. A sticky note holding the verbiage confronted me every time I looked in the bathroom mirror. It served as a reminder that the worst battles had already been faced. If I could overcome those, any new obstacle could be conquered - I just needed to remind myself of my courage.

Raven Saunders once said, "When you're an athlete, you live two lives. You have a life outside your sport, and you have a life inside your sport." In my new reality, I was waging a war between two opposing worlds, and I soon became a shadow of myself in both spheres. I found myself trapped in a perpetual high-speed interval, gasping for air, suffocating from the weight of my silence. My heart longed to be honest and open, melding my two worlds together like two interlocking puzzle pieces to complete my new identity. And yet, the trauma puzzle piece was rough and uneven, fully deviating from the smooth and structured running piece.

For a long time, I reflected on these two parts. A question ruminated within: what would happen if I unveiled my story? Would it elicit pity, discomfort or even ostracism? Perhaps. However, a habit that was once crucial for my survival, concealing my truth now suppressing my authentic self with all of its imperfections. I felt as though I was clipping my own wings. In the end, all I wanted to do was to fly.

When I initially sought support, I contacted the local sexual assault centre to access counselling. The response was wrapped with a discouraging truth - an excruciating thirteen-month waitlist.

Thirteen months. A daunting 395 days. In total, 9,480 hours for someone to go without any support if they did not have alternate resources to access.

My heart ached at the silence that echoed around me and the thought of so many others navigating their pain alone. Katherine Center says, "You need to be brave with your life so others can be brave with theirs." If I could be brave enough to live through the unimaginable, I could be brave enough to be a voice for others who hadn't yet realized their own immense strength.

My voice steadily grew louder as I took ownership of my story, merged my two worlds and meticulously adjusted the puzzle pieces. With each uttered word, the jagged edges softened, the pieces melting seamlessly into my journey. Sharing my story publicly was intimidating but it was also freeing. My willingness to verbalize my history opened space for others and myself to talk about the things that scared us the most. Fear was something I was aware could breed isolation, but I was certain that being vulnerable about our fears could create something even more powerful - solidarity and love. Moving beyond a surface level connection with my fellow runners and towards the stories that make us who we are, were the truth-telling moments I knew would truly make us move.

My mind was on fire. As I gained control, the fire that originally felt like it was scorching me from the inside out was slowly beginning to light me up.

Running will never, ever be just about the run. It is my form of meditation on the best of days, and my desperate escape on others. My mind slows down as I step onto the trail, allowing for my soul to take over. Running guides me into nature where I feel most connected to the earth; intertwined with the rustling leaves, hum of the insects and birds and the warmth of the sun glowing within me. Running continually reminds me to look at the bigger picture, especially on the worst of days; the world still goes on and I will too.

In all of our journeys we will encounter new challenges, often when we least expect them. The crux lies in how we let those chapters guide us. Similar to a race - overcoming adversity takes believing in yourself, pushing through discomfort, finding joy in the small things and of course a strong community. The psychological hurdles I've faced will never equate to the physical struggles I will ever encounter in running. Yet, both have reminded me that no hurdle is insurmountable. It is through the most rigorous battles that we find the strength we never knew we had.

We all have the courage within us to move mountains. I hope you can let the fire burning within you shine bright and allow it to not only light your own life, but to guide the paths of others.

-- Epilogue --

The gun fires in the cobbled streets of Courmayer, Italy. Jitters from my fellow runners send electrifying pulses through my veins. Our collective nerves fill my chest, overshadowing the comical reality that this event is participatory. About one year has elapsed since the traumatic memories of my past resurfaced and even less time since I toed the line at Javelina Jundred. I have opted for a shorter race today - merely 100 kilometers spreading across three European countries. Weeks before my feet touched these tracks, I grappled with an anxious fear of showing up. Though, here I am; surrounded by the chaos of cheers and cameras, heightened emotions and the unknown. My resolve is that today, I'm not here to perform my physical best. At this moment, medals or podiums aren't reflective of that, but rather the bravery to show up.

Immediately, I stay with the front of the pack, clutching onto the hope that I can metaphorically piggyback off of another runner. The thought to hold back crosses my mind as quickly as it vanishes. I persist, expecting my body to lean into what my mind is urgently longing for. This unsystematic game plan is fading but not without the trace of my aching body and fluttering heartbeat. The proceeding kilometers see my stomach plummeting on a winding rollercoaster while my hands death-grip my poles and my nose trembles at the smell of food. I feel 'off' and uncomfortable; whatever the state you call the opposite of flow.

In my head, I whisper, "You can do hard things," and zero in on the immense gratitude I feel for this exciting adventure I am on.

Glancing up from my daze, I ponder what country I am in. Have I left Italy yet? Or is this what Switzerland looks like? Regardless, the mountains before me are jagged and imperfect, strong and unmoving. Each peak is a reminder of the struggles I have overcome, the valleys indicative of the lows I've faced. The scars of the trail mirror the scars in my heart. Each wound tells a story of endurance beyond a physical domain. Altogether, just like nature, these parts of me interlace - each necessary to feel whole. My stomach is in knots and yet I am like smoke in the wind. A sense of calm begins to rush over me as I become in sync with nature's grooves, flowing through the trails in perfect harmony.

Entering an aid station, a young girl rings a cowbell, cheering as she giddily runs downhill alongside me. She is sweet and innocent. For a moment, I feel sad for my own lost childhood, a part of me that was long ago stolen. Then I glimpse at the joy in her eyes. Soaking in the appreciation that she is out here, I smile at the thought that she might be a future, badass ultra-runner. Looking around, I sense tranquility pouring over me and consider my life of abundance. I remind myself that I could stay fixated on my past, but then I'd be missing out on all that is being offered to me in the present.

There are moments throughout the race when the protective walls I've built break open, exposing my vulnerability. A dark memory seeps ominously through a crack, attempting to wash away my feelings of serenity. I casually dismiss it. Those thoughts are not welcome in this peaceful moment of mine. There is no space for that darkness in this beauty. As I float down the trail, the kilometers roll by and carry me further away from the voices of my past.

Passing by a few runners, simple words of encouragement are exchanged but I remain focused on my wrestling stomach and unstable heartbeat. Words aren't necessary on the trail. The energy is felt in the soil; abundant with our struggles and perseverance, connecting us all organically in silence. Racing into a stream, I hungrily reach for the coolness. I am halted by the giant poles fixed to my gloves, exiling me from the cold relief. In the past, I might have belittled myself for such a simple mistake. Now, I giggle at the theatrics, finding laughter in my imperfections. "Amateur," I joke, in a playful, loving way. The gap between the front runners and me grows bigger, though I feel anything but inadequate. I can now recognize that those comments made to myself before, questioning my worth, were never really true. They were statements I learned as a young girl from someone in my past. Things that were said to keep me small and silent.

As time goes on, I get louder, and the fire inside me grows into a radiant blaze.

I race towards the arch, surrounded by intoxicating cheers. Tears well in my eyes, releasing down my cheeks with no barriers there to hold them back any longer. I've conquered 100 kilometer races before, but this feeling has nothing to do with the feat I have just physically overcome. It is all about the strength and peace that I feel inside. I smile to myself. That person could not take running from me, and they never will.

Running will always be mine.

"You can't run, you don't have a bike and you only swim breaststroke – good luck with that!"

by Sarah Hughes

Dedication

I am dedicating this to my son Jack and my gal pal Dawn, who I lovingly blame for all my running and triathlon activities. They were there the day it all started and continue to be there to this day.
Thank you.

August 2nd, 2009, was a Sunday. It was hot and sunny in Calgary, and I spent eight hours standing and pacing within the same 50 metres with two people: Jack, my son, and Dawn, my soon-to-be running mentor and friend for life. I'll let you in on a secret right now. If you want to run but do not know how, chat with a runner. If you want to be supported in your running, run with runners. I have never met a more supportive, less judgemental group of people in my life. Runners want runners to succeed. They are always trying to recruit you because the people we meet while running make our lives better. That's the secret. Another secret I'd like to address before I continue on: the "runner's high" that you always hear people chasing after... it does not exist. At least, not in the same way for everyone. However, I can assure anyone that you will see your life improve when you include running; even if it's just peace of mind and the satisfaction that you've done something good. I share these now because we are all different. We all run differently and for different reasons. I don't "run." I plod, and I plod as fast as my boobs allow! Now, back to August 2nd, 2009.

It was a hot, sunny day, and I was volunteering at the finish line of the first-ever Calgary Ironman 70.3. The charity I worked for was the charity of choice and so I was there to represent them. I took my son along, convincing him it would be "fun." I must have done a good sell on it because he was an active 13-year-old who had just returned from a rugby tour. We were giving out medals and finisher t-shirts, and truly, I had no clue what this race thing was. I knew triathlons existed, but the concept of the distances did not compute. Cue Dawn.

Dawn is a local guru of everything triathlon and running. She explained the whole race to me and I was instantly hooked on this sport.

Quietly in my head I was pondering if I could ever do this but it took me many hours to say it out loud. The main reason for this was: prior to Jack's rugby tour I had promised his coach that I would ensure he stayed fit on our holiday before the tour. This grand statement led to me nearly passing out one early morning trying to run around a block with my son. The concept that after a swim and bike I would need to run the equivalent of 50 of those blocks to finish this race was wild. Two key characteristics of runners are the absolute belief that with training, you can do anything and you must have an unrelenting relentlessness. After eight hours standing next to Dawn, I finally stated, "I think I can do this!" Jack's response is the title of this chapter; "You can't run, you don't have a bike and you only swim breaststroke – good luck with that!"

He was not wrong. That day, a seed was planted that would be fed and watered, pruned, replanted, and nurtured for years, leading to so many good moments in my life. It also led to a broken foot with five pieces of metal needed to fix it, hours running track inside when it was -29°C outside, a lifetime of friends, a world of travel and a new self-identity.

Three days after my big proclamation, my office phone started ringing, oh the annoyance. I truly hate my phone ringing, but this was work and I was being paid to answer it, so I did.

"So, were you serious when you said you wanted to start running?" the voice on the other end said.

"Excuse me, who is this?" I replied, confused.

"It's Dawn from the weekend, I tracked you down. Do you want to start running?" she replied with a chuckle.

I said yes. I'd declared I would. After years of telling my son he could "do it," telling him to show up and encouraging him to try new things, it dawned on me (no pun intended) that I needed to do this. Within minutes I had found a local race I could sign up for, a five kilometers in my hometown. I had a training plan emailed to me and I walked through a maze of corridors at work to see if this mythical room I'd heard of, the gym, actually existed. Lo and behold, it did!

That weekend, Jack and I went to buy my first "running" shoes. Pro tip: if you're ever feeling blue about running, buy new shoes. Ignoring the training plan, I started to run on a treadmill at work. I did not know what the numbers meant on the machine, and I went when there was no one else around. It was my secret. I told no one I was running. Somehow, just four weeks later, on Labour Day weekend, I lined up for my first ever five kilometer race.

I still have the shoelaces from those shoes and the bib from that iconic race. Jack was there the day of the race, and I called

Dawn the next day; I did it. I ran five kilometers. Well, I didn't run it *all*, but I did it all. No Garmin, no music, no water bottle, just me and a reasonable sports bra, plus other clothes, too. No naked running here!

Five weeks later, Dawn and I did a run together. Four weeks after that, Jack and I did our first trail race together in the snow. I proceeded to run another five trail races, plus my first ever 10K, all with Dawn. I was hooked!

Over the next few months, I travelled to Malawi, Africa, for work, the Cook Islands on a rugby tour with Jack, and then a 16 kilometer trail run on Moose Mountain in the foothills of the Rockies. That was the day I discovered there was a thing called trail running shoes. I didn't have them but I needed them. About the time I came back from my travels, I found out that I had become extremely anaemic. It had gotten to the point that my whole body ached daily and I couldn't stay awake for more than five to six hours at a time. Running rapidly fell off my radar until the winter trail running season started again.

Here is another runner's truth: running is all about the post-race food. The winter trail running group I used to run with met on Saturdays. It was a noon start, there was a soup lunch afterwards and, more importantly, potluck desserts. I love food. With trail season started, my appetite was called to action. The season lasted three weeks before I broke my foot in a race. Recovery was slow. Physio wasn't something I looked into because I didn't feel athletic enough to merit this treatment.

For the next two years, I metaphorically stumbled along in my running, not training but occasionally racing as I waited for foot surgery, only to have it cancelled four times.

Finally, in December 2012, I was referred to a new surgeon. On the day I met him, he gave me a surgery date and assured me it would not be cancelled. He was correct, it wasn't cancelled. However, what none of us saw coming was Jack damaging his second knee. He had surgery on his first knee just eight months earlier. So, in a series of unfortunate events, Jack had knee surgery on a Friday, and three days later, on Monday, I joined him in post-op recovery. We were both on crutches for 12 weeks. This was not going to set us back and we were going to come back stronger. That was the plan. Sure enough, Jack recovered and played rugby for Alberta again that summer, and I registered for my first Spartan race with a team from work. After a sign-off from my physio, because I did it right this time, I had eight weeks to train and be ready. What we didn't foresee was a "once in a century flood" tearing our world apart, including my training facility, but luckily it was only a five kilometer course. The joke was on me! As it turns out, a Spartan race is not just a five kilometer run. There are obstacles too! I was definitely underprepared. To top it all off, none of my team showed up. Still, I was determined. This was my restart!

I slogged across the finish line 45 minutes after beginning the Spartan race. I did it! I had never been so muddy and I have not done one since. With that goal accomplished, it was time to come up with a new and improved plan. I had run five and ten kilometer distances without ever properly training. Three years in, I was still no closer to my triathlon goal. I needed a plan.

The plan came to me as a result of being really angry one day. Over the previous year, three beautiful ladies in my life had all passed away because of cancer and it seemed so senseless. I knew I needed to run a half marathon to finish the triathlon so my theory was to start with that and then build from there. On March 1st, 2013, I declared to the world that I was going to run my first half marathon in three months and that I was going to raise funds to support cancer research. When the training began, I LOVED IT! There was something about having the right plan, having a goal and a purpose that made it all click for me.

After that race came another plan. I'd survived a half marathon and even enjoyed the training. I convinced myself that if I did a full marathon, then it would make the triathlon run seem easy. What's more, my parents were coming to visit at the same time as the Calgary Marathon the following year. My dad was a highly successful marathon runner so another plan was hatched. I decided to train for a marathon without telling them and arrange to meet my parents at the finish line. The training was challenging, long and cold. My back hurt and my toes hurt. Training was not joyous. Nutrition and hydration became a very real concern and yes, for the record, I even tried that fate-tempting experiment of running in new shoes on race day.

Picture the scene: dinner with my parents and family the night they arrive. "Hey Dad, do you have plans on Sunday for lunch?" We knew they didn't as they had just arrived in the country. "Want to meet us at the stampede grounds around noon?" This brought a raised eyebrow. "I'm running a marathon, that's the finish line." I will never forget his reaction. "Well, that's very silly!"

Thanks, Dad. They were there, though, and in fact, they popped up all over the city like gophers with encouraging signs. They were with Jack and my friends at the finish line and it was awesome. Afterward, they stood by me as I burned my running shoes and declared, "Never again!"

So how do we get from "Never again!" to four Half Iron-man's, four marathons, about a dozen halves and a whole ton of physio? Unrelenting relentlessness and absolute belief that with training, you can achieve anything. Add that to having a plan, goal, and purpose, and here we are.

Weeks after my marathon, I signed up to run on a relay team for a kids' cancer fundraiser. At the team dinner, I casually mentioned I'd love to do a triathlon as that was the real reason I started to run, but I didn't have a bike. Not thinking much of this conversation over the next few weeks, I was stunned when one of the relay team showed up at the race with a spare bike for me! He had won it and it wasn't the right size. Look at me now,

Jack, I CAN run. I have a bike, and maybe I am going to get this done! The next season, I decided to make the switch. Triathlon, here we come.

I still had no Garmin, I was on a mountain hybrid bike, and yes, I would swim breaststroke, but I was starting this new journey. Jack bought me a book called *Women Who Tri* by Alicia DiFabioa. That summer, my first triathlon had no bike section because it snowed, so we swam and then ran five kilometers in the snow in May as our clothes froze to our bodies. Two weeks later, I had a do-over, and it was +28°C, but I got my first triathlon done. Thanks, Alberta weather, for being so unpredictable! I had gone gently into this world, starting with pool swims, as I didn't have a wetsuit. Somehow, I found myself over-confidently registering for an open water triathlon with a rented wetsuit, a hilly bike course and my hybrid bike. It was not the best recipe for success, and to top it off, my front wheel was stolen four days before the race! Luckily, my good friends who embraced my "crazy" literally showed up at work with a new wheel for my bike so I could race.

It was awful - the race, not the wheel. I'd forgotten how to swim in a wetsuit, I hadn't put it on properly, and halfway into the first lake lap, I genuinely found myself considering undressing in the lake (I didn't). This was good, though. I now had three sprint distances: a one kilometer swim, a twenty kilometer bike, and a five kilometer run, including experience in the open water. I was getting there.

The following year, I had a plan to complete two Olympic distance triathlons: 1.5 kilometer swim, 40 kilometer bike, 10 kilometer run. What I didn't plan for was falling off a horse while on holiday in Belize and damaging my back so badly that I still have issues to this day. Those two Olympic distances became three sprints as I rehabbed myself back to fitness. Then it hit me. The following summer of 2018, it would be the 10th edition of the race that started this whole journey, the Calgary Ironman 70.3. That fall I registered, bought my first wetsuit and booked myself into adult swim lessons. Time to ditch breast-stroke. I joined a club called Triathlete Within. I got a coach (thanks, Chris). I trained hard, went to camps and did warm-up races.

On July 29th, 2018, I finally crossed THE finish line of THE race that started it all with Jack and Dawn both there in person and my family across the world tracking my progress.

Throughout all my training, someone had asked, "What will you do next?" and my answer was simple. I would do nothing because this was all my goal and purpose had ever been. But, now there was more to completing the Calgary Ironman than just that. I had not counted on the friendships, achievements, experiences and the times I only got up off my couch because I had to run, swim, race or volunteer; that would shape me along the way. I hadn't banked on how that would become part of my life and identity. I hadn't realised how much I loved that. I have never met a triathlete who didn't want another triathlete to succeed on race day. We're normal people, we just know a few secrets and really want to share them with everyone. Over the next few years, I ran the London Marathon (my favourite event so far), the Las Vegas Half with my cousin and the New York Marathon in a heatwave. I ran a quarantine marathon inside a small house during COVID. I managed two individual virtual half Ironman's, another in-person, and recently, the Marine Corps Marathon. I have run with all my siblings and best friends while also finding new friends. I have trained for an Ironman, but it didn't happen for four years in a row due to COVID and forest fires. It has been hard work, blood, sweat and tears. There have been early and cold mornings, hot and late evenings, hours of training and learning, thousands of kilometers covered, and many pairs of shoes used, and I would do it all again. Now, once again, I am staring down a training path yet to be refined.

Dawn and Jack have continued to support my "crazy." In fact, I'll never forget the day Jack walked through my front door and declared, "Mum, I'm going to start running." A week later, Jack and I went shoe shopping. Mere months later, I had the coolest race weekend ever as Jack and I both ran the same half-marathon, his first and my twelfth.

I am a runner who plods as fast as my boobs allow. My journey continues and the friendships continue to grow. It has been an adventure, and if I have one regret, it is not starting earlier. Go on, take that step....

Dennis on the Run

by Dennis Kreba

Dedication

I dedicate this chapter to my number one cheerleader and supporter, my dearest wife and best friend, Paula.

I want to thank Mike for sharing his truth with me because without that moment, I might still be floundering.

Finally, I want to thank my best running buddies, Dale and Tammy.

I love you all!

Not this again. Another morning, another hangover. Most of my mornings were like this.

Since COVID-19 hit in March 2020, I had been working from home. I was feeling isolated. I was idle, overweight, and out of shape. I was drinking heavily and tired, exhausted, and hungover most days. I was lying to myself and others. I was in a dark place in my life, and I didn't realize it until it was too late.

Then "the incident" happened.

It was Friday night on December 17, 2020, when my life would change forever. I was drinking (as usual) and playing a new game online with a group of friends, including my best friend, Mike. It is important to know that I am a perfectionist and a planner. I like to know all my options before I pick the next move. I was coming into a new game where I did not know the rules or strategies. So, that night I was tentative and anxious. Add drunk on top of that and the whole scenario was a recipe for disaster.

That night, I sat with a drink in my hand and asked the other players for advice. They all knew how to play, so they should want to help me, right? Despite asking over and over again, I just was not getting help and I desperately needed it. Maybe they thought they were helping but I felt utterly lost. I felt stupid and I lashed out - "F*CK YOU!" I immediately disconnected from the online game session and spent the night fuming.

This was not the first time I had an outburst during a gaming session, either in person or virtual. Honestly, I always had a hard time with games in general. My friends were really good and they played often. More often than not, I wouldn't understand the game and end up asking a lot of questions but the help they offered was never enough to satisfy my drunk self or I would take game moves too personally. I would become frustrated because I felt stupid. No one likes to feel that way but being drunk made it so much worse.

The next morning, I told myself that it would all be fine. I had done this before and I considered myself a little lucky. Last night's outburst was amongst friends, so no big deal. My best friend, Mike, would be fine. We would both apologize, and I would promise to be better next time. Maybe I would not play that game again, I thought. The problem was the game, not me. Mike will call me this morning. He will call for sure. This was all a misunderstanding. Mike will be sorry that he did not help. We were all drunk, right?

Mike never called and I had a pit in the bottom of my stomach.

Later that morning, I called him to make sure that we were okay, and the next words would shake me to my core, "No, we are not okay."

Hi, I'm Dennis, and I have a drinking problem. Through perseverance and determination, I turned my life around and became a long-distance runner and endurance athlete. I hope you enjoy my story.

-- Sobriety --

I have always been hesitant to call myself an alcoholic. There is a stigma that comes with calling yourself an alcoholic. To soften the blow, I used to call myself a high-functioning alcoholic. I honestly did not think that alcohol was impacting my life. I never drank during work hours. I was a fun drunk...the life of the party! Besides, my friends were drinkers and were all drunk with me; most of the time.

December 18, 2020; the day after "the incident." I was sick and disgusted with myself. My best friend had some harsh things to say to me. I listened. After the call, I broke down on the floor crying. I screwed up big time. I was no longer a high-functioning alcoholic. I had damaged my life and I feared to know if my relationship with him was recoverable.

December 18, 2020. I did not know if I was going to quit drinking forever, but I did know that I had to get a handle on it. I had taken breaks successfully before. I had committed with friends to have sober nights. Realistically, an occasional sober night does not fix the problem long-term.

December 18, 2020, was, as it turned out, the day that I stopped drinking. I had to change. I could not survive the way I was living. However, I did not realize that sobriety would have such a big impact on me.

No more getting up in the middle of the night to go to the bathroom from a full bladder. No more hangovers. No more mornings filled with fatigue and tiredness. No more fuzzy morning brain. No more upset stomach and untimely bowel movements flushing the toxins from my system. No more heartburn or acid reflux pain. No more drunken shopping. No more drunken outbursts.

Instead, I had more energy. I woke up refreshed. I had so much more time on my hands that I hardly knew what to do with it. In a few weeks, I felt alive. My brain felt vibrant...I was living, not just surviving!

With all the free time created by not drinking, I was a little lost. To be honest, it was not as nice as it sounds. I had too much time to think and no way to cope. Alcohol numbs the brain. Without alcohol, I kept thinking about that night. What had I done?

I decided to get healthy. After December 18, 2020, I changed my morning routine. Instead of watching YouTube in the morning with my breakfast, I worked out. I made my coffee, went downstairs, and jumped on my treadmill. I picked a series to watch and walked. And then I walked some more. Here I am years later and I still make my coffee and walk on the treadmill six mornings a week.

I felt great. I got healthy. Fitness and walking were the outlets for my sobriety.

-- Running 2021 --

Things got more serious in the spring of 2021. My walks were slowly turning into runs and I was carefully adding on the kilometers. In April 2021, I treated myself to a new Apple Watch for my birthday. This was the little device that introduced me to a world of tracking statistics and watching my progress with eager anticipation, always pushing myself just a little bit further than the last run. In July 2021, I committed to my first marathon!

In nine short months, I ran and walked nearly 3,000 kilometers.

Phew! That was quite a lot of walking and running. I was starting to become confident in my new passion and my commitment to fitness and training.

Something magical was happening. Running and walking were no longer just a coping mechanism for me, nor a replacement activity. Fitness was quickly becoming a part of my life.

Most days followed a formula.

- Wake up and walk on the treadmill with my coffee for four kilometers.

- Walk at lunch for four kilometers.

- Run after work three to four times a week doing a variety of training runs including hills, speed runs and interval runs.

- Sunday became "long run Sunday" to my family and friends.

The training was intense. If I was not running, I was eating, sleeping, stretching or recovering. I was always hungry! Sundays were a write-off. After my Sunday run, I was exhausted (in a good way). I spent the rest of the day on the couch, recovering with a big smile on my face. Who had time to think about drinking? Not me!

I have had some crazy training sessions, including a five kilometer loop around Pigeon Lake, Alberta (complete with nearly suffocating from dust clouds and being chased by terrifying dogs) and a week amassing 63 kilometers on a tiny loop around the backcountry retreat Sunset Guiding near Sundre, Alberta. Sundre had a harrowing moment of walking very slowly past an angry wild stallion protecting his family and putting in enough kilometers to drink two milkshakes a day! I became the crazy-running-milkshake-guy!

I guess this is all to say that I was dedicated. Between running and walking, I was ready for my first marathon.

-- The Marathon --

September 19, 2021, was here. It was race day, BABY! I was nervous. I was anxious. COVID-19 was still scary and being in a race with thousands of other runners was intimidating. Luckily, I had my friends and fellow runners with me. My buddy, Dale, agreed to run the entire race with me. The Calgary Marathon was an incredible and fun experience. I loved it. There are a ton of supporters and volunteers cheering you on every year.

At one point, someone yelled, "Go Dennis!" I was a little surprised. I did not know them. How did they know me? Duh...I forgot that my name was on my race bib! We ran by the Calgary Zoo. There were picturesque moments during the run that were stunning. There was even an Elvis sighting on the course.

I had a blast and was in my glory! I was doing it! I stuck to my training plan. Ten minutes of running, one minute of walking. I had done it so many times in my training. I recited my run-walk intervals: 10-11-21-22-32-33-43-44-54-55-65, and so on. I kept at it. Ten minutes of running, one minute of walking. Dale had never raced like that before, but he stuck by me. He taught me the art of posing for race photographers; always look for the person holding the camera. Our race photos were fantastic!

I held onto my pace for most of the race, which was a little faster than eight kilometers per hour. I was on track to break my goal of a sub-five-hour marathon!

I was feeling great through the first ten kilometers. I was feeling better than expected through 21.1 kilometers and smiling just a little bit bigger, knowing that I was halfway there! I was still feeling pretty good through the 30 kilometer mark, and I was taking it all in. Dale was with me every step of the way.

Then I hit the wall.

My running slowed down. My knees started to hurt. My feet hurt. I started to question whether I could do it. My training plan faltered. Eight minutes of running. Two minutes of walking. I just needed another minute of walking. Seven minutes of running. Three minutes of walking. I was not alone. All around me, others were hitting their walls and together we were pushing through the pain. Dale was still there, right by my side, with encouragement and positive thoughts!

Endurance sports will test you in a lot of ways. I just wanted to finish. That was my test. Run. Walk. Run. Walk. If I could just keep my feet moving, I could do it. The feeling is still so vivid in my mind. I can remember the struggle. I kept running. At that point, it was sheer determination. This was my moment.

I wanted it. I kept running. We turned several corners. Still... no finish line. I yelled out in frustration, "Where is the finish line?" I scared a couple of runners around me (my apologies if that was you! I was talking to myself!) Then, I started talking to anyone around me. "We have got this!" I shouted in encouragement. We rounded another corner. Still no finish line. "Where is the finish line?" I shouted again. What a cruel ending to a long race.

I knew we were close. I picked up my pace again. Finish strong! You have got this! And I finished strong. I turned the last corner, and there was the finish line. Dale and I raised our hands together in victory as we crossed the finish line! If tears weren't already flowing, the flood started immediately after the finish line. I had finished a marathon! Wahoo!

5:02:20. I missed my goal by less than three minutes, but it did not matter. I was super close, and the most important thing was that I finished.

I spent the next ten minutes in the finish area, enjoying the moment with my friends and my wife. I cried and let my emotions out. I enjoyed this accomplishment. Achievement unlocked and medal earned!

I remember getting back to my home away from home. I hydrated, ate and napped. Then I remember going outside in the backyard by myself, and crying. I wanted to be alone with my tears and emotions. I did it. I finished a marathon. Even today, I choke up thinking about that marathon.

Completing a marathon is the toughest thing I have ever done in my life. Nothing else compares. It is physical, mental and spiritual. The training and the race pushed me to my limits. I loved it. I loved the challenge. I loved setting a goal and reaching it. And the medals...the medals are cool!

-- Meditation --

Sobriety introduces a new problem in life. Free time to think. Drinking is a coping mechanism. Alcohol numbs pain, both physically and mentally. Want to forget about your problems?...no problem...get drunk! However, sobriety offers an opportunity to be with your thoughts. Nevertheless, that is the toughest thing in the world if you have spent years avoiding it. I no longer numbed my pain. I felt the pain and thought about the pain. I lived through the pain.

I have spent many years working with a psychologist. We have sat for hours working on mindfulness, meditation and awareness. I find it difficult to find time for meditation, but when I do, I seem to have all the time in the world. I devote hours on the road running by myself, with only music and my thoughts. Running became meditative and I started practicing mindful running.

Meditation and running go hand and hand. I use a lot of meditative practices to help me have a clear mind when I run. Mindful running is focusing on your environment while not letting any thoughts take over. All the focus is on your feet hitting the pavement and the beat of your heart. I also like allowing thoughts to pass through without judgment while I am running. For example, it is okay to think about a problem at work but just let that thought disappear and bring your attention back to the running. I find it can be fun to focus on a body scan type of meditation while you are running; it can be enlightening on where you feel pain and hot spots. Finally, breathing techniques from meditation are great to use on long runs.

I think that the meditative quality of endurance sports becomes lost when talking about the benefits. You cannot spend that much time alone without thinking. That much quiet time can be difficult. I think it is very important for endurance athletes, like runners and cyclists, to practice meditation outside of their sport. You will become a better athlete because of those practices.

-- Where am I now? --

I am now three years sober and still going strong. Endurance sports are part of my life.

Sobriety and running have changed my life forever. I feel healthy and vibrant. My mind is clear. I no longer shy away from quiet time and instead embrace the quiet, meditative state. I have learned how to love myself. I am now into my 50s, and I am in the best shape of my life, both mentally and physically.

As for Mike and me, we reconciled and remain good friends. We hang out, chat on the phone, and vacation together. Our relationship is different, but that is okay. I remain grateful for the incident because it resulted in a new me. I really like the new sober Dennis.

So, that is my story. I hope I have inspired you a little bit. Step out there and walk or run! Get fit. Drink less. Trust the process. You will be changed forever if you take that first step. Do it...today!

Running Last is My Cardio

by Stephanie Krebs

Dedication

Thank you, Vince, for being at almost every race (sometimes surprising me) and being my cheerleader. I love you very much. Everett and Samuel, my young men, you are constant inspirations for me, and I am so incredibly proud of you, and I love you. To my dad, I promise next time I'll have Vince with me, so you don't have to worry. To my mom, thank you for the advice that is always on point and inspiring. I want to thank my family and friends for supporting us in our crazy adventures, sharing in the laughter and for trying out new things with us. And to Marla for pushing me to write this story. You are an inspiration to so many.

I am not what people would call an athlete. I do not have an athletic build, lean body, or long legs. I am short and a little chubby but determined. Since I was a child, I have been accident-prone. I tend to trip and hurt myself, even on level ground. I am a wife, mother, daughter, sister, auntie, friend and a teacher. I lead a busy life, doing so many things and time gets tight.

This story revolves around the Canadian Death Race (CDR) in Grande Cache, Alberta. This ultra-marathon is a 125 kilometer race with five legs, each varying from 18 to 38 kilometers. At the start of the race, you get a timing chip and a coin. The coin is given to the ferryman, Death, to cross the river on a jet boat from Hell's Gate road to the other side of Smoky River near the end of the race. This follows the legend of Charon's Obol. Leg One starts downtown and goes to Flood Mountain Station. It's got five kilometers of road and then goes into a single track before turning into a quad trail. Leg Two consists of going up two mountains, Flood and Grande, and back into town. This leg has the Bumslide, Stairway to Hell and the Calf Burner. Leg Three leaves town and then heads to the base of Mt. Hamel. Leg Four is essentially straight up Mt. Hamel and back down. The last leg goes from the base back to town. In this last leg, Leg Five, you need to pay Death to be ferried across the Smoky River, so hopefully, you didn't lose your coin because if you did, your race is over. The CDR is no joke. You can have hot blazing sun, rain and snow on the same day. That's Alberta weather for you.

In 2009, the atmosphere was electric; the whole town got involved in the race. The ladies from some of the local churches provided a spaghetti supper the night before. The Town of Grande Cache helped with the finish line barbecue. There was a farmers market with supplies and activities for the kids to do. It was a very big celebration.

This race is one of the toughest and most independent races you can do. There are minimal supplies at each aid station: water for sure, some gels and granola bars, and applesauce. You have to be self-sufficient. That was part of the appeal.

If you run as a team and one of the members misses the cut-off time, they allow you a courtesy run. Basically, start at the missed cut-off time and run that leg. If you are solo, once you call your race done, you are done.

For years, I watched my husband run the race, either as part of a team or solo. I ran with my children in the kids race, to be honest it was more of a long walk with their little legs. While I was a great support person, in my heart, all I wanted to do was run just one leg of the Death Race. I wanted to have a story to tell, like the many experiences that my friends and family talked about. Like when my friend Ben was running Leg Two and was so excited to do it. He cooked potatoes in chicken stock on Thursday, added salt to it, and once cool he packed it in a Ziplock bag and stuffed them into his backpack, which then sat on the dash of his car, in direct sunlight, for two days. When he started to get some cramps during his run, he inevitably turned to his potatoes for support. What he found in that bag had him contemplating his life choices. He stared down at the now rancid potatoes. To eat or not to eat? Out of desperation, Ben ate. Let's just say it was a very rough run for Ben. It involved vomiting and a few moments of desperation involving licking the rancid bag for any remaining salt. His story and others made me laugh so hard that my abs hurt the next day. I couldn't wait to have some stories of my own.

In 2014, I got together with my cousins to make a team named after our Chilean roots. Enter the Red Hot Chilean Peppers. We brought our Chilean flag, bought a Death Race flag and walked around with them both the night before. 'Eye of the Tiger' blasted in the car as we got ourselves pumped for the run and headed to the start line. Paola ran the first leg well. My other cousin, Cindy, fainted on the trail in Leg Two and was taken to hospital to be treated for dehydration. She had chugged her water at the beginning of the run and had nothing left for the second half. When we saw her at the hospital, she was covered in dirt. She had scraped her knee and ripped her pants, her red thong poking through. She had rolled off the trail and needed other racers to help her get to the aid station so she could be taken to the hospital.

Meanwhile, my cousin, Nibia, did her courtesy run for Leg Three. While waiting for her to finish her run, we saw a group of people that were waiting at the 2/3 transition, with a case of beer beside them. I asked them what they were doing, and they said it was for the folks that didn't make the cut-off time. They needed to have someone cheer them on, and they needed someone to be sad with, too. The racers needed acknowledgement of a good job and sometimes a beer is just the thing to do that. Nibia persevered, and despite the sweeping crew suggesting that she quit, she finished her leg proudly.

I was originally supposed to run Leg Four, but since courtesy runs are optional, I opted to run Leg Five with my cousin Carlos in the middle of the night. My kung fu teacher was volunteering on that leg as a sweeper and very clearly told me that if she caught up with me, I would have extra push-ups back in class.

It was a beautiful run that night. It was so quiet and peaceful. The only thing you could hear was your footsteps. The smell of the trees was so fresh as you passed by them. The headlamps illuminated the path, but sometimes I turned them off because the moon illuminated the forest. You could see the stars at one point on the trail where the crowns of the trees parted. Carlos and I watched the sunrise through the trees in the wee hours of the morning. We knew we could only go up to the river, so our courtesy run would end at the riverside. Our family would meet us there.

It was a bittersweet meeting with the family. Sweet because we were all together and bitter because our team did not get to cross the finish line.

In 2016, I signed up for the Near Death Marathon, which consisted of 42.2 kilometers. Between working full-time and raising kids, it was a challenge to find time to train.

Training for the run consisted of a multitude of five kilometer runs. With two little boys in tow, it often turned out to be a run to the convenience store for a washroom, a run to the park so they could play, and then a run back home.

At the pre-race meeting, we were told that there were a lot of bears in the area and that if you encountered one, you should huddle up with other racers, make yourself big, and make a lot of noise. On the way back to the campsite I wondered what you should do if you were alone.

The next morning, Race Day, I couldn't eat much for breakfast. My nerves were so bad that I vomited my breakfast right back up. It was definitely not a good start but my mom gave me some amazing words to remember on the trail: "The only person you are racing against is yourself, Stephanie. Do what you need to do."

The gun blasted and we were off. I felt strong at the start, but five kilometers in, I was getting further and further behind the pack. At one point I looked up and realized that everyone else was pretty much gone. A lady on the street said to me, "Keep that smile on your face until the end of your race." I nodded and politely said thank you, but deep down I was not sure if I could. I didn't realize how important those words would be as the race went on.

During the race, I wore a t-shirt that read, "Running late is my cardio." A more accurate slogan would have been, "Running last is my cardio." I kept going at my pace and continued on, earbuds in place, jamming to my tunes and enjoying the scenery. My tactic was to simply put one foot in front of the other, run as far as I could and then walk for a bit to recover. I was running down a single trail when I rounded the corner and saw...

MR. BLACK BEAR.

I freaked out a bit. His eyes were about as big as mine, maybe even a bit bigger. Through my panic, I remembered the words they told me, "Make yourself bigger than the bear." Short little me probably looked like a crazed lunatic waving my arms and yelling. Thankfully, the bear took off relatively quickly, leaving me to wonder what to do next. Do I run faster or do I walk? Make loud noises or stay quiet? Maybe I should start running faster to get past him? Decisions, decisions...

I kept going but decided to start singing songs very loudly, my eyes peeled and my dog spray at the ready. I envisioned myself sounding like Scuttle, the seagull from The Little Mermaid while waving my arms like crazy. I am sure it would have been quite a comical sight to behold. I speed-walked through the forest for about 15 minutes until I thought I was in the clear. I started running again, watching the ground so I wouldn't trip on a root. When I looked up, there he was again.

Crap!

This time, the bear's eyes were definitely bigger than mine. I did the whole thing again. The waving, the singing out of tune, and the walking. The sweeper crew came up behind me a little later on a quad, and they wanted to check on me since I was the very last runner. The first thing that came out of my mouth was, "I am so sorry for singing so badly, but there was a bear, and I didn't want to scare him (or me) again." One of the first things that the sweeper said was, "That'll make an epic story." They were right!

I continued on, crossed the highway, and saw more fresh bear scat, which, to my relief, didn't appear to have any Death Racer remains in it. I ran a little faster.

When I arrived at the location where the photographers took epic pictures of each runner, there was no one there. I stopped and cried. I LOVE pictures. They always tell a story worth far more than a thousand words. After I settled myself down, I took a selfie. To this day, I look at that picture, and it makes me feel sad because, at that moment, I felt alone and like my attempt at the race was not as important as others'.

It took me way longer than anticipated to get to the next transition, and I thought my race was over. When I arrived, there was no one there. No cheers, no sounds. Just a lane to the table. My family was located on the other side of the table and didn't see me come in. I ran up to the station and the volunteer told me to give her my chip, thinking I wouldn't be able to make it to the next station in time. I still had 25 minutes before the cut-off.

My husband, Vince, came to the rescue and encouraged me to keep going.

That's exactly what I needed to hear.

I kept going with some support from Ben, Vince, and our boys, who ran with me for a little bit to get me started on Leg Two. Having them by my side was so good for my soul.

Starting on my own again, I reached the road. It's a long road, and I fired up my music. Tom Petty's 'Time to Move On' played, and I felt my confidence flare.

At about the five hour mark, I had to make a washroom stop. Knowing I was the last runner, I took my pack off and laid it on the path in case the sweeping crew passed me. When I came out of the bush there was a sweeper staring at my backpack, wondering what happened. I explained why I left it. He said that was very smart to do, so they knew I was still in the race. He told me to continue on with my run and kick ass.

The time crunch was still on when I reached the next checkpoint, but they encouraged me to continue on if I felt good. I opted to get it done!

Next up were Slugfest, Stairway to Hell and the Calf Burner. A volunteer sweeping the race named Nelson became my partner in crime. He was awesome. Eventually, we ran out of the nasty hills and into the prairie outcrop. It was gorgeous. Again, another spot where the photographer usually takes pictures and they weren't there. This time, their absence didn't hurt as much. I took a happier selfie here.

I was so thankful for the training session that I had done prior to the race because I knew what was coming up next. I set little goals: get to the next creek crossing, get to the grassy spot, get to the mountain prairie. I also reminded myself, 'What must go up, must come down!' My legs were burning and I really looked forward to the downs. Nelson looked at the time and tried to get me to the aid station, but I was struggling. I kept hearing the classic line, 'you're only two kilometers away from the next checkpoint....' but that was a very long two kilometers.

I remembered the advice of the cheerleader at the beginning of the race, so when I made it to the aid station, I was smiling. It was official; I had to hand in my timing chip. I had arrived at the aid station 15 minutes past the cutoff. My race was officially over. I know that many people who get timed out are pretty choked and some are downright angry. But not me. I was elated. That was officially the farthest I had ever run in my life. 32 kilometers! Why wouldn't I be proud of that?

The sweepers then loaded me up into a side-by-side and took me back to town. On the way back to town, I asked myself why I did it. All I had ever wanted was to run just one leg of the Canadian Death Race. That's it, just one. I did more than that, and I was the happiest person ever. Hence, the huge smile I had on my face.

Success isn't in the medal that you get or the coin that sits on your mantle. Don't get me wrong, they are beautiful things, but they are just things. They aren't who you are; you are so much more than a thing. Celebrate all that you have accomplished, big or small. You've earned it!

If there is something I have learned, it's that the last of the pack are pretty special people. They know they are last, but they are still going for it and trying their best. They are survivors. They are finishers. They are amazing.

Stephanie is planning to try the Marathon again, this time with her teenage boys and Vince, who will be the biggest cheerleader ever!

Gaining Ground

by Dave Madole

Dedication

However far I have run, I have never run alone.
Thank you to Tessa for shaping my story.
To Nadine, Kelsey, and Rita for sharing the road,
and to my family for always welcoming me home.

Picture a buck toothed, bowl cut, eighth grade boy wearing thick glasses, home sewn clothes and dental headgear; the kind of overbite-correcting contraption that most teenagers only need to wear at night. Now imagine him in gym class, running laps long after his peers have finished theirs. At first, he does not notice he is alone. He is too much in the zone. Actually, now that I think about it, he enjoys the increasing ache, the nagging pangs and the sharpening strain. That is, until a classmate chases a stray ball across his path. Then... SMACK! All bets are off. Instantly, the collision knocks him breathless and scatters stars across his vision. Once he is back to breathing, another problem arises: No one, not the boy himself, nor his accidental attacker, nor even the teacher, can free the headgear from his face. Let me tell you, the only thing more painful than a mouthful of mangled metal is the humiliation of being whisked away (for all the school to see) on an emergency evacuation to the dentist. For a junior high school student, there is no bouncing back from that. I should know. This story's unfortunate, accident prone protagonist is me.

After such a shameful setback, blaming genetics becomes easier than dusting off my pride and trying to run again. "I am too flat footed. My knees are too weak. My lungs are too wheezy." The list of excuses lengthens until my mortifying middle school memory paralyses me. Decades pass. Angsty and inactive, my teens and twenties slowly slip away. I am much too out of shape to catch up to them. Only when I am about to turn thirty do I finally come to my senses.

To mark the occasion, I decide to hike Kilimanjaro, Africa's tallest mountain - a feat for which I finally accept I will need to exercise, but only as a means to an end. Jane and Krysty, two athletic teacher friends, agree to take me running with them. Almost immediately, I question both my and their intentions. This. Hurts. So. Much. Sure, no one has body checked me into oblivion (my headgear history still haunts me) but just the same, I feel like death. After running up another steep hill, without stopping I might add, I ask, "When are we going to take a break?" Jane laughs, leaving Krysty to explain, "The flat stretches ARE our break." From these two fitness freaks, I learn a valuable lesson: Desire never rests. In order to achieve, you have to embrace the aches. In the end, I hike up Kilimanjaro in four days, despite my sleeping bag's best efforts to strangle me. Take it from me, never trust a harmless-looking drawstring.

The summit success notwithstanding, I still do not consider myself an athlete. Months pass without shedding another drop of sweat. Then, given the right inspiration, perspiration floods forth once more. What is this? I am dating a woman who loves to run? Me too! Oh no, she is breaking up with me for being clueless. Apparently, you are supposed to run WITH your partner, not ten steps ahead. Woefully alone again, I lapse into my former couch potato ways. When an acquaintance suggests joining a boot camp, I seize the chance to get back into shape. It couldn't hurt, I suppose. If only I had known the boot camp is led by actual soldiers. The very first day, I come within an inch of puking up my supper. Stubbornness alone wills me to survive. Eventually, I am towing truck tires uphill, shouldering sandbags for miles upon miles and crawling on all fours until my knees bleed. Over time, I thrive in the company of like-minded masochists. They must see something in me too because one day a fellow 'run-nut' invites me to join her relay team. She assigns me leg two of something called Sinister 7. I have no idea what any of that means but how hard can it be? In an acronym... OMG. As soon as runner number one arrives, I am underway for my leg of the race. To be honest, I have no idea what I am doing. Pretty darn quick I realise Sinister 7 is also known as death by a thousand climbs. Long story short, I finish slower than I might have liked. I would do it again, though hopefully with a lot less naivete next time.

Fortunately, a runner's fate affords as many second chances as second winds. My shot at redemption comes when a spot opens on another Sinister 7 team a few years later. In the interim, I have learned my lesson about pacing. This time around, I am given legs six and seven, the anchor positions of what is now grown into a 148-kilometer race. The first five runners finish their tasks fast enough which means I begin my turn in daylight. My breathing is quick but even. My strides feel fluid and efficient. My heart thunders steadily. I can do this. Much like a season changing, night settles over the mountainscape;

cooling the air, enlivening the senses and narrowing my focus to the headlamp-thrown halo spotlighting my strides. This shaky shortsightedness should keep me from counting my kilometers before they have passed, 'should' being the operative word.

Suddenly, the floodlit transition between sections brightens into sight. There is just one leg left. Victory is mine, I mean my team's. I can almost taste it. Except I trip and fall flat on my face in front of everyone. Blinded by brilliance, I have overlooked a root knotted across my path. "Are you okay?" a volunteer asks. "Yes," I lie while clambering to my feet. "Do you need first aid?" the volunteer asks. "No, just scan my timing chip and I'll be on my way," I say. Though doubtful, she honours my request. Just around a bend, I double over in pain. I am not okay. My palms, put forth to protect me, are gashed. Searing pain radiates up my wrists. Farther still up the trail, this affliction eases only to be eclipsed by a deeper grievance throbbing from my right foot. By the time I limp across the finish line, the injury is unmistakable. When I finally visit the doctor days later, x-rays reveal a fracture. Scans also show a clot which, thank God, resolves on its own. Recovery may be weeks away but at least I have emerged with a compelling story to tell.

Once my foot heals, I set my sights on marathons; not a leap to be taken lightly. To prepare, I train five times a week, alternating between lifting weights, running hill repeats, and increasing distances until 42.2 kilometers looms within reach. Along the way, I confront a few hard truths. On hot and humid days, for example, bandaids become essential or a man's nipples might bleed through his shirt. Conversely, cold weather requires windstopper underwear for reasons I would rather not detail here. Let's keep this story PG, shall we? Without incident, I complete my first marathon in Edmonton, my second in Las Vegas, and my third in Vancouver. Success encourages ambition. My endurance flirtation soon becomes a love affair. Inspired, I make completing a marathon in every province and territory in Canada my mission. Why not combine my passion for travel with my newfound running career?

Twice a year, I crisscross the country to race. In Saskatoon, I discover the Berry Barn; a great place to stock up on pre-race carbohydrates. In Barrington, I am so starved midway that I beg for a bystander's chocolate bar. In Winnipeg, I cannot find a cab after the fact so I have to trudge two more miles back to my hotel. In Toronto, I achieve perfection at last. My total time is split evenly between the first and second halves. Huzzah! Whitehorse, Yellowknife, St. John's, Fredericton and Charlottetown soon add to my growing list of accomplishments. Notably, I have left the most challenging event for last. Quebec City, you are lovely but your marathon shows no mercy. Touching down at the airport, I succumb to a full-blown flu, and every symptom imaginable: sore throat, brain fog and achy bones. I swear I left home feeling fine. Confined to bed rest for the next forty-eight hours, I cannot stomach anything more than pain medication and cough lozenges.

Then, on the eve of the race, my fever breaks. Might as well run, right? Ten kilometers in, I am questioning the sanity of my decision. Twenty, I am wondering why people pay to suffer like this. Thirty, I have slowed to a crawl and the medics on course are asking me, "Ça va?" which loosely translates to, "Are you okay?" Clearly not. Like an extra in a zombie movie, I am lurching along brainlessly. Stupor aside, I finish with pride. Nothing, not even the day's 38°C heat, can steal this almost-last-place victory from me. My cross-Canada conquest is complete! Well, almost. No folks, I have not neglected to mention Nunavut. If there is a marathon in Iqaluit, I have not found it yet. Someday, I will make my way to Baffin Island to run laps around Nunavut's humble capital city; organised event or not. One must never let a dream die.

Not only has running flown me coast to coast but it has also kept me grounded; mainly due to Ernie, my hernia. Yes, I have given my pain a name. That way I know precisely who is to blame for my poor performance. For years we have been constant companions, rain or shine running buddies, some might even say sparring partners. Ever since Ironman Canada, an unforgettable race squeezed between my earliest marathons, my successes have occurred despite Ernie's irksome presence. I am his frenemy and he is my weakness. Like a cranky conscience, Ernie grumbles backstage until curtain call. Then, whether mid-race or just during a regular training day, he interjects by screaming out obscenities; or maybe that is me. These sudden spasms and subsequent tirades are typically triggered by sneezes, and/or coughs. I call them Showstoppers because, whenever one occurs, my runs stumble to a standstill. Finally, I have had enough. I am done gripping my groin in agony. The time has come for Ernie and I to part company.

During a surgical consultation, I learn there will be no running post-operation until I can recuperate. For active people, two weeks of recovery feels like a life sentence. On the other hand, Ernie's antics make running miserable anyway. You know what? Let's just get this over with. Thirty minutes is all it takes for the surgeon to slice me open, insert a Kevlar patch and stitch me shut again. From then on, my crotch will be certified bulletproof, though I would rather not put that claim to the test.

Albeit humbling, this injury pales in comparison to perhaps my life's greatest loss: another hospital residency. This one being my mom's. She is losing the battle with lung cancer. As the disease steals her away, I spend hours at Red Deer Regional Hospital (and later a hospice) visiting her, entertaining her and struggling to explain why this is happening to her. She does not even smoke. I wish she could continue hosting family dinners and maybe watch me run in a few more races. Easing my sorrows, the local running community adopts me, an Edmontonian, as one of their own. Runs with the group balance visits alone with my mom. Red Deer's support lifts the weight from my chest and lets my troubled mind rest; a temporary reprieve I will not soon forget.

As Dickens wrote, "It was the worst of times, it was the best of times." The next several years are an emotional rollercoaster of lows, highs, and lows yet again. First low - my mother's death. She was only sixty-five. My dad died when I was a kid, so I naively believed my family was immune to further tragedy. I was wrong. High - because I cannot find a Nunavut marathon, I decide to do the next best thing: run three marathons in one month, Red Deer, Calgary and Banff. Squeeze in two shorter races (Edmonton's 25 kilometer River Valley Revenge and St. Albert's Run Wild Half Marathon) and I figure I will either be on top of the world or six feet underground. Who has time for half-measures? As it happens, running Calgary one week after Red Deer hurt much more than Banff which was the last of the three sufferfests. Why? Because once you reach a certain level of torture, things cannot feel much worse. You just have to grit your teeth and endure.

Another low - hot on the heels of my triple-marathon triumph, I try to solo the Canadian Death Race; 125 kilometers of gnarly, singletrack trails located in and around Grande Cache, Alberta. Keep in mind, this is all happening in the same race season. A victim of overtraining, a bashed knee and a bee sting, I fail at my attempt. This is my first, and hopefully only, DNF (did not finish). Despite squeaking under the cut-off at the third transition, my head and heart are not in the game. I guess

I am mortal after all. High - after being dejected, I abandon running altogether and take off to travel the world instead. For four-hundred consecutive days, I behold marvels and rituals, peoples and wildlife. Though physically exhausted, my battery is recharged and my spirit restored. I am ready to go home and resume running once more. Low - the pandemic strikes six months after my return. A modest (under the circumstances), final high - social distancing results in training solo and then registering for the Virtual Boston Marathon. Honestly, this is the only means by which average runners like me can participate in such an elite event, unless we survive to our nineties. Then, when the qualifying time becomes a multiple of our blood pressure's numbers, we just might get in. Arthritic fingers crossed!

Though in my late forties now, I feel like a comeback kid. I have recast my Death Race 'failure' in a new image - as unfinished business. In other words, I am using dissatisfaction to drive me to conquer further challenges, specifically ultra-marathons. So far, I have managed six longer-than-marathon distances: three 50-kilometer races (Canmore's Grizzly - twice - and Edmonton's North Sun), two 80 kilometer races (Devon's River's Edge and Sinister 7's Reverso), and one 108 kilometer wonder (Kimberley, British Columbia's Blackspur, the highlight of my running career). Why would someone inflict so much distance on himself? There is something soothing about watching the sun timelapse across the sky and seeing the moon rise above silhouetted trees. I feel at peace hearing a night breeze stirring black leaves and knowing I am not alone in the stark darkness. Running amidst magnificence, this wilderness writ large, I am amazed at every turn. Just look at how far I have come, literally and figuratively, since my brace-face, middle school days.

When I started running, competitiveness was everything. I obsessed about beating other runners, measuring my success against their personal bests. These days, I am much truer to myself. I believe in gaining ground. Not against other runners, however appealing reeling people in would be. As a rule, I focus instead solely on achieving my goals. While progressing one stride at a time, no one's pace or place matters but mine. Collecting kilometers mindfully allows me to meet people, see the world and amass wisdom. For these reasons, I refuse to let a year go by without registering for a race. I dub this my approach renewing my running license. After all, can a man call himself a marathoner if his finish line photographs have faded? I think not. Running is a passion, a compulsion and an appetite for living in the moment. Nothing feels quite so basic and insatiable as movement. Whatever misgiven memories preoccupy the past, the farther we run now, the longer our bliss will last.

It Takes a Village – Racing and Training as a Blind Runner

by Daryl Lang

Dedication

This work of nonfiction is dedicated to the many people who have made my running journey possible. I won't name names because I am likely to forget someone, and I would hate for anyone to feel unappreciated. Supporting a runner – whether disabled or not – involves many sacrifices: time, transportation, use of a shower, monopolization of conversational topics, and "holidays" that double as race weekends. As a blind runner, my guides have also sacrificed minutes, hours and months of their lives to train with me so I'm race-day ready. My support system has made it possible for me to cross that finish line on race day. I am grateful for each and every one of you.

-- Disclaimer --

Writing this was more emotional than I expected it to be. I have deliberately not named names in this piece, though if any of my guides or regular running companions are reading this, you will probably recognize yourself or someone you know. That being said, memory is a tricky business. I may be known as someone with a freakishly good memory. If you remember the same event differently, and your memory is more flattering than mine, let's just admit that your memory is more accurate. Any factual errors are mine.

-- It Takes a Village --

As I write this, I am a few weeks out from my fourth marathon. I am in no way race ready. My training has not been what I wanted, hoped or expected. The last six weeks have seriously made me question whether I should be running this race at all. Nevertheless, I am nothing if not stubborn and I am choosing to run this race despite massive changes in how it's managed for visually impaired athletes... in for a penny, in for a pound. I've run this race before – twice, in fact – and this year, I have nothing to prove to myself, unlike my previous races in 2019 and 2022. Maybe this is the year I will run a marathon, just for fun.

The fact that I am blind is, to me, probably the least interesting aspect of my life. I love animals and have seven of them at home, including my retired guide dog, Jenny, and my working guide dog, Yasha. I have a job that I love and last year I let someone talk me into going back to school. Running brings me zen in a way that nothing else does. It has also given me a community of people from all walks of life that I likely would never have met. For some reason, that boggles my mind, me being a blind runner seems so inspirational to people! More than one guide runner has told me that they receive more cheers on a race course while guiding me than they do solo, which I find so very strange. The fact that my eyes don't work is sometimes, though not always, just a thing I've learned to live with. Compare this to someone having large feet but can never find shoes without special ordering. However, most people don't make comments about that when you run, do they?

All I will say about my actual visual acuity is this: I've lived with it all my life, and you do not want me driving your car. I cannot see well enough to run completely solo. Unless I'm on a treadmill, I'll be running with one of my dogs or with a human guide who sees better than I do, with each of us holding one end of a tether.

Everyone who has ever guided me has given me something more than just the kilometers we run together. I've come face to face with my own doubts, as well as been reminded of my strengths. I've been met wherever I'm at. At various points, this has included being in the midst of an injury or a mental health crisis and being gently coaxed to push a bit further. Different guides have varying communication styles and I've had to learn, sometimes on the fly, how a guide communicates in order to get the information I need. I have run with many different guides. Some have clicked with me on day one. However, I've also memorably once run with a guide who completely disregarded what I needed during a race and I paid for it later. Every single person who has guided me, even once, has made me a better runner, even if the lesson they taught me is to push harder for what I need.

Guiding is both easier and harder than most people think it is. I forget this sometimes because, to me, it's just enough to hold the tether and talk...a lot. Now, while it might be completely normal for me, it's outside of most peoples' day-to-day experience. In the past year, I've met more than one new guide who was up for the challenge but also incredibly nervous about it. There are helpful video tutorials on how to guide a blind runner that do give a great overview of how it's done (see the resources section at the end of my chapter for more information). But... am I ever nervous running with a new guide? Honestly, no. Yes, I trust my guides for runs ranging from five kilometers to a marathon but I am still responsible for how I pace myself or plant my feet. The only time I have ever not had decent chemistry with a guide was more of a pacing mismatch than anything they did or did not warn me about. My gut told me the day we met, the night before the race, that those kilometers we would run together would go sideways... and I was right.

Now, let me go back... Waaaaaay back to the first guide runner I ever ran with. It was more than a decade ago and I was doing a fundraising run for our local blind sports association. Together, we did a ten kilometer training program to prepare for the run. I was not a runner. I had what I know now were absolutely inappropriate clothing and shoes. My guide was an ATHLETE and, to their credit, tried very hard to give me pointers that I stubbornly ignored. They were the first person who believed, even before I did, that I could be a runner... even as I ran very very slowly for what felt like hours but must have only been a minute or two, and then walked for five.

Fast forward a few years. I still wasn't a runner, but I had trained with a cute, smart spitfire of a guide dog, a black Lab named Jenny. Jenny's motto in life was (and still is) "carpe diem!" – and do so quickly. After more than one "walk" that was more like a jog, I had an idea. Let's try running! I got myself a lightweight harness, and started running with Jenny around the block. Over the next several years, we worked our way up from three kilometer runs - getting lost in our residential neighborhood and finding our way home again – to the pinnacle of her racing career.

Our first half-marathon in Billings, Montana, was the start of mine and Jenny's racing career. Jenny and I had never run a race before and this one had water stations and everything! Even though Jenny would be with me on race day, and had been at my left side during all of the training runs, I knew that we would need a human to run with us. This was primarily to keep us on course in an unfamiliar area.

My human guide for that first half marathon had run many marathons before, and introduced me to racing – including the idea that getting to the start line is a victory in itself. Fun fact: I slowed myself down that first race by absolutely refusing to put my race cups anywhere but a garbage can. My Canadian sensibilities would not allow me to "litter." I was shown so much kindness on that race course. I am so grateful for that stranger who took time out of his day to run with rookie racers Daryl and Jenny, and didn't laugh (too hard) at my racing faux-pas.

After finishing my first half marathon I scarfed a banana, lounged on the grass, listened to a band playing medleys of '90s music and swore I would never run another half marathon again. Fast forward two weeks and I decided that Jenny and I would try something different and run the Hypo Half. Yup, a half marathon in Edmonton in February. I suppose it helped that I signed up for this race on a late September day that felt more like August than November, but the choice was made. We were going to do this!

I signed up for a training clinic, which is where I met the person who would become a dear friend and a consistent guide for the next several years. During one run, Jenny and I started a bit early so she could use the washroom before we got started. Somehow, we took a wrong turn in catching up to the group. My new friend caught up with us and we ended up running the entire run as just the three of us. A friendship which I cherish to this day was born. Over the next several months, Jenny (now nearly seven years old) and I got faster. I also figured out more about running in a group – Jenny sometimes has no manners and insists on being first. My friend ran with us when he could and, after a few weeks, asked if I minded if he joined us for the Hypo Half.

Officially, due to a faulty chip, I ran Hypo faster than I've ever run a half before or since. Truthfully, I am still proud of running

Hypo in the time that we did. I beat our first half marathon time by a full seven minutes, which is nothing to sneeze at!

Jenny **made** me a runner. I'm a better service dog handler and a runner because of her. I cried the day when she was eight and made it very clear that she didn't want to do these long runs anymore. Jenny is retired now and loves carpe diem-ing from whatever comfy place she can find. She graciously passed on the harness to Yasha, a serious yellow Labrador trained by Guiding Eyes for the Blind to safely guide while walking or running. I look forward to many running adventures with Yasha in the years to come, and the lessons she will teach me as Jenny did before her.

However, long before Jenny's retirement in 2019, I decided that this was going to be my year. This was the year that I was going to run a marathon. Surprisingly, while I didn't intend to, I ran two!

My friend who ran with Jenny and I for Hypo became my first tethered guide runner – and he didn't have Jenny to back him up! Running with a guide dog's harness in your left hand, and a friend who provides verbal cues just in case is very different from running tethered to another person. Communication needs to be quick, your paces need to match (or the guide needs to slow down to accommodate a slower-paced blind runner) and it was a new experience for both of us. We tried it out first in my neighborhood, which was not the best idea on residential streets during a freeze-thaw cycle – that ice was brutal!

Over the next year, my friend guided me for long Sunday runs. He cheered me on when I thought I could not run one more step, and came out for a run in all types of weather. He believed in me in ways I did not yet know how to believe in myself. Our first marathon together was glorious. We crossed the finish line and I was over the moon! The running of our second marathon was much more eventful. The run was a full ten minutes faster than our first, but it also resulted in my visiting the medical tent. Much of this is not my story to tell – largely because I remember so little of it, but here is what I can remember: I was running the race of my life! The kilometers were flying by – five, ten, fifteen and I let out a cheer at the halfway point when I realized I could absolutely make my race goal. I felt invincible! Then came kilometer 35. One of the aid stations (or was it a cheer squad at the side of the road?) had oranges. I wanted one more than anything I think I have ever wanted in my life. Although, any experienced runner will tell you, "Don't try anything new on race day," so I chose to not take it. As I ran past, leaving that glorious orange behind, I knew that I had made a mistake. I ultimately paid for it later. I fell and had to get helped up. I fell again at about kilometer 41, and my guide asked if I was done. I remember thinking, "Yes, I am done! I want to go home!" Then, another voice in my head – a much louder one – screamed, "You did not come all this way to run 41 f***ing kilometers and not finish; **you are not done!**"

There is video evidence of me crossing the finish line, but I honestly don't remember doing it. I woke up in the medical tent, being asked questions like, "What day is it? Do you know where you are?" My guide couldn't come in with me, so he stood around waiting before I finally convinced the medical team to guide me to a porta-potty (I might have threatened to pee on the floor). After the relief of knowing that I had, in fact, crossed the finish line, I kept on kicking myself. I should have eaten that damn orange!

After our second marathon together, my friend wanted to explore new goals of his own. Unfortunately, in March of 2020, the world shut down during the Covid-19 pandemic. My friend did what he could on his own. I did what I could on my own, and we ran together over the next 18 months when COVID restrictions, time, and the lack of illness or injury allowed. I was happy to cheer on his accomplishment of running a virtual 50 kilometers by being a walking cheer station on the course. I felt as though I was giving so little back in exchange for what he had given me. He showed me so much kindness and generosity that any kind of thanks seems so inadequate, but every run I try to show my guides how much I appreciate them. Unfortunately, I do not feel like I always succeed.

The past four years of running have been full of fits and starts. Between illness, injury and mental health issues, I felt like I had to start from scratch once racing started back up again in 2022. My friend guided in the Hypo half and Edmonton half in 2022 and was so patient when I grew frustrated that I was not running at the pace I previously had. My guide for the Vancouver Half was likewise patient and encouraging when my post-covid-fatigued body slowed down with four kilometers to go. Guiding is a selfless act. I am so very grateful to have had many racing and training guides who met me where I'm at, even when it's not where I (or they) want to be.

For my third marathon, in December 2022, I was matched with two guides I had never met or run with before. The plan was to run with one guide for the first half and then run with the second guide from the exchange point. I had a gut feeling that the first guide and I wouldn't click, but I ignored it. The guide pairings had already been assigned for the US Association of Blind Athletes (USABA) Marathon Championships, and I figured I could run with anyone for a half marathon distance. I wish I had spoken up. My first half guide was faster than me and either would not or could not slow down. More than once I thought about throwing in the towel at the exchange point. I was undertrained, injured and now exhausted. Nevertheless, I wasn't going to leave my second guide waiting there for a couple of hours just to send him packing with no run to show for it. I'm glad I toughed it out! I clicked so much more with this guide and finished the marathon upright and smiling. I had eaten the damn orange **and** avoided the medical tent!

Since that marathon, I've had the privilege of running with several guides. I ran my third Edmonton half marathon in August 2023, giving my guide the accomplishment of running her first half while I simultaneously ran a faster half than I have in years. Even with all of this, I wonder how long I can continue to train for marathons. Due to injury, illness, and life circumstances, the reality is that I have not always been able to find a guide to train with. Particularly, it has become harder to train for the longer distances necessary to run a marathon. Even though for most races it's up to me to plan most of the racing logistics – support for visually impaired runners is only officially offered at a handful of races in North America – I am grateful that I can still run. Social media and United in Stride, an online resource that matches blind runners with sighted guides, have both put me in touch with guides and friends outside my immediate social circle. Experience is a great teacher, and for any long-distance run, the best piece of advice I can give is, 'Eat the damn orange!'

-- Resources --

United in Stride

This site helps connect blind runners with sighted guides. If you or someone you know is blind or visually impaired and wants to get started or continue running or walking, you can sign up here. If you are interested in guiding a blind or visually impaired athlete, either on a one-time or long-term basis, please sign up! I've met several guides through this resource, particularly while one or both of us were traveling. Please note: meeting someone online comes with risks. Please check your intuition, and follow Internet safety guidelines when meeting someone from online.

How to guide a blind runner – Handy Resources

https://www.athleticsontario.ca/wp-content/uploads/2021/04/OBSA-Guide-Running-Pathway-2018.pdf

https://www.unitedinstride.com/get-started/become-a-guide

https://www.youtube.com/watch?v=kOnKauvk2oI

Achilles International Currently, they have Canadian chapters in Ontario, Alberta, and Manitoba. The more people who know about Achilles, the more likely it is that more will be created!

Guiding Eyes for the Blind

This is the guide dog school that trains running guides. I am grateful they trusted me with Yasha, and while we have not run as much as I hoped we would since the start of our partnership, I hope for more miles with my girl over the years to come.

A Seven-Letter Word That Changed My Life

by Austin Sedgwick

Trigger Warning
Reference to suicide

Dedication

I am dedicating my chapter to those who brought my running journey to life. Serge Archambault and Sydney Hockey.
There are honestly too many people to thank. I have never felt so much love in something as simple as running.
To my parents for being my number one supporters. To my siblings for always being there. To my friends and family for sharing, donating, and supporting in any way they can. To my friends for

picking me up in the middle of a highway, you know who you are. To all the strangers who have donated. To the news stations and newspapers for getting the word out.

To Kristy Koyata, for ensuring I was completely safe. To Carley Shimoda for helping me with EVERYTHING ever imaginable. I could not have run across Alberta without you and Tiara. Thank you. To the Calgary Marathon for making this all possible.

To anyone going through a hard time in their life. YOU HAVE GOT THIS!

R.U.N.N.I.N.G. A seven-letter word that I never believed in. I used to tell people who ran marathons, "You know, you don't have to do that."

I am not sure if I chose to be a runner or if running chose me. I have played sports my entire life. I have always been stubborn and always told people that running is not a sport. Oh, how naive I was. Go run longer than the thirty-minute warm-up jog before a hockey or baseball game, and you will find out the truth.

Running as a sport is different. The training is different. The people are different. The vibes are unreal. I fell in love with the sport. I fell in love with the game. Yet despite the kilometers run, and the medals earned, I still don't classify myself as a runner, and here is why.

In 2019, my running journey began because of a friend. My then-girlfriend and I were visiting a friend and his wife in Calgary for the weekend and it just so happened that the Calgary marathon was going on at the same time. His wife and her mom had been putting in a lot of volunteer hours, which brought me to the sidelines of this iconic event. Watching the runners do amazing things, crushing their goals, and raising money for a charity of their choice, I still found myself thinking, "This isn't a real sport." Again, how naive I was.

I proceeded to say that running was "easy."

Serge Archambault, my best friend, said, "Yeah? Go run 50 kilometers! You are too chicken!" This was said at the 2019

Calgary Marathon. I got back from that weekend, and while it was still a joke, that comment was ingrained in my head. I told my sister about it and she laughed and said, "You can't run 50 kilometers."

Of course, I was willing to bet on that.

I am from Lethbridge, Alberta, and I bet my sister right then and there that I would run to Taber, which is exactly a 50 kilometer distance from where I lived at the time.

There I was, loafers on (because who needs running shoes?), with a backpack slung over my shoulders and not nearly enough water. Are you even a little bit surprised when I say that I struggled every minute of it? I made it 25 kilometers; running, walking and just trying not to die. I ended up having to call a good friend to come pick me up, which I am so thankful for, or I would have been sleeping on the side of the road. Needless to say, I lost the bet.

I didn't run for a while after that failed attempt at showmanship. This was in part because I could not convince my legs to move like that again, but it was still in my head as something I would need to try again.

On December 29th, 2019, I signed up for the Calgary Marathon 50 kilometer ultra. I went to the sign-up page to prove that I could. However, as I filled out the form and came to the question,

What are you running for? What would you like to donate to? It all suddenly hit home.

My dad suffered from cancer twice. I have lost friends and family to cancer, just like we all have. This was no longer something I simply wanted to do, it became something I needed to do.

Immediately, I chose to run for the Alberta Cancer Foundation. For every $10 donated, I would run one kilometer before the event. I raised $250 right away, meaning I would have to run 25 kilometers of training. Yay...my lucky number.

This time, I wanted to amp it up and see how fast I could run. I hopped on the treadmill, strapped on the loafers, and pushed start. I would be lying if I said I wasn't tired after one minute. I'd be lying if I said I wasn't tired after two kilometers. I finished the 25 kilometers but didn't realize this would put me into a state of what my doctor classified as a heart attack. Through perseverance, a bunch of heart tests, and one angry doctor, I got back to training. I was running for one reason and one reason only: because some people can't.

When COVID hit, the Calgary Marathon was canceled, but my personal race wasn't. I set a goal to run 50 kilometers on this date at this time, and that's exactly what I was going to do. There was one reason I was doing it: for the Alberta Cancer Foundation. I was going to raise that money by running an ultra marathon and do whatever it took. Same goal. Same time. Everything stayed the same. I would finish what I started.

With good friends and family helping, we were able to raise just over $7,000 by the end of my run. With the official race cancelled, I ended up having to make my own route, and I ran in the worst weather you could ever imagine. There was hail and lightning, but there was that same best friend, Serge Archambault, suffering right there beside me on his bike, ensuring I had everything I needed. We absolutely conquered this goal, and I could not have done it without all of the support I received. However, this is not what I am the proudest of. I will touch base on that at the end of the story.

The Calgary Marathon took the liberty of doing an interview with me, asking the big question, "What's next?" I told them, "I am done running. It's back to biking and drinking beers. I am never running again." I wrapped up the interview with a huge apology to all of the real runners out there. It is a real sport. It takes blood, sweat, tears, and not to mention the loss of a few toenails. The mental strength required is something I realized cannot be taught.

When I was training, I didn't notice everything I had lost at the time. I also didn't notice the pandemic at first. I was out to accomplish one goal and one goal only, to finish 50 kilometers. I did that and quickly learned that post-marathon depression is real. My post-run depression became life-threatening when I realized everything that had I lost in 2020. What I had before my run, before the pandemic was gone, and everything that I loved was seemingly gone. My run was over, I could not see my family. I could not see my friends. I lost myself. My days kept getting darker, and I did not have a purpose anymore. I did not want to be a part of a world that I could not truly live in. Now, this was not COVID's fault. Whichever side you stand on, I am on the side of being a good person. I think we all lost some sort of faith in humanity. My days got longer, my sleeping got shorter and I could not find a way out of this never-ending darkness and never-ending pain. A pain that I had never felt. A pain that I previously didn't even believe in.

The days were filled with not wanting to be alive and wondering what was the point. Many days were spent crying myself to sleep every night or being awake all night when the insomnia took over. Showing up with a smile on my face but dying inside became the norm. Imagine the worst pain you have ever been in, happening on repeat for every single second of every waking hour, and yet you can not find a way to stop it. The desperate pain of hurting yourself just to feel something becomes increasingly overwhelming.

In 2020, everything in my life continued to get worse. I broke my shoulder in three different places and my bank account became just as broken as my body was. When I took one step, I seemed to fall fifty feet below. I felt as though I was moving through quicksand, praying something would happen to take all that pain away.

My job was gone along with my purpose and it felt like my family and friends were gone as well. I needed help but I was too stubborn to admit it. During the worst moments of my life, the moments when I needed a hug the most, my own mother felt like she could not hug me thanks to the pandemic. I think if she had known what was going on, maybe she would have. Mothers do anything for their children. They are the strongest people I know. I am happy to say I am here today and I thank her for everything she has done for me. Both my parents, all of my family and friends have made me a better person and have helped me grow. I could not see that in 2020.

What I saw back then was a never-ending darkness. The further I went, the darker it got. I used to be able to look on the bright side. I would think, "How can someone's life be that bad?" Suddenly, that false resiliency was gone and I was the one fighting against an unbearable pain that I just needed to stop. The only way I could see to make that happen was classified as the "selfish" or the "coward" way. I would not wish the pain I felt on my worst enemy. People ask me how I push through all my physical pain, asking how it is possible. It is only possible because it is nothing compared to the mental pain I once had.

This is a topic many people don't *want* to hear about, but it is a topic they *need* to hear about. If anyone has watched me run a marathon, they will see that when I am in pain, I look up into the sky and remember why I am doing it. My generation has lost so many people, so young. I too, felt the pain of loss.

On the week of my birthday, I had a friend commit suicide. As torn as I was and as much as I cried for him, I understood. It is scary when you can physically and emotionally understand the same kind of pain as the person who is no longer with you.

Although we never know exactly what someone else is going through, we can see the never-ending pain rampant in today's society. Depression is an illness that has been looked down on for so many years, an illness that is "not real."

That same week, on my 27th birthday, I took a drive to the Riverbottom. I climbed up the high-level bridge, choosing to take the hard way up because if I slipped and fell, at least then it was an accident. When I was at the top, I looked down and said, "See you soon" to that same friend who recently passed due to their own mental illness. As I was about to jump, I felt a cold breeze go through me, as if someone was suddenly there with me. It freaked me out and I needed to calm myself down. What I was about to do was meant to be irreversible. I wanted to do it with a clear head. I climbed down the bridge the same way I went up. Three hundred fourteen feet up became three hundred fourteen feet down.

It was a winter day, so the water below was frozen. During my walk, I broke through the ice and dropped into the frigid water below. I was stuck underneath. To this day I have no idea how I got out, maybe someone was looking over me that day. All I remember was that the only thing I wanted to do was live. Ironic. The day I tried to take my life was the day I would end up fighting for it.

I fought for my life that day and found a new purpose in life. I remembered who I was. I opened the dialogue around my mental health, knowing that if it can happen to me, it can happen to anybody. I knew that if I didn't speak about it, everything would stay the same. Everything I went through would have been for nothing. The people who are no longer with us and the ones who still need to be heard.

Through training, raising money for the Canadian Mental Health Association, and creating videos about my mental health, I unconsciously started to help people open up about theirs. I found myself stepping into the role of the friend that everybody needs. I was not prepared for the hundreds of messages I received but I am so happy that people trusted me with their own personal struggles. I was still on a marathon of my own journey, but I now knew that it was okay to not be okay. I constantly reminded myself that I had survived 100% of my darkest days so far, and I continued to remind others that if you give yourself a fighting chance, you still have a chance. A chance to be okay and a chance to be happy. There is a saying that goes, "If you want to die, throw yourself in the ocean, when you find yourself drowning, you will find yourself fighting for your life." That's exactly what happened to me, by a stroke of luck. Some people say I saved their lives, but in reality, they saved mine.

I have now become addicted to helping people through running.

What I failed to mention when I broke my shoulder was that the doctors also thought my neck was fractured. I am into extreme sports. I know the risk involved. I have buddies who are paralyzed, but when you hear those words, all those fears come alive. *What now? What am I going to do? I can't work. Will I be able to walk? Everything I love will be gone.* Choosing the charity for 2022 was easy. Spinal Cord Injuries Alberta, here we come. With the help of local businesses, friends and family, we hit my target goal for the third time in a row!

In 2023, I signed up for the Calgary Marathon, but I let my friends and family choose what I would be raising money for. They chose Autism.

Now that I was signed up and the organization was chosen, I thought to myself, "How do I raise money? By now everyone knows I can run a marathon any day of the week." I decided to run border-to-border, from the west to east borders of Alberta. From beautiful British Columbia to Saskatchewan. The event was live-streamed on my social media with a timer set at 96 hours, counting down. The timer would start at 07:00 A.M., but I would not start running until a donation was sent through the link provided. If there was a duration of greater than two hours without a donation, I would stop running. I did decide to put a cap on my running days at one hundred kilometers per day, and I would sleep, but the timer would continue to count down. To put it into perspective, this is just over nine marathons in four days.

With the support of my friends, family, and amazing strangers, along with news and radio stations, we crushed the run across Alberta with less than twelve hours to go. This was one of the hardest things I have ever done. Incredibly, we were able to raise over $8,000.

To wrap this up, I want to tell you what I am most proud of. Of everything I have done, all of the money raised, and kilometers run, what I am most proud of is my sister and Dad. In 2020, my sister also had the goal to run 50 kilometers. Even after my race was complete, she continued raising money for the Alberta Cancer Foundation. She and my Dad crossed the finish line together, with her running and him bicycling. I cannot tell you what it meant to watch them, a two-time cancer survivor and his daughter, crossing the finish line of a 50 kilometer run. Running for cancer is something they should truly be proud of, and I hope they know how proud I am of them.

I always enjoy the marathons I run, but more importantly, I love the people. No matter where you are from, no matter your ethnicity, gender, or sexuality, we are all runners. If you are slow or fast, working on a personal goal, raising money for an organization, or running for someone you love, we all have the same finish line in sight. The atmosphere of a marathon is what we need in this world. Nobody is looked down on or judged. We are all going the distance to accomplish something amazing. We cheer each other on, and that is what the world needs. That is what I love. People say I inspire them. If you are reading this, know that you are the inspiration. Thank you for everything. I would not be here if it weren't for you.

Being called "chicken" was the catalyst for so much. This one simple, silly word has helped me raise over $30,000 for a variety of organizations.

It has never been about running. It has always been about giving back. And I will continue to do so for as long as I can.

Running is a seven letter word that changed my life and if it helps even one person along the way, it will all have been worth it. Lord knows it helped me and it is my hope that this chapter helps you.

The COVID Half

by Zoe Antaya

Dedication

To my incredible parents and sister, who support me every step of the way. And to Papa, who inspired me to live life to the fullest.

Positive. The thick black line was etched across the test as though drawn on with sharpie; piercing and permanent. It had only taken a few seconds for this line to creep across the plastic, and yet it felt as if a lifetime had passed. Millions of regrets immediately rushed forwards as the doubt and sadness clouded over my mind.

All those track practices I had done leading up to this weekend, the Personal Records (PR's) I had achieved and the accomplishment I had felt in sprinting down that final stretch; that amazing long run I had completed the previous weekend, feeling like a gazelle as I pranced across the trails. All those training sessions I had pushed through in the blistering winds and thick snow of winter; the hundreds of times I forced myself to stay inside and strength train in our gloomy basement, pain sizzling through my quads until I wanted to collapse.

It was all for nothing.

Now my lungs were lined with mucus, infected by a virus that had taken over the world. My nose was clogged; my throat felt as though someone had dragged a knife through it.

Why?

Why did this have to happen to me today?

I had made it through two years of the pandemic without once succumbing to sickness, and now I had finally contracted the virus a week before the race I had trained six months for.

Before my mom could reach out to console me, I sprinted to my room and slammed the door, throwing myself onto my bed.

Burying my face in my pillows, I let the sobs ripple through my body, my voice escaping in screams from my torn throat.

Why?

Why?

Why?

Each time my cries slowed, an image of the finish line, the medal, the post-race high, or my family cheering from the sidelines would loom in my consciousness, and I would collapse all over again. It felt like the world was falling down on me.

I have no idea how much time passed until the tears finally dried up, leaving my cheeks salty and my eyes puffy and strained. However, it didn't matter because I had nowhere to go: I was stuck in this room for the unforeseeable future.

Eventually, I gathered the strength to roll over, and my medal wall came into view, causing me to burst into tears again.

I reached forward and grabbed the largest piece of hardware off the rack, its shiny outline swimming before me.

21.1 kilometers.

It was from the Calgary Marathon, my very first half: a race that held a special place in both my family's and my heart. Still sniffling, I thought back to that week.

My papa had been sent to the hospital and diagnosed with COVID-19. Due to many other complications, the virus was able to quickly penetrate his body, and by the time I got to come visit, he was barely there. His mouth had been open at an odd angle, collecting all the oxygen possible. His eyes were closed, and he seemed so tiny in that hospital bed. We had gone one at a time into his room, gowning and masking and gloving up. I remember how terrified I had been of getting the virus myself. The closest I could get without being overtaken by fear was touching his foot, where I tried to send as much love as I could through that tiny little squeeze. It was devastating, sitting there and watching this invisible virus suck the life out of a person we all knew so well. Even more so, it was horrifying to watch the impact it had on my mom who stayed at the hospital around the clock to be with him.

Seven days. That was all it took for the virus to take my Papa away. That was all it took for my mom's world to completely change.

The day of the funeral, when our family was in shambles, I had forced myself to head out for my shakeout run. For a short twenty minutes, everything faded away and I remembered what it was like to be happy. But as soon as I stepped in the door, I was plunged back into reality. I had no idea how I was going to do this; I had no idea how I could truly enjoy the experience that awaited me the next day when it felt as though a piece of my soul had been ripped out.

Despite my trepidation the day before, I was up bright and early the next morning. Lining up beside thousands of other runners, I bounced up and down as the race day energy buzzed through the crowds. Then, somehow, I raced faster than I had ever thought possible: a 1:56:40 for my very first half. As soon as I found my Mom at the finish line, I fell into her arms, and she thanked me. She thanked me for being a light in such a dark time, for giving her some happiness in this weekend full of sorrow.

As we drove home, I remember thinking about how life will always keep moving, whether you like it or not. I could stew in the despair of this horrific event, wishing I could turn back time; or I could put that regret aside and move forwards. I could choose to enjoy each and every moment as though it were my last on this planet.

Now, hanging the medal back on my rack, I wiped away my tears and sat up a little straighter. It was not over yet. I wasn't about to let this virus take away another part of me. I was young and healthy; I had not been given a death sentence. Sitting down at my desk to start some school work, I tried my best to enjoy these solitary moments by myself. I tried to tell myself that resting was helping my body recover from all the rigorous training I had just completed. All the work was in the tank, and now I just had to trust myself and hope that I could fight off the invader.

I would not allow this one result to define me.

The next few nights were pure horror. I couldn't breathe and lay awake all night, darkness swarming around me, a claustrophobic cloud. Images of the races in which I was sure I wouldn't be able to compete constantly flashed through my mind, producing silent tears that slowly trickled down my cheeks. A saw cut through my throat each time I swallowed. I was so alone in my little bubble, feeling helpless as I stared up at the dark ceiling.

Why did this have to happen?

Why?

Why?

Why?

Each morning, I woke up to a deep ache in my stomach. I felt a longing for something that I couldn't have, something which was just out of reach. I would make breakfast and then sit at my desk for the rest of the day, completing schoolwork. Golden sun rays streamed in through the curtains, tantalizing me and electrifying my legs. They wanted to move, my mind wanted to be free, and yet the rest of my body had me trapped. Each time I saw a runner or a biker, or even just someone walking out on the pathways; I squeezed my hands into tight little fists, trying to overpower the torment of burning desire with a physical, tangible pain. I thought back to all the days where I had to drag myself out the door, when I had to force my legs to move and just wished I could be done running with every passing minute on my feet.

I would give anything to go back to that time, I thought. I realized that I had never really thought about it as getting to run; it was merely something that I had to check off the list.

Why had I been so ungrateful?

Slouching back in my chair, I vowed to enjoy each and every moment when I was finally allowed back out there. I vowed never to take movement for granted again because life is clearly too short: you never know when the home you've built — the structure of your life — could come crashing down over you.

After what felt like a lifetime, I was finally permitted to slip on a mask and leave the house. As soon as I stepped out the door, a smile crept across my sullen face. The sun's rays tickled my cheeks with their comforting warmth — as though engulfing me in the hug I had dreamt about for the past week. Stopping in my tracks, I held my face up to the sky and closed my eyes, allowing the heat to seep in. The sun suddenly felt like a miracle, and I took in its rays as though they were chocolate, savouring each and every granule. For one glorious moment, I felt so lucky. So lucky to be alive and finally, *finally,* outside.

That happiness quickly faded as my mind reverted back to the constant worries I had been fighting since the COVID test. All that gratefulness immediately evaporated as the fear began to pour out of my mouth.

"What if racing hurts me even more? What if it causes my symptoms to worsen, and never go away?" I asked my Mom as we walked down the path. While locked away in my room, I had been researching if it was okay to run with COVID. I had found many sources warning against running with the virus, as the weakening of one's immune system while running could cause the symptoms to worsen and last. Also, my dad had gotten COVID just a week before me, and had recently developed a cough that would not leave him alone. I was terrified that it would take over my lungs, too, and make me incapable of running.

"What if racing the half will cause me to never be able to run to the same level that I could before COVID? What if it damages my lungs forever?"

I could not even imagine what my life would be like without this sport. If I couldn't go for a run after a hard day, if I couldn't pull myself out of that dark place, I would be so lost. This sport had become a part of me; possibly entwined *too* much with my identity.

"Zoe," my Mom reassured me, "you can't worry about that right now. No one knows for sure what will happen. But you are young and strong so I am sure it will be fine. Let's just take this one step at a time, and deal with everything as it comes. You have no idea how you will feel in three days." She smiled as she spoke and gently placed her hand on my shoulder.

Tears pooling in my eyes, I nodded, hoping that her optimistic answer would be true. I needed to be able to run. I hated to think about the fact that COVID might take it away, just like it had stolen so many other things from my life.

"If everything happens for a reason, then what the heck is the reason for this?" I asked her, a tear dripping down my cheek.

Silence quickly overtook our walk, both of us racking our brains for an answer.

It was T-minus one day until track city finals and two days until the Calgary half marathon. Finally, I was allowed to go for a run, as I needed to see how everything felt. Even though I had only taken a five day break, it felt as though it was my first time back after a year of injury. I was so happy to be doing what I love again that I sprinted off the driveway in pure bliss. I was like one of those pro marathoners, my legs floating across the pavement, my arms pumping effortlessly at my sides.

Unfortunately, a minute later my lungs caught up to me, and I immediately fell into a slow shuffle. I was barely moving, and breathing felt like I was pushing against a pile of bricks. Each time I tried to suck in air for a deep breath, my chest was on fire, and there was a feather tickling the back of my throat.

It reminded me of how quickly things can change. How quickly a good moment can turn into the worst one of your life.

After ten minutes, my legs were burning too, and the only thoughts running through my mind were: *How am I going to do this? Why did this have to happen to me? I'm going to come in last in the finals. I'm not going to be able to finish the half.* My thoughts quickly reduced me to tears, and I slowed to a walk. I was at the point in training where a 5k was supposed to feel easy, where each time I stepped out the door, I would picture the start line and get a little extra boost. But the last thing I wanted to see right now was a start line of expectations; a start line to a race I wouldn't be able to finish. I sat down on the sidewalk and put my head in my hands, crying again. The tickle in my throat became more pronounced and coughs erupted out of me.

Why?

I woke up the next morning a bundle of nerves, forcing my overnight oats down my throat and wincing at the scratchy pain. The dull ache each time I swallowed had turned into a thousand little needles. My nose was constantly running, though it was not as clogged anymore. Things were changing, but I wasn't sure if it was for the better.

"You don't have to do this if you don't want to," my Mom reminded me as we got in the car. "We can just see how you're feeling when we get there."

I nodded, on the verge of tears again. I really had no idea how I was going to complete this race, but I was not one to quit. I knew if I didn't run it I would be left forever wondering what I could have done: I would feel so disappointed in myself. But at the same time, I was worried about it impeding my ability to race the next day, as the half was the race which I cared about the most.

Staring out the window, I wished I could time travel. I wished I could fast forward through this race and the pain I knew it would induce. But soon enough we were at the track, and it was quickly getting real. I sped to the bathroom as I always do, and then forced myself to warm up. My legs were jello, wanting to collapse underneath me at any given moment. My stomach was just about ready to project its contents onto the track. *I just have to finish,* I thought. *Who cares what happens? Hopefully no one will be paying much attention to this race anyways,* I told myself.

"Runners on your mark," the announcer blared, and we all shuffled up to the curved starting line.

BANG!

Everyone sprinted off the line, and I tried to follow suit, getting pushed from left and right until I was funneled to the back of the pack. After one lap, my breathing had already become erratic, and the figures of the girls before me were quickly shrinking. After the second lap, my lungs were burning, and my legs had escaped from my control. *I want to stop. I want to stop. I want to stop*, I thought over and over, wondering what would happen if I just stepped to the side.

Coming around the bend for the fifth time, I was on the verge of tears, shaking my head at my mom. I had never felt like this before. I was so nauseous, and the world was swirling around me. Every fiber in my being wanted to stop. *Why am I doing this to myself?*

"Just step off the track!" she screamed, terrified that I was going to pass out. But there was no way I could do that. I only had two laps left. When the girl in front of me surged, I had no desire to go with her. *I can't do it,* I thought, allowing the fact that I would be last to seep into my brain. As I sprinted down the final stretch, tears pooled in the corners of my eyes. I was so disappointed in myself. *I should have just skipped the race altogether, then no one would have known how slow I was.*

The minute I crossed the line, I collapsed to the ground; a pile of defeat. The girl who finished first gave me a high five, but it only made me feel like more of a loser. I was the pity card, the one that she had to congratulate to show true sportsmanship. Coughs bursting from my body, I shakily stood up and shuffled off the track. As soon as I found her, I fell into my Mom's arms, and she cried and told me how proud she was.

"You are amazing," she exclaimed, and I wished so badly that I could believe her.

After the race, we stopped at the BMO center to pick up my half marathon race package for the next day, and my foul mood quickly dissipated. There was a certain buzz when you walked in, the building crowded with groups of people in leggings and sneakers; tables of energy gels and protein bar samples. With my first half marathon being immediately post-pandemic, I had not had the chance to experience this pre-race exhilaration. Even so, each time a wave of excitement rushed through my body, a dull ache quickly followed. If I didn't have COVID, I would have come here bouncing from the post-race adrenaline, my eyes bright with excitement for the day to come. This expo would have been a celebration, a treat, not a reminder of what I was missing out on. The track race kept playing through my mind, making me feel sick to my stomach. I wished so badly that I could go back and do better. I didn't know how I would get over this, especially in time for tomorrow.

I'm just setting myself up for disappointment by lining up at the start line. It's going to feel terrible.

Everything in my body was screaming that I couldn't do it, and I just wanted to quit.

Why did this have to happen to me? Why couldn't I be healthy like everyone else?

Why am I even doing this?

I think my mom saw the tears brewing in my eyes, so she directed me to the table where my package would be. We grabbed it and as I followed her out, I stared longingly at those ecstatic runners, wishing so badly that I could be them.

Soon enough, 9:30 pm rolled around — my pre-race bedtime — and I dragged myself upstairs; I needed to attempt to sleep for at least a few hours. As I lay under my covers in the darkness, I stared up at the ceiling, and a shadow of Papa's face floated into my mind. I thought about how he must have felt laying in bed for hours and hours, rapidly losing control of his body, and fighting to keep his eyes open. How he had put every single little effort into lifting his chest and letting it fall, until he just couldn't lift it anymore. I thought of how quickly he was gone, how rapidly his life had been sucked away. Suddenly, as though a lightbulb went off, I realized that I had to run tomorrow. My legs were working; my heart was still beating, so why shouldn't I use them?

A few short hours later, it was 6:57 am — three minutes until race time.

Crisp morning air tickled my nose, and nervous voices floated above the crowds around me, causing my heart to flutter with excitement. I fingered my jacket pockets for the cough drops and tissues I had stuffed within them and then bent down to triple knot my shoelaces.

I am doing this.

When I got back up again, I spotted my dad on the sidelines of the corral. I fought to be at the edge, and he smiled and wished me good luck. Under my mask I smiled back, knowing I would need every ounce of luck that I could garner.

"3, 2, 1, go!" the announcer blared, and we were off. Adrenaline surged through my body and I sped off with the crowd, quickly stuffing my mask into my pocket. The rhythmic pounding of feet took over, and I stared in awe at all the different

bodies surrounding me. All the different people, backgrounds, shapes, sizes, ethnicity, all of us moving forward together as a whole. Families stood at the sidelines bathed in the early morning rays, holding signs which read "Where is everyone going?" and "Is it worth the banana?" and "You run better than the government!" Each one brought a smile to my face and I floated along effortlessly, allowing the energy to carry me. At the eight kilometer mark I saw my family, and detoured to the edge to high-five them.

"You okay?" my Mom asked as I ran past.

To my own surprise, I answered yes and continued on my way. An Elvis Presley impersonator was singing as we crossed over a bridge, and then more families with cowbells and signs pushed us forward. The atmosphere was so amazing that I had forgotten about the fact that I was still recovering, all my worries had cleared from my mind.

And then, around kilometer fifteen, it got quiet: I glanced down at my watch to see my heart rate at 180. Suddenly, I felt as though I was having trouble breathing, and I watched in horror as my heart rate slowly rose from 190 to 200.

I knew I couldn't do this, I thought, slowing down and watching helplessly as crowds of runners sped past. Each time I took a breath, a dagger punctured my chest. A cramp had appeared under my ribs, and I wanted to walk. I wanted to walk so badly. As I rounded the corner and began to slow, I spotted my Mom, Dad, Nana and Poppa. They were cheering as loud as they could, my Nana ringing her cowbell and reaching out for a high five. Anger surged through my body — anger for this reason to speed up, a reason to push myself further when I was so ready to give in. Reluctantly, I increased my speed and plastered on a smile, but slowed again as soon as I rounded the next corner. My legs were seizing and my breathing was coarse: I could feel the bile rising up my throat.

I can't do it. I can't do it. I can't....

"You're doing amazing!" an older man exclaimed as he ran up beside me. I looked up and stared at him for a second, not quite believing that he had spoken to me. But when no one else responded, I realized that he had.

"Thank you!" I replied and watched as his back moved through the crowds. Suddenly, the sun poked through the dreary sky and engulfed my face in a warm hug. My mind flashed back to earlier that week when I had stepped outside for the first time. Back then, I truly thought I wouldn't be able to race.

I am here now.

I was doing it.

I had come last in the track finals, but had anything really changed? Glancing once again at the people around me, I thought about all the different lives and the different backgrounds that were gathered here on these streets, moving seamlessly together. This man, he didn't know me. He had just seen a little girl holding her own with the masses of adults and wanted to recognize her for her strength. He didn't know of all my shortcomings. He didn't know of all the strength that it took to get here.

However, I didn't know anything about him either. Maybe he had seen something in me that reminded him of himself. Looking around, I realized that I didn't know anything about any of these people. None of them knew anything about me. And yet here we were, spending hours on our feet together, gaining a sort of unspoken camaraderie that I knew could not be created anywhere else.

Breathing in the pain, Papa came to mind, and I realized how lucky I was. I was still here, I was pushing my body to its maximum while it was at its weakest. This virus hadn't sucked the life from me like it had him; I had been given a second chance.

I knew I needed to use this moment.

Picturing Papa's face in my mind, I clenched my fists and pushed harder, accepting the sizzling pain in my quads, the sting of my (likely bleeding) toes. I was moving with the pack again, in more pain than ever. Yet, I knew I could keep going.

I can't...

Nope.

Not a chance. Closing my eyes against the agony, I moved my legs even faster to prove to myself that I could. My breathing was rapid, my legs tight and numb. The world was spinning more than it had during the track race, but I kept going. As the runners around me sped up, I did too, and soon enough, the 20 kilometer mark appeared.

My legs moved faster than ever beneath me, the screaming crowds and cheers of my family in the grandstand were merely blurs as I dialed in on the finish line. Sprinting those final steps, it became clear in my mind that I had just unlocked something new. I had unlocked a part of me that I never would have known existed had I not been in this situation.

Hands shooting into the air, I crossed the line, disbelief clouding my mind. Immediately, I sped over to my family on the sidelines, who hugged me with huge smiles on their faces.

"You did it! You just ran a half marathon with COVID!" Nana exclaimed, staring at me in awe. I smiled sheepishly and glanced down at my watch.

1:54:20.

I had run a personal best.

With COVID.

My mind had seemed so robust in producing the belief that I couldn't do it: finally, I realized that I could overcome it. Tears brewing, I locked eyes with my Mom and fell into her arms one more time. I now understood that I had found the answer to my question: the reason behind this horrific situation.

It was essential in proving to me that I could overcome my own destructive thoughts. And only once I persevered could I discover the expanse of possibilities waiting for me in their shadows.

It's Fun Doing What They Say Isn't Possible

by Morrie Ripley

Dedication

Mom, if you could see me now

Yes You Can

I have always contemplated the prompt of "What's your Dream?" For me, walking, talking and being able to look after myself were all things I took for granted when suddenly I couldn't do those things anymore. I was left dreaming of a time when I would be able to do all these things once again for myself! Little did I know how running would become such a big part of my future when this dream came true. This is my story.

The date was September 25, 1999. I had two kids, had built my first house and was fast becoming overweight. I was a "healthy" 209 pounds with a heart attack waiting to happen. My wife and I were on our way to a friend's barbecue party in our Pontiac Grand Am. It was dusk, the sun was just above the horizon and the smells of harvest hung in the air. Suddenly, out of nowhere, a swamp donkey (AKA a moose) decided to venture across the highway. This is why you should always look both ways before crossing the road! I hit the moose pretty much dead center and it took all of a second to create quite the gory scene. I had two dents on my front bumper from where I took him out at the knees, flipping him on top of our vehicle. Somehow the moose's head was cut off, leaving the body to land in the fast lane of the highway. It was then hit two more times. Once by a Chevy Cavalier, causing him to roll over into the ditch, and again by a Ford one-ton that drove right over it like it was a speed bump. Miraculously, my wife didn't have a scratch on her. Bullwinkle however, well... never made it home.

All things considered, a ground ambulance was there quite quickly. After a quick assessment of me, the call was made to STARS air ambulance to come pick me up. When my call came in, STARS was already responding to an emergency in Camrose, Alberta. As luck would have it, when they got to Camrose, their call was cancelled. So, while still in the air, they turned around, and within seconds, they were landing on Highway 14 to pick me up. A quick call was made to the University of Alberta to let them know I was coming in. It was determined in the air that they would do a rooftop transfer and in less than 15 minutes after hitting the moose, I was landing atop the hospital. The quick rescue and medical attention are why I'm here today.

I can only imagine how long of a night it was for my parents, my wife Michelle and the rest of my family waiting to hear from the doctors. There were many uncertain hours wondering if I would even make it through the night. Multiple tests, CTs and X-rays were needed and took a lot of time to complete.

The next day, it was determined that I had broken my neck in four places and had also sustained a brain injury, effectively putting me into a coma. While waiting to determine how they would fix my neck, I was put into traction. Doctors wondered whether my neck was stable enough to fuse together on its own, or if surgically placed plates and screws would be needed. It was later decided that they would leave my neck alone for a while. They decided to screw a halo apparatus to my head to keep my neck from moving and wait to see what happened. As for my brain injury, the swelling was so intense that there was no way for them to assess how much damage there was. The waiting game began.

Roughly three weeks later, I woke up from the coma and was able to tell the doctors how and what I felt. I was so scared as I had no vision at this time, but doctors told me this was normal with the amount of swelling I had in my brain. Only time would reveal if my vision, or the ability to walk would come back. In the medical field, time is hard to borrow!

However, I was able to give them a better picture of the damage done to my spinal cord. At this time, I was still paralyzed from the waist down, with little function of my arms. Determining any nerve damage this early after my accident was almost impossible. It was the nerves that wrap around the spinal cord that were damaged. Unfortunately, with these particular nerves, if they get damaged they don't regenerate themselves. Doctors have a hard time telling the difference to assess nerve damage when there is significant swelling in your spinal column. With time, medication, and keeping me still, we were all hoping that the swelling in my spinal column would come down and reveal just how much nerve damage I had incurred. At first, I had no feeling in my legs but some in my arms. I often complained that my right side and lower back hurt, giving doctors hope that I still had sensations in the lower part of my body. This would obviously be a great thing, but days and days of bed rest can often cause pain and discomfort on their own. Yet again, let's try to borrow some more time.

Roughly another week went by, when one morning in the hospital, I thought I felt the nurse touching my leg while getting cleaned up. Often, this can be characterized as a phantom sensation. This is where your brain sees someone touching your leg and you know you should feel it, so your brain says 'hey, you're being touched.' Of course, I was excited and wanted my doctor to come see and hear what was going on. Mister "Never-give-a-guy-hope", also known as my doctor, walked in and immediately started doing some assessments.

The first test is one I do not like, even to this day. The doctor had me close my eyes and he touched my leg. It sounds simple, but I still have trouble with it. When I close my eyes, I have a hard time knowing exactly where my legs are. Without me having that extra sense to know where things are, my brain relies on the only thing that's left to test, my sense of touch.

The sense of feeling touched isn't that simple. One may be able to feel the pressure of being touched, but there are other parts of that sensation that our minds use to interpret what that feeling is and how to respond to it. Is it a feel-good touch? Is it a warm touch? Cold? Sharp or dull? Does it require my body to do something to keep my legs from getting hurt?

So, the doctor tells me to close my eyes and he pulls out a pin and starts to poke me like a pin cushion, trying to figure out if my nerves are firing properly, and if they weren't, to what degree they were damaged. As it turns out, I did have sensory damage in my legs, but I was lucky enough to have some leg function. My legs now seem to take off at times when they want to, thanks to some uncontrollable muscle spasms, but with medication I've learned to cope with them well.

After all of my assessments that morning, I was on cloud nine. Things seemed to be finally moving in a positive direction with my recovery. I distinctly remember saying to my doctor, "Now that I have feeling coming back in my legs, I'll be running the Boston Marathon soon!" Now anyone who knows me, knows that I was not a runner at all. This was obviously some sort of attempt at sarcastic humour intended to lighten the severity of my situation. My doctor turned, looked me straight in the eyes, and said, "Keep your dreams realistic. You won't be running no Boston Marathon."

After hitting a moose a month earlier, hearing what my doctor said felt like I was just now hit by a truck. Doctors do not prescribe hope. I'm not sure it is even in their vocabulary, as it is just something they cannot do. It's safer for them to give generalized statements as to what may or may not happen with the injuries one has. They aim not to get a patient's hopes up too high nor to prepare them for any changes in life after their accident. Little did I know, that day was the turning point in my recovery.

I never asked for a disability, never really even knew what one was but I knew I had to learn how to live a new kind of life. A seed was planted, and a fire was started in me that day. I wanted to prove my doctor wrong. I was frustrated with the words he had said to me. For the next few weeks, I wouldn't even look at him when he came into my room to do his morning rounds. This led to my doctor thinking that perhaps I had a more serious brain injury than he originally thought. I was not only angry at him. I was also angry at the world. This was the first time the doctors had seen me show any signs of anger, which can be a sign of brain injury. Doctors can only assess what they see and hear from their patients at that moment in time. Doctors are not lucky enough to have a before and after snapshot of their patients, making it difficult for them to determine what may or may not be normal.

As I was discharged from the University of Alberta Hospital and moved to the Glenrose Rehabilitation Hospital, my doctor was left to decide whether I should be admitted to the brain injury unit or the spinal cord injury unit. I was put on the brain injury floor for an assessment to see which unit would be the most beneficial for me. I am so thankful that my stay in that unit was a short one. Two days later, I was admitted to the spinal cord injury unit and my official rehabilitation process began.

My first day on the spinal cord injury floor I was introduced to my rehab team. I met my physio and occupational therapists and got a grand tour of the spinal cord unit. This hospital was so different from the trauma hospital I had just left. In trauma hospitals, there are a ton of restrictions as to what family and friends are permitted to do, and the reasons these rules are in place make sense. It is the doctors' and nurses' job to get patients stable and off to the rehab hospital. Since the rehab hospital knows I'm eventually heading home, they want all the help they can get from friends and family. Essentially, they want to teach everyone around me how to help me once I'm home again. My family circle was taught endless tasks such as: giving needles, medication and other daily routines. Thankfully, I was able to learn these tasks quite quickly on my own. Family and friends were shown how to help me transfer from my wheelchair to my bed and into a car which were two common tasks that one would need help with. All of these things would be critical to my recovery.

I knew my path to recovery would be a long one and the element of the unknown was huge. Would I walk again on my own? Would I need a walker or my wheelchair to get around? My physical therapist immediately began working with me on this, standing me up with harnesses. After basically lying in bed and sitting in a chair for six to eight weeks, one's body forgets what it is like to stand up. When my physio team stood me up, I became lightheaded and dizzy, and then I got sick all over the place. I was so embarrassed and thought for sure once I was cleaned up that they would not want to see me again! It wasn't long before I found out that I was wrong.

The next morning, I was rolled right back into the rehab gym, harnesses put back on and we did it all again. We slowed things down, adding something else every day until they could stand me up and let my legs start to regain strength and stability. Things went along like this for the next few weeks until one day, I rolled into the gym, but I was put in a different area. Instead of nothing around me, I was placed in front of what looked like a sidewalk with railings on both sides. As usual, they put harnesses on me and stood me up in front of these bars. I was told to hold onto the bars and told to try to take a step. My legs felt like they were concrete. They were so heavy. I couldn't lift my foot off the ground. My legs weren't listening to me.

There are things in my rehab process that I cannot remember due to my brain injury, but I can vividly remember this day. After what I thought was an eternity, they sat me back in my chair and said that just standing up and holding the bars on my own was a huge step. After that feedback, they determined that was enough for the day. Stubbornly, I refused and asked them to stand me up again. I had to try again. In my mind, I could not comprehend why my foot would not move forward when I asked it to. I just could not quit. I desperately wanted to walk again. If only there was a light switch that I could turn on for my legs to get them working again. My frustration levels grew, no matter how hard I tried, progress in my rehab slowed to a snail's pace.

A couple months after my accident I was rolled down to the gym for my physio session as usual. Somehow, this morning felt different. I wasn't sure what it was, but things felt different in my legs. We went through the normal process of stretching and setting me up in front of the bars and I was stood up. I squeezed those bars as hard as I could, and thought, 'Ok foot, let's go.' I looked down at my feet and tears welled up in my eyes. My legs just would not move. *I thought this was the day.* My legs were getting stronger every day, but my mind just could not move them. Stubborn, I asked yet again, "Stand me up. I gotta keep trying." My physio said, "Let's try something." She said she was going to push my right foot forward to see what would happen. She pushed it forward, and in doing so, it turned my hips, making me lean forward. With them holding onto me there was no way I could fall. It was right then and there, like a light switch had been flicked on and my left leg moved forward. Boy did I cry, along with all of the people around me. I can honestly say I remember my first steps!

In the end, I required surgery to help stabilize my neck. Nevertheless, 11 years later, after tons of rehab and training, I eventually ran the Boston Marathon. I've since crossed the finish line for over 30 marathons all around the world. I've had the opportunity to run in major marathons of the world, several ultras, and four Ironman triathlons. Far from crossing my own finish line, I hope to hit many more. The friends I've met and the places I've travelled to while running are moments I'll cherish for the rest of my life!

No Pain

by Herbert Camat

Dedication

Dedicated to my mom, dad, and friends who always support me, push me to be my best and cheer for me at the finish line.

When I was a kid, I was always jealous of the kids who played tag and soccer. Seeing them run around in the school field and not gasping for air made me jealous. Unfortunately, I was severely asthmatic. From the ages of three to five, I was hooked up to a nebulizer for a few minutes a day just to make sure I could catch something close to a full breath. On the bright side, I was able to transition to a spacer. This device just held the inhaler mists so I could breathe it in, but still required the use of an inhaler throughout the rest of my childhood. Running and any form of exercise as a kid was essentially my kryptonite. I was not able to run for very long, let alone very far. I had a negative outlook toward running, much like a lot of people. Why would I want to engage in something that costs energy and makes it difficult to breathe? Why would I want to do something that doesn't make me feel good physically? As a result of my disdain for exercise, I ended up having negative body image issues. This outlook stemmed from when I was an overweight child, but we'll get into how running ties in with all of this.

Flash forward to 2020, when I had a bit of a health scare. That year was not good for anybody who already felt isolated in some form or another. All I would do is order take-out and play video games, not concerned with the outside world and the current pandemic that was happening across the globe. When I went for my yearly check up, my doctors were concerned about my blood pressure. This was most concerning to me. Relatives on both sides of my family have passed from heart related conditions. There I was, a 20-year-old with high blood pressure. This wasn't how it was supposed to be. Then and there, I made the decision to change my habits and get into shape. I bought my first pair of running shoes and went on jogs throughout my neighborhood. I will admit, it was hard and hurt my feet, especially my arches. Every step hurt to breathe, and my muscles were sore, but I kept at it. Luckily, at this point, I had outgrown my asthma and did not need an inhaler anymore. As with all forms of progress, my running was not linear. Nevertheless, I started to feel better about my body, how I looked and how I felt. I was fascinated by my own progress. I started to fall in love with running, but by no means was I a long distance runner; nor did I have any intention to run long distances. Running showed me that consistency and dedication could go a long way toward self-improvement, much like all things in life. If you want something, you have to stick with it no matter how inconvenient, uncomfortable or painful it can be.

Through it all, I took up a love of Rocky, the fictional underdog boxer from Philly. I resonated with a famous phrase from his coach, "No Pain." Rocky's trainer would echo that mantra over and over again until it was drilled into his mind and mine. I do not know what it is about the Rocky theme song, but it always gets me going. I think that a lot of long distance runners have some sort of mantra that they tell themselves when things get tough. "No Pain" became mine. With my mantra in hand, I started to fall in love with running. I was slow, but I was doing it. In Edmonton, running through the River Valley is something to behold. The landscape through the seasons and the many friendly people and lots of furry friends make each run unique. While running is a great sport, I started taking on other physical activities, including climbing and weight lifting. However, like with all physical activity, there is always a risk.

In January 2022, I was the strongest I had ever been. I could continuously run just over ten kilometers. I was becoming a well-rounded athlete and I was starting to actually like what I was seeing in the mirror. Around this same time, I was doing a difficult bouldering problem while climbing. There was a tiny foothold that was supporting my right foot, and when I leapt up towards the next hold, I heard a pop and felt excruciating pain from my right foot. I fell onto the climbing mat and immediately ripped off my climbing shoe. My foot did not look good and it swelled up right away, turning purple and becoming very painful. The day of, I thought I could walk it off. I'd get some sleep, and just like magic, the pain and purpleness would dissipate overnight. Oh, how wrong I was. I could barely sleep because the pain was excruciating, and my foot somehow turned even more purple while I tossed and turned. This was when I became quite concerned, so I took myself to a walk-in clinic and the doctor recommended going to the Emergency Room. I was terrified as I had never been to the ER. Furthermore, on the news they were always talking about long wait times and to top all off, COVID came back in the form of another wave. I was ready to be in the ER waiting room for over eight hours. Thankfully, all the health care professionals were welcoming, efficient and kind even though they were strained by the state of the health care system. Luckily, I was able to get an X-ray and verbal confirmation that I did not have a fracture. I had sprained my big toe on my right foot and I was out of commission for a few months. I had to take time off from running and climbing to heal from the injury and this hurt me emotionally. My mind raced. How was I supposed to stay in shape? How was I going to get through this?

I could not properly walk for three months, I could not run for four and I was not able to boulder for five. Every time I got up from bed, it hurt to walk and some days I had to use crutches. Fortunately, at this time, school went back online, so I would not have to make the treacherous winter commute to the University of Alberta campus, which was a mini-city in itself. The most challenging thing about this injury was the physiotherapy. Recovery was painful, but my mantra of "no pain" really pulled me through. Doing my physiotherapy exercises helped put me in a better spot. My physiotherapists were extremely supportive, but I discovered that the real power to heal came from within myself. In my mind, it would have been better to just stay in bed and not be subjected to pain from physio, but I knew that deep down I needed to get back to my baseline. I wanted to return to walking and running without inhibition and pain.

Once again, my progress was not linear and overcoming any form of physical ailment is challenging, but I made it through. After a few months of sticking to my physio and keeping my mantra close to my heart, I was finally able to walk without pain but running... running was a whole different beast. I was slow and not at the same fitness level I once was. Plus, there was some pain in my right foot. It took a lot of practice and patience to get back to where I was. Once the pain dissipated, I set my sights on something bigger and more challenging.

One of my best friends is a long distance runner. Throughout high school, he would run on the treadmill for hours, which baffled me. When he told me he had run marathons, many half-marathons and an ultra marathon I was completely shocked! I asked myself: how could anyone run that far and for that long? I mean, I can run around ten kilometers but doing that another four times? Impossible! Or so I thought....

I was inspired by him. I wanted to do what he did but I had never run a formal race! I had never worn a bib with a race number. I had never crossed a start or finish line but I knew that I wanted to have the satisfaction of doing so under my belt.

I remember vividly a conversation I had with one of my best friends, Mark, in April 2022. I was asking him a plethora of questions related to running such as: How can I run that far? What if I need to pee? Don't you get hungry? This list was endless in order to gauge if I could pull this official running goal off. After all the questions I looked at him and said: "Mark, I think

I'd like to run a race this summer! Maybe a half marathon!" He looked at me and said: "Herbert, I think you could do a whole marathon!" It took me back a little bit. Me? Herbert Camat? Running a full marathon, 42 kilometers, with only four months to train? There was absolutely no way, I thought. I sat with that idea for a few hours. Many people run marathons, I told myself. Talent can only take you so far, but consistency... that could take me a lot farther. The very next day, I signed up for the Edmonton Marathon. It would be my first marathon and my very first race.

I didn't know where to start, I had never trained for anything. I hadn't played recreation sports, never competed in anything, but I found a training plan and I wanted to stick to it. I wanted to prove to myself that I could do it, which meant I could do anything.

The training was hard. There were long hours filled with loneliness, sacrifice and literal blood, sweat and tears. I had no idea that I would run for hundreds of kilometers only to do a fraction of it on race day! The toughest part of training for me was the long runs. Running anything longer than ten kilometers was extremely challenging. My knees ached, my muscles ached, and my feet hurt but I kept pushing. I knew that I had to push through the pain in order to become better than I was. To echo what Haruki Marukami once said, "Pain is inevitable. Suffering is optional." That, combined with my own personal mantra, "no pain," got me through some of the highs and lows of not just training but life. At one point, despite the pain and discomfort that persisted, I started to enjoy running. Pushing myself through the pain, past my own limits, and impressing myself. I remember the first time I ran over 30 kilometers. I was so proud of myself. The feat took a lot out of me, but I did it. I was sore for a few days after, but I was so proud of myself. The idea of doing a full marathon started to feel within reach. It was no longer an impossible task, but a palpable challenge. In a huge world, where I felt like a speck of sand, I had the sense that I could do anything and I could conquer the world.

Something runners do not often talk about is how lonely training can be. I remember the countless early mornings when the sun was not even up, but I was out there to get my kilometers in before work or before my shifts at the hospital. Outside of encountering the odd runner, giving each other a nod of acknowledgement, or the odd person walking their dog and the dog playfully chasing me... the training was lonely. There were times when my family and friends would gather but I was so busy training or recovering that I couldn't enjoy these gatherings. I knew that in the long run it would be worth it, but that didn't make it any less difficult. Through the hardships, you still have to push through. There is no other direction other than forward. No pain.

Despite my lack of presence within my social circle during my training cycles, my friends and family were still there for me, supporting me and cheering me on. One person's strength is only as strong as the company they keep and I kept some strong people around. During my various training cycles, I felt an enormous amount of pressure. Not from society, nor from the people around me but from myself. There were times where I woke up and burst into tears because I wasn't sure that I could finish, or if I could beat my own personal record.

I was an anxious mess the day before the race. I was hyperventilating and my heart was going a hundred miles a minute. Thankfully, my friends and family were there to console, encourage, and get me through the tough times. There were many challenges leading up to my first race. There were lots of aches and lots of doubts, but one way or another, race day arrived just the same. It was August 2022, and the Edmonton Marathon loomed. I was in a panic. I kept going back and forth in my mind about whether I would get injured or if I could even reach the finish line. The rational side of me became emboldened and I knew I had to honour myself and the harsh training I had put myself through. I knew I could do it, I just needed to prove it.

At the start line I watched all the people and thought, "Wow, all these people are crazy like me and want to run far!" It was so encouraging to see people coming together with the same goal. I met many friendly faces all throughout the course of the race. I knew that if those people were here to finish, so was I.

In the second half of the race, the grueling heat and dehydration were catching up with me. I struggled with the sheer discomfort and pain I felt, but I knew I could fight it off just as

I had before. The last ten kilometers are always a mind game. I had never said my mantra so many times in my life. No Pain!

Waiting for me at the finish line were some of the most important people, all there to support me and see me finish. The euphoria I felt when I was about to finish was unbelievable! All the pain, suffering, blood, sweat and tears no longer mattered after I crossed that finish line. It took me a few moments to realize what I had done. I had completed my first race... my first marathon! As my friends and family approached me, after I grabbed my post-race snacks and banana, a wave of tears hit me. Not tears of sadness or pain but tears of happiness. I managed to pull off what I once thought was impossible. I did something that not many people can say they have done in their lifetime. As tears flooded my face, I was surrounded by the warmth and love of the people who cared about me. At this point, there was *no pain*. What remained was the love I had for these people, the love I had for myself and the love I now had for the sport of running. Running has taught me more about myself than I could have ever imagined. I am capable of doing so much more than what I was ever led to believe.

Life is hard, life is painful. So is running. When training for a race, you're training for life. Pain is inevitable, suffering is a choice. Having people in my corner to root for me is such a privilege and I don't know how I can ever repay them. I hope they know I am forever indebted to them. Being able to circumnavigate challenges and build resilience has been difficult, but I am a better person for it. I am forever changed by the sport of running and now feel as though I can push through anything life throws at me. I want you to know that anything you want to do in this life is achievable. Sacrifice and pain are inevitable, but if you want it, you can do it!

Chasing Shadows, Finding Love

by Christy Holt

Dedication

This chapter is dedicated to my "crew" - my partner in life, Sean, my family and the incredible community we've surrounded ourselves with. I wouldn't be where I am today if it were not for every last one of you.

-- Not-So-Healthy Beginnings --

Truth be told, the reasons I started running were probably not "healthy" reasons. In fact, if I'm completely honest, my intentions were quite the opposite of healthy.

When I picked up running as an adult, I was in an unhappy marriage and trying to maintain my sanity as an exhausted mother to three vivacious boys, all under five years old. I was struggling to keep it together when it all happened... by accident. It was a beautiful summer evening and I was running late (see what I did there?) to see some friends in a nearby neighbourhood. On a whim, honestly not sure what had possessed me, I decided to *jog* the one to two kilometers to see them rather than drive. As it turned out, I missed meeting up with them and ended up running back home. Since I was actually feeling really good at that point, I decided to "top up" the run, continuing past my house to make it an even five kilometers.

As I ran, I felt my heart pumping and the energy building in my legs. It felt empowering – I felt truly alive! Most notable of all, I realized that I had momentarily forgotten about the heaps of everyday challenges that seemed to plague me day in and day out.

This came at a time when not only was I feeling painfully disconnected from my then-husband, but I was also simultaneously suffering from what I call "just-a-mom-itis." This term equates to being so fully entrenched in motherhood that one forgets their own individuality and sometimes forgets entirely to care for their own well being.

Running gave me a fresh new sense of purpose and some exciting personal goals to work towards. I relished the potential new source of validation.

Running gave me an 'out'. If circumstances were too difficult to face, I went for a run. If I was experiencing "too many" feelings, I went for a run. If I didn't know what to do or where to turn, I went for a run.

Before long, running was my "valid" excuse for escaping all of the difficulties I had been facing in life. It was better than couch marathoning on Netflix, I rationalized. Running further or faster was a challenge I *could* overcome, even if it took a little more effort. Running gave me a small sense of control in a world where things seemed to be spinning further and further out of control.

-- Running From Myself --

My mind has always been very busy, and while running it was no different. Given any downtime, my mind would often go wild with my endless to-do list, doubt about my marriage, and anxieties about all the things. There were so many days that I would wake up already feeling the anxiety of my life hitting me square in the chest before my eyes could flutter open. Even the would-be release of energy exerted during an intense run was no longer enough to ward off the stress that was building in my relationship.

So, in an ever-evolving attempt to avoid my own mind, I did what anyone would do. I started obsessively checking my stats and focused on beating myself - going further and faster with every run. I did anything I could to distract my mind while I ran away from my uncertain home life. Truthfully, I worried that if I looked directly at it, my whole world might implode.

Time spent alone in my head often resulted in an intense kind of discomfort that I very much desired to avoid and so as I increased my time and distance, my game plan changed again. I began to schedule more and more runs with groups of other runners, packing my schedule with social event after social event. This was all in a desperate attempt to avoid hearing the inevitable voice inside my head. Its most common mantra: 'you're not good enough'.

Meanwhile, in my marriage, I had found myself doing a great deal of blame shifting and finger pointing - I mean, hey, it's so much easier to deal with a failing marriage when it's *not your fault*, isn't it? When it *wasn't my fault*, I didn't have to put in the work to do things differently. From where I was standing, I was (with confidence!) telling myself that all I could do was *wait.* Wait for him to change. Wait for the circumstances to change. Wait for time to pass. I didn't feel like I had any power, and it certainly seemed like all potential ways out of the mess were life-threatening. It was all simply too heavy a weight for me to carry, and so I ran from it.

In addition to running and a packed social calendar, in my "down time" (as much down time a mom has while staying home with three young sons) I distracted myself with too much wine, hours (days?!) of Netflix and more than my fair share of blaming and complaining in the name of venting my frustrations. I had this insatiable need to be truly seen and heard. Since my relationship was giving me somewhat of an opposite experience, I sought out this recognition in other ways.

-- Running in a New Direction --

Knowing the sense of accomplishment that comes with finishing a race, I set out to create this experience for others. There was just something about crossing the finish line and being adorned with a medal that begged to be shared. During this time, I led numerous learn-to-run clinics, and held small, local 5K and 10K runs. All of these events were complete with high fives AND medals to celebrate our hard-earned victories! It was truly such a blessing to contribute to the running journeys of hundreds of people.

What began as leading run clinics eventually set me on a new career path, one that felt far more aligned with my desires for life. Despite many fears and worries (and confirmations from the world around me) that I was not "good enough," I still took the leap to become a personal trainer and nutrition coach. I truly wanted to help people to feel better in their bodies. I wanted to guide them back to themselves in a similar way that I had done for myself. So, I passionately shared what I had learned and thus set into motion my mission to make a significant impact in the world.

Interestingly, something else happened. In my efforts to help others grow and change, I had to take a hard look at what I was running from. Here I was, telling my clients that we couldn't just "fake it till we make it," rather we need to "be it till we see it."

We are the cause, not the effect. After years of trying (and failing miserably) to control the circumstances and people around me, I realized that the only thing I had the power to change was myself.

Just like with all my clients, my journey started with baby steps. As I began to journey deeper within myself, I began to slowly build the foundation within. I was finally starting to rediscover who I truly was – without the labels and identities the world had assigned me. Some parts of this identity were accepted willingly, while others were begrudgingly accepted, yet accepted nonetheless.

As I reflect back, I now see that while everything in my world truly seemed to be falling apart, it was *actually* falling right into place. As I began to build a solid relationship with myself, one in which I gave myself the unconditional love and acceptance that I had craved, my world around me began to shift. As I followed the inner nudges, the way became clear.

At one point, I had a life-changing realization: I am the common denominator in all of my problems. It hit me like a semi-truck. It was me. *I* was the problem. I had spent years blaming, complaining and placing responsibility everywhere outside of myself. Somehow I had missed what was before me all along: I am the solution!

Awareness of my true inner power had been cracked wide open, and it became infinitely clear to me that there were some changes that needed to be made. It wasn't easy, but it was truly worth the effort. It was time for me to take radical responsibility for my own life.

The more I practiced giving myself the love and validation that I longed for, the less reliant I was on others. I no longer needed anyone else to meet my expectations in order to feel in control of my life. My new perspective allowed me to release expectations of others while simultaneously loving myself to my highest capacity.

I cleared away the overthinking and overwhelm through the use of some strategies that I now refer to as The Spiral Stopper Method. I went on a self-discovery journey, curious and open to meeting a whole new me. I eventually began to love myself enough to set healthy boundaries - not in an effort to keep people out, but rather to lovingly show the right people the way in. Ultimately, these boundaries served as an invitation to a deeper connection with me for those who were kind, loving and supportive. It won't surprise you that some people in my life were not ready for that deeper connection and fell away, but I was grateful nonetheless. This made space for new connections and gave me some much needed clarity around my marriage. Sometimes, love alone is simply not enough to make a relationship work.

After years of clinging to hope and a prayer that somehow my relationship could be saved by some sort of miracle, I finally exited my marriage. Choosing *me* in that moment, I finally understood that I was already whole. I no longer felt that something was missing from me, so I was no longer seeking and chasing. I felt whole and complete, happy and at peace.

Things weren't perfect in life. I certainly had some very dark days during the divorce process. Approaching this with a new understanding of who I was and what I was here to create made all the difference. After years of holding back, nothing was going to get in the way of creating that destiny for myself any longer.

-- The Turn Around Point --

If you've ever run a race that has a turnaround point, you know how much it can suck to have to run the same ground twice (or more). The upside of this doubling up is that you get the opportunity to reflect on what you've been through and how far you've come.

What I came to realize was that no matter how hard I tried, and no matter how far I ran...I could never outrun what I had ultimately been trying to: myself. No matter how far I went, my shadows always followed right behind.

All the time I spent running away finally led me back to *me.* In a full circle kind of moment, it led me to the love I had longed for.

I realized that love had never been "out there." It had always been abundant within me. I already knew that happiness was not something to be chased and pursued. Fulfillment was something to be created first within and then expressed into the world. Connecting this very same principle to love opened the door for me to experience love like never before.

Here are the top five realizations that truly turned life around for me:

1. I needed to go first and set a positive example for my kids.

For years, I stayed in my marriage – to protect my children is what I told myself – but I finally realized that this form of "protection" was merely an illusion. My kids didn't need a perfect mom who held her family together with a hope, prayer and a lot of caffeine – they needed a mom that loved them SO MUCH that she bravely went first to show them *how to love themselves*. The truth is, as a parent, our relationships are a model for our children. It is our responsibility to demonstrate healthy relationships for them so that they can learn to create the healthy and loving relationships they too deserve. By going first and choosing myself, I paved the way for my children to express their own needs. I wholeheartedly encourage my children to be authentically themselves and to create a full life with relationships that absolutely light them up.

2. People pleasing was keeping me from the life I truly desired.

I discovered through much pain, frustration and resentment - that the more I pleased others with forced smiles plastered on, the more alone, unloved and unworthy I ended up feeling. I could continue to try to force life to happen the way I desired, but frankly, it seemed like a lot of effort with no result. As every runner knows well, no matter how well trained you are, some days are still tough. I knew I had to take radical responsibility for myself. Nevertheless, I had to gently remind myself that no amount of contorting myself to make others happy was going to work. I had to release the illusion of control and surrender to the way life was meant to unfold.

3. Life is full of lessons, if only we are willing to learn.

Looking back, every single moment has contributed to the wisdom and understanding that I now have. My life experience has led me to unconditionally love and accept myself. It has also brought me to a place in my life where I have such an abundance of love and acceptance that it cannot help but overflow onto others. Chasing podiums and Personal Records can definitely highlight your perceived shortcomings. However, the perfection we often chase is merely an illusion. The challenges and hardships I faced have grown and refined me in ways that are profound, and for that, I will be eternally grateful.

4. "Finding" my authentic self was a process of *un-learning*.

The protective masks I had been wearing were preventing me from the very experiences I craved most. I realized I could not truly be seen while I was hiding behind so many 'good girl' masks and societal expectations. I tried increasingly harder to be whomever I thought others wanted or needed me to be. While trying to keep up with a world of "shoulds," I was losing my own self. True freedom came as I slowly cleared away the beliefs about myself that had actually been keeping me from my fullest expression. Leaning into authenticity is less about discovering *who we are* than it is about stripping away *all that we are not*.

5. In order to be truly heard, you have to be willing to use your voice.

In the past, I would not and could not fully express myself. The fear of punishment, loss or hurting another was too great. I discovered that the only way to feel truly seen and heard is to show up and boldly express yourself in a way that only you are capable of doing. There is absolutely no one in the world that is just like you – you truly are a living, breathing miracle and you are so much more than good enough! When we are unapologetically and authentically ourselves, we are able to speak our truth in love. Furthermore, not only do we create the opportunity to feel truly seen and heard just as we are, but we inherently give others permission to do the same. What a gift to both yourself AND the world this is.

It has certainly been a fascinating adventure, reflecting on where I've been while simultaneously discovering myself anew. It's been a years-long journey with no finish line in sight. I am certain this path I walk, and occasionally run, is guaranteed to be the adventure of a lifetime!

Not long after the turning point, things shifted quite quickly. Since I no longer needed to run away from life, I finally began to run towards the life of my dreams.

-- Love at the Finish Line --

The deeper work that I have done to get to know myself has allowed me to create a healthy relationship with myself, inside and out. All of these milestones have created space for me to become aware of what is and isn't in alignment for me. As a result of this increased awareness, I began to set boundaries. First I set these new parameters with myself and then with others too, which proved to be a recurring practice. As a result of my increased expression, I developed confidence with speaking my voice and I have felt far more heard. In fact, my entire personal journey has led me to this place in my life where I can finally give back and help other people to create the happy life, relationship and impact that their soul longs for. Accepting myself and offering myself unconditional self compassion led to no longer resisting the shadows. There was no longer something chasing me, no longer something to fear... instead, the shadows became something to love.

My favourite part of this story is near the end, though what I'll share here was only the beginning of what has truly been an epic adventure of a lifetime.

Picture it: Edmonton, August 2018. The morning skies appeared apocalyptic orange, complete with a haze that stretched for miles over the beautiful river valley. The smoke blowing in from the wildfires barely held at bay and questionable air quality had loomed for days before the race. Luckily, the air quality had dropped to a reasonable range just in time. The race was on.

This was my third marathon and I was ready to make my goal a reality (4 hours and 15 minutes). I rushed up to the start line, simultaneously nervous and excited after getting there a little too late. I was anxiously hopping from one foot to another in an attempt to ease the pre-race jitters.

When the gun went off, I was ready to race. I had managed to make my way closer to the front of the crowd with maybe a minute to spare! As we took off, I kept my eyes locked on the pace "bunny" who was toting the '4:15' sign. The training hours were complete, and the time to make it happen had come. I knew what my body was capable of and what I needed to do.

What I didn't know was that this race would mark such a pivotal moment in my life.

And so, off we went. I set my focus on staying in step and on pace with the crowd of 4:15 runners. I wanted to ensure that I remained on track for my goal. There was quite a pack of us running together for the first half, but as we approached the 30 kilometer mark, the crowd really began to thin. At the same time, my body was starting to catch on to my most excellent plan of pushing it to the limit that day. My knees were starting to convey their discomfort, but I popped a couple of painkillers and kept putting one foot in front of the other. I was determined to stay on track despite the discomfort.

My mind was as busy as always, especially when I started to hit the mental wall, and I decided that I needed to get out of my head temporarily. The pace bunny seemed friendly, and I thought - hey, it's essentially their "job" to help me get this done. I have always taken this job very seriously when I have paced various races, and I was grateful to have this guide. I was struggling a bit with my thoughts when I looked around me and realized it was just him and me. He seemed, conveniently, to be running this ridiculously fast pace with an ease that had me in awe. I remember thinking, there's less than one hour left. All I have to do is not stop. Just keep going. It will all be over soon enough.

I could barely breathe. On top of that, the thoughts of doubt crept in. Would I really be able to accomplish this goal? So, I chatted him up.

At first, I asked him some short small-talk-esque questions. We covered our run history, and I peppered him with short questions that necessitated long answers. I hoped it would give me the distraction I needed mentally while giving me a chance to catch my breath, too. He was encouraging every step of the way, not just towards me but towards everyone running the race. I could tell immediately that he had a huge heart.

I kept running, and we kept chatting. The mission was purely distraction as I plodded out the final 10K of the race. As an added bonus, I got to know this calm and kind runner who was wearing a turtle shell on his back *for a full freakin' marathon.* As an added bonus, I thought he was cute, too, which made the conversation easier and my motivation to keep running stronger.

Less than an hour of small talk and getting-to-know-you later, the finish line was in sight. I was even ahead of schedule by at least a few minutes! With a final burst of adrenaline, I took off and ran with everything I had left in me. Experiencing the rush of running down the middle of Jasper Avenue to finish my third full marathon was incredible! This time I crushed my prior marathon bests (both in the range of 4:30). I finished in 4:10:53 and I was elated. Goal unlocked! Personal Best achieved! Post-race donuts fully merited! I was so grateful.

The most epic part of accomplishing this goal was not actually about the run. Instead, it was about who I met along the way. It did not take me very long to realize that this pace bunny was meant to come into my life at precisely this time. Connecting on that hazy Sunday morning while running a marathon was perfect for us. Neither one of us expected to find love that day, but I truly believe that the perfect time to find love is when you least expect it.

Fresh out of my divorce, I had not worried myself at all about finding a new lifelong partner. In fact, I had not been single for very much of my adult life, and I did not want to take any chances of rushing into anything. I truly wanted to take the time and space to heal this time around, and to really focus on just being me.

Being authentically myself was the most liberating part of the whole experience. I finally felt safe to just be myself – I felt like I'd come untethered, *and I liked it.* I decided to fully accept my human self and respond to myself with greater compassion. Armed with unconditional love within, I no longer felt trapped in a cage. I was ready to soar. I finally felt the freedom, peace and unconditional love I had longed for. And, I hadn't needed anyone to come and save me - I saved my damn self. That's when my experience and understanding of relationships shifted.

We were two whole people coming together, with no expectations for another to fix us, complete us or make us whole. The result was magical! There truly is no better feeling or experience than pure unconditional love and acceptance. Even life's incessant challenges seemed so much easier to navigate from this new perspective. All of that running away from my life had come full circle.

I started out Chasing Shadows and ended up Finding Love. In the end, every last step was worth it.

Author Biographies

Brought to you by Next Page Publishing Inc.

Next Page Publishing Inc. is an Alberta-based publisher. We partner with aspiring authors through one-on-one support to create a five-star experience for readers. Our team of coaches, editors, designers and funnel experts work alongside our authors to create a book and book ecosystem that sells.

This passion project, while a step out from our usual focus of solo books, was one that we could not pass on.

Discover more from Next Page Publishing Inc.

Larissa Soehn- CEO of Next Page Publishing Inc.

Larissa Soehn is an international best-selling author with works ranging from self-help to science fiction and children's books. She is the CEO of Next Page Publishing Inc.

As the company's founder, Larissa's mission is to help aspiring authors unleash the power of their books on the world and use them to grow their businesses. As the mom to a beautiful little girl, her goal is to set an example for her daughter that they can both be proud of. As a wife, she hopes to inspire her husband and create a life that is full of love and laughter.

Larissa loves mysteries and is usually the first one in line to a new escape room. She has a deep fondness for unearthing the ever-changing and evolving dynamics of the human mind, which is the greatest mystery of all. In her spare time, she likes to play video games, even if it does mean the odd bought of curse words. If she isn't muttering annoyance toward the T.V., she can often be found hunched over a jigsaw puzzle, which, if you ask her, is one of her greatest skills, as her ability to focus intensely allows her to complete a 1000-piece puzzle in less than 24 hours (if she doesn't eat, sleep, or go to the bathroom). If neither of those suits the mood, Larissa is likely to be found with a book in hand.

Olena Sadovnik
Author of *Regaining Hope*

Olena Sadovnik is a Mother, wife, refugee, runner and life lover. She has never been a sporty person, but motherhood and Covid gave her the impetus for jogging. Prior to the large-scale Russian – Ukrainian war, she blogged about her experiences of getting from her worst shape to the best; empowering other mothers to pursue emotional and physical well-being. According to Olena, the most difficult part for a mom is not running but leaving the house.

Upon Olena's arrival to Canada in July 2022, running became her coping mechanism for processing the trauma of war and navigating challenges of starting life from scratch in a new country. Running remained one of the few parts of her identity not taken by the war. It is something she carried over with her to Canada, as if it were a treasure trove of resilience and stability.

In the beginning of the war, Olena's biggest fear was to be separated from her daughter during air strikes on Kyiv. Olena never slept a minute in those five nights they spent living in a walk-in closet in the first week of the war. Now she supports charities who help to bring forcefully deported Ukrainian children back home from Russia.

Currently, Olena works as an Employment Counselor at an immigration agency in Calgary, AB, helping newcomers like herself to find their footing in Canada. She continues to run, write and raise her daughter in Canada with hopes to one day reunite with family and friends who remain in Ukraine.

Tania Jacobs
Author of *Running Through Grief*

Tania Jacobs is a Registered Psychologist living in Edmonton, Alberta. As a self-identified bookish kid, Tania liked gym class the least growing up. However, she was particularly good at the "endurance test," a long run around the school yard, when being fast mattered less than being able to last. She embraced her athletic side as a teenager after making her school's field hockey team, where her primary contribution was outrunning her defender. She then began to spend more time in the mountains hiking, backpacking and skiing.

Before having kids, Tania discovered trail running and began pushing herself to run longer distances. She was surprised to discover that she wasn't as slow as she thought. At her first trail race (5 Peaks Sunridge), she found herself on the podium for her age group and was hooked. "Runner" shifted to the foreground of her identity.

After being widowed suddenly in 2017, at the age of 37, Tania set her sights on running her first ultramarathon as a way to begin to rebuild for her future. Her ability to endure turned out to be crucial to surviving both widowhood and ultrarunning; each of these life experiences easing the other.

Tania continues to love being outdoors, exploring the scenery of new places while running, helping her clients find their joie de vivre and raising her two incredible children as they cruise rapidly toward adolescence.

Ed Bickley

Author of *Sumer of Miles*

Ed Bickley is a homegrown Albertan and has lived in Calgary for the past 40 years. He has a wife, raised two kids and was an IT executive for several decades. He likes to read, write, travel, work with his hands and, of course, running. Now that he is retired, he is devoting a lot more of his time to writing.

Ed started running regularly in 1989. Since then, he has run 120+ marathons/ultras and 1000+ track, cross-country and road races across North America, Europe and Australia. He enjoys competitive running as he finds it is pretty close to being a real meritocracy. "The clock measures everything; it has minimal politics (usually); it involves a bit less capitalism than most sports; in general, the time and effort you put in is what you get out."

Having completed 50 of his marathons in under three hours and 100 of them under 3:20, he was inducted into the Calgary Marathon Hall of Fame in 2012, and his race number (501) was retired. Currently, he is a member of the Calgary Road-runners club, as well as a local training gang and has coached a long-standing running group of people of all abilities for the past 20 years. He is also a UESCA-certified Distance Running Coach. His future aspirations continue to revolve around running and writing throughout his years of retirement.

Priscilla Forgie
Author of *Finding My Fire*

In 2018, Priscilla Forgie hit the pavement and discovered an immediate connection to the running community. Although, it was when she stepped foot on the trails a year later that she found herself. As someone, somewhere once said: "There's no wifi in the forest but I promise you'll find a better connection."

Priscilla thrives in the mountains and embraces longer distance races. She has various course records and wins across Canada, including the Squamish 50/50 course record and Canadian Death Race and Ultra-Trail Hurricana wins. In 2023, she stepped onto the global stage of ultrarunning, earning 8th place among female competitors in her inaugural 100-mile race at the Western States Endurance Run.

Beyond competitions, Priscilla strives for balance within her running world, deriving joy from group runs, extra days off when needed and loads of baked goods to fuel her runs. She advocates for openness and inclusivity within the running community in recognizing the endless possibilities it offers for everyone.

When not flowing through trails, she indulges in the warmth of coffee shops, cozying up with her pup and immersing in nature. Priscilla's passions extend beyond running as she dedicates her free time to volunteering at FARRM, a local animal rescue. Her commitment to animals and love of nature seamlessly align with her vegan lifestyle of plants fueling her path forward.

Sarah Hughes

Author of *"You can't run, you don't have a bike and you only swim breaststroke."*

Sarah Hughes is a gal from Humboldt, SK, who sounds like she's from the United Kingdom. Running became the start of a crazy adventure in travel, life lessons and personal growth. Sarah has cultivated a lifestyle that has seen her live and work on three continents, travel the world and make a ton of friends along the way. Discovering her passion for running and triathlons later in life saw Sarah running her first half-marathon as her son turned 18 years old. She is a passionate non-profit fundraiser, volunteer, arts fan and winter sports nut. Sarah is the first to say, "That sounds terrible; when do we start?."

Sarah grew up with her family in the United Kingdom. She was involved in many activities that saw her start her on-stage "career" as a snowball at age five. Her last musical performance before moving back to Canada was playing for the late Queen of England with her eight-year-old son. A keen youth leader, Sarah was usually found hanging off a rock face, camping, kayaking, on stage performing or generally causing organised chaos within one of the groups she led.

Moving back to Canada with her pride and joy, eight-year-old son, and four suitcases almost 20 years ago, Sarah has built a life she loves. She has managed multiple different youth sports teams, touring them across the world, directed kids choirs, volunteered for multiple organisations and raised millions for charities. You will find Sarah always smiling while adding her own dash of chaos to everyday life.

Since her first half-marathon, Sarah has raced in temperatures from -34c up to +32c, fulfilled epic dreams, and bought a plethora of running shoes along the way. She counts her running and triathlon world as one of her best 'things' she's achieved, along with her work and raising her son.

Dennis Kreba
Author of *Dennis on the Run*

Dennis is an information technology professional who is passionate about wellness and self-care. In 2020, during the apex of COVID-19, Dennis experienced a traumatic moment in his life and he decided that his life had to change. He quit drinking and has been sober for more than three years.

During his recovery, he became an avid walker, runner, and long-distance athlete. He completed his first marathon in September 2021. Due to an injury in early summer of 2022, Dennis took up road cycling and completed a 135-kilometer race in August 2023. He plans on completing his second marathon in 2024.

He started a blog in January of 2022 called 'Dennis on the Run' to share his journey. Through his blog and his experience sharing his story, Dennis discovered a new passion for writing and will be published in "Run for Your Life" and his own book "Dennis on the Run" in 2024.

Dennis lives by the mantra "next shot." He is an avid golfer and the next shot is the golf equivalent of being present. In golf, you cannot look backwards, all you can do is look at the next shot in front of you. This matches the "one day at a time" mantra shared by recovering alcoholics across the globe.

He believes through self-awareness, mindfulness, meditation and gratefulness combined with professional support and finding your focus that you can build resilience to survive the hard days and learn to love yourself.

In 2023, Dennis opened an Etsy print-on-demand t-shirt shop. He initially saw a niche to create sobriety shirts for recovering alcoholics to show their sobriety loud and proud and has since branched out to other passions such as fitness and dogs.

You can follow Dennis on his blog, Facebook or his Etsy store:

Stephanie Krebs
Author of *Running Last is My Cardio*

Born in Calgary, Alberta, Stephanie Krebs is a wife, mother, and teacher. Her family went to "Live the Life of Ryley" in Ryley, Alberta when she was 14 years old. In 2004, she and her husband made the move to Edmonton. Stephanie has three children; two have become amazing men who are changing the world one day at a time and one daughter who left this life too soon.

According to family, she is a klutz and isn't allowed to go into shops with a lot of glassware, since she has a tendency to knock things over. She is passionate about her family and the large extended Chilean family in Calgary, of whom she visits often. She loves to listen to music loudly and dance with her family in the kitchen. Stephanie adores the color red and her favorite animals are pandas. She cried when she saw a panda in real life in Calgary on her 40th birthday. She is passionate about helping others and always goes the extra mile both on and off the running path. After the loss of their infant daughter, Isabella, the Krebs family and friends make identical blankies, so dubbedIsabella's Blankies. The Kreb family donate them to the local hospital for babies that are going to pass away. Every year on Isabella's Birthday, her family goes off to some new place in Alberta for a hike. They have hiked places such as Troll Falls, Mt. Yamunsca and Ribbon Falls. In her spare time, Stephanie takes mountain adventures, takes many photographs, bakes up a storm in her kitchen, and winds down with sewing. She loves supporting her hubby and sons in their trail running, backpacking, rafting and fishing adventures. Her life is full of wild adventures which are readily told to those who are curious to learn of her exciting escapades. Stephanie loves to try new and unique things and that's how she wound up running the Marathon in the Canadian Deathrace and the MudHero. Her journey continues one step at a time.

Dave Madole
Author of *Gaining Ground*

Alberta born and raised, Dave Madole is proud to call the city of Edmonton home for the past two decades. As a graduate of the University of Alberta, he makes a living teaching English to angsty teenagers. In addition to lessons in literature, his students look forward to hearing Dave's tales about gallivanting around the globe. There are plenty of stories to regale his students with, considering his sixty passport stamps and running cross country. With a flair for being a self-proclaimed klutz, his students enjoy the hilarity that comes with a Mr. Madole marathon saga.

As an aspiring author, Dave started out writing poetry at sixteen years old. At that time, he was just a wannabe nihilist mimicking his favourite rock stars' lyrics. Long gone are the days of his long hair, pierced ears, and jean jackets, which he wore even in winter. Nevertheless, Dave's motivation to write still remains. Over the years, his oeuvre has grown to include a trilogy of dystopian novels, a treatise on growing older than his father and a selection of travel haikus. Quite the diverse collection! With renewed vigour, Dave's passions once again find their stride in "Gaining Ground," an average runner's firsthand account of overcoming challenges and exceeding expectations. Much to Dave's amazement, the boy who once struggled to complete laps in gym class now routinely finishes ultramarathon races. The gift for going the distance is a dream that no one, least of all he, knew he possessed way back when those first few fateful steps humbled him in middle school. Dave continues to gain ground both on the marathon track and in the classroom, shaping young minds to live to their full potential.

Daryl Lang
Author of *It Takes a Village*

Daryl Lang is, of course, a runner; that's why she's part of the Run for Your Life project! When she's not training for races, you will find Daryl at her day job as a legal assistant or taking finance courses through Athabasca University. She lives with her partner and seven animals, including her retired guide dog, Jenny, and her working guide dog, Yasha.

Daryl flatly rejects the narrative that she does things in spite of or to overcome her blindness. Being blind is just a part of her life that she finds inconvenient sometimes. Honestly, Daryl perceives her blindness as the most boring part of her life! She'd rather talk about running, the courses she's taking, her animals, jewelry-making (which she does when she has a few minutes) or her blog at blindbeader.ca

If she had a life motto, it would be: "Do the best you can with what you have in any given moment. Your best today will not necessarily be the same as your best tomorrow. So do the best you can when you can, even if the path to your best is a little circuitous." Daryl continues to live by these words through every run and obstacle she faces on the meandering path of her life.

Austin Sedgwick
Author of *A Seven-Letter Word That Changed My Life*

Austin has been running for charities since 2020. His journey began in 2019, when he was called a chicken who wasn't capable of running fifty kilometers. As a high-endurance athlete in many other sports, he couldn't take that challenge lying down. Despite having run many long-distance events, Austin still doesn't classify himself as a runner. To him, it has never been about running but about giving back in the only way he knows how. He has raised over thirty-thousand dollars through his running journey thus far. Austin was a person who thought running wasn't a sport and was pleasantly surprised to find that he was wrong.

Austin continues to run for charities year after year and has gone from not being a runner at all to a long-distance runner who has a goal of running sixty kilometers backward for the YWCA in 2024. Austin not only runs for charities, but he also wants to leave a lasting message behind in each run he does.

After finding himself in a dark place, a place he wouldn't wish on his worst enemy, a place he almost didn't make it out of and a place that he didn't know was real, Austin speaks openly and often about mental health. Sometimes, he wonders what gives him the right to speak on mental health, when there have been people fighting mental illness their entire life. Nevertheless, he has come to the realization that no problem is too small and that if it can happen to him, it can happen to anybody. We all fight battles nobody knows about.

Austin writes short poetry and a poem written by him has to be one of his favourites titled ***"Echo's from the dark."***

You can look happy when you're sad.
You can laugh with your friends even though they don't know about the darkest days you've just had.
You say you're fine, but you spend all night crying.
You say you'll be okay but you're just waiting for something to happen, to take all that pain away.
People say your darkest hour is just one hour, but in that hour, you want to jump or smell that gunpowder.
People say they are always there but are never there.
You find life a little unfair; you've tried everything, pills, counseling, but nothing works and gets you nowhere.
Feeling empty inside and jealous of the people who have died, you say you're fine, but you know you lied.
And now you think that the only way to be okay

is to take your own life away.
And now they'll finally understand.

Austin's wish is to lend a voice to people who no longer have it and need it the most, and to let people know they are never alone.

What started as a joke became so much more. Helping people through running might just be the very thing that saved Austin's life.

To follow Austin's journey, scan here:

Zoe Antaya
Author of *The COVID Half*

Zoe Antaya is a seventeen-year-old who was born and raised in Calgary, Alberta. She started running during the COVID-19 pandemic, inspired by her parents, whose races she had always attended as a kid. Since then, she has run five half-marathons and placed first in her age group twice. She runs for her school's cross country and track and field teams, and her senior track season is right around the corner. Through every running accomplishment, Zoe brings along her Papa's memory. Having had underlying medical conditions, he died of COVID-19 the weekend before her second half marathon — the race featured in her chapter. Although it was heart wrenching, it showed Zoe that she needs to utilize every moment she has on this earth. She hopes that this message will resonate with her readers as well. Zoe has always had a knack for writing, ever since the first short story she wrote and illustrated when she was five years old. Hence, she is so grateful for this opportunity to write about one of her most prominent passions for the world. She is also an avid academic, and just received early admission into Neuroscience at the University of Calgary. She hopes to continue on the path to medicine, bringing her running passion along for the ride. None of this would be possible without the support of her incredible Mom and Dad — Cathy and Brian Antaya — and her sister Kenzy Antaya.

Morrie Ripley

Author of *It's Fun Doing What They Say Isn't Possible*

Morrie Ripley was born and raised in Edmonton Alberta. While Involved in the home building industry all his life, physical fitness was never a priority. At the age of 25, he experienced a life-changing accident that nearly cost him his life. With a broken neck and a young family in tow, he was forced to learn to walk and talk again. Morrie was told these simple tasks were most likely not going to be possible. Displeased with that diagnosis, Morrie took his own route to recovery. With a little bit of luck, an intense rehab program, and the will to walk and run again, his diagnosis was run right off the road! Morrie has successfully crossed many finish lines, proving that with dedication and perseverance, anything is possible. Spending time with his two boys and four grandkids is a huge part of his life. Morrie continues to prove that life is what you make of it with a little luck and a whole lot of support from family, friends and a running community to keep you on the right track.

Herbert Camat

Author of *No Pain*

Herbert Camat calls Edmonton, Alberta home! Herbert is an avid long distance runner, and is relatively new to the long distance running game. Herbert loves hiking, bouldering and powerlifting when off the marathon tracks. He is also in nursing school with an ambition to become a registered nurse. He also has ambitions to move into ultra-marathon territory eventually. Herbert is a foodie and a lover of a good pun. If you're curious to try Herbert's favourite dessert, jog on over to ***Made by Marcus*** for their Sea Salt Goat Milk Caramel Ice Cream. When Herbert is not running or studying for an exam, he loves spending quality time with his friends and family and reading. Herbert's motto is: "Tough times never last, but tough people do."

Christy Holt

Author of *Chasing Shadows, Finding Love*

Christy Holt, affectionately known as the 'Happiness Hussy,' is not just a supporter of personal growth and emotional intelligence; she's a living testament to the power of transformation. Christy brings a wealth of experience and a heart full of empathy as a podcast host, international best-selling author, speaker, and mentor. Her podcast, "Create Your Happy," goes beyond surface-level advice. She readily dives into the art of consciously creating healthy and happy relationships, starting with the self.

In "Unstuck For Women," her acclaimed book, Christy introduces The Spiral Stopper Method. This practical toolkit is designed to help readers overcome overthinking and emotional overwhelm. As a result, they become empowered to consciously create the life, relationships and impact that they desire. The book is celebrated for providing a clear pathway to break free from limiting cycles and embrace exponential growth.

Christy's journey as an adventure guide is deeply personal. Driven by her own life experiences, she uses her signature CRE-

ATE methodology to help others navigate their inner worlds, transforming life's hurdles into stepping stones for growth and success. Her mission is to impart the lessons and wisdom she's gained while leading the way for others to achieve freedom and peace with greater ease and speed.

Emphasizing emotional intelligence and self awareness, Christy's work is a call to unapologetically embrace authenticity and vulnerability. She believes that unconditional love and acceptance are the necessary foundation for building meaningful connections and creating lasting change.

In a world that often feels chaotic, Christy Holt stands as a beacon of peace, hope and clarity. Her approach to life isn't merely about overcoming personal challenges; it's about learning how to truly thrive in the #messyfuckingbeautiful adventure that is life. Visit www.coachchristyholt.com for additional resources and programs designed to help you navigate life's complexities with grace and confidence so that you can consciously create the healthy and happy relationships that you desire and deserve.

Companion Journals

Feeling inspired by the stories of our brave authors?
Grab your companion journal and join the fun.
Available on Amazon.

Manufactured by Amazon.ca
Bolton, ON

Made in the USA
San Bernardino, CA
29 September 2013

ABOUT L.C. CHASE

Cover artist by day, author by night, L.C. Chase is a hopeless romantic and adventure seeker. After a decade of traveling three continents, she now calls the Canadian West Coast home. When not writing sensual tales of beautiful men falling love, she can be found designing book covers with said beautiful men, drawing, horseback riding, or hiking the trails with her goofy four-legged roommate.

L.C. is a 2013 EPIC ebook awards finalist for *Long Tall Drink*, 2013 Ariana cover design awards finalist, and 2012 Rainbow awards, honorable mention for *Riding with Heaven*.

You can visit L.C. at www.lcchase.com.

ALSO BY L.C. CHASE

Pickup Men

Love Brokers: Mister Romance

Riding with Heaven

Three to Tango, *with Chloe Cole*

THE COMPLE

LONG TALL DRINK

L.C. CHASE

To Diane,
Thank you so much!
Happy reading and keep
spreading the love!
LC Chase
:)

Long Tall Drink

Cover Design by L.C. Chase
Photography by Rob Lang
Interior layout by L.C. Chase

ISBN: 978-1492177777
Printed in the United States of America

Also available in ebook:
ISBN: 978-1-61118-499-0
Edited by Jana J. Hanson

THE COMPLETE AND UNCUT EDITION

LONG TALL DRINK

L.C. CHASE

For my mom,
who taught me I could do anything I set my mind to.

CHAPTER 1

Hands braced at ten and two on the steering wheel, Ray Ford locked his elbows and pressed his shoulders firmly into the solid backrest. Forty minutes in the cab of his pickup hadn't helped the kink in his spine. A kink that had less to do with last night's lumpy motel bed than his and Landon's horizontal acrobatics.

With a satisfying *pop* he relaxed into the heated leather seat and dropped his right hand from the wheel onto the center console. His fingers tapped along with Toby Keith, who was singing on the radio about bullets and guns and Mexican hotels. A slow smile stretched his lips. Today was a good day to be alive.

Landon had been as wild as a Pryor Mountain mustang—nearly a year and a half later and still endlessly creative. It often surprised Ray when he thought about how that one-time Internet hookup had turned into the mutually beneficial relationship they had now. The hour-plus drive for a night in Billings with his secret lover had always been exactly what he'd needed to take the edge off.

But Ray wasn't sure how much longer he could keep up with the younger man, even if it was only every other month. After forty years on this earth, he was beginning to feel every hard-lived day. There was more to it than age. Landon was tiring of the secrecy and had begun to drop subtle hints about wanting a relationship he didn't have to hide. If Ray were honest with himself, he was tiring too. And that scared the shit out of him. Landon was a good man and deserved much more than Ray could, or would, give him.

For now though, he was content as things stood, and those few stolen hours that allowed him to be himself. But if Landon pushed—

A moving flash of gold light ahead, like a distress signal, pulled him from his thoughts. Focusing on the source of the signal, Ray

made out the shape of a lone cowboy camouflaged in faded jeans and a tan jacket, walking along the cracked edge of rough road, a beat-up dust-colored duffel bag was heaped over his shoulder. If the sun hadn't reflected off a buckle, Ray probably wouldn't have noticed the man until he was on him.

Closing in on the wanderer, Ray realized the smooth, effortless gait couldn't really be called a walk, more like a swagger.

The cowboy turned around and hooked his thumb to the sky. Long legs planted shoulder-width apart staked his ground. The collar of the well-worn ranch jacket was flipped up, shielding against the chill spring breeze that danced across the plains from the East.

Even though dark sunglasses and a cowboy hat that sat low on the brow worked together to hide most of his face, it was his presence alone that seemed to command attention.

Ray wasn't one for picking up hitchhikers—not that there were many, if any, on this deserted stretch of US-310, especially in the early hours of a Sunday morning—but something about the man on the side of the road compelled him.

Before he'd thought it through, his foot had moved from the gas pedal to the brake. As if on its own accord, the truck pulled off the two-lane highway, steel-belted tires growling over rumble strips, and came to a stop fifty yards beyond where the cowboy stood. Dust billowed into a small tornado in the wake of the vehicle's draft, obscuring the man from view. Ray watched in his rearview mirror as the cowboy stepped out of the swirling cloud like a rising phoenix—or the hero in an action movie emerging in slow motion unscathed from a fireball.

"Well, would you look at that," Ray mumbled. "There's a long, tall drink of sexy if I ever did see one."

Lean legs ate up the pavement with an unhurried stride only a truly confident man could master. Now that the cowboy was facing the bright morning sun, the concealing Stetson and sunglasses couldn't hide the slightly crooked nose, strong square jaw, cleft chin, and lips worthy of exploration.

An odd niggle of anticipation teased the edges of Ray's consciousness.

He turned off the radio and pressed a button on his armrest to lower the passenger-side window as the cowboy reached the truck. The hitcher removed his sunglasses and leaned in. Intelligent, deep green eyes flecked with bronze, a hint of mischief sparking in their shadows, gazed back at Ray.

"Where you headed, cowboy?"

"Bridger." Just one word and the deep, resonant voice sent an unexpected spike of heat through Ray's nervous system.

The words escaped before his brain caught up. "You're in luck. Hop in."

The cowboy flashed a magazine-cover smile that revealed impossibly white teeth and inclined his head. "Thanks."

He opened the door, tossed his duffel on the backseat, and climbed gracefully into the cab. A rush of cold air followed him in and swirled around Ray's legs.

The quad cab of the fire-engine red Dodge Ram 3500 shrank to the size of a Mini Cooper as the man settled into the leather bucket seat beside him. Ray watched as his passenger hit the button to close the window and buckled himself in. He was tall, solid, and exuded a kinetic energy that could knock a bottle off the fence at a hundred paces.

The cowboy turned to face him, and time stretched out in weighted silence. A glint in the man's eye held Ray captive, as though he were on the verge of sharing a great secret—a secret Ray suddenly wanted to know. *Needed* to know.

A crooked grin spread across the ruggedly handsome face. "Name's Travis."

The skin at the back of Ray's neck warmed. He nodded. "Ray."

Time continued to saunter on without them as they sat facing each other, immobile, truck idling smoothly. Travis broke the time glitch by tapping his forefinger to the brim of his hat, his intense gaze not leaving Ray's. In that deep, whiskey voice, he drawled, "S'a pleasure, Ray."

The air in the cab buzzed. Perspiration broke out between Ray's shoulder blades. He pushed his hat back on his forehead a little. He

briefly contemplated switching the truck's heater off in favor of the air-conditioning.

Ray had experienced the occasional instant attraction in the past, but nothing at this level. Not this . . . biting. Not to the point where if he squinted his eyes, he'd see electricity arcing between them.

His groin tightened. *What the hell*? Had he not just left Landon's bed less than two hours ago? At the moment, however, it felt as though he hadn't seen to the need in years. The sudden urge to lean over and run his hands over Travis's solid legs, peel off his jacket and shirt, and feel smooth skin under his hands was overwhelming. And more than a little disconcerting.

Ray cleared his throat. "Okay then."

He forced himself to face forward, shifted the big truck into gear, and pulled back onto the deserted highway. Both hands tight on the wheel, he was acutely aware of the man sitting on the other side of the cab. He stole a sideways glance at the strong, rugged profile. Dirty-blond hair long enough to fist spilled over the jacket collar. A lean-fingered hand splayed loosely on a muscular thigh. What would that hand feel like on his own thigh, strong and sure, inching slowly upward . . . ?

Ray looked away, cleared his throat again, and shifted in his seat. He had Landon when he needed him. Landon was safe. Landon took care of him. What he didn't need was some crazy attraction to a drifter that could only come to trouble. The kind of trouble Ray had managed to avoid his whole life.

The quicker he got rid of his passenger, the better. "What's in Bridger?"

"Ranch job," Travis said. "Hopefully."

"Hopefully?"

"Heard there might be work."

Ray chanced another look at his passenger, staring longer than someone behind the wheel of a three-ton machine should. "There are only two working ranches near Bridger." *And please, God, say you're headed to the Double T.*

Travis shrugged a shoulder in response, gaze focused on the passing Montana landscape. The man seemed completely at ease,

unconcerned with the possibility of having to turn right back around to wherever he came from.

Ray forced his attention back to the long, straight road ahead of him—a feeble attempt at ignoring the increasing discomfort of his jeans. Wide-open empty highway, sparsely treed plains, and endless blue sky left entirely too few distractions from his entirely too sexy passenger. "Any ranch in particular?"

"Ford Creek."

Ray nearly choked. His heart kicked up a triple beat. He looked over at his passenger again. "Ford Creek Ranch?" He winced at hearing his voice crack on the last word.

"Yep." Travis angled himself to face Ray, one eyebrow cocked, that mischievous glint in his eyes. "Know the place?"

"You could say," he said quietly and turned away from the heavy gaze that burned his skin. *Rein it in, Ford.* "What are you hoping to do there?"

"The best quarter horses in the country deserve the best trainer."

Silence filled the cab again as Ray struggled for an air of indifference. "You're a horse trainer?"

"The best."

"Not lacking for confidence, are you?"

Ray caught another nonchalant shoulder shrug from Travis in his peripheral. "What's your last name, Travis?"

"Morgan."

Ray released a breath he hadn't realized he'd been holding. This far too attractive hitchhiker was Travis Morgan. Headed to Ford Creek Ranch. What were the odds?

"*The* Travis Morgan?" He risked a glance at Travis and was once again trapped in that impossibly magnetic gaze. Travis nodded, a checked smile playing on his lips. Lush, kissable lips...

"Well, shit." Ray turned back to the road ahead of him, hands tightening on the wheel.

Travis Morgan's reputation traveled far ahead of the man himself. A world-class trainer, Morgan was one of those people with a rare ability to draw the best out of even the most dangerous, untamable animal. Any ranch fortunate enough to have him cross their gates

was left with champions in his wake. And having that trademark signature on your stock was akin to winning the lottery. Morgan chose the ranches he wanted to work on seemingly whimlike. He couldn't be contacted or contracted. The man was elusive, an enigma, an apparition emerging from a swirling cloud of dust.

Ray distractedly lifted the top panel of the center console and reached in for a pouch of cinnamon sticks. He'd quit smoking years ago, but in chewing on cinnamon sticks to help break that habit, he'd gained another. At least the new one was healthier.

The Morgan name would catapult the price of Ford Creek's already top-dollar working and performance horses substantially, further cementing his family's legendary reputation.

Having the man on his ranch, working beside him day-in day-out, however, would be dangerous. He'd overheard the whispered rumors about Morgan having a penchant for the company of men. With the crazed reaction Ray was having to him already, "danger" wouldn't even begin to describe the situation it could put them both in. The damage it would cause if he lost control of this sudden desire, the risk to his family's reputation and livelihood—his own life—would be too great.

He'd never forget what had happened to Dwayne Harrelson all those years ago, and there was no way in hell he was going to suffer the same fate.

And despite all that he was going to anyway. It just wasn't good business sense to pass on having the Travis Morgan name tagged onto Ford Creek's horses.

He'd just have to make a few extra trips into Billings.

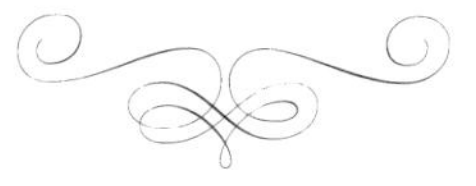

"Was that a good 'shit,' or a bad 'shit'?" Travis asked, studying Ray as his thoughts played across a strong, angular face. He hadn't missed the telltale flare in those dark, amber-flecked eyes, nor the hard-set jaw. A master of body language—in both horse and man—Travis could read every subtle nuance, shift, and sound, giving him the unique ability to anticipate and counter actions.

The man at the wheel would probably be shocked to know just how eloquent his unspoken language was.

Ray cleared his throat and shot Travis a quick, almost nervous glance. "No rancher in his right mind would turn down the opportunity."

Travis nodded.

He'd noted the wary shift in other man's expressive eyes. It was clear Ray had heard of more than Travis's reputation with horses. The man had appeared interested but was obviously not about to act on it now. Not after hearing Travis's full name. Even though Travis felt a thread of annoyance at that, he wasn't surprised. No one was willing to play a role in the rumors that rode alongside him. No one dared take the risk.

Good for the ranch, bad for the rancher.

Just as well. With that last debacle in North Dakota, he wasn't willing to risk letting the truth behind the rumors see the light of day. It had been three weeks, and the bruises had faded, but his ribs were still sore.

But damn if Ray didn't make him think things, want things, he couldn't have.

With a drawn-out sigh, he turned his attention from the driver with the soulful brown eyes and sexy five o'clock shadow to the untamed Montana landscape.

Wild arnica and Indian paintbrush colored waving pale green brome and sage grass with bright splashes of yellow and red. Sparse clusters of ponderosa pine followed snaking, unseen tributaries. The Pryor Mountains reached for the heavens on the eastern horizon, and the carpet of desert grasslands raced up its base.

The state's famous big sky stretched far and wide above them, stirring a brief, unwanted memory of the massive Texas spread he'd grown up on. That sky had been as big as everything else Texan, but somehow the skies currently overhead seemed more immense, intimidating.

A reminder of how insignificant he was in the grand scheme.

Twenty minutes of silence passed before Ray slowed the big truck and turned onto a graded dirt road. From this vantage point, all Travis could see was wide-open land.

They bounced over a cattle guard and passed under a log archway with FORD CREEK RANCH burned into its smooth bark.

"I hadn't expected a doorstop lift," Travis said. "Much appreciated."

Ray shrugged without looking at Travis. "Like I said, you're in luck."

Travis hadn't expected to come across a man he wanted to run into again either.

An odd twist akin to disappointment pinched in Travis's gut when a large homestead came into view over a small rise. It went against his better judgment, but he'd hoped the drive to the ranch would have been longer. Something about the driver had him wanting more, even though he couldn't risk taking the chance. No matter the signs he'd read. His reputation wouldn't survive much longer, and with his reputation, so went his only source of income.

He'd thank Ray for the ride, wish him well, and never see him again. Judging by Ray's reaction, it would be best for the both of them.

Ray pulled up in front of the rambling log home with a burnt red roof and wraparound veranda like he owned the place. Not as splashy as some, but it didn't need to be. The house felt comfortable; even looking through the bug-splattered windshield, he knew it was the kind of place he'd be happy to call home. Travis frowned. *Home* hadn't entered his mind in eighteen years.

It had to be the comforting scents of leather and cinnamon that permeated the interior of the big cab.

Ray put the truck in Park, turned off the engine, and exited the cab without so much as a glance back. Travis reached into the backseat and grabbed his bag. Unfolding from the truck, he walked around to meet Ray in front of the near shoulder-high hood.

"Thanks for the lift, Ray," Travis said as he hefted the duffel over his shoulder. "Don't suppose you know the owner?"

Ray cast a long gaze over him, unmistakable desire flashing in those telling eyes. Then he shuttered his expression with a near audible thud and opened his mouth to speak.

"There you are, Raymond." A strong female voice cut the man off. Travis turned to find an older woman with silver hair pulled back in a loose ponytail and piercing pale blue eyes. She wore faded jeans,

a tan western shirt, and an unlaced pair of beat-up barn boots. She stood on the veranda, hands on her hips, scowling at Ray as though he were a disobedient child. "I hope you've sown your oats. We have a ranch to run here, young man."

Ray sighed. "It's Sunday, Dot."

Travis slanted a glance at Ray, intrigued by the somewhat chastised tone of the man's response.

"Stock doesn't take a day off eating just because you take a day off working."

Dot stepped down the three steps off the porch and shifted her sharp gaze to Travis. She was a good half foot shorter than he yet seemed to tower over him. He shifted his feet apart, attempting to balance himself under the weight of her stare. He felt exposed somehow and certain very little escaped the woman's notice. Travis knew right then, without a doubt, she was one woman he'd be wise never to cross.

Ray's response to her wasn't quite so intriguing anymore.

"And who might you be, son?"

He removed his hat, held it against his chest, and stepped forward as he extended his hand. "Travis, ma'am. Travis Morgan."

She eyed him as if deciding whether or not to believe he was who he said he was, and took his hand. Her grip was strong and sure as they shook. Then her eyes softened, and a smile lit them from behind, putting him immediately at ease. This one would no doubt keep him on his toes. He liked her already.

"What brings you to Ford Creek, Travis Morgan? Besides Raymond here?"

"Looking for work, ma'am. I train cattle horses."

"Dot. Call me Dot, please."

He smiled warmly. "Dot. It's a pleasure to meet you."

She regarded him for a moment. "Travis Morgan, you say?"

"Yes'm."

"Yes, I've heard of you. Well, you're certainly welcome here."

"Thank you, ma—Dot. Don't suppose you could introduce me to the owner?"

Dot looked from Travis to Ray, laughter dancing in her sharp eyes, and chuckled. She shook her head and turned back for the house.

"You're standing next to him, son," Dot said over her shoulder as she opened the door and disappeared inside.

Travis turned to face Ray, the man's expression locked down and unreadable. *Well, shit* was right. If he had any sense at all, he'd turn around and hightail it out of there right now.

Ray struck out his hand. "Ray Ford. Owner of Ford Creek Ranch."

Travis reached for Ray's hand, ignoring the need to run. The rancher's grip was firm, confident, and the warmth of his skin tingled in Travis's palm. They stood facing each other, gazes locked, hands clasped but no longer shaking. Ray let go after an extended beat. Travis felt the instant absence of the simple touch.

Ray cleared his throat, but his voice sounded rough when he spoke. "Just so happens I have a herd of green horses fresh off winter pasture in need of training."

"Just so happens I train horses." And shit if his voice didn't sound the same.

"So it would seem."

"You'll be needing what I'm offering then."

Ray paused, and the muscles in his clenched jaw twitched. "As I said. You're—"

"I know," Travis cut in with a half smile, "I'm in luck."

Ray didn't move, his eyes and body language once again giving his thoughts away. For a second—a drawn-out, charged second—Travis thought Ray would take a step forward, reach out, touch. Travis almost made the move to do so himself, but Ray took a step back, shutters dropping firmly into place.

Ray cleared his throat and gave Travis a cool smile, but he wasn't fooled. The man was just as affected as he was.

"I'll introduce you to my foreman. He'll get you sorted out."

Travis tipped his head, tapping the brim of his hat with a forefinger. "Boss."

Ray regarded him a moment longer, then nodded and turned toward the barns. Travis grinned as he hiked his duffel bag higher on his shoulder and followed Ray, enjoying the view of that tight ass wrapped in snug jeans.

CHAPTER 2

"I have about a dozen men on the ranch at any given time," Ray began as he led Travis across the yard. "Being that it's Sunday, most of the hands are off-site. They'll start rolling back in toward dinner time."

Travis was only half listening. The words didn't matter as much as the smooth, musical intonation that carried them. The low, thudding scuffle of their boot heels striking hard-packed dirt laid down a steady bass track.

He couldn't deny how attracted he was to Ray and found himself regretting that they hadn't met at a different time under different circumstance. But for all intents and purposes, this man was his boss for the next few months. Fucking around with nameless strangers picked up in nameless bars was one thing, but with a man like Ray Ford? Travis shook his head and ran his gaze over the length of Ray's frame. Nope. Getting too close would only put both of their hard-earned and well-established reputations in jeopardy.

Attempting to deflect his visual imaginings of the man walking a step ahead of him, Travis turned his attention to the surroundings.

A small, inviting lake stretched out behind the ranch house. On its banks, a copse of tall pines huddled against the ever-present Montana winds that rustled harmoniously through their limbs—nature's singsong. A long rope with two knotted handholds at the end hung from the thick branch of a tree that extended out over the water. An image played out in his mind of a young Ray, gangly and uncoordinated, laughing as he swung back and forth on the rope, gaining enough momentum to launch himself far into the lake.

It wasn't too much of a stretch to imagine that the somewhat serious-looking adult Ray could have been a playful and carefree boy.

And like a bee drawn to honey, Travis found his gaze pulled back to the handsome rancher.

Beneath the band of Ray's black cowboy hat, dark brown hair trimmed just above the collar rested neatly against his neck. He was of average height, a couple of inches shorter than Travis's six feet. His build was stocky with broad shoulders and thick legs, complementing Travis's longer, leaner frame. An image of that strong body shot through his mind, one not quite as innocent as kids playing on rope swings during the dog days of summer.

Mind on the surroundings, Travis. Mind on the surroundings.

The surroundings weren't overmuch different from most working ranches: main barn flanked by two outbuildings, one of which revealed farm equipment and vehicles through an open bay door. Beat-up trucks covered with so much dust and dirt their original colors were indistinguishable, parked alongside the barn. Two gooseneck horse trailers sat on wood blocks beyond the trucks.

On the far side of the barn were two large corrals—one of which held a small herd of horses, a single horse in the other—a couple of round pens and cattle runs, and beyond that, open range as far as the eye could see.

Ray led Travis into the barn, down a double row of large box stalls separated by a tidy concrete hall. The stalls were empty, but the indigenous odors of an active stable—cedar shavings, timothy, leather and liniment, that unique salty-sweet scent of horse—were a soothing balm to his soul. There wasn't anything else he'd rather do, could imagine doing, than working with horses. They were the only living creatures that truly accepted him as he was.

They turned into a small office at the end of the hallway. An older man with thick salt-and-pepper hair sat behind a cluttered desk toward the back of the room. His attention was focused on a sheaf of paper as he gnawed on the end of a pen, shoulders scrunched tight. The man looked up with a frustrated sigh as they entered; his brows furrowed, and a slight frown was on his mouth—what could be seen of his mouth anyway. The fellow had the thickest handlebar mustache Travis had ever seen.

"Morning, Holl."

"Mornin', Ray." His voice was thick and graveled. He nodded toward Travis. "Who you got here?"

"Travis Morgan. My foreman, Hollis Ames."

Travis stepped forward as Hollis rose and stepped around the desk to take Travis's hand in a quick shake. "Mr. Ames."

Hollis chuckled. "We don't stand on formality around here, son. Hollis'll do."

"Hollis then."

"Travis will be training the horses for the Remuda midsummer."

Travis shot Ray a surprised glance. Having the horses he'd trained going to the Remuda competition and sales would be a major coup on his résumé. And more reason to stay clear of the rancher and focus on the job at hand.

Hollis cupped his chin with a sun-baked, leather-skinned hand and rubbed at the thick stubble on his cheeks with his thumb. His gaze shifted over Travis's shoulder, going distant for a second before returning. "Travis Morgan, eh. Yeah, I've heard of you."

He dropped his hand, reached for a well-worn cowboy hat, and plopped it on his head. "All righty then, let's get you settled."

Ray nodded to the two men, then turned and disappeared from the office.

"This way, son," Hollis said as he led Travis in the opposite direction. Travis resisted the urge to look over his shoulder and catch a glimpse of Ray's retreating backside.

"We'll stop at your quarters first." Hollis gestured to a horseshoe-shaped cluster of small log cabins behind the barn, hidden from the main house. A large fire pit sat in the middle of the semicircle, flanked by three halved logs for benches. The faint smell of campfire smoke permeated the air.

The soft lowing of nearby cattle and the snorts of restless horses in the corral sang in chorus with the quiet buzz of insects.

"Five hands live on-site. The rest have families to go home to. Cabin on the end there is empty. You can call that one home while you're here." Hollis stepped up onto the small porch and opened the door to a simple room with basic but comfortable-looking furniture: narrow bed, small desk with a chair tucked under its ledge, dresser, and

wood-burning stove—and his own private bathroom. It may as well have been the Waldorf compared to some of his past accommodations. But then, he wasn't a picky man when it came to taking a load off his feet. He tossed his duffel bag on the bed and followed Hollis back outside.

The tour and running commentary finally ended at the corrals. Both men rested their arms on the top rail and hooked a boot on the bottom rung.

"Just brought this herd down from winter pasture last week. Some are a bit wild, but most had some ground work last season. Mostly three- and four-year-old mares and geldings, but we got one stallion. That boy back there"—Hollis motioned to the horse with a corral to himself—"that's Diablo."

The stallion stood head high, ears pricked forward, chest out. Dark, intelligent eyes sharp and observant. His coat was a rich blue-black, the only marking a crescent moon-shaped white snip on his muzzle.

Travis's curiosity was instantly piqued. That horse was going to challenge him, and damn if he didn't thrive on a good challenge.

"Tough son of a bitch," Hollis continued. "Be sure and watch your back around that one. But you won't be getting near him anyways. Beast is too wild for anyone but Ray to handle, and he's done past lettin' anyone else try."

"Good thing I'm not just anyone," Travis said. "If the horse needs training, I'd like to take a crack at him."

Hollis stepped back from the rails with a chuckle and clapped Travis on the back. "Good luck with that, son."

"What?" Aggressive horses were his specialty. Why he wouldn't be allowed to work with one that obviously needed the most attention didn't make sense.

"Breakfast and dinner are up at the main house there. Six a.m., six p.m." Hollis continued. The Diablo subject clearly closed. "Try not to be late if you want a full plate. Boys around here got a hearty appetite and burn through Dot's cookin' like a pack of rabid dogs. Lunch is a serve yourself deal whenever you get hungry. Dot leaves a stack of sandwiches in the kitchen.

"Sundays are quiet. Rest of the day is yours. Wander around. Get yourself settled. Plenty to be done come mornin'." The older man tapped his brim and ambled back to his office in the barn.

Travis turned back to the corral with the big black stallion. The proud horse met his gaze and held it in silent challenge. Travis smiled. "You and me, boy. You and me."

Travis made a point of being on time to the main house for dinner, and the moment he opened the door, that sense of home hit him again. Warm air soothed over skin cooled from a biting evening breeze. Fresh-baked rolls and the mouthwatering scent of roasted beef and garlic assaulted his senses. His stomach growled, reminding him that he hadn't eaten since he'd stopped at a roadside café at five that morning.

He stepped into a large foyer with cowboy boots stacked along the wall, jackets and hats hanging haphazardly on pegs above. Adding his gear to the collection, he exited the foyer. To the left was an inviting living room with a dark brown leather couch and two matching oversize chairs, distressed oak accent furniture, a rocker in the corner, and a large stone fireplace. Off the far side of the room, a hallway and stairwell led deeper into the house. To the right of the foyer was the dining room. Western-themed black-and-white photographs hung on the wall; a grandfather clock stood guard next to a door he figured led to the kitchen. Taking up the majority of the room sat a massive rectangular wood table.

Travis nodded at Hollis and the few men already seated. "Evening."

He'd met the men who lived on-site as they'd trickled back to the ranch over the course of the afternoon, as well as a few who lived off-site. With the exception of one disapproving glare, they'd been friendly and welcoming.

"Pull up a chair and dig in while the diggin's good," Hollis said.

Travis took the chair next to Ross Dennison, who'd taken it upon himself to ensure Travis knew the who's who and what's what. He was a jovial sort in his late thirties with Elvis Presley sideburns and had

been a fixture on Ford Creek going on twenty years. Aside from Ray, Hollis, and Dot, no one knew the comings and goings of the ranch better. When Hollis wasn't around, which was rare Travis was told, Ross was the man in charge.

"I could hear your stomach growling before you opened the door," Ross said as he handed Travis a platter loaded with thick slices of steaming hot roast beef. "Load up, man. I ain't carrying your ass out of the mud when you keel over from starvation."

Travis couldn't help grinning. He thanked the man and took the proffered platter. Only a few hours, and it already felt like he and Ross had been friends for years.

Jesse Davis, an eager kid he'd met earlier, pulled up the chair on Travis's other side and plopped down. "Evening, Travis. Mind if I sit here?"

"Not at all."

"I mind." The voice was sharp and hard, drawing the table's attention. Sam Davis. The one cowboy who'd glared at Travis during introductions. "Switch seats with Clay."

"Dad—" Jesse began.

"Move." Sam's order brooked no room for argument. Travis noted the flush of pink rise up the kid's neck as he got up and traded seats with Clay Fisher, a young man about Jesse's age. Embarrassment poured off the poor kid in waves.

"What's your problem, Sam?" Ross asked.

"Don't want my boy sitting near the likes of him." Sam jutted his chin across the table in Travis's direction and leveled him a hard, meant-to-intimidate look with his steel gray eyes.

"Jesus Christ, Sam," Ross started, his cutlery clanked loudly as it dropped to his plate. "What the hell kind of thing is that to say to a man you just met?"

"It's all right, Ross," Travis said, meeting Sam's gaze head-on. "I'll handle it."

He nodded his head slightly, giving Sam the floor to start the same old song and dance.

"Heard some rumors about you."

Here we go. Travis sighed inwardly and regarded the man with controlled outward calm. The men about the table held their collective breaths at the clear challenge in Sam's words. There was one like him on just about every ranch. But Travis had hoped he wouldn't have to deal with one so soon after North Dakota. And he was getting so tired of having to deal with it at all.

He could usually put the rumors to rest early on and avoid being hassled, but every now and then he came across someone who wouldn't let up, which usually had him departing earlier than intended.

Fucking rumors. One of these days he was going to say "fuck it all" and come kicking out of the chute like an angry Brahma bull. But not today.

"Have you now?" Travis held his voice level and gaze steady.

"Heard you're one of them queer boys."

The steady *tick-tock* of the grandfather clock was the only sound in the large room. Meals forgotten, all hands' eyes were riveted to the potential showdown at the end of the table.

"S'pose you heard that I trained grizzly bears in Alaska too."

Confusion clouded Sam's eyes as the comment obviously made no sense to the man. "What the hell does that have to do with anything?"

"Exactly," Ross muttered.

"Not a damn thing. But then, I've never been to Alaska, so obviously that isn't true. Although I have encountered a few bears." Travis paused. "But unless I'm mistaken, we've never met before today. Have we?"

Sam shook his head, barely.

"Didn't think so," Travis continued. "That being the case, I don't see how you'd have any idea one way or the other what is or isn't the truth."

Sam remained silent, but his gaze never wavered from Travis's. The man's clenched jaw ticked, his cheeks flushed the ruddy color of his scruffy beard, and storms broke out in his cold eyes. His voice was flat and challenging as he practically spat the words out. "Ranchin's a *man's* business."

Travis let that comment settle in the space between them for a moment. Then made a point of flashing a half smile he knew wouldn't come close to reaching his eyes. "Last I checked I'm all man."

A snicker from Clay's direction encroached on the edges of Travis's hearing. Tension vibrated thickly in the air. Neither man broke their hard stares. Any second the antique clock would chime high noon, and the standoff would be settled by the quickest draw.

Hollis put an end to the silent showdown with a dramatic clearing of his throat. "What matters is the man's reputation training horses. And that's solid. Rumors don't mean shit."

Ray chose that moment to enter the dining room with Dot at his side. All eyes dropped to the table, throats cleared. The men finished loading their plates and began digging into their meals. Travis held his gaze steady on Sam, his body rigid, until the other man broke and dropped his eyes.

"Don't worry about Sam," Ross leaned in to whisper. "He's always been a prick. Can't help himself. Doctors couldn't remove the stick stuck up his ass."

Travis nodded, appreciating Ross's attempt at lightening the mood. He drew in a long, slow breath and shifted his gaze to Ray as he exhaled. He couldn't stop from admiring the strong set of the rancher's muscular shoulders, the easy stride, smooth vibe, and warm expressive eyes. Those eyes were going to be his undoing if he didn't watch himself.

At least he wouldn't have to spend overmuch time in the other man's company. With twenty head to train, his days would be fully occupied, and they'd never be alone at mealtimes. The chances of him having an opportunity to lose control would be highly unlikely.

Ray held out Dot's chair for her and took his seat once she was settled. His gaze met Travis's and held for a second or two longer than wisdom dictated. Travis turned away first—and caught Dot watching him with an observant glint in her eye.

Too damn sharp.

He quickly looked to his plate and began loading his fork as heat fanned up his neck. Suddenly the sounds of forks and knives clanking on plates grated on his eardrums.

"I trust y'all met Travis Morgan," Ray addressed his men. "I'm sure you're all aware of his reputation and what it will mean for this ranch. He'll be working with me training the herd for the Remuda."

Travis barely managed not to choke on the bite of food that was currently halfway down his throat. He quickly reached for his glass of water and took a long, deep pull. *Dammit.*

This job just got much harder.

CHAPTER 3

"Well?" Dot's voice broke into Ray's reverie as he stood on the back porch, sipping his coffee in the chill Montana spring morning. He loved this time of year. Still cold enough in the early hours for his breath to billow in puffy white clouds, and warm enough by midday to consider a dip in the lake. Almost.

A sliver of pale light had just peeked over the eastern horizon as the sun began its relentless blazing path across the heavens. A vibrant canvas reflected on the undisturbed glass surface of the small lake: warm yellow bled into peach, then lavender, and finally crisp, endless blue.

"Good morning, Dot," he said without turning.

Plumbeous Vireo trilled a broken burry of cheery phrases as they greeted the new day. Sharp, invigorating scents of pine and sweet clover coaxed Ray's senses to life.

"Are you going to tell me about your date the other night, or do I have to beat it out of you?"

Ray closed his eyes and silently counted to five. Sandra. The latest unwitting candidate in Dot's quest to see him married. Ever the happy little matchmaker, she was always trying to find the perfect woman for him to settle down with. He'd worked the date with Sandra to his advantage—as he did with the majority of Dot's setups—dropping her off right after dinner and then spending the rest of the night with Landon Graves.

He hated the denying, hiding, and lying, to Dot especially. He just didn't have the heart, or courage, to tell her the perfect *woman* would never come along. And risking the truth would be far too damaging. Not just for him, but for the ranch's reputation, his family's

hard-earned name, and everyone who depended on Ford Creek for their livelihoods.

If it ever came out that he was gay, he'd be run out of town like Dwayne Harrelson—if he were lucky enough to still be breathing.

He'd only been seventeen when it happened, but it had set the course for the rest of his life. When it was discovered Dwayne's roommate was much more than that, local suppliers refused to sell him grain and provisions, others refused to buy his beef or bid on his horses at auction, and hands walked off the job and left him short staffed. His fencing was sabotaged, property vandalized. And when Dwayne still wouldn't be intimidated, wouldn't back down, it escalated. His barns and home were torched, and he and his partner were beaten to within an inch of their lives.

No one had stepped forward to help the men. No one was ever charged for the crimes against them. Dwayne had lost everything he'd spent his life working for.

Ray knew his own dad had been part of the posse that ran him out, as well as Chester Davis, Sam's dad—they'd both smelled of smoke that fateful night. Those men, because of their ignorance and discrimination, had destroyed a man's livelihood, forced him from his own home, and almost taken his life. Ray would not see that happen to himself or to his ranch.

No, that itch was too far dangerous to scratch in the open.

So, he appeased Dot's need to see him settled by enduring a seemingly endless string of uninspiring dates. It wasn't that the ladies she'd set him up with were unlikable or unattractive; he simply didn't swing that way.

A horse squealed aggressively in the distance, interrupting the morning songbird's conversations.

Ray turned around with a smile he hoped didn't look as strained as it felt, that the weariness wasn't evident in his voice. "It was fine."

"Fine?" Dot's bright eyes popped as her brows shot up. "What kind of date is that? Fine?"

Ray inhaled slowly. "Sandra was a lovely young woman. We had a nice evening."

Dot rolled her eyes. She was clearly becoming frustrated with his complete lack of interest in the women she'd tried so hard to match him up with. He really couldn't blame her. It had gone on long enough with the same outcome: "Yes, we had a nice time, yes she was lovely, no—"

"Are you going to see her again?"

"Don't think so."

"When are you going to stop beatin' the devil around the stump and find yourself a good woman, Raymond?" She threw her hands up and huffed a small cloud into the space between them. "There are only so many available ladies in these here parts, young man. I've gone through just about the lot of them trying to find you the perfect ranch wife."

"Maybe you should stop then, because I don't need a wife." The words escaped harder than intended.

Dot's eyes narrowed, and her sharp gaze bore into him. A shiver of fear ran up his spine. Did she know? Could she see behind his mask, see who he really was? Nothing terrified him more. Dot was the closest thing to a mother he'd ever known, having lost his own in childbirth. His father had never remarried and had tried his best to raise Ray. But he had a ranch to run and not enough time to properly care for a small child. Dot had unselfishly stepped up and added surrogate mother to her long list of ranch duties. She'd given so much of her own life to ensure Ray grew up wanting for nothing and knowing he was loved, no matter what. Even still, he couldn't chance disappointing her, or worse, having her turn away from him.

"I'm too busy, Dot. You know how it is around here. I don't have time for a woman."

"Every man needs a good woman, Raymond."

Not every *man.*

Ray held his tongue and his gaze until Dot cowed, ending their short stare-down with a shake of her head. Her shoulders slumped slightly, just enough to send a spike of regret through his chest. He hated letting her down, but this was one argument she was never going to win. The hardest part of it all was that he couldn't seem to find a way to tell her why.

"I just want you to be happy, Raymond." The fire died out of her voice and twisted the spike.

"I know, Dot. I know."

She gave him a small smile and rubbed her hand up and down his forearm, then turned back for the house. "Breakfast is just about ready, son."

His ranch hands were already seated and loading their plates when Ray entered the large dining room through the kitchen door. The first pair of eyes he made contact with belonged to Travis Morgan—and they stayed on him until he'd made his way across the floor and pulled out his chair. A rush of heat caught him off guard, scoured his insides, and pooled in his lower abdomen. He cleared his throat, tore his gaze from the cowboy who was quickly overrunning his thoughts, and took his seat beside Dot.

He nodded. "Morning, gentlemen."

A chorus of mumbled, sleep-laden "mornin's" followed his subdued greeting to the crew.

Once Ray's plate was loaded, business began as usual with the men giving him a status report on the livestock, pastures, supplies, and any other issues in need of consideration or direction. He tried to pay attention but found his thoughts, and his gaze, traveling back to the sexy cowboy at the far end of the table.

"Lost some more cattle on the north range," Jesse said between mouthfuls of sausage. "Don't have a head count yet."

That caught his wandering thoughts. Ray looked around the table only to be met with blank stares and shoulder shrugs. Broken fence lines or rustlers—hopefully not the latter.

"Okay, Jesse. Take an ATV and run the lines. Don't forget to take a two-way radio with you."

"Will do, boss."

"On second thought. Clay, grab an ATV and go with him just in case we have a rustling problem. I don't want anyone out there alone."

Clay Fisher was Jesse's best friend and had been living and working on the ranch five years now. Clay was a year older at twenty-three,

though Jesse was clearly the "older" of the two. But what Clay lacked in maturity, he more than made up for in sheer physical force. He was well over six feet and solid as an ox. He was hardly ever serious but had an incendiary temper if pushed too far. Fortunately that limit was long and wide. But the boy was nothing if not loyal. He could trust him to watch Jesse's back if they came upon any trouble of the gun-toting, thieving kind.

It wasn't that he didn't think Jesse could take care of himself. With a father like Sam, the kid had to have some decent defensive skills, but in general, he was too...sweet. And for whatever reason, Ray had always looked on Jesse like a younger brother, had some sort of innate sense that he needed to look out for him.

"You got it, boss," Clay answered, then turned to Jesse and elbowed him in the ribs. "Race you to the ravine."

Jesse elbowed him back and laughed. "Loser gets shit duty for a week."

"Get your gum boots ready, dude," Clay teased, shoving Jesse with his shoulder.

"Boys," Dot said with a firm, authoritative voice. Jesse and Clay immediately quit horsing around and returned to their breakfasts. Clay snickered under his breath.

Ray shook his head and once again caught Travis's eye. Ray dropped his gaze to his plate and kept it there.

With the morning meal finished and the day's tasks set, the men rose one by one and placed their dirty dishes in a plastic tub on a trolley for Dot before heading out. Travis hung back until the last man had cleared the dining room and placed his dishes in the tub.

"Can I help you clean up, Dot?" His deep voice was sincere and respectful.

Dot looked up at him, as surprised as Ray was, but she shooed him away with a smile. "You go on and do your own work, young man."

Travis hesitated a moment and glanced at Ray. Ray nodded toward the foyer as he rose from the table. "Daylight's burnin'."

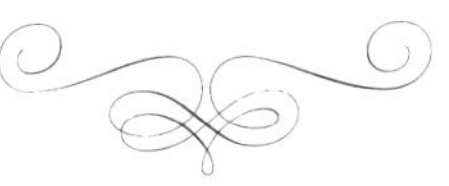

"I have a rule against working with a partner," Travis stated, matching Ray's stride as they walked across the yard toward the barn. Ray inhaled the subtle scent of livestock and fresh hay that rode the ever-present eastern trade winds.

"You aren't working with a partner," Ray said, his voice a bit tighter than intended. He took a breath. "We've got two round pens there, and we'll split the herd. We'll be working on our own."

"Sounds fair enough, I suppose. Any preferences on which horses you want?"

"Nope. Go ahead and take your pick."

Travis tipped his head in the direction of the corrals. "And Diablo over there?"

Ray shot a sideways glance at Travis.

"Hollis told me about him yesterday. I wouldn't mind taking him on."

Ray had had enough trouble with that horse, though he had an unusual bond with the animal. Diablo's dam had died when he was just five weeks old, and Ray had assumed nursing duties, bottle-feeding the youngster to keep him alive. For the first eight months of his life, the colt followed Ray like a lost puppy. That time had laid down an unshakable foundation for the rare understanding they now shared.

Even if Diablo made a point of testing it every time Ray brought him down from winter pasture. Four years now.

Few people believed the feisty stallion was actually well trained. He just played at wild. Still, Ray wouldn't trust that horse with anyone else, no matter how experienced a horseman. Diablo's volatility with everyone but Ray had sent more than a few men to the hospital over the years. He wouldn't chance another being hurt. And for some reason he didn't care to explore, the idea of Travis hurt bothered him more.

Ray shook his head. "Nope. Any horse but."

"You know I do this for a living, Ray."

"Of course. And so do I. But that doesn't change the fact I won't chance anyone's safety with that animal."

"Ray—"

Ray stopped and faced Travis. His voice snapped. "Are you going to argue with me?"

"No, of course not. But training horses like that, it's what I do best."

"He doesn't need training."

"But Hollis told me n—"

"This is starting to sound like arguing."

Travis squared his shoulders infinitesimally. "I'm not arg—"

"*Travis.*" Ray used the man's name like a weapon and received the desired effect. Travis snapped his mouth shut. "Whose ranch are we on here?"

Bronze fire flashed in Travis's eyes, and a muscle ticked in his clenched jaw. He pursed his lips, looking for all the world like a rattler poised to strike. Instead of being annoyed with the man for arguing with him, Ray found it . . . arousing. *Damn it all to hell and back.*

With a firm tone and pointed enunciation, Ray said, "My ranch. My horses. My rules."

Facing off, the sudden urge to grab the man by the back of the neck and pull him in for a hard kiss shocked Ray. Travis threw his hands up in surrender, though Ray doubted the acquiescence would last. The enticing fire in the other man's eyes abated, replaced by that mischievous glint Ray was too quickly becoming familiar with—and tempted by. A crooked half smile popped a dimple in Travis's cheek.

"Fine." Travis matched Ray's verbal delivery. "*Boss.*"

The sun had reached its highest point in the sky when Ray's stomach began to growl. He was working a big bay gelding with curious brown eyes that was proving to be one of the better horses he'd handled in a long time. Some horses he just clicked with. Those were the ones he had the hardest time letting go.

With their training session at an end, Ray stood in the middle of the pen and waited. The big bay sauntered over to him, nickered softly, and nudged his shoulder. Ray smiled and scrubbed the animal's strong jaw.

"You're just a big pushover, aren't you?"

Ray turned away from the horse, who followed right on his heel like a well-trained dog, and reached through the railing for the bucket of carrots he'd left on the other side. Running his hand over the thick, muscular neck, he handed the gelding his treat for a job well done. He returned the horse to the herd and made his way over to the other pen where Travis was working with a red dun mare.

Ray swiped at a light sheen of sweat under the band of his hat with a bandanna he'd pulled from his back pocket.

"Time for lunch, Travis."

"Few more minutes," Travis said without turning away from his charge. "She's just about got it."

Ray leaned his forearms on the railing and crossed one booted foot over the other to watch the famous Travis Morgan at work. That effortless swagger he'd noticed when Travis was walking along the shoulder of the highway translated into a quiet confidence with his equine counterpart. His every movement, every sound, had been sharply honed to earn trust quickly. But then, Travis wouldn't be the best trainer in the country if he didn't command that sort of respect.

It was impressive to watch the man communicate, understand, and intuitively anticipate the skittish mare to settle her with ease. Given how Travis's kinetic energy had so unsettled Ray, he was somewhat surprised it had the opposite effect on the horse. Perhaps it was the man's focus.

Which drew Ray's focus from horse to man.

The heat of the afternoon sun had forced them to remove their heavy jackets. Travis stood with his back to Ray, the sleeves of his blue-checked shirt rolled up to his elbows. The material pulled across his back as he moved, flattened against taut, defined muscle. Ray found himself mesmerized by the play of lean muscles as they contracted and extended from shoulder to hip. He imagined that back bare, his hands sliding slowly over warm skin, tracing the curves and contours of each muscle with his tongue.

Travis reached behind and shoved a red bandanna into his back jeans pocket. The movement grabbed Ray's eyes and pulled them along with it. His gaze remained focused on piece of cloth—in the back

pocket of well-worn, butt-hugging Wranglers—a red flag taunting an angry bull.

Ray couldn't pull his eyes away, so he squeezed them shut. The lack of sight only amplified sound. Travis's even breathing and the low murmur of his deep whiskey voice as he soothed the horse's anxieties.

What Ray wouldn't give to have that soothing voice murmur in his ear, encouraging him, coaxing him to obey the other man's commands? His skin tingled, and heat rushed south as his cock agreed.

Ray cursed under his breath.

"What's that, Ray?"

His eyes popped open, and the blood that had been pooling south suddenly reversed engines and raced north, flooding his neck and cheeks. He took a deep breath and said a short prayer of thanks for small miracles. Travis still had his back to him. Ray rubbed his own bandanna over the back of his heated neck. He cleared his throat and, wincing at the roughness of his voice, said, "Uh, I see why you're the best in the country."

Travis glanced over his shoulder. Those magnetic eyes locked with Ray's, and Travis flashed one of the most stunning smiles Ray had ever seen. The sheer brilliance of it hit him like a hoof square in the center of his chest with enough force to shove him back a step.

Shit on a stick.

He was done for.

CHAPTER 4

"Hold on, I'm coming," Travis hollered as he stepped out of the small bathroom and wrapped a towel around his waist. He crossed the room in three long strides, dripping a trail of water as he went, and swung the cabin door open. The blanket of cold air that attacked his exposed, wet skin was more refreshing than chilling after his hot shower.

Jesse stood on the porch with his mouth open, about to speak, but the words had apparently died on their way out. The kid's gaze suddenly riveted to Travis's bare chest, traveled slowly downward, until it got hung up on the bulge behind the thin blue towel.

Well, well, well. Travis hadn't seen a perusal that blatant outside a gay bar. So, it seemed Jesse Davis was gay. *How the fuck about that? Wouldn't Sam just shit a brick?*

He bit back a laugh at the irony, but couldn't stop the smile breaking out across his face. "Something I can help you with, Jesse?"

Jesse's head shot up to meet Travis in the eye; shock and embarrassment played out on his young face. The kid's neck and cheeks flushed such a brilliant red, Travis thought he'd pop an artery. Jesse's jaw worked silently a couple of times before he was able to force sound out of his mouth. "I, uh, we"—he cleared his throat—"we're... me and the guys...we're gonna light a fire and toss back a few beers."

Travis looked over Jesse's shoulder and saw Clay and Ross throwing logs and kindling into the fire pit, creating a tepee. He hedged. "Okay."

"Uh, yeah, so...you want to join us?" Belatedly, Jesse held up his hands, a bottle of Wild Fly Ale in each. A cold beer actually sounded pretty good.

"Sure. Just let me dry off and throw some clothes on."

Travis rarely made friends on the ranches he worked. He made a point of keeping his head down, doing his job, and moving on the second he was done. No attachments or commitments meant no problems, disappointments, or hurt.

But these men sitting around a roaring campfire—relaxed and laughing, genuine and straightforward—had a way of putting Travis at ease, as if he'd always been here. They'd befriended him quickly and easily, made him feel like he belonged. It was a rare feeling, and one he was afraid to get too comfortable with.

Good things never lasted. The bottom always dropped out, and he was the one who always paid the price.

Jesse sat on the log bench beside Travis, nervous and fidgety. He kept glancing at Travis with awe, excitement, and that blatant flare of desire in his guileless gray-blue eyes. Clay sat on Jesse's other side, and Ross shared the next bench with a cooler of beer. The fire crackled and popped. Red embers rose to twine with bright stars in a swirling, lackadaisical dance.

Travis observed how the men interacted with one another as they regaled him with their adventures on Ford Creek. The other two treated Jesse like a kid brother. Both seemed genuinely fond of the young man. Not that it was a hard thing to do. Travis had to admit the kid was instantly likeable. Jesse's best friend Clay was watchful of him. The young cowboy may come off as an immature clown to most, but it was hard to miss Clay's astute observance, like an ever-faithful guard dog. The kid was smarter than he let on, and Travis was grateful Jesse had a friend like him in his corner. Especially after the little run-in with the kid's father at dinner that first night on Ford Creek. And now discovering that the kid was gay, with a hot-tempered, homophobe dad, Travis's own protective instincts had flared.

A brief memory of the first time life had shot him down rose to the surface. He took a solid draught of his beer and pushed it away.

"Well. That's it for me." Ross stood and dropped his empty bottle into the cooler with a sharp *clink*. "This old man can't keep up with you young bucks anymore."

"Whatever, Ross," Clay said. "You still kick my ass at arm wrestling."

Ross winked. "That's because I have a secret family maneuver."

"One of these days I'll get it out of you," Clay teased.

"Taking it to the grave, boy." Ross laughed and headed for his cabin with a wave over his shoulder.

Clay chugged back the last of his beer, exchanged a look with Jesse, and stood up.

"I'm calling it too. Don't want Dot giving me shit for being late for breakfast again." He clapped Jesse on the back. "Later, dude."

"Later," Jesse said.

"Make sure Cinderella gets home before curfew," Clay said to Travis.

"Shut. Up." Jesse spluttered and smacked Clay on the thigh. He laughed and knocked Jesse's hat from his head, then sauntered off.

Silence fell around the campfire as Jesse retrieved his hat, dusted it off against his knee, and settled it back on his head. Travis waited for Jesse to bring up what he knew was coming. It didn't take long.

"Can I ask you a personal question, Travis?" There was a timid note in Jesse's voice, and worship and lust in his eyes.

Travis shrugged his shoulders.

Jesse cleared his throat, squared his shoulders, and sat up straighter. "Those rumors my dad was talking about the other night . . ."

Travis regarded the kid for a moment. He didn't make a habit of outing himself to many people, but it seemed apparent Jesse needed some guidance, support, someone to turn to. Still, he held back saying anything definite.

"Anyone else know?" Travis asked, using the same gentle and assuring tone he used with his horses. "Anyone you can talk to?"

Jesse's eyes widened, fear flashing through them.

"It's okay, kid. I understand."

Jesse relaxed, and his relieved exhale nearly drowned out the crackling fire. "Clay knows, but he's straight. No one else."

Travis nodded. Poor kid thought he was alone. He had no idea Ray could have been there for him all along, if the stubborn man wasn't so deeply closeted, and Jesse wasn't so green.

Travis found himself skipping back in time to another young man, this one much younger than Jesse, with that same youthful innocence, wonderment, and fear.

That boy hadn't had anyone there for him either. He'd been fifteen years old, discovering who he was on his own, when his father had found him behind the barns kissing Bobby Joe MacCabe.

It all played out so clearly in his mind, as though it were only yesterday.

One minute Travis was enjoying the most earth-shattering experience of his life as he and Bobby Joe clumsily kissed for the first time. The next minute, he was yanked by his collar and slammed up against the side of the barn, splinters digging painfully into his back.

His father, the man Travis had always looked up to and trusted without question, punched him in the gut so hard he felt like he was drowning, unable to pull air into his lungs. Still gasping for breath, the second punch rocked his head back against the hard wood. His vision grayed out, stars danced in a chaotic cloud, and he thought, Huh, you really do see stars. Just like in the comics. And it was almost comical. Until he crumpled painfully to the ground in a bloody heap when his father let go with a kick to the ribs, and told him to get off his property.

It took close to an hour before he could pick himself up off the ground and stagger to the house. His body was on fire, and there was dried, crusty blood on his face. One eye was swollen near shut, and his side hurt so badly he could only take short, shallow breaths.

He didn't make it into the house. His father stepped out onto the front porch, arms crossed over his broad chest. "You don't live here anymore. You're no longer my son or a member of this family."

"Dad . . ." Travis pleaded. He couldn't believe his dad was doing this. The man who'd taught him how to lasso a calf, shoe a horse, ride like the wind—the man who'd always been there for him.

But apparently love was conditional.

"Where am I going to go?" He spit dirt and blood from his mouth.

His father yelled at him, face flushed with anger, "I don't give a shit!"

Travis's head snapped back like he'd been physically slapped. He saw the faces of his family watching from behind the front window, and looked to each one pleadingly. His mother wouldn't meet his eyes. His own fucking mother! His older brother Randy sneered at him in disgust, and the oldest, his sister Gracie, was crying. She turned from the window and a moment later charged through the front door. Their father grabbed her by the collar and hauled her back.

"Dad!" she screeched. "He's hurt. He needs help."

"He's nothing to us now. Go back inside."

"He's my brother." Gracie was crying, wailing, flailing her arms at their father, but the man didn't even blink.

"Get off my property before I get my twelve-gauge."

His father was gone. The man who stood on the porch with dark, killing eyes was a stranger. Travis had no choice but to turn around and leave. Gracie's cries echoed in the distance as he lurched slowly down the long drive, leaving the only place he'd ever known.

That was the last he'd seen of White Deer, Texas, or the people he'd once called family.

A shudder ran through him. Travis slammed back the last of his beer, hoping it would drown the painful memory once and for all.

He would be there for Jesse, like he'd wished someone had been there for him eighteen years ago.

"Yes," Travis said quietly.

"Yes what?" Jesse asked confused.

"The rumors are true." He turned to face Jesse. "And that's strictly between us. Understand?"

Jesse nodded. "Understood."

"Not even Clay can know," Travis warned.

"I got it, Travis." Jesse nodded again and his eyes turned serious, revealing comprehension beyond his years. "Between us. You've met my dad."

"Unfortunately." Travis sighed. He stood up and added his empty beer bottle to the collection in the cooler. "And don't hit on me. I'm too old for you."

Tension hung thick and palpable in the air when Ray and Dot walked in to the dining room for breakfast. Just like the first night Travis had joined them. Ray scanned the men crowded around the table focused intently on their meals, with one exception. Make that four. Sam's face was flushed with anger, lips pursed, flat eyes glaring across the table. He looked like a lone bandit, pissed off, cornered, and holding out to the very end against a determined, unyielding posse. A posse made up of Ross Dennison, Clay Fisher, and Travis Morgan. Jesse sat between Travis and Clay, body held tight, head down, nostrils flared.

"Gentlemen," Ray said as he pulled out Dot's chair and after she was seated, pulled up his own, still watching as he sat. The silent standoff continued. "Ross? Do we have a problem here?"

"No sir," Ross answered Ray, though his words were directed at Sam. "We're all good. Aren't we, boys?"

Sam agreed begrudgingly with a curse under his breath and snatched the platter that was being passed his way.

"Don't you be cursing at my table, Samuel Davis," Dot admonished.

"Yes, ma'am," Sam said with obvious effort at civility. He loaded his plate in sharp, jerky movements.

Aside from bare-bones business at Ray's requests, not another word was spoken. Meals were eaten with vigor as the men seemed to be in a great hurry to get to work. The first to finish, Sam rose abruptly from the table. His chair scraped loudly on the hardwood floor. As he walked around the table to drop his dishes in Dot's trolley, he stopped to lean over Travis's shoulder and whisper into his ear. Whatever Sam said, Travis showed no outward reaction—didn't even look like he was listening—but the vibrating rigidity of Sam's body told Ray it wasn't "have a nice day."

As was becoming habit, Travis hung back and offered to help Dot with the cleanup. She absently shooed him off, telling him to behave himself. Travis turned and gave Ray a long, unreadable look. Then he nodded and left the room.

"You've got trouble brewing between those boys, Raymond," Dot said matter-of-factly.

Ray sighed. "Yes, it appears that way."

He dropped his dishes in the tub, leaned down to give Dot a quick kiss on the cheek, and headed out to get to the bottom of the morning stare down.

Travis was still in the tack room gathering gear when Ray caught up to him.

"What's going on with you and Sam?" Ray asked as he entered the crowded room. Two rows of saddle racks, three-high and seven-deep, took up the majority of the small space. Tack lockers took up one wall, floor-to-ceiling, and half of another wall sported hooks holding bridles and halters, leads and lunge lines. Interspersed with the headgear were framed photos of Ford Creek's legendary equine history.

"Nothing."

"Didn't look like nothing." Ray followed Travis down the narrow row of saddle racks. The sharp, buttery scent of leather and earthy horse sweat hung thick and comforting in the air.

"Just Sam posturing." Travis pulled a saddle off one of the midlevel racks and turned around to meet Ray's gaze, a flash of merriment lighting his changeable eyes. "Nothing to worry about."

"What is he posturing about?" Ray pressed. "I won't have tension between the hands on my ranch."

Travis gripped the saddle by the horn, slipped his hand through the gullet, and held it comfortably at his side. He placed his free hand gently on Ray's hip.

Ray froze.

Travis flashed a half smile and tilted his head to the side. "Excuse me."

It took Ray a second to realize he had Travis trapped in the narrow walkway. He angled his body away and pressed his back up against the saddles. A horn dug into his spine as Travis moved past deliberately slow, taunting—the bastard. His magnetic gaze didn't waver from Ray as he went.

Ray's hip burned where Travis's hand had been. Scorched right through the thick denim and branded the skin. He silently counted to five, cleared his throat, and followed.

"I want an answer, Travis."

Travis regarded Ray. The light changed in his eyes like he was weighing how much he wanted to reveal. "Who was sitting beside me?"

"Ross and Jesse."

"There you go."

Ray frowned. "'There you go' what?"

Travis stepped in close, and once again Ray froze. Travis looked down into his eyes, searching, intense. He was close enough for Ray to see the bronze striations in those captivating green eyes, the darker rim around the outside of the iris, and those goddamned long, thick lashes. Travis reached over Ray's shoulder, leaning even closer, a hairbreadth from touch. The man smelled of cedar leaf, ginger, and a hint of woodsy smoke. And damn if Ray didn't want to press his nose to Travis's neck and inhale, open his mouth and taste that tanned skin.

His entire body was strung tight, every nerve heightened into acute awareness, and there was no force behind his voice when he spoke. "Back the fuck off, Morgan."

Travis smiled, seductive and cocky and knowing. His dancing, fiery gaze didn't falter as he lifted a bridle from one of the hooks behind Ray and stepped back.

"Think about it, Ray. You're an intelligent man."

Travis dropped the bridle in a tack box on top of a collection of assorted grooming and training gear, a bucket of carrots wedged in the corner. He picked up the box and held it out for Ray. "Your tack, boss."

CHAPTER 5

The day was coming to a close, and Travis was having trouble focusing on the ornery buckskin currently testing his boundaries.

Thoughts and images of a certain sexy rancher were taking up far too much of his available brain space. It had only been a few days, but he had to admit he truly enjoyed working with Ray. While they weren't exactly working together, per se, they were working side by side. Relatively. And even though their training techniques were similar, Travis had picked up a couple of new tricks from the man. That right there didn't happen often. In fact, Travis could count the number of times it had on one hand. It moved Ray yet another notch up in his estimation.

Travis had been paying more attention to Ray than he should, absorbing the man's every detail and nuance, imprinting the musical cadence and inflections of his deep, rough voice. Learning the man from a distance. And he knew without a doubt the feeling was mutual. Travis hadn't missed the surreptitious glances, the sudden darting of eyes to avoid being caught watching, and the throat clearing and slightly flushed cheeks when he had.

Not to mention the spike in atmosphere in the tack room earlier, when Travis had laid his hand on Ray's hip and invaded his space. He'd had Ray on the edge.

And damn if that didn't completely turn Travis on.

The man put out a hard, uncompromising air, but Travis knew that was only for show. He'd observed the sensitive hand Ray used with the horses he trained and how quickly those horses trusted him. It was also clear how much Ray respected and cared for Dot, respected the men who worked on his ranch. Ray cared more than he let on.

Travis had come across more than one genuinely hard man in his life, and there was nothing gentle or kind to be found in them. Those men were born that way, whereas Ray wore it like a shield. And Travis understood why.

If he weren't in a situation where people knew who he was, if he hadn't just had the shit beat out of him back in North Dakota, Travis would have already had Ray under him faster than a rodeo bronco out of the chute.

But folks did know him here, and Ray was his boss. It wasn't just his reputation at stake. Ray had even more to lose if they were caught.

And the recent beating was still too fresh in Travis's memory.

He'd been on the Double Diamond Ranch for barely a week, but his warning signals had been flashing and ringing from day one. He'd known better than to go against his infallible intuition, so why he'd ignored it that time, he couldn't say.

The moment he'd been introduced to the hands, the atmosphere had turned frosty. Not one person, aside from his boss and the cook, had spoken to him unless absolutely necessary. He'd been disappointed at having to quit so soon after starting but knew he was jeopardizing his life by being there.

Travis had hefted his duffel bag—that hadn't even been unpacked—over his shoulder and hightailed it out of there. Things would have been okay if he hadn't stopped at a local pub for a couple shots of tequila, if he'd kept going until he'd cleared the state line. But he'd needed something to take the edge off while he worked out what to do next, where to go. And that was when it had all gone south. He knew he wasn't getting out of North Dakota without at least one broken bone when he'd heard "Looky here, fellas. It's the Brokeback cowboy" behind him.

Travis had looked up into the mirror behind the bar and counted five men from the Double Diamond in its reflection. He was a fighter, more than confident in a one- or two-on-one, possibly even a three-on-one, but five?

Life may have thrown him more curveballs than most, but he was far from suicidal. He knew when he didn't have a chance and found no shame in walking away.

He'd slid a couple of bills to the bartender and ordered five more shots for his *friends*. When the bartender had lined the drinks up and called the bewildered men forward, Travis had shot back his last tequila and slipped away quietly while the ranch hands indulged.

He'd made it two miles down the road before he'd finally breathed a long sigh of relief. Unfortunately it had been too soon. If only there had been at least one passing vehicle he could have hitched a ride with.

The Double Diamond hands had caught up to him, banked their truck hard onto the shoulder, and piled out ready to rumble.

Travis unconsciously rubbed a hand over his ribs at the memory.

But that was Double Diamond and this was Ford Creek. He'd been welcomed here without question or reservation. With the exception of Sam Davis, that is.

Travis stole another glance over his shoulder. Ray was leading a sturdy-looking paint back to the corral on his way to swap for another steed. For such a solid man, his stride was effortlessly fluid.

Logically, Travis knew they both had far too much to lose to take the risk, but it didn't stop his mind from coming up with a way around it. There was no denying they were attracted to one another, and they both had reputations neither wanted damaged or destroyed. But that didn't mean they couldn't take advantage of the situation regardless. They were both mature and experienced enough to stay under the radar. Ray had obviously done so thus far without the slightest hint of rumor or speculation. It would be mutually beneficial for the both of them, and it would only be for a few months.

The tension was already growing at a rapid pace between them, and it was only a matter of time before one of them snapped. Even though the urge to move on hadn't struck yet, Travis knew he wouldn't be able to stay put longer than a few months anyway—never could.

Mind made up, Travis turned back to his charge, feeling a little more relaxed and able to focus clearly once again.

Turned out the ornery buckskin wasn't so ornery after all. Not once the animal figured out who was in charge. Travis finally had the gelding following him obediently around the pen when he heard an aggressive bray from the other ring. A heavy, thudding crash against aluminum railings followed. He whipped around just in time to

see Diablo rearing, raking his hooves through the air, ears flat back, nostrils flared—and Ray on the ground against the rails.

Impulse and adrenaline catapulted Travis up and over the six-foot fence as though it were nothing more than a highway guardrail. There were less than two hundred yards between the round pens, but it may as well have been two miles. Travis's boots felt weighted with cement as he ran.

"Ray! Get out of there!"

A furious Diablo charged at Travis—ears flat back, teeth bared—when he grabbed the rails and started to climb over. Ray didn't even flinch. Just shot a quick glance over his shoulder and raised one hand, signaling Travis to stop. The warning in his expressive eyes was stern and immutable, his voice level and forceful when he said, "Stop."

"Stop? What the hell—"

"Unless you want to lose a limb," Ray said, his voice unchanging, "I suggest you back away from the fence."

"Dammit, Ray. You need to get out of that pen."

"And you need to back off."

"That horse is going to kill you." Travis's voice had pitched a touch high, and he had yet to break his stuck-to-the-fence-like-Velcro imitation.

Ray cracked an infuriating half grin, and his eyes twinkled. "No, he isn't. You're just pissing him off."

The stubborn son of a bitch thought this was a game? He didn't know what Ray had been drinking, but whatever it was it had clearly impaired the man's judgment.

"Fuck that. I'm coming in." Travis made to move up another rail, intent on pulling Ray's dumb ass out of the ring. Diablo charged again with an angry squeal.

"You can stay right where you are, Morgan." Ray's rough voice cracked like a whip, the twinkle gone from his eyes. "Better yet, go back to your own horse."

Diablo tossed his head and stamped the ground in agreement, attention focused on Travis.

"Ray—"

"Go." The stubborn man shook his head once and turned back to the dangerous stallion.

With a frustrated sigh, Travis jumped off the fence and took one step back to appease Ray and the angered horse, but he was reluctant to leave the rancher alone. Just in case. "I'm staying right here."

Ray didn't respond.

Travis crouched down to make himself less threatening to Diablo and willed the pounding in his ears and rapid, short breaths that made his throat drier than the Nevada desert to settle down.

At that first, quick glance, Travis had thought Ray was in serious danger, and panic had immediately set in, coloring what he'd actually seen.

Now that the disconcerting blinders were off, the ones he didn't want to think too much about, he could see what had really been going on.

Ray had been sitting on the ground—as he still was—cross-legged, hands palm up on his knees as though mediating, with his back against the rails. His posture relaxed, his shoulders rose and fell with an easy, even rhythm. He had simply been waiting Diablo out, letting the horse act out until he settled on his own.

The less threatening Ray was, the less aggressive the horse would be. Travis shook his head. He practiced the same tension and release and approach and retreat methods as Ray, but sitting on the ground, that vulnerable to an angry twelve-hundred-pound animal, was taking it a bit too far.

And he was damn well going to give the man a piece of his mind for it later.

Gradually Diablo's volatility meter began to ease back to the right. The rearing became a stamping of the earth, snorting, and head tossing, which then settled back further to a few snorts and head tosses. Then the animal stood his ground looking anywhere but at Ray. Tension Travis hadn't realized his body had been holding finally released when the big horse lowered his head and looked at Ray with a calmer air.

"Hand me a carrot," Ray said, his voice low and even. The man hadn't moved a muscle the entire time Diablo had put on his show.

Travis turned to the bucket of carrots a few feet away and reached for one. He placed it in the open, waiting palm. His fingers brushed

the skin, brief and gentle, as he retreated. Ray's shoulders tensed infinitesimally, then settled back. Travis smiled at the telling reaction. That small touch had affected Ray as strongly as if Travis had grabbed hold and squeezed tight.

Ray broke the carrot in two and placed one half on each palm. Then lowered his hands back to his knees and resumed his Zen-Buddha routine.

Half an hour later Travis was smiling, and his chest swelled with pride as he watched Ray standing in the middle of the pen. Diablo's neck was draped over his shoulder as he nibbled at Ray's shirt while Ray scrubbed the big animal's jaw. The horse had tugged at the shirt enough that it had come loose of his jeans. Nibbling again, Diablo pulled the shirt up enough to expose a flat stomach, pale skin, and a trail of dark hair that disappeared into the jeans waistband.

Travis unconsciously licked his lips.

Ray chuckled softly at Diablo's antics and murmured inaudible, low-toned, dulcet words of praise in the now tame-as-a-kitten animal's ear.

A sudden screaming thought slammed into Travis's brain that had him instantly straining and uncomfortable against the zippered fly of his jeans: Ray would be an amazing lover.

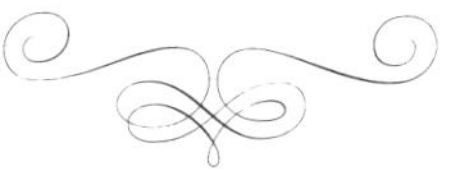

Ray sat in a chair on the front porch, absently chewing on a cinnamon stick as he waited for the men to come in for dinner. More specifically, waiting for Travis.

He had a bone to pick with the man.

Wind chimes trilled melodically in the dying evening breeze. The temperature had dropped as the sun began its descent, but warmth crept into his chest and fanned out as he recalled the afternoon. How panicked Travis had looked when he'd come charging to the pen when Diablo was playing his games. Charging to Ray's rescue. He couldn't ignore the feelings of pride and desire that the action had sent spiraling through his nervous system, but he could push them aside, force them into the background.

Travis came around the side of the barn with that unmistakable swagger of his, Jesse Davis in tow. Though he couldn't make out the words, the harmony of their voices carried across the yard—Travis's deep baritone and Jesse's eager tenor. Jesse kept looking up at Travis as he spoke, hanging on his every word. Travis laughed at something Jesse said, and the sound reverberated in Ray's chest, a sound he wanted to hear again, to cause. A ping of some strange emotion he refused to identify bubbled below the surface. Ray narrowed his eyes slightly as he watched the two men approach.

"Evenin', Ray," Jesse said in his youthful exuberance as they climbed the short steps.

He nodded. "Jesse."

Then he shifted his gaze to Travis and was once again trapped in those impossibly captivating eyes. Amusement and mischief danced in their shadows, withholding the secret Ray had wanted to learn the moment Travis had hopped into the cab of his truck.

"A minute, Travis."

Shit. Why did his voice always seem to come out rougher or sharper than intended around this man?

Jesse paused with his hand on the door and looked back at Travis questioningly. Ray wasn't sure what to make of that. He was the boss of this ranch. Not Travis. But Travis was whom the boy had looked to with his should-I-stay-or-should-I-go expression. When had that happened? And why did it piss him off?

"Go on in," Travis said.

Jesse shot a quick sidelong glance at Ray, then nodded and disappeared inside.

Chirping crickets and the quick *zzzzzttt* of insects electrocuting themselves on the ultraviolet bug zapper hanging near the door played in practiced concert with the swaying wind chimes.

That rare flush of jealousy rose again, and this time its buddy anger came along for the ride.

Ray glared. Travis waited.

"I appreciate your wanting to help this afternoon, but you needn't bother," Ray began once they were alone on the porch, and he could

temper his warring emotions. "I've got things under control with Diablo. We have a history and a...special way of working together."

"Special or not, it won't stop me from reacting how I do when I see anyone in any sort of trouble."

"I wasn't in trouble."

"Didn't look that way from my vantage point," Travis challenged.

"What you saw"—Ray lowered his voice, but couldn't prevent the snap the words were delivered with—"was Diablo playing."

Why did the man have to argue and rile him up so easily? What really rankled his hide was that he, again, seemed to find himself aroused by it. Which only aided in pissing him off more.

"Twelve hundred pounds of angry horseflesh bearing down on you is not what I'd call play." Travis lowered his voice to match Ray's but, unlike Ray, his edge remained controlled.

Ray stood up to face Travis. The man was a couple of inches taller, but Ray made a point of stretching to his full five feet ten and met Travis at almost eye level. "Believe it or not, that horse is actually well trained."

Travis didn't back down from Ray's attempt at intimidation. Didn't even flinch.

"I don't," he answered annoyingly unaffected. "So again, I will continue to help those who appear to need help."

Ray ground his back molars together until his jaw hurt. He counted to five, fighting the overwhelming urge to take Travis's mouth in a hard, punishing kiss—or punch him. Either would be equally satisfying right about then.

"I don't need a sitter, Morgan," he snapped.

Travis matched his tone. "Not my intention."

"What is your intention, then?"

The air between them crackled. Both men were once again rendered immobile under locked gazes. The muscle in Travis's strong jaw clenched, and bronze fire exploded in his eyes, scorching a path straight down Ray's spine. Silence wrapped around them, and the world closed in. Ray felt cocooned inside a kinetic bubble that had the fine hairs on his arms standing on end. Even the low buzzing nocturnal orchestra failed to penetrate its imperceptible walls.

"What do you want, Ray?" Travis's tone had changed, the pitch dropped, the edge roughened. Right then Ray knew exactly what he wanted—inside Travis. One stride and he'd cover that long, lean body with his own.

Heat spread out from his abdomen and sent electric shocks in every direction. Blood rushed to his cock, filling it quickly, demanding. His gaze dropped to Travis's lips; the upper not quite as full as the lower flushed deep pink. Then those lips parted, and the slow whisper that spilled over them was almost a growl. "What do you want?"

Ray felt a groan bubbling up his throat and forcibly swallowed it back. He dug his fingers hard into his thighs in a poor attempt at countering his reaction to the frustratingly sexy cowboy, but it didn't help. He opened his mouth to tell Travis exactly what he wanted, what he was going to—

The front door banged against the wall like gunshot, and Ray damn near shed his skin. His head snapped around so fast, he knew he'd be feeling the whiplash before the night was over.

Dot stood in the doorway with an amused glint in her eyes. "You boys quit staring each other down like a couple of roosters in a henhouse and get your butts in here. Dinner's getting cold."

The burning heat that had run rampant over his body a moment ago suddenly turned cold under Dot's bucket-of-ice-water presence. His lower body chilled, literally, but his face was now an inferno.

Travis casually removed his hat, holding it against his chest as he ran a hand through his unruly blond hair. Ray's eyes followed the movement with a frown.

"Sorry, Dot," Travis said, a sheepish grin on his face and a playful tone in his voice, as if they hadn't just been a heartbeat away from tackling each other to the ground. "Just discussing a difference in training methods."

"Must be a pretty serious difference," she said.

Ray didn't fail to notice the humor that laced through her words. Her bright eyes were sharp and speculative. Ray knew she saw more than she let on. She always saw more than she let on. A shiver raced up his spine. *Not good. Not good at all.*

Travis leaned down and gave her a quick, chaste kiss on the cheek.

"You said something about dinner?" Travis asked politely.

Dot regarded the two of them a moment, then without another word turned for the door. Travis placed his hand on the small of her back and followed her inside without so much as a glance back.

Ray stayed outside a moment to pull himself together, still staring at the spot where Travis had stood. He dragged his hands down his face.

"I am so fucking screwed."

CHAPTER 6

All through dinner Ray's gaze kept straying to the sexy cowboy at the far end of the table. Much as he tried, he couldn't seem to veer his thoughts off the track that kept replaying how close that body had been to his. He could still feel the heat that had wrapped around his own body, still smell the masculine, earthy scent that had his every nerve vibrating. All he wanted was more.

And every time Travis caught his gaze, that mischievous glint taunted him.

It was the most uncomfortable, yet arousing dinner he could ever remember sitting through. The risk of taking what he wanted, and being caught for it, was at once terrifying and enticing.

Dammit, he had to get a grip on this growing obsession. Why couldn't he push the man from his mind like he'd pushed every other desire away all his life? What was it about Travis Morgan that drew him like a magnet? It was like he had no control, was almost completely at the man's mercy. And being under someone else's control didn't bode well in Ray's estimation.

He trained his eyes to the dinner plate in front of him, pursed his lips, and speared the potatoes with excessive force, counting the minutes until dinner was over and the men cleared out.

Travis prolonged the torture by hanging back and trying to do what he did after every meal: help Dot with the cleanup. And Dot responded the same as always by shooing him off. The man was nothing if not persistent.

"Stop messin' with an old woman," Dot admonished.

"You, Miss Dottie McCray, are far from old," Travis drawled with laughter in his rich, resonant voice, sincerity in his eyes, flashing that award-winning smile that made Ray's pulse quicken. Then Travis

scooped her up in his arms and waltzed her around the room. "Let's go dancing, Dottie."

To Ray's complete surprise, Dot giggled, actually giggled like a little girl. Two turns around the room, and she slunk out of his embrace. "Now you stop, young man. Even if I were your age, we both know I'm not your type."

Travis gasped dramatically and splayed a hand over his chest. "You wound me, Miss Dottie."

"Oh hush! You go on now and let me do my chores." Her cheeks were flushed, and she gave him a playful shove. Travis laughed, genuine and heartfelt. The affectionate friendship growing between the two warmed Ray. And hearing Dot giggle was damn near priceless. For some strange reason it was important to him that they got along, that Dot care—

Travis turned and caught Ray's gaze just then. The smile on his rugged face faltered, and the light in his eyes darkened. And it was there. That heat spread out again, reaching for him, covering his skin. Time crashed to an agitated halt, and Ray couldn't hear anything over the heavy pulse that beat on his eardrums like a fist. His face felt like it was falling, and with a start, he realized he'd been smiling. Not a grin or a half-cocked lift of his lips, but a full-on, teeth exposed, cheek-cramper of a smile. Ray dropped his gaze and frowned.

The grandfather clock tick-tocked relentlessly.

"Well." Travis cleared his throat. "I'd best be going then."

He took Dot's hand in his and chastely kissed her knuckles over a slight bow. "Good night, Miss Dottie. Thank you for the dance."

Dot laughed, sounding more like herself, and playfully smacked Travis on the arm. "Good night, Travis."

Travis graced Ray with a sly smile, his voice low and deliberate, "Good night, Ray."

He nodded sharply. "Travis."

It was then that Ray noticed Dot had been watching them, gaze flipping back and forth, expression contemplative. He stood up abruptly and walked over to the large dining-room window that looked out over the barns and the plains beyond. The thick blanket of night had fallen and gently covered the land as it rested.

Ray tracked Travis in the window's reflection as he left the room. He heard the front door bang softly in its frame as it closed, followed by the dull echo of boots as they trod across the wooden porch. Dot came up beside him. Together they watched Travis walk across the yard with that easy, confident swagger, his sidekick Jesse—who'd obviously been waiting for him—in tow. Floodlights on the barn roof corner silhouetted their bodies. Travis pushed the hat off the younger man's head and ruffled his hair. Jesse picked up his hat, and Travis deftly dodged an incoming hit with said hat.

Ray frowned, not liking the feeling their camaraderie caused in him.

"Good man, that one," Dot said at his side. "Be good to have him stay on."

Ray shot a sideways glance at her, but she kept her gaze fixed forward. He didn't need to see her eyes to know they were dancing with sage amusement. A coy smile struggled to overtake her face.

"He's a drifter, Dot."

"Every seedling roots itself eventually, Raymond. No matter how far the wind carries it."

He countered. "Winds blow strong and constant in these parts."

"And the soil is fertile."

Ray gave up. No point in arguing with the woman.

Dot gave his arm a quick rub, stretched up on her toes to give him a light kiss on the cheek, and left him with his thoughts.

Ray pulled in a deep breath and exhaled on a long, weighted sigh as his thoughts returned to Travis. He was beginning to look forward to seeing the man each day a little too much. Dot and Jesse were quickly growing attached as well. Travis wasn't the stick-around kind, and sooner rather than later he was going to make his silent exit. Three damn days, and the man had managed to burrow under their hides. Even Clay and Ross acted like he'd been on Ford Creek forever.

Travis was going to take a huge chunk of this ranch with him when he left. The tornadolike force that was Travis Morgan would leave a path a mile wide in its wake.

And Ray had a sinking feeling the damage would be permanent.

CHAPTER 7

Ray looked across the narrow Formica table and watched Travis dip his burrito into a dish of thick salsa before taking a hearty bite. They'd stopped for lunch at Ray's favorite Mexican café before heading back to the ranch with the newest addition to his herd.

He wasn't entirely sure how he'd got himself roped into taking Travis with him to check out the stud in Billings. He'd blame it on Dot. It was all her doing, practically pushing the man out the door and into Ray's truck after breakfast.

"Travis can give you a second opinion," she'd said. "He knows his horses."

Yes, Travis knew his horses, but so did Ray. It was his damn ranch, and he would make the damn decisions. Without Travis's two cents.

Travis hadn't seemed fazed with Dot's insistence as he sat in the passenger seat messing with Ray's stereo like it was his God-given right. The man had zeroed in on the only rock station in range. His knee bounced, and long fingers tapped on his muscular thigh in time with the fast beats. Ray had been too tense to talk but had found himself relaxing as Travis shared tales of his many adventures and travels training across the country. He had to admit he'd felt an odd pang of envy at the carefree lifestyle Travis enjoyed. Ray had never had that kind of freedom. Nothing to tie him down, no roots or responsibilities—the ability to pick up and go wherever the wind took him in a heartbeat.

A fleeting wave of disappointment passed over Ray. Travis would be moving on before too long. That was something he needed to keep in the forefront of his mind when his body tried taking control. And a good reminder of how much he had to lose. Travis would pack up

and disappear, carried away on the ever-present trade winds, and Ray would be left alone to deal with the fallout.

Mind once again firmly in control of body, Ray took a long swig of his iced tea.

"I didn't thank you for your help back there." He broke the easy silence that had fallen between them while they ate their burritos and enchiladas.

He hadn't needed Travis's input to ascertain that the tall, blue roan quarter horse had stellar bloodlines, confirmation, and disposition. There was no question the stallion would be a valuable asset to his breeding operation. What Travis had helped with was his star-status name.

The owner of the roan had been so excited at the prospect of selling his horse to none other than Travis Morgan, he'd tripped all over himself to sweeten the deal. Ray had attempted to correct the man's misconception, but Travis had placed a hand lightly on the small of Ray's back, effectively disconnecting his brain. The shock of that hot touch, Travis's touch—in public—had frozen Ray in place. He swore his heart had even stopped beating.

Travis let his hand slide slowly, like a caress, from Ray's back and casually stepped forward without missing a beat. He shook the man's hand and haggled on the price. The owner had dropped it considerably for bragging rights and, of all things, an autograph. Travis had turned back and given Ray a surreptitious wink that made his breath catch.

"Don't mention it," Travis said with a shrug, loading up another dollop of salsa on his burrito.

Ray's gaze fixed on Travis's mouth as it opened to take a bite. Deep pink lips closed around the thick cream-colored tortilla. One hand gripped it firmly at its base, holding it in place, and Ray's abdomen clenched at the sight. The burrito fell away, and a wet tongue shot out to run along the top lip. A missed chunk of red salsa clung to the corner of the sensual mouth. Ray saw himself leaning over the table, sticking his own tongue out and lapping up the spicy hot sauce. Then he would trace the seam of those enticing lips, ensuring he hadn't missed a drop, and they'd part, allowing him entrance. Blood drained from his brain and fled south in response.

One side of that delectable mouth lifted and held motionless—waiting. Ray raised his gaze to find Travis staring back at him. Darkened eyes flashing with fire, burning him, singeing his skin. Travis raised his thumb and wiped at the salsa, then put the digit between his lips and sucked. He opened his mouth, and his tongue made a display of circling around the tip before he closed over it again. Then he slowly pulled it out, finally letting go with a small *pop*.

Good. God.

Ray was mesmerized, fully erect and pressing painfully into rough denim and an unforgiving metal zipper. Why didn't he wear button-fly jeans? His cock throbbed, and he shifted to accommodate himself as much as possible, short of yanking his pants off to free his aching dick.

The smile on that rugged, handsome face across from him widened, and that single dimple deepened in his cheek.

What the hell was he doing? Mind controlled body. Not the other way around.

Annoyed, Ray tore his gaze away, suddenly finding his enchilada extremely interesting. He could not look at Travis again, not without jumping his hired hand right there on the table in the middle of Santos Café. The good people of Billings, Montana, likely weren't ready for that kind of lunch-hour entertainment.

He would never look at a burrito the same way again.

Ray shifted in his seat again, willing his blood to retreat so his brain could function properly. He cleared his throat. Twice. And without looking up, asked, "So . . . uh . . . what got you into training horses for a living?"

Travis's extended silence forced Ray to look up and meet the eyes of the man who was too easily driving him around the bend. With a satisfied smile and unaffected casualness that pissed Ray off, Travis said, "Always had an affinity for them."

Ray's voice was sharp. "I have too, but I'm not world renowned."

If he hadn't been watching so closely, he'd have missed Travis's slight wince. "I'm far from world renowned. And your ranch is legendary."

"That's due just as much to the cattle as the horses."

Travis shrugged and returned to the task of making his plate look as if it had come straight out of the dishwasher.

Pissed at being pissed, Ray checked his tone and said, "So what's your secret?"

Travis shot Ray a quick, almost wary glance. A dark flash scored the green depths of his eyes, sending a ripple through their usually resident merriment. For a fleeting moment, Travis looked . . . vulnerable. Not something Ray had ever expected to see in the confident and carefree cowboy.

"No secret. They're just . . . unconditional . . . in their trust. I give that back. Simple."

There wasn't anything at all simple about that. Whatever experiences Travis had lived through, it was clear that not all were the exciting, high-times adventures he'd shared earlier. Something sharp and uncomfortable nipped at Ray's edges. He ignored it, curious about the history of the man sitting across from him.

"You ready?" Travis asked without looking up. He placed a napkin over his now spotless plate and waved for the waitress to bring their check.

"Nope." Ray held up his hand, palm out, as Travis reached for his wallet. "I've got it."

He pulled a couple of bills from his wallet and dropped them on the table. Before Travis could argue, he quickly added, "For saving me a bundle on Blue out there."

Ray slid out of the booth after Travis and followed him out the door into a warm and breezy afternoon. It was a small town, as far as cities go, but exhaust and heated concrete competed with the fragrant spring flowers and blooming trees that filled the air. His big red Dodge and matching trailer were conveniently parallel parked across the street. A lazy snort echoed from the trailer as Blue waited patiently.

He was just about to step off the curb when someone called out his name. Ray turned around and spotted his lawyer, Henry Cordero, walking briskly up the sidewalk. Henry wore a gray suit, the jacket buttoned tightly across his potbelly, black cowboy boots that always looked like he'd just bought them an hour ago, and a ten-gallon cowboy hat that hid his near completely bald scalp. Sunglasses

disguised permanently bloodshot eyes, and a thick mustache capped his thin mouth.

A young man dressed in a dark blue suit that better fit his tall, lean frame walked confidently at his side. He too wore black cowboy boots, though his actually looked as though they'd kicked around a while. Blond hair was slicked back instead of under a hat. When Ray's gaze met the young man's deep hazel eyes, his stomach clenched. The enchilada he'd eaten contemplated an immediate and inappropriate exit, and a wave of panic threatened to send him running. *Jesus fucking H. Christ.*

"Ray Ford," Henry said as the pair stopped a couple of feet away. *Too late to run now.* "Not often I see you in town."

"Afternoon, Henry," Ray said, his was voice strained and hoarse when he spoke. He caught the sidelong glance Travis shot his way from the corner of his eye but could only handle one thing at a time.

Henry struck out his hand and gave Ray a hearty shake with his too-firm grip and too-soft skin. "I don't think you've met our newest partner at the firm, Landon Graves."

Travis looked from Ray to the two men and back. Ray's skin had paled, and panic flooded off him in heavy waves. Travis looked back at the suits. The older man, Henry, seemed relaxed and genuinely friendly—for a lawyer. The other man, Landon, mirrored Ray in expression and stance. They knew each other. More than acquaintances, Travis ventured, and frowned.

Ray stuttered. "Uh, I-I'm not sure . . . I don't think so."

That was not the serious, self-assured and in control Ray Ford Travis had come to know, and he didn't think he liked it. Ray was stoic, unshakable, unless Travis was the one doing the shaking and shattering of the rancher's iron control.

Landon reached out hesitantly and took Ray's hand in a quick, awkward shake. He nodded once. The younger lawyer seemed as unable to form a cohesive sentence as Ray and didn't attempt to speak.

Landon slanted a measuring glance at Travis, who met it head-on with one of his own. The man was good-looking, a bit taller than he, just as lean, and too young. He couldn't imagine Ray with a suit like him and didn't want to. Travis clamped his jaw tight and ground his teeth. He instantly disliked the younger man for having had what he wanted, what was his.

And Ray was his.

Travis moved subtly closer and slightly behind Ray, sending a clear message to the young lawyer. Landon was no slouch in the silent-language department if the narrowed eyes and hard, challenging stare he shot Travis were any indication. Travis answered with a smug grin. Lines drawn and ground staked.

He'd think on that sudden possessive streak later.

Henry drew Travis's attention by striking his hand out. "Henry Cordero," he said with a slight inflection in his graveled voice.

Travis took his hand in a quick, firm shake and nodded. "Travis Morgan."

Henry inclined his head. "My associate, Landon Graves."

The young lawyer looked like he'd rather chew nails, but cordially took Travis's hand. His skin was hot, and his grip deliberately crushing, sending a message of his own. Travis smiled, ignored the message, and in his most pleasant and sincere voice possible said, "'S'a pleasure, Landon."

Landon's mouth was a hard slash across his attractive, clean-shaven face, his voice clearly forced when he spoke. "Travis."

Oblivious to the silent battle to claim Ray as their own, Henry continued, "How's that beautiful Dottie McCray doing?"

Travis looked to Ray. He could feel him vibrating, agitating the calm afternoon air. A thick muscle ticked in his clenched jaw, but to the unobservant eye the man looked cool as a cucumber. "Great. You know Dot."

A sharp *thud* from the trailer signaled a much needed easy out to end the awkward situation.

"I think that's our cue, Ray," Travis said.

Ray jumped on the opening. "Yes. Sorry, Henry. Got a new stud we need to get out to the ranch and settled."

"Sure, sure." Henry didn't seem at all offended by the subtle brush-off. "Give that Dot a hug for me, will you?"

"Will do," Ray said over his shoulder as he dashed for the truck.

Travis nodded to the men and followed after Ray. He felt the burning heat of Landon's glare on his back and smiled.

"So . . ." Travis began, as they merged onto I-90 West, leaving Billings behind. "You and Landon, eh."

"Shut the fuck up, Morgan."

Travis smiled and settled back into his leather seat for the silent ride home.

CHAPTER 8

Ray leaned back in the well-worn leather office chair and dragged his hands over his face. Stubble scraped under his calloused palms. It had been a long, draining day. Thank fucking Christ it was finally over. He'd run the gauntlet today and really couldn't take one more hit.

"You okay, Raymond?" Dot entered the den, carrying a steaming mug of coffee in each hand.

He cleared his throat and sat up. "Just going over Hollis's weekly report."

She placed a mug on the desk for him, then moved to the leather couch on the other side of the room and sat down. She pulled her legs up and tucked them underneath her.

Ray brought the steaming mug up to his lips and took a sip. Hot liquid with an unmistakable kick burned a pleasurable path down his throat and splashed warmth into his belly. Spanish coffee. *Heaven*. He lifted his cup toward Dot. "Thank you."

She nodded. "Good-looking horse you brought home."

"I think he'll earn his weight in gold come next season."

Dot was silent for a moment before asking casually, "What's up with you and Travis? You've had your back up ever since you returned home."

Ray was used to Dot's habit of jumping topic tracks when she was fishing. It was her bait and switch method of squeezing out what she was really after. But Ray was too spent to play the game with her tonight.

He sipped his coffee and waited. Fiery liquid softened his stressed, jagged edges.

Best way to play the game was to simply sit back and let her start when she was good and ready to get going. It usually didn't take more than a minute or two.

And right on cue . . .

"Do you remember my friend Martha Reeves? She used to spend the summers here with her charming grandson, Gregory?"

Ray nodded. He hadn't heard that name in decades, but Gregory Reeves was not someone he'd ever forget.

Martha and Gregory had come to the ranch every summer as long as Ray could remember. But it wasn't until he'd turned fourteen that he found himself increasingly captivated by their houseguest. Gregory was two years his senior, tall and lanky with messy, surfer blond hair, piercing blue eyes, and a smile that could turn a raging Brahma bull into a gentle lamb. And he was the star of Ray's every wet dream.

Gregory was his first. Had shown him who he really was and confirmed to him what he'd been questioning for a long time—that he was gay. It had been frightening and liberating and exciting.

He was fifteen the last time the Reeves came to visit, but those two summers with Gregory had been the best of his life.

"We've received an invitation to Gregory's wedding."

Ray almost spluttered his coffee. *Wedding*? The boy he remembered was most definitely gay.

Dot regarded him for an unnerving moment before she continued. "Poor boy had to move to Vermont because it isn't legal for him to marry in Michigan."

"What?" Ray choked. Dot had jumped too many tracks at once and lost him, sent him skidding off the embankment. "Since when is marriage illegal?"

A speculative shine glinted in her bright blue eyes as she searched his intently. "You boys seemed so close. Didn't you know Gregory was gay?"

And there it was: the final hit. His entire body locked up, synapses shut down.

Dot may as well have tagged him with a stun gun when she sent him careening over the edge.

Had Dot known Gregory was gay back then? And by default, suspect *he* was too? Cold sweat broke out between his shoulder blades as his system jerkily restarted itself. He reached for his cup with a shaking hand. Slowly took another sip of the coffee to disguise his shock and corral his stampeding thoughts. But mostly, he needed the fortification. He needed the rum straight up. Better yet, a shot of whiskey. Or three. He still had a half-full bottle of Glenlivet in the liquor cabinet, didn't he?

"I'd never suspected." Dot's strong voice reclaimed his scattered attention. "But that's neither here nor there. The young man and his boyfriend of seven years are getting married. Gregory is over the moon and rightfully so. And we've been invited." Her pause was calculated. "Don't you think that's wonderful, Raymond?"

Ray shifted uncomfortably in his seat. It was a yes or no question, but even that seemed too much to process. He opened his mouth, and all that came out of it was a barely audible, husky, "Um . . ."

Dot smiled proudly, like she'd just figured out one of the world's greatest mysteries. He tried to rein in his reactions, keep his outward expressions checked. But that was a difficult task around Dot—also known as the font of the universe—at the best of times.

"I think it's so wonderful that he found his perfect match. Though it's a shame those boys had to uproot their lives and move to another state to make it legal. What the hell right does the government have to dictate who you can marry anyway?"

Ray raised an eyebrow at Dot's cussing. That wasn't something heard very often, and it usually meant someone had better start running—and running fast.

"They need to wake up and let people be. Love is love. Man or woman. What business is it of anyone else's anyway? And don't even get me started on those damn churches. Spreading hate when they're supposed to be spreading love. Bunch of narrow-minded, hypocritical, big—"

"Dot!"

Her back was ramrod straight, feet flat on the ground, skin flushed. Fire blazed in her eyes with an intensity that made Ray sink back into his chair. He rarely saw her riled up. Had no idea she'd

thought that way, with such vehemence. And, quite frankly, it scared the hell out of him.

Dot stood up abruptly and huffed. She smoothed her shirt down, tucked a stray strand of silver hair behind her ear, and shot Ray a piercing stare.

"I'm sure you agree."

Panic exploded in his chest.

She nodded her head in agreement with her silent deduction and gathered their mugs. She gave him a light kiss on the cheek and made her way to the door.

"I'll send back the RSVP tomorrow for all of us."

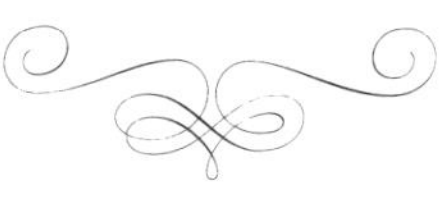

The first thing Travis noticed when he entered the dining room for breakfast was Ray's empty chair—and Dot's far too shrewd eyes on him.

Quickly diverting his attention to the table, Travis said good morning to the men and took his seat between Ross and Jesse. Sam's glares from across the table had become par for the course, but Travis and the rest of the hands simply ignored him. Fortunately Sam had been keeping his comments and opinions to himself. At least at the table.

"Branding's just about done," Jesse said as Travis loaded fluffy scrambled eggs, honey-glazed ham, and crisp hash browns onto his plate. "So maybe tomorrow morning I could come over to the corrals? You could start teaching me?"

Travis couldn't help but smile at the eagerness in Jesse's voice. The kid had been working cattle since he was old enough to command an animal ten times his size, but what he really wanted to do was train horses. Ray had offered to teach him, but with roundup and branding always short of hands, there'd never been a good opportunity. By the time Jesse was free to start, the training was done, most of the herd sold, and the working horses they stabled over winter were already seasoned.

"Said I would, didn't I?" Travis drawled.

Jesse hooted a quiet "sweet," drawing a hard, flinty stare from his dad.

Travis's attention was drawn back to the empty chair at the other end of the table almost against his will. Like passing by an accident he didn't want to see but couldn't stop from craning his neck to look anyway.

Voices around the table faded into the background as Travis's mind wandered. He wanted to know where Ray was, but damn if he was going to ask. The man not being there bothered him. And why that bothered him he didn't care to examine. Yes, he liked Ray. Yes, he wanted Ray. Who wouldn't? The man was sexy as hell. But he wasn't staying. Couldn't. Anything beyond physical enjoyment didn't matter.

Yet it did.

Travis wasn't quite sure when it had begun to matter. It might have been after dinner the other night when he'd caught Ray's unguarded, heartfelt smile. That smile had done something to his insides, lifted him somehow. There was warmth and promise and hope in that smile, and for the first time in a long time, Travis had felt like someone cared about *him*. He'd found himself suddenly wanting to do whatever it took to earn that smile again and again, to be worthy of earning it.

Or it might have happened yesterday at lunch when he'd caught Ray staring at his mouth as he ate his burrito. Ray's gaze had been riveted to every small movement. And when he'd raised those deep brown eyes to meet Travis's, they were dark chocolate flashing with lust and desire so intense he'd felt electricity spike between them. The hair on his arms had stood up. His cock had grown painfully hard. And he'd thought Ray was damn near going to climb over the table when he'd teased him by sucking the salsa off his thumb.

But it was for sure after lunch when emotions long since dormant had flared to life with roaring force. When Landon had silently challenged him. And that was one challenge Travis Morgan was not about to step down from.

Shit. He was becoming too attached to the sexy rancher. No. Strike that. He was already too attached.

Fear tap-danced across his chest. He didn't do attachments. Not to anyone or anything. He knew all too well what lay down that road.

He couldn't stay on at Ford Creek any longer. But as much as he needed to leave, he wanted to stay more.

Fucking hell.

A nudge against his shoulder pulled him out of his reverie.

"Where'd you go, man?" Jesse asked.

"What? Nowhere." Travis made the mistake of glancing at the empty chair again, catching Dot's watchful eye.

"You zoned right out. Didn't hear a word I said, did you?"

Travis snapped. "Of course I did."

He immediately regretted the whip-snap tone of his voice and inhaled deeply. The kid didn't deserve taking the brunt of Travis's frustration, but Ray wouldn't leave his head. All he'd wanted was a damned fling, some mutual hot sex. No strings, no emotions, no regrets. They hadn't even kissed yet, hardly even touched, and he was already screwed.

"Seriously, Trav." Jesse leaned closer and whispered in a conspiratorial tone. "If you got something on your mind, you can talk to me. Right?"

Travis nodded and with a calmer tone said, "You best get to branding them cattle if you want a training lesson."

Travis stood up from the table and carried his dirty dishes to the trolley. The last thing he wanted to talk to anyone about was how deep Ray Ford was getting under his skin. And how much that scared the shit out of him. He dropped his dishes into the tub and turned to leave.

"Travis," Dot called after him. "Why don't you help me clean up here?"

Travis stopped stock-still halfway across the room. It took him a few seconds to register what Dot had said. The first time he didn't offer, and now she wanted his help? Or was it because she was too damned observant and had something to say, something he likely didn't want to hear?

He mentally sighed and turned back.

"Sorry, Dot," he apologized. "Yes, of course. Let me help."

She smiled that I-know-what-you're-up-to smile of hers and nodded.

Travis hung back and stacked plates and silverware on the trolley as the men cleared out, ignoring the death stare Sam leveled at him as he dropped his dishes carelessly into the tub. With the last of the men gone, Travis and Dot finished clearing off the table in companionable silence. Dot tossed him a damp cloth, and they wiped down the dark wood beginning at opposite ends. When they met in the middle, she spoke in her motherly tone he'd become familiar with. "It's been nice having you here, Travis."

"Thank you, Dot. I've enjoyed being here."

"Sure would be nice if you stayed on. I'd like that."

I'd like that too. "I don't know, Dottie. I'm not much for planting roots."

She didn't say anything in response as they made their way into the kitchen, Travis pushing the cart. He rinsed the dishes in the sink and handed them to Dot, which she then loaded into the industrial-sized dishwasher in an orderly fashion. Their rhythm was as smooth and practiced as if they'd been working side by side for years.

Everything was too comfortable here. Too *right.* Not even a fucking week and already it was going to be painful to leave.

"Ray was up and off before the sun to run fences on the north range," Dot offered, seeming to know his unasked question. Travis only nodded in response, afraid that anything he said would come out wrong. Not many people could tie his tongue up like she could.

When they were done with the dishes, Dot turned and regarded him with that shrewd, intense gaze of hers. The one that always made him feel naked and exposed.

"You'd be good for each other."

Everything inside Travis screeched to a crashing halt. It was all he could do to keep his jaw from hitting the blue-and-white-checked linoleum floor. But he had a feeling the cartoon character eyes-popping-out-of-his-head thing was a dead giveaway.

Bright light flashed in Dot's eyes, and she graced him with a warm smile. "Don't you have some horses in need of training, young man?"

When Travis didn't respond, couldn't respond, she chuckled and gave him a gentle shove toward the door. "Off you go, son."

What the hell . . . Travis made his way to the corrals in a mild stupor. He'd known Dot was too damned sharp for her own good. Known if he let his guard slip, even a fraction, she'd find him out. And it seemed she did. Fortunately, it seemed she not only approved of her discovery, but also encouraged it.

Fear eased and something else settled in his chest, something pleasant.

Travis was about to enter the barn to gather his tack when a loud snort and whinny drew his attention. He glanced over his shoulder to see Diablo looking his way, tossing his head.

He grinned and whispered, "Hello, Diablo."

CHAPTER 9

It was approaching the lunch hour when Ray ambled unhurriedly back to the ranch, feeling relaxed. Sweet grass and the sharp scent of first-cut timothy drying in the sun rode the gentle breeze. He'd told Dot he had to run the lines, but he'd ridden out before sunrise for some time alone. Yesterday had been about more than one man could handle in a single day, and he needed the peaceful solace of nature to recharge.

He'd saddled up Rebel, one of his favorite working mounts, and ridden west following a creek that tried to be a river. An hour's ride had him dismounting at a secluded spot shrouded by a copse of Ponderosa pines as the first fingers of daylight splayed out across the waking land. He'd thrown a blanket on the ground and leaned back against a tree, closed his eyes, and listened to the earth's gospel. Morning birds cheerily welcomed the day. Insects buzzed around opening wildflowers. The gurgling creek coaxed his mind into a quiet, unthinking state.

But even that couldn't keep Travis Morgan from his thoughts for long.

Eventually he'd hauled himself up, climbed back in the saddle, and ridden the lines. The fencing Jesse and Clay had repaired was secure, and except for one break that he'd tagged with a red strip of synthetic ribbon, the rest of the lines looked strong. Fortunately, it didn't appear they had a rustling problem, and most of the stray cattle had been recovered. In no hurry to return, he'd taken a turn through the south pasture as well. They'd soon be moving the herd of Black Angus out there for the summer.

Riding in behind the corrals, Ray noticed the round pens were empty. No Travis. And then he immediately berated himself for the

sliver of disappointment that needled inside. Something else caught his attention as he reined Rebel toward the barn. Diablo's corral was empty. Missing horse; missing cowboy. Cold dread pricked his skin. If Travis had tangled with that horse and been injured . . .

The rhythmic beat of hard hooves on soft ground drew him to the indoor arena. He pulled Rebel up when he reached the gate at the open end of the ring.

In the brief moment of blindness that hung in the shift between bright sunlight and dark interior, Ray could make out the silhouette of horse and rider turning into a smooth figure eight at the far end of the ring. Seconds later his eyes adjusted, and his heart stopped.

Travis was astride Diablo.

And the sight was breathtaking.

Travis sat the horse with understated confidence and ease, Diablo well in hand. They moved in perfect synchronicity, Travis's commands so subtle he may as well have been psychically communing with the black stallion. For a moment, Ray couldn't quite believe it was Diablo under saddle. The horse moved with effortless grace through a series of obstacles placed randomly about the ring. He displayed flawless flying lead changes, collected trot and canter, sliding stops. Sleek black coat stretched over solid, sharply defined muscle, sinew and bone, reflecting blue-and-white sparks under the dim arena lights.

Travis held the reins loose in his left hand, right hand splayed on a strong thigh, posture relaxed and languid. There wasn't much more striking than a man who knew how to sit a horse.

Impressive show aside, it didn't change the fact that Ray had specifically told Travis not to go near that horse. And there he was, first chance he got, disobeying a direct order. It was like the man was on a personal mission to rile him up, knock him off-kilter.

Ray remembered all too well what had happened to the few cowboys who'd tangled with that horse in the past: broken bones, punctured lung, stitches, and one cowboy in a three-week coma. That was the last time he'd let anyone near Diablo. Ray shuddered, forcing back images of what could have happened to Travis. Arrogant bastard.

Fear shifted into anger with frightening intensity.

Ray's voice boomed across the arena. "What the fuck do you think you're doing?"

His roar spooked Rebel into a jolting sidestep. Travis and Diablo barely twitched.

The frustrating cowboy glanced over his shoulder. Ray didn't know what affected him more, the sheer joy that lit Travis's handsome face or the blinding magazine-cover smile. Travis reined Diablo his way and casually trotted over.

"Hey, Ray." Travis beamed as they approached. "You weren't kidding about the training. He's a dream."

"Get off that goddamned horse right now, Morgan."

Travis's smile faltered only slightly. "Easy, Ray." His tone was placating, but his eyes were amused. "I figured out what his problem is—"

"I don't give a shit what his problem is. Right now the only problem around here is you."

Travis grinned. "No. Actually, you're the problem."

"What the—" Blood pumped hot and furious through Ray's veins and burned his throat. "You looking to get fired?"

"Listen," Travis continued undeterred. "Those other men who tried to work with him, were you near?"

Goddamn if the man wasn't pulling a Dot tactic with the track-jumping thing.

"What that hell does that have to do with anything?" Ray barked.

"Were you?"

"Of course!" Ray threw his free hand in the air.

"Well, there you go." Travis nodded, looking quite pleased with himself. "Diablo thinks you're part of his herd and saw those men as a threat. Damn horse has been protecting you."

Ray opened his mouth and snapped it shut with a shake of his head. How did he get from frustrated and angry to dumbfounded and mute in the space of a breath?

"Do you have any idea how amazing this horse is? You know what you've got here, don't you?"

"That doesn't change the fact that I specifically told you to stay away from him."

Travis regarded him for a long moment. The animated light in his green eyes dimmed as though just now realizing Ray was well and truly pissed. And Ray would not let the loss of that shining amazement derail him.

"Why are you so bent out of shape? You know this is what I do. It's what you hired me on for. I'm the best there is. And the only way to test my theory on Diablo was without you present."

The smooth, controlled tone of Travis's deep voice only increased the sharp edge in Ray's. "That's beside the point."

"Is it?"

"Dammit, Morgan. Diablo is unpredictable. Volatile."

"In case you failed to notice, *Ford*"—Travis paused to take a breath before continuing—"I'm a grown man. I've spent my whole life with these animals. I know what I can and can't handle. And I can handle this one just fine."

Travis was right. Ray couldn't discount that Travis knew exactly what he was doing. And obviously, the man was fine. Better than fine, actually. Diablo was completely under his control.

The anger he'd been riding began to ebb; the bitter taste of fear lingered in his mouth.

Ray's voice was lower and a touch hoarse when he said, "You could've been hurt or worse. And there's no one around to help if you were."

A weighted silence fell between them. Lowing cattle and indistinguishable male voices echoed in the distance. Flies buzzed in the lazy midday heat. Diablo stamped a foot and snorted. Rebel swished his tail. The atmosphere shifted. Travis's eyes darkened, his expression turning serious. The sun suddenly felt hotter on Ray's back.

"Is that what you're concerned about, Ray?" His voice was low, seductive. "Not mad that I went against your orders but worried I could've been hurt?"

Heat rushed up Ray's neck, he clamped his jaw tight and pressed his lips into a flat line. What the fuck was he doing?

"Would serve you right if you were," he snapped.

Travis flashed that captivating smile of his, and Ray's whole body coiled tight. He didn't want to feel the things Travis made him feel.

Didn't want to want what the man offered. The problem was he did, and it was getting harder to remember why he shouldn't.

"I'm going to put Rebel away." He reined the chestnut gelding for the barn. "Diablo had better be unsaddled and in his corral when I get back."

Ray couldn't release the tension that vibrated dangerously through his limbs. Not wisely anyway. One minute he wanted to hit Travis, and the next he wanted to strip him down, wrap himself around that long, powerful body, and sink in deep.

But he couldn't. He had no doubt the sex would be amazing, maybe even worth the potential risk, but nothing would come of them. Nothing could. It wasn't like the nomadic cowboy would stick around. Not that Ray wanted him to. Really.

Ray cursed as he dismounted Rebel and cross-tied him in the hall outside the tack room. He unbuckled the cinch and flank straps, and slid the saddle and sweaty blanket from Rebel's back. He carried the saddle into the tack room and slammed it down on its assigned rack.

"Fuck."

He went to the tack locker and grabbed a brush, curry comb, and hoof pick. He'd call Landon. Call him right after lunch, maybe before. Landon could work off this sharp edge and get Ray back on an even keel.

He turned around and crashed into a solid wall. Air whooshed out of his lungs; the hoof pick fell from his grasp and clattered loudly to the concrete floor. So completely focused inward, he hadn't realized Travis had entered the tack room, let alone stood right behind him.

Ray staggered back a step, but Travis didn't move, his eyes darkly intense.

"Sorry, Ray. Didn't mean to spook you." The trace of amusement underlining his words belied that sentiment.

"No, no. It's . . ." Ray shook his head, looked to the door, and moved to step around Travis. The crowded room was growing smaller by the second. Walls were closing in, the air thick and stifling. He

had to get out. He stepped to the left, and Travis mirrored his move, blocking his way. Ray shifted to the right, and again Travis followed.

Ray released a frustrated sigh. "I'm not doing this dance."

Neither man moved. And Ray made the mistake of looking up into Travis's gaze. The fire in those mesmerizing eyes welded his feet to the ground—and then it was too late. All the worry and anger he'd felt washed away in a flood of desire that carried him helplessly downstream.

He wanted to fight the currents. He wanted to ride the waves.

Travis took a tentative half step forward, and Ray didn't retreat, couldn't move. Travis was the green-eyed cobra, and he was the fatally entranced prey.

Heat poured off Travis in dense, erotic waves. Scents he'd begun to associate with the cowboy—cedar leaf and ginger and wood smoke—mingled with leather, horseflesh, and witch hazel. The combination sent a depth charge of lust straight to Ray's cock.

Travis took another half step, invading Ray's space, filling his vision. Too close. Too far. The atmosphere crackled, the room disappeared, and Ray was wrapped inside Travis's ethereal cocoon again. His skin tingled, pulse pounded heavily in his eardrums, heart stampeded in his chest like a herd of runaway cattle.

Travis placed his hand lightly on Ray's hip. An electric jolt skittered up his spine. Still he couldn't move, couldn't break the trance, couldn't stop the telling shudder he knew Travis wouldn't have missed.

"Tell me what you want." That deep, sonorous voice drawled pure sex.

Ray hadn't noticed where Travis's other hand was until the pad of a calloused fingertip lightly traced the line of his jaw. Ray ground his molars together, fighting the urge to moan, to lean into the man.

"Don't." His voice was husky, nearly inaudible.

"Don't what?" Travis asked, so close now his breath ghosted warm and moist over Ray's cheek. "Don't stop? Is that what you're saying?"

No. Yes. Oh, God. Ray closed his eyes. Fear of repercussion fought a bloody battle with desire. And he was losing sight of which side he was fighting for.

Two warm, strong hands cupped Ray's face, and his eyes snapped open. Travis leaned in, his gaze predatory, and slanted his head. Ray's lips parted.

"Take what you want," Travis whispered into Ray's mouth with a featherlight brush against his lips. And all Ray could do was inhale. He sucked Travis's intoxicating essence deep into his lungs and held his breath. He didn't want to exhale, didn't want to let go, just wanted to breathe Travis.

"Ray . . ." That one single drawn-out syllable, a raw plea heavy with need, snapped Ray's resolve. Brushes clattered to the ground unnoticed as Ray fisted his hands in Travis's shirt and shoved him hard against the lockers. Travis's hat fell and joined the party of disregarded items at their feet. Ray reached a hand behind Travis's neck, pulled his head down, and claimed his lips in an aggressive and desperate, openmouthed kiss.

And Lord, have mercy.

Lips firm and soft as silk, that had haunted his dreams since he'd first seen them in the rearview mirror of his pickup, tasted so . . . felt so . . . he didn't know, didn't care, just needed. Needed the feel of them under his own, moving with him, giving and taking in equal measure. Whiskered chins scraped together erotically, teeth clashed. Then Travis's tongue slid boldly into Ray's mouth—explored, tasted, teased. Travis moaned and sent Ray's every nerve ending aflame. But it wasn't enough. It would never be enough.

Travis shifted, and Ray fell into the full length of that lean, strong body, each with a leg between the other. Travis's hands gripped Ray's ass and pulled him in tight. Thighs and hips and cocks and chests pressed hard against each other. Travis lifted his knee, and Ray groaned deep in his throat, the pressure under his balls nearly too intense. Ray rocked his hips into Travis, sliding over the rock-solid erection trapped behind restricting denim.

Ray reached for Travis's jeans, yanked the top button open—

A metal pail hit concrete and clanged sharply in the barn hallway. Hollis's gruff curse followed, and reality came crashing down with bruising force.

Ray wrenched himself from Travis's embrace and stumbled backward. The corner of a saddle rack jabbed sharply into his shoulder blade, unnoticed. Ray stared at Travis, the dangerous cowboy whose dark expression was unreadable, breath coming in harsh, rapid huffs.

Ray's heart pounded out of control for an entirely different reason now. He cursed under his breath and spun on his heel. He stormed from the tack room, barely avoiding colliding with a bewildered Hollis. Ray didn't acknowledge his foreman, didn't look, didn't stop. From far away he heard the man's voice, registered concern in the tone, but couldn't decipher the words.

"And groom that goddamn horse!" Ray yelled without looking back.

CHAPTER 10

Ray's worn boot heels struck hard-packed earth with enough force to send shock waves reverberating up his legs as he stormed from the barn.

He'd been a heartbeat away from bending Travis over a saddle and had almost been caught with his pants down. Literally. He'd come far too close to destroying his reputation, the ranch's reputation, everything his family had spent decades building. His life. Travis would be nothing more than a fling. Gone with the wind in a couple of months, a distant hollow memory.

And he'd thought the man was dangerous? What a joke. Travis Morgan was downright treacherous.

The terrifying thing was, a part of him didn't care. He'd jumped that fence, and now he wanted to ride that wild horse into the sunset.

Ray clenched his hands into tight, bone-snapping fists.

There was no way he could go back out to the corrals and train alongside the too-goddamn-sexy cowboy today. Not without remembering how that solid body had felt against his. No way he could sit at the dinner table tonight and look into that sublime face and those magnetic green eyes that had controlled him. No way he could watch those entrancing lips move without wanting to feel them against his mouth again. Kiss and lick and taste every inch of the man they belonged to.

Oh God, he was in so much trouble.

He felt like a walking stick of dynamite. Had to get off the ranch before his wick burned to its base. Had to get to Billings and douse this bonfire.

And just because it pours when it rains, Dot was sitting in a chair on the porch as Ray approached the house, watching him intently. He sighed a silent curse. Too late to hide his anger now.

"You look mad as a peeled rattler, Raymond," she said, concern and amusement dancing in her bright eyes. "What's got in your craw?"

The dull thud of boot heels approaching from behind had Ray straightening his spine in automatic response. He didn't have to look over his shoulder to know who owned that long, sure stride.

Dot looked past him to the advancing man, then back to Ray with narrowed eyes, her shrewd gaze not missing a beat. Ray ground his teeth hard enough to crack his jawbone. He strode past Dot without a word, yanked the front door open, and charged into the house straight to the phone in his den.

After arranging to meet Landon, Ray threw a change of clothes, lube, and a whole box of condoms into a duffel bag before making his way back through the house. He'd deliberately waited until Travis had returned to the corrals so he could make a clean break. No such luck. Travis was gone, but Dot had come inside and was now sitting in the living room on an oversize leather chair that almost swallowed her whole. He barely suppressed a groan as he put his head down and made a futile attempt at escaping the "Dot McCray Inquisition."

"What's going on, Raymond?" she asked in her soft, motherly tone. "You boys have some sort of spat?"

The implication grated. Ray stopped halfway across the room, eyes locked on the front door, and counted to ten when five wouldn't do. "It's nothing, Dot."

"Really? So 'nothing' that you're dashing for the door with a packed bag and won't look me in the eye?"

He sighed and turned to face her. "Just a difference of opinion is all." It was a struggle to keep his expression flat and voice level, even though he knew he could never truly fool her. "Like I said, nothing to worry about."

"Where you running off to in such a hurry then?"

"Business in Billings."

Dot studied him a moment, brilliant blue eyes dancing. "That so?"

Ray steeled himself under her scrutiny. He knew she wasn't buying it, not for a second, but whatever he said right now would come out too hot. He was too riled to keep his words in check. *Dammit*, he needed to get out of there.

"Be home for dinner?"

"Don't think so."

Dot nodded. She picked up her glass of lemonade from the companion table and rose from the chair.

"It'll get better when you boys accept what's right in front of you." She smiled and left the room, leaving Ray to stew in his warring desire and denial.

CHAPTER 11

"About fucking time," Ray snarled, crossing the room in three long strides.

He yanked the motel door open before the soft *rap-rap-rap* on the other side had stopped. A surprised Landon Graves stood outside in the dying light of an early spring day. Having come straight from work, he was dressed in an expensive-looking steel gray suit with a light gray shirt and deep plum-colored silk tie. His eyebrows shot up comically when Ray grabbed the tie and hauled him roughly inside like a roped steer. Ray might have laughed if he hadn't already downed four glasses of whiskey while waiting for Landon to arrive. If he weren't dead serious about killing the serrated knife-edge Travis had him riding.

Ray kicked the door shut with his boot heel, wound his fist around Landon's tie, and pulled the man's head down. His mouth slammed into Landon's in a hard, angry kiss. A kiss meant to purge and cleanse, erase and forget.

The lips beneath Ray's were firm and soft, but not quite as full. They moved with him, following his lead, but they didn't challenge, didn't battle for control. The tongue that met his, while not timid, wasn't demanding. It didn't taste quite right, wasn't the flavor of sunlight and sweet feed his body suddenly craved.

After a brief second of stunned hesitation, Landon responded with a long moan. And that wasn't right either, the sound not deep nor resonant enough.

Ray broke the kiss abruptly. He loosed his hand from Landon's tie and stumbled back a step from his longtime lover.

"Shit." He ran a hand through his short hair. "Sorry, didn't mean to come on so strong."

Landon tugged off the tie. "Actually, Ray, I think I liked it." Bewilderment laced Landon's short laugh. "But I think I'd like it more with less clothing."

Landon tossed the tie to the chair by the door, slid the jacket off his broad shoulders, and began unbuttoning the shirt.

Ray felt an odd sort of disconnect as he watched Landon undress. They'd been meeting in secret, having great sex for nearly two years, but he'd never really *looked* at his young lover. Not close. Not deep. They gave each other only what they needed, and that was enough. Though Ray knew Landon wanted more. He wanted a relationship in the true sense, one he didn't have to hide—one Ray could never give him.

"Going to join me, cowboy?" Landon asked in a dulcet voice.

Shirt added to the pile of clothing building up on the chair, Landon's bare chest was lean, skin pale under the weak lighting of the motel room. Broad shoulders tapered into a narrow waist. Long legs had Landon standing a couple of inches taller than Travis—taller but not bigger.

Landon's eyes were more hazel than green—open and expressive, withholding no secrets. His face was smooth-skinned, features classically handsome whereas Travis was rugged and wore life's experiences in the fine creases around his eyes and mouth.

Ray knew what he'd be getting with Landon. He knew that although Landon wasn't an aggressive lover, he was generous and endlessly creative. But heaven above, even having not yet fully experienced Travis, Landon didn't match up.

Travis, Travis, Travis. Goddamned Travis Morgan. Even here with a willing body ready for him, wanting him, the cowboy wouldn't leave him alone.

"Yeah," Ray said as he tore at the buttons, opening his shirt but not shrugging out of it. He reached for the button of his jeans as Landon stepped out of slacks that had pooled at his feet. His erection jutted eagerly from his groin. Ray closed the distance, grabbed Landon by the hips, spun him around, and shoved him face-first onto the bed.

Landon grunted something Ray didn't catch as he climbed up on the bed and knelt between Landon's spread legs. He tugged his

zipper down, freeing his semierect cock, then fell forward and covered Landon's body. The man under him was warm and firm, but not solid. A white-collar physique created and maintained in a gym, not one carved by hard living and working the land. Still strong, but not powerful. Not Travis.

Unblemished pale skin smelled of rainwater and mint that for some reason made Ray think of summer picnics. Pleasant, but not enough to overpower the lingering trace of cedar leaf, ginger, and wood smoke that still clung to his clothing, his skin. Not enough to overpower Travis.

Fucking Travis.

And God help him, that's exactly what he wanted to be doing right now.

With a curse, Ray pushed himself off Landon and stalked across the room. He zipped up his jeans—no point in leaving them open—and reached for the half-full bottle of Glenlivet sitting on the faux-oak dresser. He grabbed the empty glass beside the bottle, poured himself a three-finger shot, and downed it in one swallow. Liquid fire blazed a path to his stomach, dulling the sharp edges. He winced.

"It's him, isn't it." Not a question. "That cowboy. Travis."

"Hell no!" Ray snapped. He frowned at the defensive tone of his voice, promptly dismissed it, and poured another hearty shot.

"I saw the way you looked at each other yesterday," Landon said, a touch of sadness underlying his soft voice.

Landon was a good man. He deserved someone who would treat him right, be proud to walk down the street at his side, give him what he so clearly wanted. But as much as Ray cared about him, and he did, he just wasn't that man.

He checked his tone but didn't turn around. "Don't go there, Landon. We both know this was only ever going to be about sex."

"I don't know the story between you two, of course, but it's plain to see it's about more than just sex."

"Not true."

"Really? Then why are we sitting here talking about it instead of having it?"

Ray opened his mouth to refute, but his vocal chords flatlined. He peered into the glass in his hand, searching for the words he'd lost. Tiny diamonds winked and danced in the amber liquid, promising temporary oblivion instead of wisdom—and a raging hangover come morning.

"You won't drown him in alcohol or forget him in another man's bed," Landon said close behind Ray. "Not even in mine."

Defeat pressed down on Ray's body like a cement blanket. His limbs felt heavy and cumbersome. He couldn't deny the truth. Couldn't deny that he was falling for a man he couldn't have.

Warm hands rested lightly on his shoulders, and then Landon's voice was quiet in his ear. "Don't drive tonight." The hands squeezed once, then fell away. "Good-bye, Ray."

Distantly Ray was aware Landon had just ended their relationship. Or perhaps it was he. The door clicked shut, and Ray turned around to face an empty room.

There went Tornado Morgan's first victim.

"Shit."

Ray sat down hard on the edge of the bed and polished off his whiskey. Even when not present, Travis Morgan was an annoyingly persistent man. There'd be no forgetting him in drink or casual sex tonight. Probably never be anything to make him forget the one man he wanted more than he'd ever thought possible.

Travis couldn't focus. He glanced over his shoulder, again, at the empty round pen. Ray had yet to return from wherever he'd torn off to yesterday afternoon, after things had got a little hot and heavy in the tack room.

After they'd almost had sex.

Travis knew he was pushing Ray when he'd followed him. Knew what Ray risked, what they both risked. But damn, the man was an irresistible force when he got all riled up. He radiated a power and passion that had Travis's body shaking with excitement in response.

And those incredibly expressive eyes, darkened to a rich espresso, had scalded his skin.

He hadn't been disappointed when Ray snapped and slammed him up against the lockers. Kissed him with such intensity, Travis had forgotten to breathe. Every nerve ending had caught fire. And holy hell, he'd nearly come in his jeans right then.

He could still taste the lingering cinnamon on his tongue.

"Hey, Trav," Jesse called out, jarring Travis from his erotic reverie of the tantalizing Ray Ford. "I'm free the rest of the afternoon if you want to start training."

"Good." *I need the distraction.* "Have some men herd half a dozen steer into the ring for us. I'll bring a couple horses over."

Travis selected two just-broke horses—Little Red, the bold and willing red dun mare he'd taken a shine to, and Wiley Dog, the high-strung buckskin that continued to test him. The mare would be a good mount to start the kid on. She was one of those horses that practically trained themselves.

"You're on Red, here," Travis said as he joined Jesse in the ring. "We'll do dry groundwork first. Then if things go smoothly, we'll see how she takes to the cattle."

Travis gave Jesse a few basic pointers as they tacked up; then he mounted up and sat comfortably in the saddle while he observed and instructed. The kid was good, and Little Red was a quick study. It was a bit of a cheat starting Jesse on her, but he needed a confident grasp on the basics before he started working a horse with an attitude like Wiley.

"She's good on the right turns, but she's not listening to you on the left. You need to get her off your leg. Give her a little spur and keep her shoulder straight, nose in."

Jesse tried to get the mare into a loose turn, but she still resisted on that side.

"Right toe forward, left foot behind the cinch, heel in," Travis instructed. "Keep your knee pressure firm."

Jesse huffed. "That's what I'm doing."

Travis rode over and dismounted, passing his reins to the kid to hold Wiley while he demonstrated. He walked around to the mare's

right side, sliding his hand over her rump as he went. "Here," he said as he positioned Jesse's foot, toe in and forward, tapping Red's elbow. Then he moved around to the left and positioned the other foot, heel in toward the horse's barrel. "And here."

Then he placed his hand on Jesse's lower leg and pressed it against Red's side. She moved off his leg immediately.

"There. That's what you want, kid."

"Sweet." Jesse smiled and leaned down to rub the mare's neck. "But I wish you'd quit calling me 'kid.' Twenty-two officially makes me an adult, you know."

"Yeah, well. Eleven years my junior means you're always going to be a kid to me." Jesse rolled his eyes, and Travis slapped him on the thigh with a laugh. "Get over it. Kid."

Travis reclaimed Wiley's reins, and as he walked around the buckskin to mount up, he saw Sam Davis standing outside the arena gate. Even from across the ring in dim lighting, Travis could see the rigid stance of the man's body, flushed ruddy cheeks, and killing glare. Travis groaned inwardly. *And the day had been going so well . . .*

Sam yelled furiously, "You get the fuck away from my boy!"

Travis almost shook his head and dismissed the man but knew that would only fuel an irrational fire. One he really didn't feel like putting out.

"And you get the hell out of there, Jesse."

"I'm just learning to train, Dad," Jesse reasoned.

Travis sighed and handed his reins back to Jesse. "Stay here."

"I'm sorry, Trav."

Travis shook his head. "We're good."

He made his way to the gate at a deliberate, leisurely pace and stopped a few feet shy. "You have a problem with Jesse learning to train horses, Sam?"

"Nope, I have a problem with him learning from you." Sam's voice was confrontational, and his steely eyes held violent storms.

Travis spoke without inflection. "And why would that be?"

"You know damned well why."

"No actually, I don't." Travis crossed his arms over his chest.

"I saw your hands on him. Saw you touching my boy."

Travis regarded Sam for a long moment. He didn't want to do this. *Really* didn't want to do this. Without pulling his gaze from Sam, he spoke over his shoulder, "Go back to working Red on her left turns, Jess. I'll be right back."

Travis inclined his head. "Let's step outside so the kid can work."

Travis strode past the angry man and headed for the far corner of the barn. A quick scan of the area told him they were without audience. As he came to a stop, he caught a flash of movement in his peripheral. He ducked reflexively and narrowly missed Sam's sucker punch.

He knew Sam was no match for him, but he was so tired of fighting, so tired of always being put on the defensive, keeping his guard up 24-7. All he wanted to do was to relax and enjoy his life—his way—in peace. Why something so simple and basic continually proved to be so unattainable, he'd never understand.

Undeterred, Sam hauled off and launched a right hook that Travis dodged neatly. The missed contact tipped Sam briefly off-balance, and Travis took advantage of the recovery lag. He spun the man around by his arm, twisting it behind his back, and slammed him up against the hard wood siding of the barn. Travis pushed his weight into the armlock and dug the elbow of his other arm into the back of Sam's neck, effectively immobilizing the irate ranch hand.

"We. Are not. Doing this," Travis ground out, giving Sam a little shove with each clipped sentence.

"Get off me!" Sam struggled in Travis's unyielding grip, his voice just shy of a scream. "You fucking perv—"

"What the hell is going on here?" Ray's voice snapped across the yard like a bullwhip that left Travis's ears ringing. He and Sam both froze on a heartbeat as Ray rounded the barn and strode toward them. Travis cursed under his breath and stepped back, roughly releasing Sam.

"Nothing, Ray." He took off his hat and ran a hand through his hair. As he replaced it, he said with forced nonchalance, "Just settling a difference of opinion."

Ray looked from Travis to Sam and back, his expression shuttered. "Looks like a little more than that from this angle."

While Ray waited in apparent calm for an explanation, Travis studied the rancher for what he was more concerned about—clues to his absence. His eyes were bloodshot, skin drawn and pale under an unshaven face, and his rough voice had a jagged edge, like it had been cut with hard liquor.

So the man had gone and got himself good and drunk last night.

"One of you want to tell me what's really going on here?"

"I'll tell you," Sam spat out with clear disdain while rubbing the back of his neck. He glared daggers at Travis as he leaned down to pick up the hat that had been knocked off his head during their scuffle. "Son of a bitch queer was touching my boy. That's what's going on here."

Other than a slightly raised eyebrow, Ray showed no outward reaction, no signs indicating what was thinking. Travis didn't miss the nearly imperceptible tick in the man's jaw, however. Ray wasn't nearly as calm as he projected.

"Had his filthy hand on Jesse's leg." Sam dusted off the hat against his thigh. "And who knows what kind of twisted poison he's filling my kid's head with when I'm not around to protect him."

"I'm not a fucking kid, and I don't need you or anyone else to protect me," Jesse snapped at Sam as he came out of the arena still astride Little Red. His gaze shifted to Ray. "All he's doing is teaching me to train. That's it."

"I know, son," Ray said.

Then Jesse looked back to Sam, pinned him with a forceful stare, and pointedly said, "Travis is my friend."

"You see?" Sam's voice rose. He flapped an arm in Jesse's direction. "He's already infecting my boy."

Both of Ray's eyebrows shot up, surprise clearly evident in his otherwise checked expression. Travis distantly registered the dull thud of nearing hoof beats followed by boot heels hitting the hard ground. Disturbed dust drifted on the breeze and tickled his sinuses. Sam was growing more agitated by the second. Volatile tension radiated off him like a locomotive without brakes on the edge of a long descent. And that was much more concerning than the growing audience.

"Infecting?" Ray repeated. The sharp, hard edge of his voice sent a shiver up Travis's spine. "Are you fucking serious?"

Sam flinched, and his gaze flickered nervously to the hands that had dismounted and discreetly formed a loose horseshoe around them, those still on horseback making up a second line of defense. His jaw worked, but Ray didn't give him a chance to say anything.

"What about Ross and Clay? They're all friends. They sit next to each other at mealtime and hang out after work. Is Travis poisoning them too? And what about me? I work beside the man every fucking day. Am I *infected*?" Ray spat that last word out like someone had dipped his cinnamon sticks in cow shit.

"I don't like him, Ray. He ain't right." Having lost a little of his hard edge, Sam's voice sounded almost petulant. For a second, Travis thought Sam would start stomping his feet like a five-year-old having a temper tantrum.

"You don't have to like him. You don't have to talk to him. Jesus Christ, Sam. You don't even have to work with him." Ray continued in a cutting tone. "The man's here to do a job. Just like you. Simple as that. I don't see how anything else should be a problem for you. Let alone your concern."

"He ain't right," Sam argued weakly.

"So you said. And you're entitled to your opinion. However. Again. I don't see how that affects your job here."

"He's bad for the ranch, Ray." Sam squared his shoulders. "Shouldn't be here."

"The only bad thing for this ranch is your homophobic paranoia," Jesse cut in, his cheeks flushed with anger and embarrassment. "You have no clue about—"

"Don't you backtalk me, boy," Sam threatened as he turned on Jesse with a raised fist. "I'll give you a lesson you won't soon forget."

The sudden aggressive movement startled Red, who jumped sideways and began a prancing dance on the spot.

Flashbacks tore through Travis like an explosion: slivers digging into his back, the painful crack of his nose breaking, and the man he'd once called father threatening to kill him. He'd do everything in

his power to prevent even one more kid from having to go through something like he had.

"You son of a bitch," Travis said to Sam, his voice deathly flat. "You lay one hand on that kid and I swear to God, you'll regret the day you set foot on this earth."

Travis took a step forward, but a hand across his chest stopped him. He glanced at Ray, who shook his head once in warning.

"Fucking cocksucker." Sam took that second of distraction to round on him. Travis ducked, but this time Sam's fist was faster than his reflexes and clipped the edge of his jaw. The horseshoe guard broke rank, and Ross and Clay quickly restrained a raging Sam, who spouted off a string curses and inflammatory slurs.

Ray stepped forward, putting himself between them, his back to Travis. It was a protective gesture Travis wasn't sure Ray realized he'd made or how telling it was. He just hoped no one else enjoying this little show was as observant.

"Settle the fuck down, Sam." The fury roiling in the bass notes of Ray's voice was unmistakable, and Sam immediately stopped fighting his hold.

"Where the fuck does he get off telling me how to reprimand my own kid?"

"Sam . . ." The stern warning was clear in Ray's voice.

"I ain't working here with the likes of him, Ray," Sam continued. "Won't fucking do it."

Ray remained still for a long moment facing Sam, then turned an unreadable glance over his shoulder at Travis. For a second, Travis had the fleeting and disappointing thought that Ray was going to fire him. He wouldn't be surprised if that's the way it went. It certainly wouldn't be the first time. What did surprise him was the sharp, stabbing pain in his chest at the prospect of it. He didn't want to leave the ranch, leave Ray. Not yet.

Light flickered briefly in Ray's eyes, and Travis exhaled. If he was reading the man right, he wouldn't be making an early exit from Ford Creek Ranch.

"Fine then," Ray said as he turned back to Sam. His voice level and clear. "You don't work here anymore. Come by tomorrow morning to pick up your final paycheck in Hollis's office."

Travis tensed, bracing himself for more violence, as did the rest of the men standing guard. Every one of them had a finger on the trigger. Ross and Clay tightened their hold on Sam. But the man's only visible reaction was the blood that rushed to his face in a frightening flush. The now ex-hand stood rigid, as though his brain was still processing how he'd suddenly ended up out of a job. Travis could feel the fury thrumming off the man's body as he bore holes through Ray.

"You're firing *me*? Over *him*? A fucking faggot?" Sam asked incredulously, like it was the most mind-blowing thing the man had ever heard.

"No. I'm firing you for your belligerent attitude and fighting on my ranch."

Sam clenched his fists. His gaze drifted over the small crowd looking for backup but clearly finding none.

"We're done here. Leave quietly, now, or you'll find yourself with an escort off my property," Ray said.

"Fine," Sam snapped and shrugged angrily at the hands holding him. Ray nodded, and the men let go but didn't step out of reach.

Sam looked over Ray's shoulder at Travis. "You're going to pay for this. Mark my words."

"Enough, Sam," Ray barked.

Sam turned his furious gaze back on Ray, then spit on the ground, just missing his boots before he spun around.

"Get off that horse, Jesse," he ordered as he began walking away. "We're leaving."

"No."

Sam stopped dead in his tracks and spun around. "What did you say to me, boy?" His voice was frighteningly flat.

"I said no," Jesse repeated defiantly. "You got fired. I didn't. I have a job here, and I'm staying." He glanced nervously at Ray, who gave an assuring nod, then back to his dad and sat a little taller in the saddle.

Sam turned a homicidal stare back on Travis. The message was clear, and Travis would be ready. He would not back down from the likes of the Sam Davises in this world.

Without another word, Sam turned on his heel and stormed across the yard to his truck. When the rusted pickup had charged

down the long driveway in a cloud of dust and its chugging engine faded into the distance, Ray turned back to the crowd that had formed.

"Anyone else have an issue here with how I run my ranch or who I employ?"

Every head shook.

"Right. Y'all get back to work now."

As the men cleared out, Travis found himself rooted to the ground, facing Ray for what felt like hours. Ray had just put himself on the line for Travis, and the gravity of that action wasn't lost on him.

"Jaw okay?" Ray asked.

"Yep."

The shutters lifted, and those warm, soulful brown eyes that Travis was coming to love looking into burned a smoldering path straight to his groin. Ray nodded once, then turned and walked back across the yard to the house.

CHAPTER 12

Two seats remained empty as Ray and Dot sat down at a rather subdued table for breakfast the next morning. Ray forced back the disappointed sigh building in his lungs. He'd hoped Sam would have let Jesse come back to work. He shouldn't have to pay for Sam's issues, and Ray couldn't help but feel responsible for it. He was the one who'd fired Jesse's dad, after all.

Ray heard the front door close as he began loading up his plate. All heads turned when Jesse walked into the dining room with his head down. He'd taken off his hat but was still wearing a pair of mirrored sunglasses. He mumbled an apology for being late and pulled up a chair beside Travis. Jesse's hair was mussed like he'd just crawled out of bed, and his shirt was rumpled. The same shirt he'd been wearing yesterday. A bad feeling slithered through Ray's chest.

"No hats, boots, or glasses at the table, son," Dot said. "You know the rules."

"Yes, ma'am." Jesse's quiet voice was ragged. He carefully removed his sunglasses, neatly folded them, and hung them in the V of his shirt. He didn't look up, didn't make eye contact with anyone, and Ray saw why all the way from the other end of the table.

There were so many gasps around the room, it sounded as if the walls themselves had heaved in dismay. Jesse's right eye was swollen shut, and the socket and cheekbone sported painfully angry shades of blue, purple, and black.

"Jesus fucking Christ." Travis's deep voice reverberated through the floorboards like an earthquake. The fork he'd been holding fell from his hand and clanked loudly against his plate. "Did Sam fucking do that?"

Cold fury laced Travis's voice like barbed wire and shocked Ray. The depth of anger in that usually smooth baritone was something he'd never have expected from the carefree drifter.

"Travis," Ray said calmly, the same tone he'd use on a skittish horse. "Settle down."

Travis didn't even acknowledge that Ray had spoken. His gaze was fixed on Jesse, his lean body beginning to vibrate.

"Don't worry about it, Trav," Jesse said quietly. "I'm good."

"The hell you are." Travis jumped from the table. "I'm going to teach that son of a bitch a lesson."

"I'm coming with you." Clay slid his chair back and rose.

"Travis," Ray barked loud enough to break through the dark tunnel Travis had begun to slide down. Travis spun his head around and shot a livid glare at Ray. Under any other circumstances Ray may have responded to the challenge in kind, but he saw something swim alongside the frenetic anger in Travis's eyes that held him back. Pain.

"You know he did this to the kid, Ray," Travis said tightly. His voice and body trembled under his tenuous restraint. "I'm not about to sit by and let him get away with it."

"No, you're just going to make things worse. Antagonizing Sam is only going to put Jess in further danger, and I won't have it."

"I don't give a shit," Travis threw back. "I'm done putting up with people like that."

"Fine," Ray conceded. "But you're not buying trouble while you're on my ranch. You'll follow my rules or clear out."

"Fuck your rules, Ra—"

"That's enough!" Dot's voice was a sharp, ear-piercing crack of lightning that rendered the room suddenly mute and froze the air in every man's lungs. The grandfather clock's peaceful *tick-tock* continued its steady rhythm, oblivious and undisturbed.

"Travis Morgan, you sit your butt back down in that chair right now," Dot commanded forcefully. "You too, Clay Fisher."

Clay plopped down like his legs had been shot out from under him and then bowed his head. Travis stood for a second longer; his hands clenched in tight fists. The muscles in his jaw ticked while a

nuclear inferno raged in his eyes. He lowered himself slowly to the chair with obvious force.

"Now." Dot looked around the room, making eye contact with each man. "No one is going off on any half-cocked mission to 'kick Sam's ass.' Raymond and I will discuss what happened and how to handle it rationally and privately with Jesse. And there will not be any more swearing at my goddamn table. Are we understood?"

Clay nodded, but Travis remained still as a statue, his gaze now fixed on the breakfast plate before him.

When it appeared Dot had the room under control, albeit tenuously, she turned her attention to Jesse, her tone now soft and motherly. "Are you going to leave home, son?"

"Yes, Miss Dottie." Jesse's gaze remained fixed on a spot on the table as he spoke. "I left right...right after. I-I told him I was going to move to the ranch. Move in with Clay." He shot a quick nervous glance at his friend. "If that's okay."

"Don't even have to ask, dude," Clay assured. "You know I got your back."

"Good," Dot said. "Except you're not moving into Clay's cabin. It's too small."

"We'll get a bunk bed for them," Ray said.

"Nonsense. You'll move in here, young man. We have plenty of room."

"Oh, no. I couldn't do that, Miss Dottie," Jesse said with another quick glance up.

"You can and you will, and that's final." Dot's voice was firm. And anyone with any brains knew better than to argue when she was in control. Facing down a stampeding herd of elephants would be easier. "Clay, honey, you take a truck and go pick up Jesse's things when you're done your with breakfast. And stay clear of Sam."

"Yes, ma'am."

"All right then," Dot said as she glanced around the table and waved her hand. "Y'all finish your meal while it's still warm. We have a ranch to run here."

Ray watched as the men returned to their meals before his gaze landed on Travis. He hadn't spoken since Dot ordered him to sit

down—he'd barely moved—and now sat staring distantly at his half-eaten breakfast. His body was still tightly coiled, jaw set hard, and the thick jugular vein in his neck pulsed a rapid tattoo. Ray couldn't see Travis's hands under the table but had no doubt they were still clenched in knuckle-whitening fists.

Travis cleared his throat and pushed away from the table.

"If you'll excuse me," he said to no one in particular. "I have a busy day ahead." He picked up his plate, remaining food untouched, and dropped it on the trolley as he made a hasty exit.

Ray had a feeling he was going to find something broken out there in Travis's wake and decided to give him a little time to vent before he went to work.

"I'm so sorry," Jesse said when the room once again fell silent. "I shouldn't have come back."

"Don't you dare, young man," Dot admonished. "You did the right thing. You have absolutely nothing to apologize for, and you're staying right here."

"Yeah, dude," Clay agreed.

With a sigh, Jesse went back to his breakfast, and Dot leveled a knowing look at Ray. He nodded his understanding. They'd all need to watch out for Jesse—and keep Travis in check—until Sam got over it and moved on.

Ray took his time leaving the house, and when he did make his way out, he found Travis working with a new horse. Fortunately nothing was broken, but Travis wasn't getting anywhere with the animal.

"Why don't you call it a day, Travis," Ray called over after a couple of hours. "Looks like you could use a break."

"Nope. Need to work." Travis didn't turn around. His voice was flat and emotionless.

Ray watched the man for a few minutes, trying to figure out what was going on in his head. Obviously the situation with Jesse was bothering him. But it bothered Ray too. Not to the point of vigilante violence, but still, Travis wasn't the only one pissed off. The whole ranch was pissed. Jesse was like a kid brother, and the first reaction he'd had was the same as Travis's, though Ray wasn't so quick to action.

And then an unwelcome thought skimmed over the surface of Ray's mind. What if Jesse and Travis were more than just friends? Anger and jealousy rose in the back of his throat, and he quickly swallowed the sharp bitterness back. No, he would not let himself be jealous over a temporary hand, a rambling cowboy. He had no reason. Jesse was just one of those bright, shiny lights in the sky that people instinctively wanted to make sure never dimmed.

"Why don't you stick around the house after dinner and have a beer with us then," Ray offered.

"Sure."

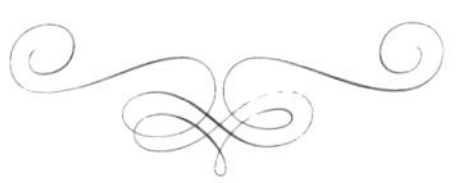

Ray watched Travis surreptitiously as the three men sat in the living room nursing their beers after dinner. Ray and Jesse were sitting at opposite ends of the large leather couch, and Travis sat on one of the oversize chairs near the front window.

"Dot got you all settled?" Ray asked Jesse, breaking the silence that had fallen after Dot had bid them good night.

Jesse nodded, plucking at the label of his Wild Fly Ale.

"I'm really sorry about this, Ray. Travis." Jesse kept his attention on the label-peeling task as he spoke. "I didn't tell him the truth. Not really. But I did tell him I wouldn't stop working at the ranch. I wouldn't stop being friends with Travis. That's when he hit me"—he paused, then added quietly—"the first time."

Out of the corner of his eye, Ray saw Travis flinch; noticed how tightly he gripped the beer bottle in his hand. If that bottle had been fine crystal, it would have shattered by now.

"I told him I was going to move onto the ranch. Stay with Clay. He went off that I'd been brainwashed by Travis and if I messed with people like him, I'd end up just as twisted. Said he didn't want a 'fucking faggot' son."

Jesse paused, and they both glanced over at Travis. His whole body had begun to vibrate, his mouth was pressed in a hard slash, his lips white, and his nostrils flared. He'd yet to say anything, and his gaze was fixed on the throw rug on the floor in front of the fireplace.

"And I started getting mad," Jesse continued, drawing Ray's attention back. "Told him being gay wasn't catching and what'd he care so much for anyway. Didn't affect him any. He started going off again, saying stupid ugly shit, and I yelled at him to shut up. Told him I was twisted long before I met Travis. That's when he hit me again."

Jesse looked to Ray with fear in his eyes, clearly wanting to say something even though he was terrified to do so. Silently imploring for understanding at what he was about to share. And Ray suddenly knew what was coming. His stomach turned. *Oh shit, no.* How could he have not known?

Jesse squared his shoulders, faced Ray dead-on, and spilled his deepest secret in a rapid rush. "I am, Ray. Gay, I mean. And I hope that won't change you letting me work and live here."

Shame needled its way under Ray's skin. All this time the boy had been working for him and living with a man like Sam, his own father. He knew the kind of fear Jesse lived with, how alone he'd have felt all this time. He thought he knew his men, but clearly he'd failed the one he should have known best. If he'd known, he could have somehow found a way to make it easier for the young man. At least let him know he wasn't alone if he needed someone to talk to, a shoulder to lean on.

Ray dragged a hand over his face and in a cracked voice said, "I am so sorry, Jesse."

Jesse nodded and quickly looked down at his hands but not before Ray caught the liquid flash of disappointment and hurt in the boy's eyes. *Fuck.*

"No, Jesse." Ray reached out and laid a hand on Jesse's shoulder, giving it a small squeeze. "I'm sorry I didn't know. I'm sorry I wasn't there for you, to help you. But believe me, I understand. More than you know."

Jesse's gaze shot up, wary but hopeful. Ray couldn't find it in him to say it out loud, so he nodded intently. Jesse swiped at his eyes with the back of his hand, and then his clear blue eyes shone brightly at Ray, so bright Ray couldn't help smiling. Jesse raised his eyebrows in silent question, and Ray nodded again.

"No. Way."

Ray dropped his hand from Jesse's shoulder and took a long draught of his beer. He'd just come out to one of his ranch hands. Granted circumstances were somewhat unique. But there it was. He wasn't quite sure how he felt about that just yet. It was a bit of a relief, but he'd also just risked opening the door a sliver, let a spear of light in to tease out the darkened corners.

But Jesse was a good kid, deserved a good life, so that little bit of risk was worth it. At least now Jesse knew he had someone he could talk to. And so did Ray.

"Well." Ray cleared his throat. "This is your home now, as long as you want. You're safe here. We'll make sure of it."

"Thank you, Ray."

Jesse looked over at Travis, then back at Ray with a concerned expression on his youthful face. Ray shook his head and stood up. "It's been a crazy couple days," he said to Jesse. "Why don't you call it a night."

Jesse nodded, stood up, and said good night to Travis, who didn't seem to notice. Ray gave him a pat on the shoulder and sent him down the hall. Ray sat back down on the far end of the couch and waited patiently for Travis to come back. The clock in the dining room ticked faintly in the background, keeping time with Ray's steady heartbeat. Floorboards overhead creaked as Jesse made his way along the upstairs hall to the bathroom. Water splashed through copper pipes buried in the walls and groaned when it stopped. Then the quiet hum of silence filled the house.

Finally Travis looked over at him, slightly stunned, like he'd just realized where he was but not quite sure how he got there—face drawn and eyes haunted.

"Welcome back," Ray said quietly.

Travis rubbed at his jaw absently. "Sorry, didn't mean to zone out there."

Ray nodded. Just like waiting for Dot to get her "go" in gear, he waited for Travis to start the conversation. He'd share where he'd gone or he wouldn't, but Ray found himself hoping the man would.

"Jess okay?"

"Yep."

"Good."

Travis looked down at the bottle in his hands as if wondering why he was holding it. Whatever had happened in the man's past, the incident with Jesse and his dad had brought something painful to the surface. Ray had already caught a glimpse of vulnerability buried in the depths of Travis's eyes at the café in Billings, and now this. Just like he didn't ever want to see Jesse's bright light dimmed, he didn't want to see Travis lose his carefree, mischievous attitude. Ray was disturbed to find that it hurt him seeing Travis in pain—the kind of pain that couldn't be healed with salve and a Band-Aid. All he wanted to do was cross the room, pull Travis from the chair, and hold him. Run his hands through Travis's hair, over his back, and soothe away whatever hidden demons he fought.

Travis looked up at Ray and held his gaze for a long moment, his eyes searching for a sign of some sort. Finally he sighed, placed his beer bottle on the companion table, and locked his gaze on the area rug again.

"I was fifteen when my dad found me kissing another boy," he began. His voice was monotone and low, elbows on his knees, hands clasped tightly. "He flew into a rage. Beat the shit out of me: my first broken nose, ribs. First broken anything actually. Then when I was lying in a pool of my own blood in the dirt, and he told me I was dead to him. Kicked me off his property. I've been on my own ever since."

"Jesus, Travis."

"I swore no one would ever hurt me again," he continued, his words growing stronger and sharper as he spoke. "Swore I wouldn't let anyone beat on someone who couldn't defend themselves. I won't stand for it. Won't turn my back on anyone in need of help. But Jesse needed my help . . ."

Travis looked up, and Ray's heart lurched. Anger and shame shone behind a brilliant glossy sheen that covered those beautiful eyes and reflected in the edge of that deep voice.

"Jesse needed my help, and I failed him. I swore I wouldn't let the Sams of the world hurt him when he told me he was gay. And look at him!" Travis's voice pitched a notch higher. "Look what the bastard did to that poor kid. Because of me. Because I failed."

Ray couldn't take it anymore. Couldn't stand to see the Travis he knew suffer and berate himself. Ray was as much at fault—more, actually. Travis had really only just met Jesse, but Ray had known him for ten years.

In one swift move, he crossed the room and pulled Travis up into his arms.

Travis fell into Ray's embrace, warm and solid and strong. So, so strong.

He needed that more than anything right then, was shocked by how much he needed it, that he even could.

And then he broke, gave in, took that comfort without hesitation and let the past wash over him. Watched it race downriver in a flood from his pores. He wrapped his arms tightly around Ray's waist and clung to him like a life preserver in the churning rapids. Fear of history repeating itself, of not being able to protect, not being enough for anyone, drowned in the safe current of Ray's warmth.

His throat constricted. *Hell no.* He would *not* fucking cry. Not in front of this man.

Ray held Travis with one arm firm around his waist and a rugged hand cradling the back of his skull. Travis leaned his forehead into Ray's shoulder, and Ray whispered in his ear. He couldn't make out the words but understood their meaning. He let Ray's strength hold him, wrap around him like a shield.

"It's okay, Travis," Ray soothed in that rough, melodic voice. "Let it out. I've got you."

A single sob escaped Travis's burning throat. He squeezed his stinging eyes shut and fisted a hand in Ray's shirt. Travis knew he was losing the fight but wasn't yet willing to give up.

Ray moved his hand in slow circles over Travis's back. "I won't let you fall," he whispered. "Let it go."

And Travis did.

He'd already passed the point of any chance at winning that fight anyway. The floodgates opened, and it all came flooding out

in a violent, gushing mess: the pain of being rejected by his father, his family. All the years of being lost and alone with no one to lean on, take care of him. He cried for the boy whose childhood had been stolen and the man he'd become, so afraid of letting himself care for anyone enough to give them the power to hurt him.

He cried for the people he hadn't been able to help, the ones he'd failed. The ones he loved but could never tell. For Jesse Davis, so young and innocent, and for Ray Ford, hidden so deep he'd need a search and rescue team to find him.

He cried until the reservoir ran dry and his throat scraped like sandpaper and his body felt exhausted. And Ray held him tightly the whole time. He didn't let Travis go, didn't stop whispering in his ear.

Finally he was empty. He stood clutched to Ray until the vice grip on his chest loosened, until his heartbeat steadied, until he could breathe again. And he breathed in Ray. Suede and sandalwood filled his senses. Suddenly it wasn't enough. Suddenly he needed more, needed *all* of Ray.

Travis began to nuzzle into Ray's neck, inhaling his scent, and Ray tilted his head slightly, allowing Travis more access. Travis sucked the warm skin into his mouth and rolled his tongue over the salty flesh as he gently drew blood to the surface.

Hot, moist breath against his ear sent shivers tearing through his body. Sure fingers threaded through his hair. He couldn't stop the moan that exploded from his throat. And then Ray's mouth was on his, but not crushing or aggressive like the day before. This time it was soft, gentle, and deeply sensual. Travis parted his lips, and Ray's tongue slipped into his mouth in lazy exploration. The tenderness of it turned something in his chest. A weight lifted, a crack opened, and light seeped inside. The sensation of being home washed over Travis once again. But now he knew why. He was where he wanted to be. The place he'd traveled back and forth across the country to find. Where he belonged—and the man he belonged with.

"Oh God, Ray." He broke the kiss and panted. "I want you so bad."

"I know." Ray's voice was breathy. "God, I know."

Then firm, satin-skinned lips stole the breath from his lungs with a ferociousness that had Travis wondering if, for the first time in his life, his knees might truly buckle.

Travis answered the commanding kiss with a demand of his own. He lured Ray's tongue into his mouth and wrestled with it: tangling, twisting, sucking. A deep, long groan reverberated between them, and he wasn't sure which of them it had come from. Didn't care. All he knew was that Ray Ford was kissing him like a man stranded in the desert who'd just discovered water. Travis prayed the well would never run dry as that clever tongue dueled with his. The taste of him was intoxicating and heady: spice and cinnamon rode sidesaddle with the beer he'd just finished.

Travis tugged Ray's shirt from the waistband. He slid his hands beneath the soft material and sank into burning hot, satin skin stretched over hard, flexing muscle. His hands moved of their own accord, trying to cover every inch of Ray. The muscle beneath his palms responded eagerly to his touch.

Ray groaned hungrily and rocked into him, grinding their erections together in erotic rhythm. Urgent hands traced over Travis's shoulders, his chest, and then began roughly unbuttoning his shirt.

They had yet to break the fevered kiss, breathing through their noses so they wouldn't have the need to. The connection was a lifeline Travis hadn't realized he'd needed until then, and he refused to let go.

Then Ray's hands were on Travis's bare skin, branding him as they traveled inquisitively over his torso. Travis stopped thinking and reached for the button on Ray's jeans for what he craved most.

Ray jerked back, breaking their impassioned kiss. His chest heaved with rapid, shallow breaths. His thick cock was a sharp outline trapped behind dark denim.

Ray pushed Travis; the backs of his knees hit the chair he'd been sitting on, and he flopped gracelessly onto the cushion. His eyes widened when Ray knelt between his legs, using his body to push them apart. Travis couldn't pull his gaze from Ray. The gorgeous, stoic man who'd stood steady in the eye of a hurricane, whose strength could carry Travis with ease, whose power, so fierce and unyielding, could at the same time be so tender and giving. But then, hadn't Travis thought that when he'd watched Ray train? That he'd be an amazing lover?

Ray placed his hands on Travis's knees and slowly slid them up his thighs. Heat burned a trail through the heavy denim. One hand rode over Travis's straining erection, tracing the outline and squeezing with just the right amount of spine-tingling pressure as the other worked the pants open. Ray pushed the clothing out of the way and then took Travis commandingly in hand. *Oh. My. God.* Travis's hips shot up into that heavenly hand. He needed to feel more of Ray. Needed to feel him everywhere, to be absorbed by him, lost in him.

And then Ray smiled. A smile Travis had never seen, sly and seductive and holy—"Shit, Ray!"

Travis's brain checked out the second Ray's beautiful lips closed over the head of his cock. The wet heat of Ray's mouth sent shivers racing over his body; electricity bounced from his balls to his skull and back like a pinball. Ray sank down on him, taking him all the way, wrapping him in blazing heat and . . . *what the fuck is he doing with his tongue?*

"Not going to last," Travis managed to pant. "Ray . . ."

Then he felt Ray smile around his shaft and cup his balls firmly, and just like that Travis was standing on the edge of the cliff. Arms spread wide, head thrown back, and body leaning gracefully forward. He tipped past the center of gravity and dropped into an exhilarating freefall. Wind sang in his ears as he soared effortlessly on a lazy summer current. He felt weightless and alive and never wanted to land.

And then skin and muscle and bone knit itself back together, and the weight of body sank deep into the leather chair that closed around him like a giant hand. Nerve endings crackled and danced in the dying electrical storm. He was back on solid ground. Bound by gravity. His breath hitched when he opened his eyes and met Ray's gaze. Amber flecks in those soulful brown eyes glittered like gold nestled in the rich bed of a clear stream. Travis suddenly wanted to go swimming.

"Fuck." Ray's was voice a rough, erotic slide over Travis's eardrums. "That was beautiful."

Travis wanted to say something, searched for the words, but his brain was still riding thermal currents somewhere far above the earth. He cupped the side of Ray's face with one hand and slid the other

down his chest, but Ray grabbed his hand, wrapped it in his, and held it tightly over his heart. He shook his head with a lazy, sated smile.

"Watching you sent me over," Ray whispered.

Travis let out a half laugh, then leaned forward and rested his forehead against Ray's, their noses touching. "Thank you."

CHAPTER 13

Travis glanced over his shoulder at Ray working a liver chestnut gelding with flaxen mane and wondered how long this was going to go on. The man had barely said two words to him since the other night—the night he'd shown him how to fly. Travis had given Ray the benefit of the doubt yesterday, being that it was Sunday, and they'd all had the day off. But that excuse didn't cut it today. Today it seemed Ray was doing his best to avoid him and had hardly even looked him in the eye.

He really couldn't buy that Ray might be regretting what they'd done. Not when he remembered the way the sexy rancher had smiled at him, looked at him, how he'd touched him with such genuine adulation. That wasn't a man doing something he didn't want to do. That was a man absolutely *loving* what he was doing.

So what was with the cold shoulder?

Not one to let sleeping dogs lie, Travis walked over to the other training ring. Ray's back was to him when he leaned against the railing and hooked a boot heel on the lowest rung.

"What's going on, Ray?"

Ray's shoulders stiffened, but he didn't turn around. He was silent for a moment, his voice flat when he spoke. "Don't know what you mean."

"The hell you don't."

Travis saw the man's sigh as much as he heard it. Ray called the chestnut to a halt and removed the lead line from the horse's halter. He scrubbed the animal's muscular neck before walking the few feet to meet Travis at the railing, hands in his pockets.

"This really isn't the best time or place to talk about it." His hushed voice sounded resigned.

"When is then?" Travis pushed. "A couple months goes by pretty quick, and I'd rather not spend it at odds with you."

"That's just it," Ray said. "You're leaving. Best to keep that in mind and not make things difficult."

"How is taking advantage of the situation making things difficult? No one's going to know anything we don't tell them."

Ray was quiet for a long moment. He couldn't get a read on the man, his usually expressive eyes firmly closed down. But he was positive he caught a flash of something like sorrow in their soulful depths.

"That's all it is for you then?" Ray asked. "Sex?"

Travis frowned. How was he supposed to answer that? Tell Ray it was more than sex when he was leaving anyway? What was the point in that? It could never be more, even though he felt like that line had already been crossed. Even though he felt at home here on Ford Creek—first time he'd felt at home anywhere in eighteen years.

And why would Ray want more than that anyway? He knew how much the man stood to lose. Ray would never ask him to stay so why put himself out there?

Fucking trick questions.

"Well, I'd say it's pretty obvious there's a strong mutual attraction going on here. We're adults. We obviously know how to fly under the radar. Why not?"

"I don't fly at home. That's why not."

"No?" Travis challenged. "What was the other night?"

"Reckless. Careless. A mistake."

Of course it was a mistake. It always was, wasn't it?

Travis did his best to school his expression, remain blank, but hearing that coming from Ray hurt a little more than it should. A warm breeze drifted over his shoulder, bringing with it mild bouquet of dry sage grass, dirt, and horse. The chestnut snorted and swished his tail from the other side of the ring.

Ray was silent for a moment but must have seen something in Travis's eyes, because the edge in his voice had softened, his tone almost a plea when he spoke. "You've already seen how Sam reacted, and that was only based on small rumors. It's just too risky, Travis.

I've seen what can happen to men like us in these parts." Ray paused, lifted his hat, and ran a hand through dark hair that Travis knew firsthand felt like silk sliding between his fingers. "This thing . . . You're leaving . . . It can't . . . It's just not worth it."

You're not worth it, Travis heard, and something pinched painfully in his chest. He was fully aware of the risks but still, some small, long-dormant part of him had held steadfastly to a kernel of hope that maybe this time, it would be different. Maybe that was the pinch he felt, that diminutive glimmer being crushed helplessly into the ground once again. He knew better than to hope for any more than he had. No one had ever chosen him first, had they? He'd never been worth the effort. Not to his father or his mother, not the one foster home he'd actually been happy at, certainly not any of the men he'd ever been with. They only wanted him so long as it stayed all nice and quiet on the down low. And people wondered why he kept moving.

"This how it's going to be then?" Travis asked, fighting to keep his tone even.

"This is how it has to be," Ray answered softly. "You know where I'm coming from, right?"

Travis looked over Ray's shoulder at the gelding dozing in the late-afternoon sun and shrugged. "Sure. I get it."

When Travis looked back at Ray, he saw regret and a touch of anger in the man's eyes. What the fuck was that about? Ray was the one who'd made the self-proclaimed mistake.

"We done talking then?" Ray asked.

"Reckon so," Travis answered flatly.

Ray opened his mouth and snapped it shut. What could he say anyway? With a sigh, he left Travis standing at the rail and returned to his charge. Travis stood where he was for a moment. It was frustrating watching Ray, close yet not. Though unsurprised, knowing Ray thought he wasn't worth taking a risk on hurt far more than it should. Ray was just another rancher on just another stop of the endless journey. No reason he should be any different.

But he is.

Travis went back to his pen with disappointment simmering just below anger, and led the bay he'd been working back to the corral.

He was done training for the day. Done watching what he couldn't have. Done hoping for things that could never be. He needed to get away for a while—away from the ranch, away from Ray, and most importantly, away from this desire to mean enough to the man to take the risk. Which really was stupid. What was he thinking anyway? He wasn't going to stay, and Ray wasn't going to ask him to. He needed to keep his own reputation clean if he wanted to keep earning a living, and really, that was the most important thing to remember.

Funny his heart didn't agree with his mind's rhetoric.

The big buckskin had wandered over to the gate when Travis entered the corral. He let the bay loose and threw the halter on Wiley. "Hey, big guy. How's about we go for a ride?"

It was close to the dinner hour when Travis made his way back to the ranch. A couple of hours of aimless riding had been exactly what he'd needed to center himself.

As he neared the ranch, he noticed a rising plume of dust following in the wake of a rapidly moving vehicle approaching from the east. When the vehicle crested the rise, bucking and bouncing along the dirt drive, he recognized it as Sam's rusty pickup. He pulled Wiley up and watched as the truck slid to a reckless stop in the yard, almost colliding with one of the ranch vehicles. Sam launched himself out of the cab and flapped his arms about, voice raised in agitation. Two more men piled out of the truck from the passenger side and came around to flank him. Travis was too far away to clearly hear what Sam was saying, but he did catch his name on the wind.

"Christ," Travis said under his breath. The day just couldn't get any better.

With a long-drawn sigh, he nudged Wiley into an easy walk parallel to the driveway. He was certainly in no rush to deal with the likes of Sam Davis and his little posse.

Unnoticed by the unexpected visitors as he approached from behind but within earshot, Travis was able to make out the colorful epithets Sam tossed out at the gathering hands. Sam was in quite a

tizzy about Jesse living on a ranch with a bunch of queer lovers, which is what they all had to be to keep a freak like Travis on but fire him, a *real* man. That was about the funniest thing Travis had heard all day, though not quite funny enough to earn the effort of actually laughing.

Jesse stood behind Ray, flanked by Clay and Ross, but didn't say a word as his dad berated him. The rest of the hands coming in for dinner formed a line ten strong behind Ray—an intimidating army.

"You need to turn around and get off my ranch right now," Ray ordered firmly, cutting off Sam's tirade.

"Not until that son of a bitch pays for what he's done," Sam countered angrily.

The *ku-cha-ku* of a round being dropped into a rifle chamber drew everyone's attention to the house. Dot stood on the front porch with a bolt-action rifle aimed squarely at Sam's chest.

"You take your bad attitude and your little hoodlums and get off my ranch, Samuel Davis," Dot said in a voice that sent an icy shiver down Travis's spine. "Your choice. Go now and live, or I drop you where you stand and call the coroner to come pick up your miserable pieces."

For an extended, tense beat, no one moved a muscle. It seemed even the cool, early-evening breeze had stilled.

"Fine," Sam spat. "But don't be thinking this is over."

He turned around and froze when he saw Travis astride the big buckskin. His storm gray eyes narrowed, the skin under his scruffy beard tightened, and he clenched his hands into tight fists.

"That him?" a short, stocky cowboy to the left of Sam asked. He had a scrunched-up face and wore jeans the same color of dirt as his boots. "That the fag?"

Sam nodded, and Scrunchy Face cracked his knuckles. Travis would have laughed if the sound of popping cartilage hadn't echoed through his memory and yanked him sharply back to North Dakota.

Five men had piled out of the mud-caked Double Diamond pickup; three grabbed two-by-fours from the bed of the truck, and the other two cracked their knuckles in anticipation of a beat down. Yes, they'd left Travis curled up in the fetal position on the side of the road with three broken ribs and countless abrasions and bruises, but

he'd given them a few souvenirs of his own. He hadn't been the only one who had limped away from that fight with broken bones.

Anger that had taken Travis so long to finally settle roared back to life with a vengeance. No more. No more hate and broken bones and hiding from life.

"You want to take me on, you ignorant piece of shit?" he bit out in a cold, flat voice. His vision tunneled, his ears buzzed, and his body began to vibrate with explosive heat. He slid from the saddle, dropped the reins carelessly, and converged on Sam and his posse with murderous intent. Whatever had shown on his face was enough to force Sam and his band of hoods back a step. Fear flashed through Sam and Scrunchy Face's eyes, but the other man, taller and harder looking, remained vacant of emotion. He would be the one to watch in this fight.

"What?" Travis asked without inflection. "Three on one aren't good enough odds for you?"

Challenged, Sam straightened his shoulders. "You're a dead man," he threatened and took a step forward.

The booming explosion of a rifle shot rent the air and echoed across the plains like rolling thunder. A small pad of dirt exploded like a bomb not more than two feet in front of Sam, bringing him and his posse to a sudden stop. Spooked, Wiley reared and nearly ran over Travis as he galloped wildly toward the corrals and the safety of the herd. Travis remained intently locked on Sam.

"That was your only warning," Dot said, reloading the chamber for emphasis. "Next bullet puts you down."

Sam glanced over his shoulder to see Dot with her rifle trained on him, square and steady. She tipped the muzzle up briefly in a quick "go on" motion. He looked back at Travis and sent him another killing glare.

"Next time."

Travis smiled, cold and feral. "You know where to find me."

Sam and crew climbed grudgingly back into the truck, and Sam gunned the engine, making a show out of peeling out of the yard and covering the small crowd in a thin layer of dust.

"Well, that was fun," Dot said with laughter in her voice when the truck's screaming engine faded into the wind. She flipped the safety interlock on and rested the long barrel of the rifle over her shoulder. "Come on then, gentlemen. Show's over, and dinner's ready."

As the men followed Dot into the house, Ray leveled a telling stare at Travis. It wasn't difficult to decipher the man's see-what-I-mean? look, not that Travis was really paying any attention. He desperately needed to release the fury poisoning his veins and clouding his mind. Decisively. Something was going to have to break dramatically.

"And next time you go gallivanting off without telling anyone, take a two-way," Ray snapped, then turned and disappeared inside the house.

Ray flipped over onto his back and stared up at the ceiling. Again. He turned his head and groaned. The digital clock radio on his night table flashed 2:57 a.m. in obnoxious glowing green numbers. He hadn't slept well for two days now, and tonight he hadn't been able to sleep at all.

Travis hadn't come in for dinner after their unpleasant visit from Sam and friends. According to Jesse, he hadn't joined the men for after-work beers around the fire pit either. He'd just silently disappeared inside his cabin and pulled the shades after moving a whole wall of baled hay from one side of the loft to the other.

Ray knew why, but dammit, there was just too much at risk—and it went deeper than his reputation now. Landon was right; it was more than sex with Travis, and Ray hadn't even seen that one coming until it hit him upside the head. He couldn't deny it any longer. He was falling for the man, hard. Getting more involved now was only going to leave a bigger hole when Travis left. A crater.

Travis showing his colors earlier, that he was just in it for the sex and would be moving on once the horses were trained, settled Ray's resolve. Even though what they'd done the other night was reckless, he couldn't regret it. He hadn't been exaggerating when he'd told Travis it was beautiful. It was. *He* was. But situations like that were going to

get him found out, and they'd already had a close call in the tack room last week.

It couldn't go any further. No matter how hard he tried to convince himself it was just sex, he knew it wasn't. With that man it never would be. If he stopped it here, now, he would still be able to let Travis go. But even that felt like a lie.

Ray sighed and rolled onto his side. He stared out the bedroom window at stars hanging brightly on a midnight canvas. A full moon cast pale luminescence over the grooved edges of the worn mullion. Warm orange light flickered in the curve of the metal window catch and reflected on clear panes. Horses whinnied in the distance.

An uneasy feeling settled over him, and goose bumps spread across his skin. The night felt too alive for this hour. Something disturbed the silence, but he couldn't quite pinpoint what it was. His gaze fell on the flickering window catch again.

What on the ranch gave off a yellow-orange glow?

And why were the horses so restless?

Ray jumped from his bed and strode to the window as his pulse sped up. That warm flickering light emanated from the other side of the barn, brighter lower to the ground. Tiny red lights rose and mingled with the bright white of the stars on a swirling black thread.

"Shit."

Ray spun around and reached for his jeans, hopping into them as he grabbed a shirt and punched his arms into the sleeves. He swung his door open, yelled out to Jesse and Dot that they had a fire, and quickly padded barefoot down the hallway, haphazardly buttoning his shirt.

Ray was still pulling his boots on when he opened the front door, and Jesse crashed into the foyer, half-asleep with his shirt hanging open. He didn't wait for the kid and bolted across the yard. Men's voices were growing louder and more frantic as he neared the far side of the barn. He staggered to a horrified stop when he rounded the corner. One of the cabins was almost completely engulfed in flames: Travis's cabin.

Two men were throwing buckets of water at the wall of fire, which only seemed to anger it more. Even from here Ray could smell the

pungent bite of gasoline. No way was this an accident, and Ray had no doubt about exactly how it had started—and who started it.

Clay ran past him, carrying another useless bucket of water.

"Clay," Ray called, fighting the panic growing in his chest. "Where's Travis?"

"Inside," Clay shouted. "He's still fucking inside."

Ray cursed silently, his mouth suddenly dry and heart racing like a thoroughbred. He grabbed the bucket from Clay's hands. "It's a gas fire. Water won't stop it. Go get the fire extinguishers from the barn. Go!"

Clay turned and ran with Ross on his heels.

The smell of gasoline this close was strong enough to burn his nostrils, and his stomach bottomed out. He swallowed back rising fear through a constricted throat.

Travis was in there.

Ray cursed as he paced the perimeter of the fire with a dull pain in his chest. Sweat began to bead on his forehead, trickle down his spine, and his shirt clung uncomfortably to his skin. Travis was trapped inside that inferno, and there wasn't a fucking thing he could do to help him.

Goddammit, what was taking Clay and Ross so long with the fire extinguishers?

Just then Ray caught a flash of movement on the other side of the window. He yelled Travis's name and rushed forward, oblivious to the angry tongues of hell that lashed out and singed his skin. And then something locked on his arm and yanked him backward as his feet struggled for purchase to fight back. He couldn't go back; he had to go forward, to Travis.

"Are you insane?" Hollis yelled at him. "Getting yourself lit up like a candle isn't going to save him."

"He's going to fucking die in there, Hollis," Ray yelled and then fell into a short coughing fit. Black smoke hung heavy and choking in the air. It sucked the oxygen from his lungs and grated his throat. His skin burned; his eyes watered.

"We're going to get him out, Ray," Hollis said with convincing determination.

Then the cabin window exploded outward from the force of a large, shapeless form tearing through it. Glass shattered and cascaded to the ground, glittering like gold confetti in the firelight. The dark form came to a hard crash on the edge of the small porch and rolled off, hitting the dirt with a loud *oof.*

Travis lay on the ground wrapped in a wet blanket, groaning and racked by a spasm of painful-sounding coughs.

But he was alive.

CHAPTER 14

The sun was cresting the horizon, painting the world in a soft orange-pink hue with masterful brush strokes when the ranch hands finally cleared out of the kitchen. Ray had given the men a flex day; it was up to them if they felt like working today or not. It had already been a long morning, and the sun was only just rising. Most had chosen to go back to bed for a few hours.

They hadn't been able to keep Travis's cabin from burning to the ground, but they'd been able to prevent the fire from spreading to the other cabins.

Hollis had called the police and fire department nonemergency lines to report the fire after they'd put it out. Essential services were all volunteer this far from town, and they didn't see the need to ruin everyone's night. The sheriff and fire investigator would come to the ranch later that afternoon to collect their statements and examine what was left of the cabin. If they confirmed it was arson, they would pull Sam in for questioning.

Now that it was just the four of them in the house—he, Travis, and Dot sitting at the small kitchen table, and Jesse standing against the wall near the doorway—the adrenaline had dissipated and fatigue began settling deep into Ray's bones. He was too old for shit like this. He wearily ran a hand through his hair. They were all tired and achy and even after showers, they still stank like smoke.

Fortunately Travis's injuries had not been serious. Other than relatively minor smoke inhalation, a massive bruise was forming on his shoulder from the impact of his hard landing outside the cabin. It was his quick thinking in soaking the bedspread in the shower and wrapping it around himself that had prevented any burns or cuts during his escape. And probably the only thing that saved his life.

He sat in a chair across from Ray with an ice pack on his bare shoulder; a trail of melting ice twisted a path down his biceps and dripped off his bent elbow. All he had on was an old pair of Ray's jeans Dot had found for him. His eyes were bloodshot, and his voice was a deep rasp. Dot had fixed a mug of hot water with lemon and honey to soothe his throat. It seemed to be helping in that he wasn't coughing as much. It'd probably be a few days until his voice was once again velvet smooth.

"Thank you, Dot. Everyone," Travis said quietly, the weariness in his voice evident on his face. "I think I'm good to go now. I'll make up a bed"—he paused to take a sip from his mug—"in one of the empty stalls and get a little shut-eye."

Travis stood slowly and placed the ice pack on the table. He hadn't yet noticed the incredulous expression on Dot's face.

"Don't be ridiculous, young man," Dot said. "You're moving into the house. The downstairs room at the end of the hall is empty and all yours."

"No." Travis protested a little too vehemently and fell into another coughing fit.

Dot raised an eyebrow and looked to Ray.

Ray knew it would be hell with Travis under the same roof—it was bad enough having him on the same ranch—but there was no way he was going to let the man sleep in the barn. Not after what happened tonight. Not after Sam tried to kill him.

"It'd be best if you stay here, Travis," Ray said.

"No, really," Travis said weakly. "I can sleep anywhere, and the barn's as good a place as any."

"Nonsense," Dot said, dismissing the idea out of hand. "You sit down, put that ice back on your shoulder, and drink your hot water. I'll go make up the bed and find you some clothes."

Travis looked to him, then Jesse and back to Dot. Seeing there would be no arguing his way out, he sat down in defeat. His shoulders slumped, and his chin dipped to his chest.

"I'm so sorry, Trav," Jesse said in a small voice, not leaving his perch near the dining room door. "This is my fault. I know my dad

did this, and I can't let anything else happen to you. So, I-I'm going to quit." He shot his gaze to Ray. "And leave the ranch."

"Nope. This is not your fault," Travis rasped firmly. "Don't even think that for a second." Travis paused with a wince and took a sip from his cup. It was obvious how much it hurt him to talk. "This is all on your dad . . . He'd have come after me . . . Regardless."

"He's right." Ray took over. "Even if you'd left with your dad when I fired him, he'd still have come after Travis. And if not him, then someone else. You know that as well as we do."

"Maybe, but—"

"No maybe. No but," Ray interrupted. "You live here. You work here. And more importantly, we want you here."

Jesse looked from Ray to Travis, who nodded emphatically.

"Okay. I didn't really want to leave anyway," he said with a timorous smile.

Travis started to laugh, but it morphed quickly into a coughing fit.

"Will you still teach me to train horses, Trav?" Jesse asked when Travis had the coughing under control.

"Of course," Travis said. "Not going anywhere."

Ray's eyebrows shot up, and a surge of anger-laced jealousy flooded his veins. What the hell did Travis mean he's "not going anywhere"? And why was he saying it to the kid and not him?

"Good," Jesse chirped. His tone turned solemn when he added, "I'm real happy you're okay, Travis. I was so scared."

Travis nodded and flashed one of his magazine smiles at Jesse. Another wave of envy washed over Ray. Jesse said good night as he left the kitchen, and Ray waited until Jesse's footsteps faded before he turned to Travis.

"I don't appreciate you making promises you know you're not going to keep," Ray said in a low, sharp voice.

Travis stared at Ray for a long moment, his tired eyes searching. "What the fuck does that mean?"

"You know damn well what that means, Travis. You can't tell Jesse you'll be here for him when you won't. You're leaving."

"Maybe I'll stick around," Travis bit out.

Ray huffed. "That'd be great. Then we'd both be screwed up the ass. And not in a good way."

"Maybe not," Travis countered, but there was no fight in his voice.

"Really? You've already made it clear you're just looking for sex while you're here." Ray paused to check his rising voice while trying to ignore the flash of pain that flitted across Travis's rugged face. "The second someone catches wind of what's going on, we both know you'll disappear faster than an eight-second whistle."

"That's not—" Whatever Travis was going to say was interrupted by Dot coming through the kitchen door.

"Here we are, son," she said cheerily, oblivious to the glares he and Travis were leveling at each other. Dot dropped a small pile of clothes on the tabletop beside Travis's elbow. He cleared his throat with slow, deliberate care and shifted his attention to Dot.

"These are some of Ray's old clothes I've been meaning to drop off at Goodwill," Dot continued. "You two are close enough in size that his shirts will do you fine. Jeans might be a smidge short, but they'll keep you clothed until we get you to town to buy your own."

"Thank you, Dot," Travis said quietly. "I appreciate it."

She nodded and smiled warmly at him, then laid a gentle hand on his shoulder. "Your room is ready. Go sleep as long as you need."

Travis nodded, and his gaze dropped to the clothing. His shoulders hunched forward just enough to make him look tired and beaten down. Something in his demeanor shifted infinitesimally, and he seemed lost, vulnerable. Ray just wanted to pull him into his arms and make him smile, make those heavy-hearted eyes dance.

"Good night, boys," Dot said as she turned and left the kitchen.

"'Night, Dot," they returned in unison.

Travis didn't move for a moment, and Ray wasn't quite sure what to say or do. Clearly their interrupted conversation had lost its momentum and looked like it wasn't going to be continued. Travis had retreated inward, out of Ray's reach.

Travis lifted his free hand and ran it over the shirt on top of the folded pile. It had been one of Ray's favorites, with blues and greens running in thick vertical bars. The material had softened with age and

had always felt warm and comfortable, like coming home. The elbows had blown out, but Dot had patched them with a square of soft leather.

Ray watched Travis's hand as it traced a lazy S over the shirt like a caress. He carefully lifted the garment, slid his arms slowly into the sleeves, and buttoned it up with deliberate focus. He rolled his shoulders back and ran his hands down each forearm, smoothing the material.

Seeing Travis in his shirt shifted something inside. Something he couldn't quite name that had been off-kilter before and now seemed to have locked back into place, where it belonged.

Then Travis raised his eyes—still magnetic, even smoke burned and bloodshot—and they collided with Ray's gaze. The moment stretched with visible energy, and Ray felt like he was still standing at the edge of the fire again. Blood rushed south; the muscles in his lower abdomen clenched sharply. He cleared his throat and abruptly stood from the table, breaking the charged connection.

"Well, I'll let you get settled then." Ray groaned inwardly at the ragged sound of his voice. Without risking eye contact again, he nodded and made his way to the door. He paused before going through and over his shoulder said, "I'm glad you're okay."

Ray took four deep pulls of refreshingly cool water and mentally followed its path as it quenched his mouth, raced down his throat like a waterfall, and splashed into his stomach. He placed the glass on the counter beside the sink and leaned against the edge, hands splayed on the grooved tile surface, as he stared out the kitchen window.

Twenty-four hours had passed, and still he hadn't slept more than a few of those hours in fits and starts.

The moon was shining in all her brilliant glory again tonight. Stars glittered and sparkled in the heavens like tiny diamonds scattered on a bed of black silk. The night was still, the earth and all its beings in quiet repose. Except for him.

How the hell was he supposed to sleep, knowing Travis Morgan lay just down the hallway? All bare skin and hard muscle stretched

out and inviting. Ray dropped his head and bunched his shoulders. He wanted the man. God, how he wanted the man. He wanted him to stay, wanted him to want to—if it were possible, if it were a perfect world.

But it wasn't a perfect world, and he wouldn't take the risk, wouldn't ask. Even if he did, Travis would either pick up and leave anyway, or worse, he'd stay and eventually resent Ray for it, and then leave. No matter how he spun it, it all came back to Travis leaving. That cowboy just wasn't made to stick.

And why the hell did he keep torturing himself over something that couldn't be? Something he shouldn't—*didn't*—want anyway?

He promptly squelched the little voice in the back of his mind that knew a lie when it heard one. He didn't want to think on that.

Ray inhaled a long, deep breath, held it for a three-beat, and then exhaled just as slowly. Somehow, someway, he had to distance himself from the sexy cowboy. Just two more months, surely he could endure that. After all, he'd been denying himself for more than three decades. Another sixty days or so should be a drop in the bucket. He huffed out a weak laugh. Who did he think he was kidding? He'd already lost the battle and now it was only a matter of limiting the casualties.

Letting his shoulders drop back down, he picked up his glass and swallowed the last mouthful of water, then rinsed out the glass and placed it in the dish rack. He turned away from the counter, took one step, and froze.

Travis was leaning against the doorframe in silhouetted luminescence, clad only in an old pair of pajama bottoms, *Ray's* old pajama bottoms. His arms were folded across his bare chest, one foot crossed over the other. His posture was relaxed, but his eyes were damn near glowing as bright as last night's bonfire—and Ray was trapped under that intense gaze, rendered immobile. His heart sped up and banged around crazily in his chest, his pulse boomed in his ears, and he suddenly felt light-headed as his blood made a rapid charge to one central location.

But he couldn't move.

Travis pushed off from the wall, their gazes locked as he stalked across the darkened room with that confident swagger of his. The

linoleum floor looked like a chessboard under his bare feet. Pale blue-white light speared through the kitchen window and gave the white squares an ethereal glow.

Sleek curves and angles of muscle caught in the lambent light created a beautiful display of motion and grace as Travis approached.

Ray felt the soft material of his own cotton pants shift to accommodate his swelling cock.

And still he couldn't move.

Travis didn't slow as he closed in on his prey, intent and determined. Didn't stop when he reached Ray and grabbed him roughly behind the neck. Even as he crushed his mouth to Ray's in a demanding kiss, he continued to move forward. It was the small of Ray's back slamming into the immovable counter that stopped the driving momentum.

Ray's paralysis broke and without even a second of internal argument, he wrapped his arms around Travis and returned the kiss with fervor. Their tongues fought for dominance; teeth ground together, and unshaven chins scraped. And it was like nothing Ray could remember experiencing. It screamed an angry roar of release, of banked desire and denied need, and the moan that rumbled up through his chest drew a match from Travis. The hand on Ray's back seared into his flesh like a branding iron and pulled him into the solid blanket of heat that was Travis's bare chest.

And the fierce avarice of their joined mouths had yet to abate.

Ray slid his hands down the smooth, hard expanse of Travis's back until the pajamas waistband impeded his exploration. Undeterred, he dipped beneath the stretchy band and filled his palms with a firm ass. Ray squeezed, and Travis rocked his hips into him, the erotic flex of muscle drawing another rumbling moan from Ray. Travis ground into Ray while the edge of the counter gouged his back.

And it wasn't enough. It could never be enough.

Ray let go of that incredible ass and pushed hard against Travis's chest, finally breaking their frenzied kiss. Travis stumbled back a couple of steps, his expression dazed. Those captivating eyes were heavy-lidded, blazing with fire and glazed with lust. Their heavy breaths echoed in the quiet kitchen, and chests heaved in rapid unison.

Holy shit, had anyone ever looked at him like that before? Wanted him that much? Had *he* ever wanted someone that desperately? This enigmatic, carefree, dangerously handsome cowboy was going to be the end of him, and at the moment he really couldn't find it in himself to care. Travis was the only thing he wanted.

"God, Travis. I want to fuck you so bad."

Ray reached out and grabbed Travis by the hand and dragged him, just shy of a full-out gallop, to the downstairs bedroom.

CHAPTER 15

Ray shut the door behind them and spun Travis around by the hand he still held until Travis's back connected with the cool, painted surface of the wooden door. But Travis didn't notice, because Ray was on him before he could take a breath. Mouth and tongue and teeth nipped and bit at his neck and shoulders and chest; sure hands ran down his sides, over his abdomen and back in a quest that felt as desperate as his own. Travis was lost in sensation. Lost in the heady scent of sandalwood and suede and their mingling arousal. Lost in the feel of Ray's hot flesh against his.

Travis pushed into Ray and walked him backward to the bed, mouths fused as they moved. Ray hit the mattress and fell back, and Travis didn't waste the advantage. He leaned over Ray, grabbed his pajama bottoms by the waistband, and pulled them off. He stood back for a moment, the soft material slipping forgotten from his hand as he stared down at the most incredible man he'd ever known stretched out before him.

Moonlight shone through the bare window and captured Ray's strong body, encasing him in a soft ethereal glow. Skin lightly dampened with perspiration glistened like a million diamonds flickering in the sunlight as his chest rose and fell with each rapid breath. Travis's gaze was riveted to the beautiful, fully erect cock that rested thick and rigid against Ray's taut stomach. It was the most erotic thing he'd ever seen.

Ray folded his hands behind his head and opened his knees.

Travis groaned at the silent invitation and roughly shoved off his pajamas. He dropped to the bed on his hands and knees and crawled up Ray's body, straddling him without touching. Finally he had the sexy rancher exactly where he wanted him, and he was going to savor

every single inch of him as long as humanly possible. After this night, there wouldn't be any part of Ray Ford he wouldn't know intimately.

Ray reached up as Travis lowered his head to take Ray's mouth in an unhurried, sensual exploration. He slid his tongue against Ray's in a slow undulating tease, traced the shape and smooth surface of each tooth, and sucked on the lower lip before gently releasing it. He nipped and licked and kissed his way down the strong, thick neck, over solid pectorals dusted with a downy layer of dark hair, and pulled a hard nipple into his mouth. Ray groaned a curse and clenched his hands in Travis's hair, lifting his hips, but Travis kept himself just out of reach.

Travis moved to the other nipple and shifted his weight to one arm. With his free hand, he swept an open palm over Ray's torso, following ridges of abdominal muscle, plowing rows through soft hair with his fingertips, and stopping on the rise of hip. He kissed a path downward and dipped his tongue into an innie belly button that earned a sharp intake of breath from Ray.

"Goddamn, Travis . . ." he panted.

Travis smiled, pleased with his effect on the stoic, serious rancher, and continued his journey. He kissed and licked down into Ray's inner thigh, avoiding the thick shaft but letting it slide against his cheek as he went straight for Ray's sac. He sucked one ball into his mouth and rolled his tongue around it as Ray writhed and groaned and mumbled unintelligible words, the fingers in his hair twisting. Travis slid his hand down to cup and squeeze Ray's balls, freeing his mouth so he could run his tongue up the length of Ray's straining erection.

His own body was coiled tight with need and desire, but he fought it back to give Ray everything he had. He would take what Ray gave, but right now he had to give Ray something to remember, had to leave his mark on this man somehow so he'd always be a part of him.

He swirled his tongue around the head of Ray's hard shaft and lapped at the escaping precum, swallowing with a purr that surprised him. He'd never purred for any man in his life. He closed his mouth around Ray and, with steady pressure of his lips, slid down the rigid length as deep as he could. Ray rocked his hips upward with a long growl, and Travis relaxed his throat, letting Ray take what he needed.

Travis let go of the tightening ball sac and rested his hand on Ray's stomach, feeling it rise and fall in rapid succession.

And holy fucking hell, Travis was on the verge of his own orgasm without even being touched.

Then Ray was pulling painfully on his hair, but Travis didn't care. Ray could do anything he wanted to him. Anything.

"Travis . . ." Ray pulled harder, forcing Travis to release him with a complaining groan.

"I want . . ." His voice was a hoarse rasp. "I want to come inside you."

Travis trembled with anticipation, but all he could manage was, "God, yes."

Ray flipped him over so he was the one who was straddled, but Ray didn't tease. He forced himself between Travis's legs and lowered into the cradle they made. He rolled their hips together and took Travis's engorged shaft in a firm hand. Now Travis was the one making incoherent sounds as lit nerves snapped up his spine and short-circuited his brain.

"You have what we need?" Ray asked.

"Shit," Travis said as his heart plummeted. "The fire."

Ray dropped his forehead to Travis's chest and groaned. After a second he took a deep breath and then lifted himself off Travis and jumped from the bed.

"Don't move," he warned in an authoritative voice. He pulled on the closest pair of PJ bottoms, which weren't the ones he'd been wearing before, and raced from the room.

Without the heat of Ray's body over his, Travis shivered as the cool air attacked his exposed skin. He pulled the bed sheets up to keep warm while he waited for the sexy rancher to return, praying he wouldn't come to his senses now that their sexual momentum had been broken. He looked over at the night table, but there wasn't a clock in Travis's room; he didn't even wear a watch. He had no idea how long Ray was gone.

Though it seemed longer, probably less than a couple of minutes had passed before Ray came back into the room with more condoms than they'd need in one night—unless Ray was Superman—and a

bottle of lube clutched against his chest with one hand. He shoved off the pants and said, "I told you not to move."

"Warm me up then," Travis cajoled.

Ray stalked across the room, tossed the paraphernalia carelessly on the nightstand, and ripped the sheets from the bed. Goose bumps charged across Travis's skin from the sudden shock of chill air, and then Ray climbed onto the bed and covered him with his scorching heat and heady scent. Travis grabbed him behind the neck and pulled him down for a hard, passionate kiss.

Strong hands moved reverently over his body, and fire burned a trail in their wake as their tongues dueled. And then a burning hand slid along the crease of his ass cheeks and over that one place so few had ever breached. Travis may have slept with a lot of men on his journeys, but he refused to bottom for one-nighters. He couldn't think of anything he wanted more than accepting Ray inside his body, handing over the reins and trusting Ray to take him where he needed to go, to take and give what he wanted.

Ray teased at his opening while he kissed down Travis's chest and took his cock in his mouth and sucked hard. Travis bucked from the bed with a restrained shout. He couldn't take any more. He needed Ray. Needed him now. Blindly he pawed at the night table until his hand landed on the bottle of lube. He tossed it at Ray's head and growled, "Now, dammit!"

"Bastard," Ray muttered playfully as he paused his ministrations long enough to retrieve the bottle and slick up his fingers. Then he was back sucking on Travis's cock and pushing one slippery finger inside. And it was like his entire body had suddenly been engulfed by raging wildfire.

Ray worked him with mouth and tongue and fingers until Travis felt like a writhing, mindless bundle of nerves. Every touch was an explosion that drove him that much closer to completely losing his mind.

And he wanted more.

"Fuck, Ray," he keened through gritted teeth. "Fuck me."

Ray released Travis's cock from his mouth, pulled his fingers from Travis's body, and Travis groaned in complaint at the loss. Ray

stretched over him and fumbled for a condom, but hell, it was like the man was suddenly all thumbs and knocking them all to the floor.

"Christ, Ray," Travis groaned. His body cried out to be filled, possessed. Right. Fucking. Now. "What are you? Sixteen?"

"Shut up." Rapid breath fanned Travis's heated skin in short, moist bursts. "My hands are so greased up it's like I'm at a fucking rodeo pig scramble."

Travis chuckled and reached over to grab a packet from the nightstand before Ray could knock them all off. Good thing Ray brought two boxes worth downstairs. He pushed Ray back and tore the wrapper open with his teeth. Then he deftly rolled the latex over Ray's thick erection. Ray followed Travis's hands with his lubed ones and slicked himself up. Finally sheathed and positioned at Travis's hole, the blunt head of Ray's cock pressed at him but didn't move forward. The man was determined to drive him completely insane.

Travis looked up into Ray's intense gaze, and in the bright light of the moon, he could see a war of concern and desire playing out in those dark, soulful eyes. Travis knew without asking or being told. This wasn't just sex. This was the point of no return. Last chance, Charlie.

Even knowing that he had so much more to lose and was poised on the literal cusp of taking that risk, Ray wouldn't move forward unless Travis also willingly accepted. Which made Travis want him all the more.

Travis nodded and whispered roughly, "I want you in me, Ray. I want to feel all of you."

Ray lowered his head and claimed Travis's mouth with a bruising kiss so full of passion and adoration, it wrapped around his heart and threaded into his very soul. And then Ray began to push inside, slow and deliberate. The stretch and burn caused Travis's body to tense, and he broke the kiss, sucking in a sharp breath. It had been so long since he'd taken another man into his body, but he'd never wanted one as badly as this sexy rancher.

Ray stopped, and Travis knew how much control it was taking to hold himself suspended, allowing Travis's body to relax and accept the beautiful invasion.

"Okay?" Ray asked, his forehead resting against Travis's.

Travis nodded and gave his hips a little rock. Ray took the cue and continued in one long, steady stroke until he was fully seated. And he was deep. So. Fucking. Deep.

"Fuck, yeah," Travis panted. Every nerve in his body shot rockets of fire through his system. "Come on, Ray. Ride me hard."

Ray obeyed and began to thrust in, slow and measured at first, almost fully out and then all the way in, with such devotion Travis felt like his chest would explode from the sheer pleasure of it. Travis took himself in hand and pulled in long slow strokes, matching Ray's pace.

"Sweet. Fucking. Mercy." Ray groaned. "Oh God, Travis . . ."

Ray began to rock faster, harder, and Travis bucked his hips to meet each thrust, take him deeper. And then it was as if the levee broke, and Ray burst from his tightly held control in a tidal wave of lust and need and desire. He became a fathomless, swift-moving rapid that pulled Travis under as it flooded over him, into him. He was completely surrounded by Ray. Absorbed. Joined. One. Cleansed in a river of rapture. What he had been was gone. Now he was something new, something different—a part of another. And he never wanted to be anywhere else.

Keep me.

Ray's pounding rhythm grew erratic, frantic, until he froze, impossibly deep, incredibly perfect, and Travis felt Ray begin to pulse inside. Then Ray shouted his name on a curse as he came, and Travis dived over the edge of the waterfall right behind him. Hot threads of exquisite release painted his stomach in abstract designs. Ray collapsed and rolled beside him, and the raging rapids emptied into peaceful hot springs that soothed his spent body.

Travis lay beside Ray in contented silence, staring up at the ceiling while his harsh, rapid breath and pounding heart gradually slowed. Ray's shoulder pressed lightly against his—the only point of contact. It was such a small touch, but to Travis it was the world.

"If you cold-shoulder me again tomorrow, I'm going to kick your ass," Travis teased but kept his gaze trained on the ceiling. He didn't feel as light as his tone, knowing already he wouldn't be able to handle Ray shutting him out again.

Travis felt Ray's hand search his out in the dark, grasp it, and thread their fingers together, then give him a reassuring squeeze.

"Won't happen," he said in a self-depreciating tone. "I'm a stuck pig now."

Even during that odd neither-here-nor-there moment when consciousness crept unrelentingly forward but hadn't yet taken hold, Travis knew he was alone. It was one of those things people instinctively knew—some innate awareness of living energy. He didn't need to turn around, didn't need to open his eyes to know the space behind him was empty, the sheets cold where the heat of Ray's body had been.

He swallowed back a wave of building apprehension that today would be a repeat of the past few. It wouldn't, because if anything, Ray Ford was a man of his word.

Warm sheets pooled in his lap as he sat up and looked toward the window. He hadn't drawn the curtains the night before, and soft, pink-hued light peeked through unfettered, letting him know the day was about to begin. The mouthwatering smell of maple bacon drifting under the door confirmed it. He ran his fingers through his hair and just as he was about to get up, the door opened slowly with a quiet creak. Yellow light from the hall spilled in to silhouette a familiar form in its frame.

"You're up," Ray said, his voice soft. He stepped into the room and gently closed the door.

"Morning," Travis said, his voice sleep-roughened.

Ray stood by the door for a moment, in an apparent debate with himself. A large brown paper bag was clutched in his hand. Debate settled, he walked the few feet to the bed and sat on the edge with his back to Travis. Ray seemed uneasy, and a cold shiver raced across Travis's bare skin.

Ray sighed and looked over his shoulder, meeting Travis's gaze. Travis felt his body tense, preparing for the worst, but relaxed when Ray flashed a quick, sheepish smile. He angled his body toward Travis

and looked down at the paper bag in his lap for another moment. Then Ray abruptly held the package out to him. Travis took it while watching Ray for an explanation, but the man just shook his head and turned away from him again. Whatever was in the bag, it was clear Ray was nervous about giving it to him.

Which only piqued his curiosity.

The bag wasn't overly heavy nor hard edged, which told him there was material of some kind inside: clothing, most likely, too heavy to be a shirt but too light to be jeans. He carefully opened the bag and pulled out its contents. He couldn't believe what he was looking at, had to stare at it a moment longer to be certain. His breath hitched, his mouth went dry, and his heart sped up. In his hands he held a brand-new pair of rich, chocolate brown suede show chaps, with matching fringe. The belt and side yokes were smooth tan leather with intricate flower filigree, and the matching leg trim was adorned with three silver moon conchas.

Travis ran his hand over the leather, butter soft and cool under his palm. His chest tightened. He should say something but couldn't seem to find suitable words. He didn't know why these chaps were even in his hands.

Ray cleared his throat but didn't turn around when he spoke. His rough, melodic voice was almost a whisper. "I'd like you to have them."

Have them? Shock stalled Travis's mind, a lump clogged in his throat, and his vision blurred inexplicably. No one had given him anything in so long, not anything that mattered. No one had cared enough. But these chaps, this beautiful gift—a gift from Ray—had suddenly become the most precious thing in the world. No matter what might come of this thing they'd started, Ray had touched him in a way he could never possibly forget.

He wanted to dive across the bed and wrap himself around Ray, hold on tight and kiss him, love him, never let go.

"I-I don't know what to say," he managed to push through his constricted vocal chords.

"Nothing to say," Ray said; his voice sounded equally tight. He shot another glance over his shoulder, and Travis had the impression

there was something more Ray wanted to say, that he was right on the edge.

Say it. Ask me. Ask me to stay and I will. Please.

Travis searched his gaze for a long, imploring moment before Ray turned away with a nod, more to himself than Travis, and Travis swallowed back the tightening knot in his throat.

Ray stood up quickly and in a voice a bit too loud said, "Well. Breakfast is about ready."

And with that the sexy rancher, his lover, was out the door without a backward glance.

CHAPTER 16

Travis had the feeling he was being watched, which was confirmed when he turned around and locked eyes with Ray. The sun had reached its zenith, and the normally constant eastern winds were nearly absent, leaving the afternoon unusually warm. Or maybe he just felt warmer because he couldn't stop thinking about Ray and replaying last night and this morning on his mental theater screen.

He'd long since taken off the borrowed jacket and rolled the sleeves of the borrowed shirt up to his elbows. Even though the shirt had been washed, the earthy essence of the sexy rancher lingered deep within its fibers. Something about Ray's clothing covering his skin had kept him in a semierect state all day.

Diablo came up behind Ray and nudged his shoulder. Without breaking their silent, exchanged gaze, Ray scrubbed Diablo's neck and inclined his head toward the barn in invitation.

Not wasting the time it would take to open the gate, Travis climbed the rails of the round pen and hopped down on the other side with eager anticipation. Ray copied his move and a beat later was striding away with Travis following, once again enjoying the view of that tight ass wrapped in snug jeans. The smooth rocking motion of broad shoulders as Ray walked—determined and deceivingly graceful—was mesmerizing.

Travis felt like there were springs in his boot heels as Ray led him to the barn, down the quiet hallway, and into the small tack room where they'd first kissed.

"Close the door," Ray said in that rough, aphrodisiac voice.

Travis reached behind and closed it without taking his eyes off Ray. The heat in the man's gaze, radiating off his strong body, was so fierce Travis could feel the hairs on his exposed forearms singe.

He wasn't sure who moved first as the breath whooshed from his lungs, but it didn't matter. What mattered was the full length of Ray's body pressed up against his, pinning him decisively between hard wood and hard flesh. What mattered was his cock now at full mast, straining against the zippered teeth of his jeans for escape. What mattered was Ray's lips on his, the hot, clever tongue plunging into his mouth and strong hands that seemed to be everywhere at once—and his shirt somehow half off.

He'd never been so immediately and intensely aroused by any man before, never wanted one as badly as he wanted Ray Ford.

Travis dug his hands into Ray's hips and tried to pull him in tighter, closer, as though he could merge their bodies into one as they rocked desperately against each other.

Ray groaned and broke the kiss, placed a hand on Travis's chest, and pushed himself away to arm's length. His breath came in short, rapid huffs that sent light bursts of cinnamon into the air. His eyes were dark with desire. Tiny flickers of amber fire burned around the edges of those liquid-chocolate irises.

"Not here," Ray managed on a voice so low and raspy it sent a shiver up Travis's spine. Ray collapsed his elbow and stepped back in, close enough to nip at the bare skin of Travis's shoulder but far enough that his mouth and hand were the only points of contact.

Hyperaware of the burning weight of hand and sensual lips on oversensitive skin, Travis could barely form a coherent thought, let alone words. "House?"

Ray shook his head and licked at the hollow at the base of Travis's throat with a flat tongue. Travis moaned and latched his hands onto Ray's upper arms for support. He felt like his eyes had rolled into the back of his head.

"Hayloft?"

Ray shook his head again and playfully nipped along the subtle curve of collarbone.

"Empty stall?"

He paused for a heartbeat, mouth hovering just over the surface of Travis's flesh, hot breath fanned over tongue-slicked skin. Ray shook his head again and resumed his erotic skin-feast.

"Oh God, Ray." Travis dug his fingers into the solid muscle of Ray's biceps as every nip and lick and suck sent a shock wave through his body.

"We gotta go somewhere. I need—" His brain cut out for a second when Ray bit down hard on the thick muscle where his neck and shoulder met. "Ah, fuck . . . Ray. You have no idea how bad I want you."

Ray broke off and stepped back, chest heaving. "Pretty sure I do," he said gruffly, skin flushed with desire. He carefully readjusted the shirt on Travis's shoulders and bestowed on him the most provocative smile he'd ever had the privilege of receiving.

"Saddle up."

Ray spun around, grabbed a bridle off the nearest hook, and tossed it over his shoulder in Travis's general direction without bothering to look back. He caught the leather headpiece reflexively and held it against his chest, wondering what the hell he'd just missed.

"What?" Travis croaked. One minute they were a heartbeat from having sex right there up against the tack room door, and the next—

Ray tossed another bridle at him. "We're going for a ride."

"Now?"

Ray pulled a saddle off the nearest stand and turned around. His eyes were wild, expression excited and urgent, and Travis grinned when Ray gave him a lascivious wink. The man was one horny dog, a horny dog with a plan.

"Back forty. Complete privacy."

"Hand me that damn saddle," Travis said, feeling every ounce of the impatience he heard in his own voice.

Barely twenty minutes later they were saddled up and heading west at an easy canter toward the river that cut a path through the south range. It would have been ten minutes if Ray hadn't needed to make a run up to the house and grab certain specific supplies for their ride. Ray couldn't believe he was going to do this in broad daylight. And at the same time, he couldn't wait another second. Having Travis

again had been the only thing he'd thought about since last night—longer if he were honest with himself—and the only thing he wanted.

It was a huge risk taking this thing any further. He knew he shouldn't, but in the last twenty-four hours, he'd managed to convince himself they could be discreet enough, that what happened to Harrelson wouldn't happen to them, and conveniently forget Travis would be leaving. He'd deal with that day when it came; until then he'd enjoy as much time with the man as possible.

When they were well out of sight of the ranch, Ray reined Diablo in to a walk. Travis came up beside him on Wiley Dog, and they settled into an easy gait, riding side by side in companionable silence. The familiar tang of horse, earth, and dry native grasses drifted on a breeze that had picked up speed as it swept across the open land.

Travis's knee rubbed gently against his with every sideways sway of the horses' barrels, sending a rush of electricity crackling through his body at each brush. A raging hard-on was not conducive to riding, but he wasn't about to move away from the touch. There was something oddly comforting and intimate about it, more than physical—a form of communication understood without the need for words, and Ray found himself wanting, needing, more of that.

Ray glanced over at the handsome cowboy and took in the strong, rugged profile. Travis turned and trapped him in that captivating bronze-fired gaze, but unlike the past couple of weeks—*Jesus, was that all it had been*?—he didn't dart away in embarrassment or frustration. This time he met the cowboy's gaze in equal measure. Unafraid. That incredible mouth curved up in a knowing, sensual smile, capped by a single sexy dimple. Those full, velvet lips were more enticing than he could have ever imagined. If he'd thought he could kiss Travis just once, have him just once, he was sadly mistaken. He would never get enough of this enigmatic man.

"We almost there?" Travis asked. The resonant voice was rough around the edges in a way that made Ray's cock throb. He shifted in the saddle to ease the growing discomfort. The creak of leather and the strike of hooves on hard ground competed with the pounding of his pulse in his ears. If their destination weren't already in sight, Ray would be pulling Travis down off Wiley right here.

He nodded toward the dense copse of Ponderosa pines that rose up over a bend in the river about a quarter mile ahead: his favorite spot. "Just ahead there."

Travis followed his gaze, then looked back and leveled him with a near-blinding smile, his eyes alight with mischief. "Race ya!"

Without waiting for a response, Travis gave the big gelding a kick and clucked his tongue. The pair bolted into an effortless gallop, but Ray held a prancing Diablo back for a moment. He didn't think he'd ever tire of watching that man ride: powerful and confident and truly beautiful. No matter the horse he sat, he was one with it—man and beast in perfectly synchronized harmony.

Diablo snorted, tossed his head, and stamped at the ground, letting his displeasure at being held back be known.

"Okay, boy. Let's get them."

Ray gave the stallion his head, and the big animal needed no further incentive. He dug his hind hooves into the earth for traction and launched like a thoroughbred out of the gate into a full-out, eye-watering gallop.

As they closed in on their destination, Ray was only a few horse lengths behind Travis when a flash of something dark snapped out like a whip from the low, tree-shadowed grass. Rattler.

Wiley shied sideways sharply, as if on a lateral track, then hunched his hindquarters and reared straight up. His angry squeal rent the air. Travis had barely shifted in the saddle, moving easily with the horse. Ray couldn't have stopped the proud smile that took over his face at that display of horsemanship if he tried.

But the smile froze on his face when the big buckskin overbalanced himself in his panic and went down backward, crushing Travis beneath him.

Ray's breath caught in the back of his throat, and his heart stopped midbeat.

The world screeched to a trembling standstill, sound drowned out, color faded.

Wiley found his legs and stood, leaving a terrifyingly lifeless body on the ground. Ray couldn't breathe. His lungs felt like they were being squeezed in a vice grip. Seconds that felt like hours crawled by as he and Diablo raced the last few yards to Travis's side.

He sat back tight in the saddle and slacked the reins with a "whoa" he didn't fully register saying aloud. Diablo immediately dropped into a hard slide, and Ray was out of the saddle and kneeling at Travis's side before the horse had come to a complete stop.

"Travis!" The voice pitched heavy with fear sounded foreign to his ears. Travis lay unresponsive on his back. For a brief moment of escalating panic Ray didn't know what to do. His hands hovered uselessly over Travis's body. Then he drew a deep breath and with a shaky hand, pressed two fingers firmly against the thick jugular vein in Travis's neck. Relief washed through him at the strong, fast pulse that beat steadily under the pads of his fingers. He was alive.

"Travis?" Ray gently cupped the man's face with one hand and placed the other gently on his chest. "Trav, can you hear me?"

No response.

Afraid to move him in case of spinal injury, Ray did a visual assessment of Travis's body for any obvious signs of physical trauma, and his breath froze in mid-exhale. His heart clenched into a painful fist, and a wave of dizziness tilted the ground beneath him.

"Jesusfuckingchrist."

Blood had begun to soak through the bottom of Travis's shirt and protruding from the lower left side of his torso, a broken tree branch that had run him clear through.

CHAPTER 17

"Sweet Mother Mary of Jesus."

Ray had seen his fair share of bizarre accidents, had seen horses take a fall on their riders more times than he cared to remember, himself included. That was part of ranching life. But he had never seen anything like this before. He fell back on his heels as cold panic roared forward and clouded his thinking. His mouth now too dry to swallow, and a bead of sweat trickled down his cheek. Images of a blood-soaked, lifeless Travis hanging limp in his arms flashed through his mind.

No. He would not lose Travis. Couldn't. Not like this.

A fucking tree branch.

Ray shook his head in denial. He refused to accept that something so innocuous could be the end of a man like Travis Morgan. He was too powerful, too vibrant, and *alive* to be taken out this way. Taken from him.

Anger welled up and flooded his veins, forcing the panic from his mind. He would not let that happen. Mind clear and focused, Ray snapped into action.

"You're not going anywhere, Travis," he bit out on a shaky voice. "You hear me?"

He pulled off his own shirt and carefully wrapped it around the base of the branch, immobilizing it to prevent any further damage and staunch some of the bleeding. He applied gentle pressure with both hands and assessed their surroundings.

They were too far from the ranch to be seen or heard. Diablo, although relatively close, was out of reach; even though well trained, he wasn't like a dog that would come when called. He needed to get

the two-way radio out of his saddlebag and call for help, but was too afraid of leaving Travis's side for even a second.

"Fuck!"

White-hot rage boiled under his skin. His entire body vibrated, strung tighter than a stud on breeding day. Travis was going to die out here if he didn't get help quickly. Helplessness settled over him like a suffocating, crushing blanket. Ray looked to Diablo again and gauged the distance. Looked back at Travis's too-pale face and squeezed his eyes shut.

"Okay"—he opened his eyes and said with a nod—"you hold on, Travis. Just hold the fuck on."

Ray took a deep breath, carefully let go of the shirt, and ran to Diablo. Thankful the horse didn't bolt, he grabbed the reins and quickly led him back to the supine cowboy. He dug the two-way out of the saddlebag, along with a spare shirt, and a blanket he'd tied behind the cantle. His hands left bloody prints on the leather and Diablo's coat. He dropped back down beside Travis and resumed applying pressure on the wound with his left hand. Using his right hand, Ray covered as much of Travis's torso as possible with the thick blanket and tucked it under his shoulders. The man was still unconscious, but his body had begun to shake.

That done, he reached for the two-way and radioed Hollis, sending up a prayer that the foreman would be in his office. Only seconds later Hollis's gruff voice crackled over the radio. Ray closed his eyes and thanked the heavens. He'd never been so happy to hear the man's voice.

"Hollis, it's Ray." He paused to check his pressure on Travis's wound. "There's been an accident. Travis is hurt. He needs a hospital, but I can't move him."

"Damn," the foreman responded, his voice immediately sharp and clear. "Where are you? What do you need?"

"We're on the south range along the river. I need you to get an air ambulance out here pronto. Get a pen for my GPS coordinates."

There was a pause, and then Hollis was back to take down the information.

"Send some men out here to get the horses. I'm going in the helicopter."

"Will do, boss."

Ray put the two-way down by his knee and checked the wound. The blood loss had slowed some, but there was no way to tell how massive the internal bleeding was. Travis's skin had taken on a deathly pallor that sent a spike of dread slicing through Ray's chest. He felt for a pulse again—still there but weakening. Flesh now cold to the touch. His hands were stained with Travis's blood. The bitter, metallic tang of it hovered heavy in the air and scoured the back of his throat. He wanted to spit it out, but his mouth was too dry to build up enough saliva.

Ray jumped when Hollis's gruff voice crackled over the two-way.

"Yeah?" Ray barked; his gaze locked on Travis's face.

"Chopper's on the way. ETA fifteen minutes."

Ray thanked Hollis and then said to Travis in a reedy voice, "Fifteen minutes, Travis. You hear that? Don't you dare die on me. Not on my land. My fucking ranch, my fucking rules."

Travis's eyelids fluttered and slowly lifted. His gaze was unfocused, distant, and the bronze flecks that normally flashed in those beautiful green eyes had died, leaving them frighteningly flat and empty.

"Travis . . ."

That vacant gaze followed the sound of Ray's voice and recognition sparked in their depths a moment later. He tried to speak, but no sound came from his mouth. Ray ran his fingers through Travis's silky locks in a gentle caress at his temple.

"S-so . . . c-cold . . ." Travis croaked through chattering teeth.

"Shh. Help is on the way. You just hold on."

Ray adjusted the blanket under Travis's chin, then leaned down and lightly pressed his lips to ones that had been warm and soft less than an hour ago but were now chillingly cold and tinged blue. Fear gripped his heart and squeezed it painfully, but he wouldn't let Travis see it. He would be strong for Travis. Had to be.

"I'm not letting you go, Travis Morgan," he said vehemently. "Got that?"

A half smile ghosted those unnaturally blue lips. "Con trol . . . freak."

Ray smiled back, but knew it didn't reach his eyes. "Save it, Morgan."

They fell quiet a moment, gazes locked, neither man able to pull away from the other. Travis's smile faded from his face, his expression turned serious, and a flash of that enticing fire flared in his eyes.

"I think I-I'm . . . falling in lo—"

Ray quickly placed two fingers against Travis's mouth. He didn't want to hear that. It wasn't something he ever thought he'd hear from Travis, and he definitely didn't want to hear it now. Not like this. He shook his head sharply and his voice threatened to fail when he said, "You tell me later. Okay? We'll get you patched up, and then you tell me."

But Travis told him anyway with his eyes.

"Travis, please . . ."

Travis tried to nod, and then his eyelids slid down, and he slipped back into unconsciousness.

CHAPTER 18

After what seemed an eternity, Ray finally heard the distinctive, rhythmic *wop-wop-wop* of the approaching helicopter. He vaguely registered Diablo bolting as the aircraft began to set down. He draped himself carefully over Travis's body to protect him from the swirling dirt and dry grass kicked up by the machine's spinning rotors.

And then there were hands on his shoulders, gentle but firm, trying to pull him away from Travis. But he fought the hold. He couldn't let go. Refused to.

"Sir, we've got him," a compassionate voice said next to his ear. "It's okay."

"But that . . . tree . . ."

"We're going to do our best for him," the man said. "Come on, let us do our job."

Ray nodded and reluctantly released his grip around the base of the branch. He stumbled backward as two paramedics closed in on Travis, checking vitals and assessing the wound. He didn't really understand what they were saying, but their voices and actions were reassuringly professional and efficient.

The man who'd spoken to him, one of the paramedics, led Ray to the chopper and eased him down in a leather seat. "What's his name?"

"Travis. Travis Morgan."

"He mean a lot to you?"

Ray shot a startled glance at the paramedic, looking at him for the first time. The paramedic was a young man with kind blue eyes and a warm smile—no hint of malice or judgment in his expression.

"It's okay. I understand," he said, extending his hand. "Name's Jacob. My partner and I are going on eight years now."

Ray's brain stuttered. He couldn't respond. Didn't know how. The whole situation was just too surreal to make sense of. Fortunately he didn't have to. The other two paramedics had arrived with Travis secured to a board and lifted him into the aircraft. Once they were all safely buckled in, Jacob took to the controls and the big bird lifted off. Ray reached for Travis's hand and held it while he stared at the man's pale, strained face, willing him to live, to stay.

A team of nurses and doctors were already waiting on the helipad when they landed on the roof of St Vincent's Hospital. After quickly moving Travis onto a wheeled gurney, they rushed him straight through to emergency surgery—with that goddamned tree branch sticking out of his side.

Ray didn't notice the paramedics take their leave, didn't hear what Jacob said in parting, or remember how he got from the helipad to the ER waiting room. He just felt the overwhelming, numbing fear of losing Travis so soon after having just begun to discover him. He couldn't seem to stop the tremors that racked his body, or slow the pulse that made his heart pound erratically against his rib cage.

Travis could die.

He looked down at his hands and furrowed his brows in confusion. They were covered in blood—Travis's blood. He'd lost so much, too much.

His stomach flip-flopped, and bile burned the back of his throat. Ray's knees gave out, and he plopped gracelessly onto the nearest chair. He dropped his head into his hands and squeezed his eyes shut. He refused to accept that Travis wouldn't survive this. Refused a life without that carefree cowboy in it.

Distantly he became aware of a hand resting gently on his shoulder. He looked up to see Dot and Jesse standing before him through a blurred veil. His mind registered that Dot was speaking to him, because her mouth moved, but he couldn't hear what she was saying over the frenzied buzzing in his ears. Couldn't understand her words or form any in response. Her eyes searched his with compassion and concern. He felt strangely detached from his body, as though he were nothing more than an empty husk. There but not.

They sat down on either side of him, and Dot held his shaking, bloody hands in hers.

Finally, almost three hours later, a doctor entered the tensely quiet waiting room. Ray immediately jumped from his chair.

"How is he?" His voice cracked.

"He's going to be fine," the doctor said. "We were able to remove the branch and clean the wound completely. Amazingly, the branch missed his vital organs and only nicked his stomach."

"Thank God," Ray breathed, the relief so intense he felt momentarily dizzy and his vision blurred again. His face felt oddly wet. Warm arms wrapped around his waist from both sides, and he let himself be supported by Jesse and Dot.

"Come on, Raymond," Dot said quietly. "Let's get you cleaned up."

Ray woke with a start. Panic jolted his system like an electrical shock that was quickly followed by relief when his gaze fell on Travis resting peacefully. Alive.

After Ray had taken up residence in the chair at Travis's bedside yesterday, the remainder of the day had passed in a hazy, disjointed blur.

He remembered the moment Travis had come out of recovery and been moved to a private room. He'd been instantly at his side and refused to leave or even shift from his watchful perch in a chair butted right up next to Travis's hospital bed. He ignored the nurses who'd tried getting him to leave, ignored Dot who'd tried to take him home, or at least make him eat, though he did finally acquiesce to a shower and a change into clean clothes. But then he'd refused to move until those captivating green eyes opened and once again trapped him with their secrets.

Ray straightened up in the unforgiving chair he'd fallen asleep in, and rubbed absently at the kink in his neck. He studied the man who'd somehow come to mean everything to him in such a short time.

Goose bumps spread across the exposed skin of Travis's shoulders and upper chest. Ray leaned over and pulled the bed sheets up to Travis's chin and tucked them around his cowboy's blessedly warm body. *His* cowboy. He didn't know quite when he'd started thinking of Travis as his, but he liked the sound of it.

He let his hand rest lightly on the center of Travis's chest, reveling at the warmth that radiated through the sheets under his open palm—warmth that meant he would live to ride another day. Ray slowly slid his hand to the base of Travis's neck and then upward. A strong pulse pounded under his fingertips as he made his way to the hard jawline. He liked the rough scrape of day-old stubble against his palm. He cradled the side of Travis's face and lightly caressed healthy, pink lips with his thumb. Then he leaned forward, his cheek to Travis's chin, so he could feel the soft, reassuring brush of breath on his skin.

Ray sighed. He began to lower his hand and pull back, but Travis reached up and caught him with a light grip around the wrist. Travis turned his head slightly and pressed his cheek into Ray's palm. Then he opened his eyes. Though still dulled with pain and medication, that mischievous, heart-stopping fire simmered in their depths, and Ray was positive he heard angels sing.

Travis lowered Ray's hand with his and rested them both on his chest—over his heart—and laced their fingers. Then he slid the other hand up Ray's arm, over his shoulder, and threaded long fingers into his hair. Ray closed his eyes and reveled in the sensation of his cowboy's reverent touch. Travis moved his hand to the back of Ray's neck and tugged.

Ray opened his eyes and parted his lips over Travis's mouth, but paused a hairbreadth from touching. He just needed a second to breathe in the intoxicating scent of Travis, let the heat of Travis's body flow over his skin. And then Ray closed the last sliver of space and took those velvet lips in a soft, intimate slide that said everything he didn't have words for. He poured all his fear and relief and heart into the kiss and into Travis, and something in his chest relaxed.

Travis parted his lips, and Ray didn't hesitate. He wrapped his tongue around Travis's and deepened the kiss. Suddenly it became intense, passionate. Need seared through Ray's brain, and he had

to be closer, dive deeper. Travis tried to rise up, but Ray eased him back gently and rose from his chair, leaning over Travis until he was practically in the bed with him, covering him.

Ray knew right then and there without a doubt that this man, Travis Morgan, was the most important person in his life. He would give anything for him—even his ranch.

Ray broke the kiss and gazed deep into Travis's eyes, as if he could reach his soul.

"I want you to stay, Travis," he said in a rough whisper. "Stay here with me."

Travis was quiet for a moment, and Ray couldn't get a read on what he was thinking. Apprehension began to nip at the bliss he'd been riding.

"You know I'm not one to lay down roots."

Ray nodded and quickly averted his eyes, hoping he'd dropped them before Travis could see the disappointment that threatened to split his heart. His chest felt like it had just caved in, and he struggled to breathe. He'd said his piece, put it out there, and received a response. There was no more he could do. He wouldn't push the man to stay only to be resented for it later. It had to be Travis's choice. But if it hurt this much now, Ray really didn't know how he was going to survive without his carefree, effervescent cowboy when he eventually did leave.

"But if there was any man worth staying in one place for," Travis continued, "it would be you. It *will* be you, Ray."

Ray looked up into mischievous eyes that smiled back at him with merriment and so much adoration, his chest swelled, his throat opened, and he could breathe again.

"Kiss me, sexy man," Travis drawled in a low rumble that Ray responded to with a deep groan. And then he did exactly what his cowboy had commanded. He kissed him with everything he had.

A throat cleared softly from the doorway.

They froze. Ray's eyes snapped open and met Travis's wide, shocked gaze, mouths still locked.

Ray jumped back from the bedside and stumbled into the chair he'd been sitting on. It tipped over and hit the floor with a loud *clank*

that echoed incessantly in the stunned silence. Heat scorched his cheeks so intensely, he knew they had to be a brilliant, fire-engine red. "Mortified" didn't even begin to describe what he was feeling just then. He'd been caught kissing a man, and now it would destroy not only his reputation and the ranch's, but Travis's as well. He tried to tell Travis he was sorry with his eyes, but Travis was already looking toward the door with a bashful smile playing on his handsome face.

Ray turned to see Dot walking into the room with a large paper bag in her hands. A cheek-splitting Cheshire cat smile lit her face, and amusement flashed in her piercing blue eyes. Even though Ray knew she'd suspected and seemed supportive, having her actually *see* was a horse of a whole other color.

"You sit right back down by your man, Raymond Ford," Dot admonished as she pulled a chair up to the other side of the bed. "Brought Travis a homemade meal. Don't want my future son-in-law here dying from the poison they call food in this place."

Ray still hadn't moved. Shock hadn't finished its ragged tour through his body. Travis's dancing gaze bounced back and forth between a stunned Ray and jovial Dot.

"Pick your jaw up off the floor and come sit down." Dot didn't look at him as she pulled containers from the bag and arranged them on the hospital tray. "You think I wouldn't have figured out how bad you two have it for each other? Goodness, half the ranch knows."

"What!" Ray reeled. His knees felt weak, and his stomach rolled over.

They were ruined. Yes, he'd already decided he'd give everything, but zero to a hundred wasn't quite the speed he'd planned on coming out at. Actually, he hadn't thought about much beyond keeping Travis alive and getting him to stay.

"Oh, don't you worry, son," Dot said cheerfully. "Not the off-site crew, just Hollis, Jesse, and Clay. Oh, and Ross too, of course. We've been running a bet on when you two would finally see what we've all seen since you brought this fine young man home."

She glanced up at Travis and gave him a conspiratorial wink. "Of course, I won the pot. I swear. Men will never learn not to bet against ole Dot McCray."

Travis chuckled and immediately sucked in a sharp breath and winced. “Oww. Don’t make me laugh, Dottie.”

Travis looked over at Ray and pinned him with that magnetic gaze he’d come to love being trapped by. Then his cowboy smiled, and Ray knew, one way or another, things would work out. They had to, because going back to a life in secret, without Travis in it, would be beyond unbearable.

“This isn’t an issue for you, Dot? And the hands?” Ray asked. It seemed all too surreal. He’d woken up this morning buried deep in the closet, and now, before the day was even half-over, he was out and apparently accepted. Well, at least with Dot anyway.

Numbing terror and overwhelming relief battled for control of his mind.

“I’ve only ever wanted you happy, son,” Dot said softly. “And this fine young man here seems to be the one to make that happen. I’ve no right to admonish that.”

Travis held his hand out and quietly said, “Come here, babe.”

Ray righted the chair and reached out hesitantly, taking Travis’s warm, strong hand in his before sitting back down. Travis gave him a quick, reassuring squeeze.

“Now that we’ve got that all settled,” Dot chirped. “Let’s eat.”

“But it’s not all settled, Dot. Not everyone is as accepting as you. Remember how Dwayne Harrelson was run out? And look what happened with Sam. He tried to kill Travis and will probably try again—”

“But he didn’t, and he won’t.” Dot waved her hand. “The sheriff arrested him this morning. They’re charging him with arson and attempted murder. He’ll be sent away for a good long time.”

“Thank God.” Ray breathed out a long sigh of relief. “But we have the welfare of the ranch, our reputations, and the people who depend on us for their livelihoods to think about.”

Dot regarded him for a long moment and then settled back into her chair.

“Sometimes you just have to follow your heart, Raymond.” Her voice, deliberately soft and soothing, never failed to put him at ease. “No matter where that may lead. If the heart that matches the beat

of your own comes in the body of a man, so be it. Doesn't change anything. You're the same man you were yesterday. Better, even, from where I'm standing.

"Though I would've appreciated you telling me sooner. I wouldn't have wasted my time trying to find you the perfect woman." She chuckled and glanced at Travis with a shake of her head and roll of her eyes.

"But what if everyone turns on us, like Dway—"

"That was over twenty years ago, Raymond." Dot cut him off again. "Still a long way to go, but society has progressed since then. So maybe we lose a little business, but in this day and age, big deal. There's much more to gain than lose, and you won't lose those closest to you. I doubt you'll lose many ranch hands or buyers either. Wouldn't be surprised if you gained a few more."

"Maybe, but how can this work?" Ray sighed.

"Like every relationship, son. Love, understanding, compromise, and a lot of hard work." Dot paused. "Don't worry. This town loves you. You boys are going to be just fine. You've got me to keep you in line, and some good men out there who have your backs."

Ray looked a little shell-shocked. Dark shadows tinged the delicate skin beneath his eyes, complexion pale, shoulders rolled forward, and gaze unfocused somewhere beyond Travis's chest. He hadn't yet said a word since Dot left the hospital room a few minutes ago, satisfied that Travis had been properly fed.

"You sure you want to do this?" Travis couldn't help but ask. Too many times he'd raised his hopes only to have them lopped off at the shoulders.

Ray reached for his hand and threaded their fingers. That melodic voice was rough but decisive when Ray spoke. "Without a doubt. I don't ever want to go back to a life without you."

"I don't either."

For the first time since he'd left White Deer, Travis felt happy, truly floating-on-air, to-the-tips-of-his-toes happy. Ray wanted him

to stay, wanted him enough to risk everything for. Despite the drug-dulled throbbing pain in his side, Travis couldn't remember ever feeling better than he did at this moment. Ray Ford, the serious, stoic rancher with those sexy, soulful brown eyes, had put *him* first—Travis Morgan, number one.

That little kernel of hope that refused to be dislodged could finally dig its roots in and grow. After eighteen years, he was home. For the rest of his life.

"Dammit, Travis. I almost lost you out there."

He gave Ray's hand a gentle squeeze. "I'm still here. And I'm not going anywhere without you."

Ray looked into his eyes with so much intensity, so much emotion, Travis couldn't breathe. The language this man, *his* man, silently spoke filled his heart near to bursting. He didn't need to hear the words to know he was loved. Ray said it with his soul.

"We're going to be okay," he said, his voice a low rasp. "You know that, right? As long as we have each other, we're going to be okay."

Ray graced him with a smile he felt all the way to the marrow of his bones. "Yeah, as long as we have each other."

EPILOGUE

Ray stood behind Travis, admiring his cowboy's reflection in the mirrored wall of the elevator that carried them effortlessly upward. Golden sun-streaked hair, brushed neatly back from his face, curled over the collar of his jacket in a gentle wave. Ray itched to run his hands through the silky strands and twine them around his fingers, muss them up. Nothing looked better than Travis in the morning with tousled hair—especially after they'd made love and his skin was flushed, eyes soft and heavy-lidded.

Those incredible eyes gazed back at him in the mirror—the secrets they held still not completely revealed. A single dimple capped a crooked grin on that ruggedly handsome, tanned face. And that unique, kinetic force that defined the man vibrated in the small confines of the elevator, ratcheting Ray's desire for him up another notch. It sometimes amazed Ray that there seemed to always be another level to reach.

He could barely wrap his mind around how much had happened since that black day in April four months ago—the day he'd almost lost Travis forever. But Travis lived and everything changed. He and Travis had come stampeding out of the closet with guns blazing. Well, to their ranch hands, anyway. It had been a frightening thing to do, but at the same time, liberating beyond measure. For the first time in his life, Ray had been able to breathe freely.

While not everyone had been accepting, Ray had been surprised by how many were, or who didn't seem to care one way or the other. Just as Dot had predicted, they'd lost a couple hands and a regular buyer, received the occasional sneer in town, but the violence and destruction of his ranch and the Ford Creek reputation Ray had feared all his life never came to be.

"What?" Travis asked, his voice a soft seductive growl.

He stood tall, confident and commanding, looking every bit the dashing aristocratic rake, in his tailored black silk tuxedo. Travis always looked incredible no matter what he wore—or what he didn't. Actually, he looked best in nothing at all, as far as Ray was concerned.

"Sweet mercy," Ray's voice was a hoarse rumble deep in his chest. "You are gorgeous."

Travis's grin morphed into that dazzling, magazine cover smile as the elevator came to an imperceptible stop and the doors whooshed quietly open. He reached his hand back for Ray's and when their hands were firmly clasped, Travis led him out into the hall. Life really couldn't get any better, Ray thought.

"That was the best wedding I've ever been to," Ray said as they reached their hotel room door. His first crush, Gregory Reeves, had looked incredibly jubilant standing at his man, David's side, with dancing eyes and an unshakable smile. It was the kind of happiness that ran bone deep and cast the whole world in a warm, golden glow. The bond Gregory and his partner shared was unmistakable, visible to the naked eye. And one Ray found himself hoping he and Travis might some day share.

It had been good to see Gregory after so many years. He still looked like a surfer, but had filled out and was no longer the lanky teen Ray remembered. He was still handsome. Nothing would change that, but the man had nothing on Travis. Gregory's husband was also a handsome man, dark where Gregory was light, and they were absolutely perfect together.

Travis slid the card key in and out of its slot. The green light flashed and he pushed the handle down, opening the door. "That was the only wedding I've ever been to."

Ray entered the room behind Travis and shucked off his tux jacket. He tossed it onto a chair near the entrance, then grabbed Travis by the waist and spun him around so they faced each other. He slipped his hands beneath the lapels of Travis's jacket and shoved it off his shoulders, pushed it down his arms until it ran out of real estate and fell to the floor.

"Something I've been dying to do all night," Ray said with a lascivious smile as he pulled the knot of Travis's bow tie loose.

Travis chuckled. "Why don't you grab a couple beers so we don't get thirsty."

Ray let his hand glide provocatively across Travis's abdomen as he moved away and walked over to the mini fridge. He retrieved two cold bottles, turned around, and stopped dead in his tracks.

"What the hell are you doing?"

Travis, his cowboy, his lover, was down on bended knee looking up with an expectant expression on his face and an excited, inner light glittering in his eyes. One hand rested on his knee, clenched into a fist. A rush of warmth spread throughout Ray's body, his pulse kicked up a notch, and he suddenly felt breathless.

"What the hell does it look like I'm doing, Raymond Ford?" The smile in Travis's voice shone as bright as a summer sun at high noon. "I'm asking you to marry me."

Ray heard the words, but couldn't quite connect the thought to action. Travis wanted to marry him? Travis Morgan, the man who'd spent the last eighteen years of his life drifting with the wind? Ray could never have guessed that Travis would be the marrying kind. Let alone the staying around kind. Ray certainly hadn't thought marriage would ever be for himself. Didn't see how it could ever be in the cards. But now . . . Now the most incredible man he'd ever known was down on his knee gazing up at him with so much love and desire in his eyes, Ray felt like his heart would explode if it swelled any more.

Travis turned the fisted hand over and rolled his fingers out like a blooming flower. There, in the middle of his open palm, were two silver bands. And Ray's gaze locked on them, hypnotized.

"Any time there, Ray." That deep resonant drawl washed over Ray in a gentle, erotic wave. "Don't leave a man hanging."

Yes! "But . . . Montana . . ."

Travis scrunched his nose and scoffed. "The state doesn't get to tell me who I spend the rest of my life with."

Ray blindly placed the beer bottles on top of the fridge, missing on the first try, then strode forward and dropped to his knees before Travis. He cupped Travis's face with both hands and kissed him with

enough force to knock him to the floor. Ray sprawled over Travis and let his lips and mouth and tongue answer what his voice wasn't yet able to.

Ray broke the kiss and sat up, impatiently tugging at Travis's shirt. The buttons were too much to deal with, so he yanked it roughly over Travis's head. He stared down at Travis's lean, defined chest and smooth, flawless skin, marred only by an angry jagged scar on the lower left side of his torso. A permanent reminder of how close he'd come to losing the man forever. He traced his fingers gently over the rough skin, and then Travis captured his hand, drawing his gaze.

"Hey," Travis said softly. "I'm still here. Not going anywhere."

"Don't ever do anything like that again, Morgan," Ray said solemnly. He'd never felt so terrified and helpless in his whole life; never wanted to experience a day like that again.

Travis shook his head and smiled. He brought Ray's hand to his mouth and placed a light kiss on each knuckle. "I believe I'm still waiting for an answer, Ford."

Ray reclaimed his hand, pulled his shirt over his head and carelessly tossed it on the floor so he could feel skin against skin. Travis was here and always would be, which was a damn good thing because Ray had never wanted anyone as badly as he wanted this man. Ray reached for the zipper of Travis's silk slacks. "And I believe there was something I was about to do first."

Travis laughed and grabbed Ray's left hand. "No sex before marriage."

"Little late for that, cowboy," Ray teased.

"Then answer me."

"You already know the answer."

Travis gazed up at him, his eyes flashing as he opened his hand again. Ray looked to the rings. The bands were wide, simple, polished to a bright sheen with smooth beveled edges. And perfect.

"They're engraved," Travis said in a breathless voice.

Ray lifted one ring from Travis's hand and turned it to see the inscription. *My cowboy. My love.*

His throat tightened. He could barely swallow.

Travis lifted his other hand, fingers spread. "I say yes."

Ray slid the ring onto Travis's third finger, and suddenly the room seemed brighter, the air lighter, and Ray felt as if he might float away.

Ray barely heard his own voice when he said, "I say yes."

Travis released a breath of air Ray hadn't been aware he'd been holding, and slowly slipped the matching ring onto Ray's wedding finger. Ray's vision blurred as he stared down the silver band. A symbol of what they meant to each other, what they shared, and what would be a constant reminder to always put that first. Cherish it. Cherish each other.

Travis wrapped the ring-clad hand in his and pulled Ray down, taking his mouth in a tender, passionate kiss.

"I love you, Travis Ford," Ray whispered when they broke for air.

Travis laughed, low and deep in his chest. "I love you, too. Ray Morgan. Now quit talking and show me how much."